A C

He could not believe ly
into the path of the ed
throughout the yard a it,
but she never reacted or
a moment before laun he
last possible second and they tumbled to the ground, rolling over and over until they came to a stop in the dirt.

Taking a few deep breaths, he raised his head to look at her. The woman's eyes were closed and she was barely breathing. Her hair was loosened from its braid and fell in waves onto the ground. And he found himself wanting to know what color her eyes were . . .

Praise for Terri Brisbin's unforgettable Time Passages romances

A Love Through Time

"A very special book, and a time travel with a twist. Fans of Scottish adventures will revel in *A Love Through Time*."
—Christina Skye, author of *Christmas Knight*

"Those of you who complain that your medieval romances are not real enough, this book is for you . . . The action doesn't stop." —*All About Romance*

"Classic time travel! Terri Brisbin has created an evocative Scottish tale brimming with warmth, wit, and sensuality."
—May McGoldrick, author of *The Intended* and *Flame*

"A fresh face who adds a unique twist to the sub-genre . . . Fun . . . a crisp story line . . . If this novel is any indication, Ms. Brisbin has a long future ahead of her."
—*Painted Rock Reviews*

A Matter of Time

"*A Matter of Time* blends fantasy and romance with a story that is rich in Scottish tradition and passionate in the telling." —*BookBug*

Titles by Terri Brisbin

THE QUEEN'S MAN
A MATTER OF TIME
A LOVE THROUGH TIME

THE QUEEN'S MAN

Terri Brisbin

JOVE BOOKS, NEW YORK

THE QUEEN'S MAN

A Jove Book / published by arrangement with
the author

PRINTING HISTORY
Jove edition / September 2000

For information address: The Berkley Publishing Group,
a division of Penguin Putnam Inc.,
375 Hudson Street, New York, New York 10014.

The Penguin Putnam Inc. World Wide Web site address is
http://www.penguinputnam.com

ISBN: 0-515-12906-2

A JOVE BOOK®
Jove Books are published by The Berkley Publishing Group,
a division of Penguin Putnam Inc.,
375 Hudson Street, New York, New York 10014.
JOVE and the "J" design
are trademarks belonging to Penguin Putnam Inc.

PRINTED IN THE UNITED STATES OF AMERICA

10 9 8 7 6 5 4 3 2 1

This book is for Linda Kruger, my agent.
Thanks for taking the first steps in my
writing career with me!

My thanks to Eloisa James, romance author and a goddess of Shakespearean Literature and History, for her help with English epithets.

Also, a special thank-you to Mary Stella, whose wonderful "what-if" question stirred my creativity when writing this book.

And my thanks to Teresa Eckford for her help in researching parts of this story. Any mistakes or changes to history are of my own making!

Prologue

LONDON, ENGLAND

"PROMISE ME !"

Maria Morales Browning forced the words out through teeth clenched in pain. She clutched at her sister's wrist, pulling her closer. "You must promise me now, before it's too late."

Maria felt death's presence grow stronger. She could not fight much longer and the matter that weighed heavily on her conscience must be dealt with before she died.

"I am here," her sister whispered. "Tell me what I must do."

"My writing desk . . . open the third drawer." Maria struggled to point her sister in the correct direction. "There is a packet."

Her sister opened the drawer and rifled through the contents. Then lifting an object, she held it out to Maria. Maria's eyes and throat burned with unshed tears as she beheld the proof of her gravest sin. Blinking against them, she leaned her head back and considered the high price her lie had cost her soul and her adopted country. The anger and hatred had faded in the years since her act of betrayal, but those feelings were now replaced with the dread of dying without absolution.

"Take it and hide it, I beg you. Make certain that no one, *no one,* knows where you put it."

"Maria, what is this?" her sister asked, holding out the packet of folded and sealed parchment to her. Maria feared even touching it now and shook her head.

"You must preserve it, for if a time comes when England has need of a king, this will put him on the throne." A cough rose from her chest, cutting off her breath. Pain burned a fiery path through her limbs as the spasms went on and on. 'Twas worse with each bout. Soon she would be unable to draw air into her chest.

As her sister aided her in sitting up, Maria smelled the rancid odor surrounding her own body. 'Twas coming, sooner than she'd first thought.

"Remember, tell no one."

Maria Morales Browning, daughter of Queen Catherine of Aragon's Spanish physician and midwife to two of England's ill-fated queens, closed her eyes and gave up her fight. The proof, now safe with her sister, weighed on her no longer. Death overtook her. She fought no more.

Chapter 1

"OUCH !"

The thump of her head hitting the wall and her yell echoed through the tiny dust-filled chamber. Wincing against the discomfort, Sharon Reynolds sneezed four times in a row. Crawling around the large open trunk, she tried to find a less dangerous place within the small room.

Gently, she lifted another piece of clothing and carefully examined it. If she were correct, this chest of women's dresses was one of the biggest finds of Elizabethan artifacts to date. Her optimism warred with her scientist's sense of caution and her own recently acquired cynicism as she gathered the dress for a closer look. A thin seam along one side of the bodice didn't match, in size or stitch, the seams in the rest of the garment. Flicking her nail against one end of it, the end unraveled slightly.

She knew she should probably wait until the trunk was removed from the room to do any close-up work but her curiosity overwhelmed her. Although the dresses had been carefully photographed and replaced in the trunk, Sharon could not resist the urge to have a quick look at one of them. Of course, by the time she'd arrived at the site nightfall was approaching and she'd had to postpone a true examination.

"Sharon? Are you almost finished? We're about to head out for a bite."

The voice drifted into the cubbyhole as she bent over examining the loose thread. Her classmate from her studies at the London Textile Institute soon peeked her head in looking for her.

"Mo, I'd really like to continue here for a bit."

Maureen Boylan, assistant director-on-site for the renovations, stepped into the already cramped room. "It's difficult to stop, isn't it?" Mo reached out to touch the dress Sharon held and then stopped. "And just as difficult not to hope."

"Not to hope?" Sharon frowned at her friend and looked back at the trunk before her.

"That they're authentic. It would be the find of a lifetime if they are." Optimism filled Mo's voice. A scientist through and through, Mo nonetheless always hoped for the best. That was something that Sharon was learning not to do much anymore.

"I have my suspicions," Sharon answered. "But I'll reserve judgment until you look at them in the lab and do some dating of the fabrics." She placed the dress back on top of the other garments.

"Things that bad?" Mo asked, her eyes meeting Sharon's for the first time since she'd arrived.

"I'm here, aren't I?"

"Are you ready to tell me, Sharon? I could read it in your e-mails and hear it in your voice. Telling me might make you feel better."

Sharon wasn't sure she wanted to tell anyone about it yet. The sense of failure was too new and strong to make it easy to talk about, even with her dear friend.

"Let's just say that politics are about to ruin the position I've wanted to hold for most of my professional life."

"Whew! That sounds even worse than I'd imagined." Concern filled Mo's voice. "But you had the full approval of the museum's board."

"Until Jasper Crenshaw started his campaign behind my back."

The man had been acting curator of the Chicago Museum's Historical Costume and Fabric collection until her own appointment as head curator. His objections to her youth and inexperience had gone ignored and unanswered until lately. Mistakes in displays, in verifying research, and in financial records had recently plagued Sharon's administration of the collection. Questions were being raised about her ability and fitness. She was, at thirty, the youngest woman ever appointed to such a position and Jasper had played on that as a weakness. She blew out a breath, raising more dust motes in the air.

"That snake is still in Chicago?" Mo knew Jasper by appearance and reputation, a reputation Sharon had always doubted and ignored . . . until now.

Sharon slid her glasses higher up on the bridge of her nose and sighed. This was not the time to talk about her reasons for taking this unexpected sabbatical "in the field." The outrage and embarrassment were too fresh. She didn't want her excitement about this probable historic find to be dampened by the reality of her present-day life.

"Can we talk about this later? Maybe over a drink?"

"Oh, aye. But I'll only be put off if you promise to tell me all the details." Mo cocked one eyebrow in question.

"Oh, aye." Sharon winked as she answered, mimicking her friend's soft English accent. "You will get more details than you really want after you buy me a couple of shots of single malt."

"You have yourself a bargain." Mo inched her way away from Sharon and toward the door. "We'll be securing the house for the night soon. A RenFaire troupe will be using the grounds this weekend so we want it locked up nice and tight before they arrive."

"You're letting them on the grounds even with this"—she pointed at the trunk before them—"still here?"

"We'll be moving that tomorrow. The troupe isn't due to set up until the day after that. And they are only permitted to use the far barn and fields beyond."

"I'll finish up and be ready to leave in just a few minutes, then."

"This trunk has been here for a long time," her friend said with a smile. "You'll have more time in the morning before we move it."

"I just want to look at this dress. I'll meet you downstairs in twenty minutes?"

"That's fine. Watch your step coming out of there. The floors haven't been reinforced yet."

Sharon listened as Mo's steps traveled down the corridor away from her. Turning back to the item of interest, she shoved her hair back behind her ears, slid her glasses back down onto the bridge of her nose, and leaned down for a closer look.

The dress was a classic example of a minor noblewoman's gown from the Elizabethan period in England. The only discrepancy was the tattered seam along the side of the stomacher. The shoddy workmanship was at odds with the rest of the carefully sewn dress. The dangling thread piqued her curiosity and she gave a slight tug on it. The seam gave way and a small bundle of parchment slid partly out of the dress.

Tucking the bulk of the long dress carefully over and under one arm, Sharon eased the parchment out of its hiding place. A shock traveled through her as it landed in her hands; waves of shivers moved up and down her spine, making it difficult to breathe. The parchment bore no markings on its outer cover. The vellum was of a high quality and she was amazed that it was in such excellent condition. It was then that she realized that none of the dresses displayed any signs of mildew or moths or damage of any kind.

Something strange was happening here. These dresses, even sealed inside a trunk and protected from air and sunlight, would still show signs of their age. But these garments looked as though someone had just placed them in storage. And the parchment was smooth and supple, opening with no evidence of drying.

A part of her knew she should call in the others to witness her opening the packet but a strong urge pushed her forward. Slipping one finger under the seal, she gently lifted the edge of the outer covering and eased it away from the pages inside. Gazing at the documents before her, Sharon felt light-headed. Droplets of perspiration trickled down her face and down her back. The very air in the small chamber seemed oppressive and electric as words became clear to her.

June, in the Year of Our Lord, 1560.

May God in His infinite wisdom and mercy grant forgiveness to a sinner. I, Maria Morales Browning, now an English subject, do, in fear of the Lord's wrath, write this confession.

A confession? This letter was almost four hundred and fifty years old if that date was correct. Again, from the look of it, it could have been written just yesterday. Somehow, though, instinctively Sharon was certain that this was authentic. And yet it couldn't be, could it? She tilted the page to try to get a better look in the lessening light of dusk and the poor quality of the lamps available.

I do not know if I will have the courage to confess my sin as it should be done or even if I will have the opportunity to do so. My confessor has not traveled to this land for many years and I can feel the disease taking its hold within me.

As I have watched the King of England and his households and courts over these many years, I thought that this sin would remain between God and myself. But, like so many other sins, the effects of this one have spread away from the center like waves on a pond's calm surface—affecting much as time passes.

Sharon shook her head and blinked to clear her vision. The handwriting, although of some quality, was still in the older English style with flourishes and different letters from what she was used to examining. In spite of the difficulty, she was drawn back to the document, a sense of anticipation and even dread building in the bottom of her stomach.

My actions cost a Queen her life, a son his mother, and a country her Queen. If hatred had not corrupted my heart,

Anne Boleyn might still live today. And her son, Henry Tudor, would be King after his father, Henry. If arrogance and misplaced loyalty had not blinded me, I would have revealed the truth and all would be different in England and the world.

Anne Boleyn might still live? Another Henry Tudor would be king? Sharon searched her memory for information about Henry the Eighth and his children. There had been at least one bastard son but he had died before reaching adulthood. Maybe the letter would explain more.

It was easy to hate her for the humiliation she caused for my Queen Catherine. It was simple to think of her as the Great Whore who had stolen my Queen's lawful husband. But truly, not even I should have taken the Lord's work into my own hands. Even as I bore the babe farther and farther from the birthing chamber, I knew in my soul that I sinned most grievously. I told myself that with his small size and pitiful cries he would not last an hour. But he was a true son of Henry and fought for his life.

A son? A son of Anne Boleyn and Henry the Eighth? Sharon tried to take a breath but the room seemed to close around her. The information in this letter would change history's view of Henry and his wives and children. If it were true, of course. Sharon tried to step back mentally and look at this logically, but the ramifications of this letter stunned her.

A true son of Henry's would have saved Anne Boleyn's marriage and may have prevented Anne's execution. He would have succeeded Henry and the world as she knew it would be vastly different. As possibilities filled her mind, she took a deep breath. Whoa! This was a wonderful what-if scenario but there was no proof that this woman's deathbed confession was true. Although her initial reaction was that it was authentic, only accurate scientific testing and research could point to the truth.

Glancing back at the page, Sharon desperately wanted to finish the woman's account before calling her colleagues in to examine it. Even knowing that she was breaking protocol, Sharon hesitated to share this exquisite find with anyone just yet. A few more moments would not make a difference.

He roused from his stupor as I carried his frail body to be disposed. All in the birthing chamber believed him dead. My first thought, God forgive me, was to cover his face and finish the deed. I can only believe that the Holy Mother's intercession stopped me from committing the most heinous of sins in that moment of supreme hatred and, by doing so, She saved my soul from eternal damnation.

Instead I carried the child out of the palace and gave him to a Catholic family to raise, letting them believe this was another of the King's bastards to be kept from the Whore's path. He grew to be a healthy and robust child in spite of his weak beginnings.

I have not the courage nor connections nor power to right the wrongs I have done, for I shudder to think what would happen to him if his true parentage were known. His bastardy has been and will be his best protection as the struggle to establish which faith is the true faith continues. I lost my faith long ago but not my fear in the Lord and so I do what I can do now to protect the true heir to the throne of England.

The true heir to the throne? Not Elizabeth? What would England and the world be like without her long and successful reign? Sharon shook, almost dropping the parchment onto the floor. Her knees gave out and she sat down heavily on the trunk, not trusting her legs to hold her up.

I have sealed with my confession a copy of the attending physicians' statements and descriptions of the son, born prematurely to Anne Boleyn in January 1536. The babe inherited his mother's birthmark, one passed through most of the Boleyn family and easily recognizable as belonging to them. I have also obtained and enclosed a copy of the boy's baptismal certificate, accomplished in secret shortly after his birth. With these proofs, he could take his place on the throne.

Sharon's mouth dropped open in disbelief. Her hands began to tremble and the edges of her vision blurred. If this was true, she held proof that could have changed the world.

If only the baby named Henry Tudor had lived and held this proof in his own hands. What could have happened then?

Sharon shook off her astonishment and knew she'd better inform the British authorities of the existence of this piece of evidence pointing to a different possibility of succession. It would need to be authenticated and preserved as one of the greatest what-ifs of history. Carefully refolding the pages together and wrapping the covering around them, Sharon stood up.

In her excitement, she forgot about the dress now twisted on her lap and over her legs. And about the low ceiling. And the position of the trunk in the room. Bumping her head yet again, she tried to sidestep the chest but the dress tangled around her legs and sent her stumbling. Trying to regain her balance and to protect the valuable dress and documents, Sharon turned as she fell toward the wall.

As she landed heavily against the wall, it gave way, dropping her several feet down into another room. Mo's warning about the instability of the structure echoed through her brain as she slid to a stop against another wall. She watched in disbelief as the wooden partition in front of her closed like a door but with her on the wrong side.

Sharon scrambled to her feet and dusted off the dress she still carried. This chamber was bigger but not by much. Readjusting her glasses on her nose, she noticed bright light coming into the chamber from under a door on the opposite side of the room. After placing the dress over her shoulder, she tucked the packet into the pocket in her broom-style skirt for safekeeping and walked over to where she'd entered this room.

Examining the edges of the wall revealed nothing, no sign of a latch or handle for her to open the door. This was very strange. She knew that this wall was really a doorway—that made sense since the small chamber where the trunk was had been a priesthole, a hidden room used to hide Catholics during time of persecution. But how could she open it if she couldn't find the latch?

Shaking her head at her bout of stupidity, she turned to

use the real doorway in the room. If she couldn't get back through the fake wall, she would go around through this other way. Sharon approached the door and turned the knob, pulling on it as she rotated the handle. It wouldn't budge.

The same hot and stuffy feeling she'd experienced a few minutes before returned; perspiration again poured down her back and a feeling of fear tickled her gut. She fought to control the fear and anxiety even as she struggled to open the door. Finally, footsteps approached from the other side and the knob jiggled as someone opened it from outside.

Mo! Mo must have come looking for her and knew the other way around to this room. She let out a nervous laugh and took a deep breath. As the door opened, she smiled, ready to tease her friend for taking so long. But it was not her friend standing before her. A woman dressed as an Elizabethan courtier stood before her. In shock, her words escaped before she could control them.

"Who the hell are you?"

Chapter 2

A MASK OF surprise and anger covered the woman's face as she gasped, as startled by Sharon as Sharon was by her. And as the expression lessened as bit, Sharon felt the sharp sting of a slap on the cheek. Surprised more than hurt, she raised her hand to the place of insult.

"Here now! That kind of behavior will not be tolerated in the queen's household. Your lady aunt would be sorely displeased to know of this."

"My lady aunt?" Sharon examined the woman from head to toe and then stared back at her. "I don't know who you are or what you're talking about." Still clutching the dress to her, Sharon stepped around the full skirts and headed for the hallway outside the room. "Do you know where Mo has gone?"

A tight grasp and sharp nails clutched her wrist, stopping her forward motion and then pulling her back into the small chamber. The woman's face was tightened, her eyes darkened with fury. Sharon stood face-to-face with her, waiting, prepared to defend herself from any further attacks. "You will stay here until I have had my say, mistress."

Who was this woman? The manor house was supposed to be empty except for the research team. Mo said they were securing the site for the night. Night? Strong beams of sunlight flooded the hallway and small room. It was as bright as noontime, but that had passed hours before. Sharon took a closer look at the woman who blocked her path.

She was shorter than Sharon by about an inch, and her hair was pulled away from her face and tucked under a small lace cap. Her dress, although not ornamented, was well made and costly from the look of it. The bodice was cut low and squared over the shoulders; a layer of what looked like fine beige lawn covered the shoulders and neck and ended in a short ruff around the woman's neck. The rest of the bodice and skirt was cut in the usual style of an Elizabethan gown.

Elizabethan? Sharon glanced at the dress over her arm and realized the similarities. Running her fingers over the gown, she was even more confused. Images flashed through her mind and Sharon recognized them—a Renaissance fair. Women in clothing just like this, playing the role of noblewoman or commoner. Men in matching costume . . . food . . . fun. That would explain this woman's appearance but not how and why she was there.

"Your say? If you just tell me where Mo is, I'm sure she can clear this up." Sharon shook her hand, trying to free herself from the woman's steely grip. Unsuccessful, she waited for an answer.

"I do wonder why your aunt thought you appropriate for the queen's wardrobe. With your sharp, disrespectful tongue and your most slovenly appearance, I daresay you will not be acceptable."

Sharon looked down, once again surprised by the woman's comments. Well, she did look a bit slovenly, but her fall and landing on a dusty floor explained most of that. She lifted her glasses from the bridge of her nose, folded them, and slipped them into her pocket. Her braid had come loose, and tendrils of hair curled around her face.

None of this made any sense. This must be one of the actors in the Renaissance fair being held this weekend. Okay. She could understand that. But . . .

"Here now, pay attention to my words," the woman began, snapping her fingers in front of Sharon's face to get her attention. It worked. " 'Tis obvious in your haste to attend to my summons, you have become most confused. I am Lady Randall. Your aunt sent word that you are highly skilled with needle and thread and could serve as one of the queen's seamstresses during this summer's progress."

"But where's Mo?" She was not going to fall into some role without finding Mo and gaining an explanation.

"Mo? Who is Mo?" A frown formed deep furrows above the woman's brows.

"Mo, Maureen Boylan? She's in charge here."

Lady Randall's questioning frown turned to one of annoyance.

"The queen employs none of the Irish in her household. You must be mistaken of the name. I am the one who did ask your aunt to send you to me and I have not the time to stand and play an idle game of words with you, Mistress . . . ?" The inflection said she wanted to know Sharon's name.

"Sharon, Sharon Reynolds." She held her free hand out to shake the woman's hand but it was not offered. Instead her hand was slapped away.

"Methinks if you will get dressed, clean up your appearance, and show me the proper respect and a curtsey, I will forget this ill beginning. I will await you in the hall. Knock when you are ready to begin anew."

Lady Randall released her wrist and pulled the door closed once more. The clicking of a key in the lock told her she was not getting out until the woman decided she was ready. Sharon, still trying to decide if she was imagining this or not, looked around the room. She noticed a chair and small table in one corner that she'd not seen before. A low chest sat against the opposite wall from where she'd landed. A basin sat on top, with wisps of steam rising from it.

She walked over to look closer, convinced that this could not have been here before. Dipping her finger into the water and feeling the resulting burn in that finger told her she was awake and not dreaming. Well, standing here was not getting her answers to this puzzle. She could play along until she found where Mo was hiding. Sharon picked up a scrap of linen lying next to the bowl and dipped it in the water, carefully wringing out the excess.

After cleaning her face and hands, she dusted off the dress and held it up to inspect it. The dress really did look as good as new. And clutching it in front of her, Sharon realized it looked to be about her size. But it would be totally inappropriate to try it on.

The key moved noisily in the lock and the door opened a crack. "Make haste, make haste," Lady Randall hissed.

Sharon looked down, realizing for the first time that her soft gauze blouse and broom skirt might resemble the undergarments necessary for such a dress as the one she carried. Still she resisted putting on the probably priceless dress. She folded it back as she had found it in the trunk and opened the chest, looking for a place to store it.

The chest was filled with clothes for a woman, and they included all types of chemises and stockings. Some were of a fine lawn and some were of coarser linen and wool. Sharon opened one drawer after another. These clothes should not be here, she thought. This chest should not be here. The house had been unoccupied for years and all the furnishings had been removed before the renovations and repairs had begun. Looking around the room, finally seeing it as it was, Sharon blinked in surprise.

That wooden cupboard should not be here.

Sharon took the few steps needed to cross the room quickly and tugged on the knob of the tall closet. It opened without resistance. Dresses and skirts hung neatly and a row of shoes, soft ones like ballet slippers and a pair of ankle-high boots, lay on the bottom of the closet. She was in someone's room and neither the room, the furniture nor the clothing should be here. What was going on? Could this be someone's idea of a joke?

Another knock and angry whisper shook her from her confused reverie. She decided to play along until she could find Mo and get an explanation. Taking one of the skirts from the rack, she slipped it over her own clothes and tied it at her waist. Going to the chest, she yanked open a drawer and found a matching bodice, which she tugged over her blouse and laced into place. Sharon pulled the edges of her blouse out from the bodice.

These clothes fit her perfectly! Another puzzle piece in some larger mystery. Well, getting out of this room would help her find the answers. With movements deft from years of practice, she rebraided her hair and then knocked on the door.

"Well, finally! Come along then, there is much work to be done in preparation for tonight and a pair of lazy hands is of no use at all to me."

"Tonight?"

"The banquet for the queen. Where have you been, Mistress Reynolds, that you know not of this or of the plans your aunt made for your future?"

"Obviously not here," she answered, sarcasm filling her tone, still thinking she'd landed in some kind of play. She was again the recipient of a sharp slap. Sharon raised her hand to grab Lady Randall's wrist but the older woman was faster.

"Truly, if I had not the pressing need of a seamstress, you would find yourself rightly chastised for your unruly tongue. For now, you shall go without the noon meal. If you finish the work assigned to you, I may allow you something later. Now come."

Not giving Sharon the chance to refuse, the virago clutched her arm tightly and dragged her out of the room and into the hallway. As she looked left and right, her mouth dropped open in amazement. The house was filled with people and furniture. And it was beautiful! The wood gleamed from layers of polish and the floor tiles shined from scrubbing, their original colors and patterns now showing through.

Although Sharon tried to pull to a halt, Lady Randall would not allow it. With apparently little effort, the woman dragged her through different hallways and up stairs until they reached another chamber. This one was filled with chattering women and large numbers of trunks overflowing with dresses, gowns, headpieces, and garments of every shape and type imaginable.

"Here is your seat," Lady Randall said, pushing Sharon onto a small stool not far from one of the windows. "And this is what you must finish." A bundle of fabric was placed on her lap. " 'Tis one of Her Grace's favorites and she wishes it ready for this evening's reception."

Sharon picked up the material and turned it over. It was a headdress made of a cloth of gold, actual silken cloth of gold, and fit for a queen. Reenactors rarely used the real thing because of its delicacy and exorbitant cost, but this was real. One half of the headpiece was ripped from the seam and most of the ornamentation was gone. The remaining pearls and other jewels showed the pattern that should have been matched on the torn side. It was spectacular.

She looked up at the other women in the room, who were all gaping at her. Young and old, thin and plump, all held garments of one kind or another in their hands.

"Worry not, the thief who did this damage has been rightly punished for her transgressions," Lady Randall began, "as will anyone caught stealing from Her Grace." With a stern look to each of them, Lady Randall turned back to Sharon. "Get working, Mistress Reynolds. Time grows short and you have much to do."

Lady Randall strode toward the door, then paused before leaving. "Patricia?"

"Yes, milady?" a petite young woman in the corner answered, standing as she did, but without raising her glance from the floor.

"Assist Mistress Reynolds in her work. She will need the matching pearls to place on that headpiece."

"Aye, milady," Patricia answered, as she dipped into a deep curtsey. Lady Randall swept from the room on some other mission and Sharon surely felt sympathy for the woman's next target.

• • •

The room cleared a short time later when everyone, except Sharon and Patricia, was sent for lunch. True to her word, Lady Randall ignored her looks and the sounds emanating from her noisy stomach. Well, she wouldn't take this for much longer. Something strange was going on and she would get to the bottom of it, and soon.

Although her hands were busy with sewing, lucky for her it was something she was excellent at doing, so her glance constantly swept around the room to gaze at the people and the changes in the chamber. She was certain she'd been in this room before—she recognized the hallway and the position of the windows. It had not looked like this at the time. The curtains now at the windows were striking in their design and deep burgundy color. She would have remembered these. Unfortunately, her stool wasn't placed near enough to the windows to give her a view of the grounds outside.

Every time her attention wandered, Patricia drew her back with a tug on her skirt. The girl was no older than a teenager, quiet and pretty, and she followed Lady Randall's directions to the letter. Her behavior, serious and never wavering, made this seem too real and not playacting at all. Of course, she reminded herself, that wasn't possible.

Maybe she'd fallen asleep in the priesthole and . . . No, that seemed even more impossible. But how could she explain the changes in the house—and the people who were there and those who were missing?

Lost in her thoughts, she soon finished the headpiece. It was then that Sharon noticed the rest of the seamstresses had returned from their meals and were chatting in hushed whispers as they turned their attention back to their assignments. Determined now to explore the house on her own, she rose from the stool, handed the needle, thread, and finished work to Patricia, and stepped toward the door. Lady Randall stood in front of her, blocking the way before she took her second step.

"Patricia," she said, although her gaze never left Sharon's face, "has Mistress Reynolds completed her task?"

"Aye, Lady Randall, the headpiece is repaired." Patricia's soft whisper was almost too quiet to hear.

"Mistress Dobbs, what tasks do you have for Mistress Reynolds now?" Their gazes locked in a silent battle of wills. Sharon had already had enough. From the corner of her eyes, Sharon could see Mistress Dobbs, Lady Randall's chief assistant, shift nervously at the tension in this situation.

"I need to leave."

"Nay, mistress, you have not my permission to do so."

"I don't need your permission."

The flaring of the woman's nostrils and the deepening of the shade of her eyes should have warned Sharon that she was on dangerous ground. But Sharon was tired of the charade, tired of not knowing what was going on, tired of feeling like a fool caught up in some game.

"Oh, but you do," Lady Randall said, her voice lowering menacingly.

Sharon glanced over at Patricia, whose face had taken on a terrible pallor. The room grew unnaturally quiet, as though empty. Sharon looked at the other women and found them wide-eyed and holding their breath, waiting for Lady Randall's response to her challenge. She needed to stop this before the situation got out of hand.

"Milady Randall, I beg your pardon." She stuttered out the words, lowering her gaze to the floor as Patricia had and dipping into a curtsey. "I meant only that I need to use a . . . privy."

Apparently it worked, for the tension left the woman's shoulders and she stepped aside. "Patricia, go with her and bring her back directly."

Sharon opened her mouth to argue but decided not to. Once she was out of this room and Lady Randall's sight, it would be an easy thing to get away from Patricia. She closed her mouth and bit her tongue as she added another curtsey for good measure before following the younger woman from the chamber.

She stayed behind Patricia until they reached the stairs, which Sharon knew would take her down to the main floor. She quietly turned and ran down them, holding the long skirt up and out of her way. After three flights, she reached the foyer and turned and ran toward the back of the house. She increased her speed when she heard Patricia call to her from the stairway above.

Following a long hallway, Sharon ducked and maneuvered around people dressed as courtiers and some working as servants. This was the most realistic reenactment she'd ever seen. The costuming was impeccable, down to the makeup and hairstyles. Even the smells were authentic. She noticed more than one had forgone using deodorant for this festival. Authenticity could go too far in her opinion.

The light and activity ahead of her told her that her escape was near at hand. Following a line of people going out the door, she kept pace with them until she stepped into the sunshine. Now she would find her answers.

The world exploded around her with sights and sounds she never expected. Animals and coaches and men and women were all running busily around the stable yard. The bright sunshine reflected off many of the brightly decorated carriages and even some of the horses' bridles. Stable yard? Carriages? There was no stable yard or animals at Tenby Manor. Absolutely none. And no stable either.

She raised one hand to shade her eyes as she spun around, taking in the hundreds of images that came crashing at her. Men pulling recalcitrant horses. The overwhelming odor of manure. The barking of dogs. Heat rose from the animals and activities around her, making it difficult to breathe. She dropped the skirts she'd been holding in her other hand and stood gaping.

She never realized she'd continued walking into the yard. Never saw the unruly stallion pull away from the groom who was trying to lead him across the busy enclosure. Never realized her death was close at hand.

Chapter 3

HE COULD NOT believe his eyes. The woman walked directly into the path of the rampaging stallion. Screams erupted throughout the yard as others saw the impending accident, but she never reacted. Richard Granville hesitated but for a moment before launching himself at her. He leapt at the last possible second and they tumbled to the ground, rolling over and over until they came to a stop in the dirt.

Taking a few deep breaths, he raised his head to look at her. The woman's eyes were closed and she was barely breathing. Her hair was loosened from its braid and fell in waves onto the ground. He found himself wanting to know what color her eyes were.

He shook his head and rolled off her, kneeling next to her so that he could reach her face. He patted her cheek and tried to rouse her. He didn't think she was injured from their fall. He slipped his arm under her head, intent on carrying her back into the house from whence she came, when he heard a soft moan escape from her lips. Soon he would know the shade of her eyes and her name.

"What happened?" Her husky whisper struck a chord within him. He leaned closer to hear her better.

"You walked into the path of Goliath. He was none too happy over finding you there."

"And I was none too happy to be there." Her eyes opened and she blinked against the bright sunshine.

Brown. Her eyes were brown. He wasn't sure why it mattered, but he felt that it did. He stood up and offered her his hand.

"Here, mistress, permit me to help you to your feet." When she did not respond, he asked, "Are you able to move?"

"I am not sure. Every part of me hurts." She lifted her head as she spoke, and her gaze moved up her own body as though she were assessing any damage to it. The shapely legs uncovered by her twisted skirt looked fine to him. And the curved and cushiony parts he'd felt as they rolled on the ground felt fine to him as well. But he guessed that his heavier weight on her slighter one may have knocked her breath from her.

"Come, give me your hand." He waited as she slowly reached out to take his hand. Pulling her gently to her feet, he slipped an arm around her until she was steady. After a few seconds, she looked at him once more.

Brown? Had he thought her eyes were brown? That color did not come close to the shade he now saw. Flecks of pure gold shot through the darker mahogany color. He'd never seen anything like this before. He'd never seen anything like her before. And considering his many years within and around the queen's household, he'd not have thought there was any woman not known to him in Elizabeth's service.

"I do wonder how it is that you are unknown to me? Are you new to the queen's service?" He watched confusion flit across her face. It showed itself for a brief moment as a frown on her brow and then it was gone, replaced with something else, something hidden. Ah, a woman with secrets.

"I have just arrived here," she answered, looking around the yard and toward the house. "I lost my way in the many corridors and was blinded by the bright light."

"And I thought perhaps you were blinded by my beauty."

He laughed at her disdainful expression. She was obviously inexperienced at the ways of court and of flirting.

"He's under control now, sir," Richard's new groom, John, reported as he ran up to the place where they stood. "I put him back in the stall."

"I am glad of it, but had you accomplished the task when I asked, Mistress . . . ?"

"Reynolds," she replied.

"Mistress Reynolds and I would not be wearing the yard's dirt as decorations."

"Yes, sir," John answered, bowing his head.

"Wait for me in the stables. I will be there shortly."

John bowed and left in a run. Richard watched him go before turning back to Mistress Reynolds.

"Will he be all right?" she asked, searching his face with those eyes.

"John or Goliath?" Her eyes sparkled now as she tried not to laugh at his joke. He could see it.

"John, of course. You were harsh with him."

"Not as harsh as he deserved. You could have been maimed or killed and the horse could have injured himself. Neither of those is acceptable within my responsibilities."

"And you are . . . ?" So she *was* new here. She did not know of him yet; none had shared the gossip with her.

"Richard Granville, at your service, mistress." He tilted his head and offered a polite bow to her.

"Thank you for saving me, Richard Granville."

He wanted to hear his name from her lips again. A picture of her lying naked in his bed, covered only with the finest of satin sheets and calling out for him in play of passion, flashed through his mind. Those shapely legs wrapped around his waist as he . . . Richard shook his head to clear his thoughts. Bloody hell, one would think he was an untried youth!

"Oh, damn, she found me," she said. "I have to go." She pulled away from him and walked to the doorway leading into the manor house. She paused before entering and gifted him with a warm smile. His already heated blood surged into parts of his body better left unheated when tasks were left to be done in Her Majesty's service.

He made his way over to the stables after directing the carriages and their grooms out of the yard. John waited for him outside Goliath's stall.

"Come, lad, help me brush him down. He's had enough excitement for one afternoon."

John looked grateful for the reprieve and they entered the stallion's enclosure together. Offering to the boy one of the brushes he carried, Richard began to brush the neck and shoulders of his favorite mount. This was a task that many others could have performed but Richard found it relaxing after a stressful and busy morning.

And after the arousing presence of one Mistress Reynolds.

He surprised himself with his own strong reactions to her appearance. Something about her manner called out to him—she was not just new to Elizabeth's household; he could tell by the way she spoke she was a stranger, an outsider. And no one understood the difficulty of being an outsider more than he did. He lived as one every day of his life. Noble but not quite. Royal but not quite. Family but not quite.

Richard Granville, the not-so-secret royal bastard.

Apparently she'd just arrived, for she did not seem to recognize him. A wave of sadness crashed through him, for he knew what would happen once she did. It had happened before and would happen once more. Men and women fawned over him, offering their friendship and company. But not for himself, not for who and what he was. 'Twas only to gain access to the most powerful woman in the world—his half-sister, Elizabeth Tudor, queen of England.

Mayhap she would be different? With her strange accent and unusual ways? He could hope, but he would wait to see. His hopes had been dashed before and he had learned that lesson well.

• • •

Sharon dusted off as much of the dirt as she could as she walked slowly over to the doorway where both Patricia and Lady Randall stood. Her hair was a mess, too. But at least she was alive. His, *Richard Granville's,* actions, taken without hesitation, had saved her life. She was too sore to fight this nightmare any longer. Sharon waited for Lady Randall to act. It was not long in coming.

"You may be new to our household but you will learn our rules—quickly or slowly, that is your choice."

Lady Randall grabbed her upper arm in a tight pinch and pulled her into the house. Sharon resisted but the female version of Attila the Hun didn't seem to notice her efforts. Soon, she'd been dragged back up to the small chamber and shoved inside. Sharon stumbled across the room before regaining her balance.

"Mayhap hunger and thirst can teach you to follow my instructions. You will remain here until morning." Sharon watched in silence while the woman searched through the keys she carried for the one that fit the door. Lady Randall pulled the door closed and locked it. Sharon could hear some harsh words directed to Patricia, who stood outside the door of the chamber, and then the sharp tapping of Lady Randall's shoes on the polished floor as she strode away.

Sharon looked around the room and saw that a small pallet had been placed in the corner. Well, it was better than nothing. As she lowered her battered body onto it, she prayed that her mind would go blank and not try to mull over everything that had happened to her since she'd found that packet of papers in the dress. Her world had turned upside down and she had a strange feeling in the pit of her stomach that it was not going to get back to normal for some time.

The scraping of wood upon wood roused her from her listless sleep. Sharon lifted her head from the small lump of a pillow and stretched her neck, trying unsuccessfully to rid herself of the twinges and spasms. Pushing herself onto her elbows, she looked around the room. It was the same as when she first lay down, except that the ribbon of light shining under the door was now duller. The furniture that should not be there still was. Instead of finding herself in her own room in the nearby bed-and-breakfast, she was still locked inside a room that shouldn't exist.

Straightening out the layers of clothes tangled around her legs, she rolled to her knees and stood up. Her glasses lay unmoved on the floor next to the pallet so she picked them up and slid them in her pocket. Her brief rest had left her invigorated and determined to solve this mystery.

Tiptoeing softly over to the door, Sharon tilted her head and leaned her ear close to the frame. Sounds of merriment drifted in from afar but she could hear no one close by. With her hand on the knob, she carefully twisted it, trying to judge whether it was locked or not. The knob didn't budge; the door was locked.

"Patricia?" she whispered into the small crack between the door and its frame. "Are you still there?"

The wood-on-wood scraping came again and Sharon recognized it as a chair moving across the floor. Then a voice barely loud enough to be heard answered her.

"Yes, Mistress Reynolds, I am here."

"Can you open the door?"

"I can but I may not. Lady Randall said you are to stay here until the morn."

Sharon pushed the straggling hair from her face and blew out an exasperated breath. Lady Randall again . . . still. She knew the girl was young—maybe she should try for sympathy. That might get the door opened for her.

"I am very hungry, Patricia. Can I get something to eat?"

"No, mistress. Lady Randall said you are to have nothing until the morn." After a pause, the young woman added, "I am sorry but I have my orders." Sharon could hear the reluctance in Patricia's voice.

Sharon looked around the small room, searching for something she could use to free herself from confinement. It was then that she realized what was missing from the room.

"Patricia, there is no chamber pot and I need to use one."

She could almost feel the woman's frustration through

the door and she certainly heard the sigh that followed her request. She held her breath, waiting for Patricia to make her decision. It came a tense minute later when Sharon heard the jingling of the key against the metal tumblers of the lock. The door swung open and Patricia stood in front of it, chamber pot in hand.

Patricia handed the large pail-like bowl to her and reached into her pocket. Holding out her hand to Sharon, the young woman took a step into the room. Sharon would not miss her opportunity. Taking Patricia's hand in hers, she yanked until the other woman lost her balance and tumbled to the floor. Taking advantage of the fall, she bolted from the room and pulled the door shut behind her, turning the key in the lock.

It was then she looked in her other hand, the one she'd used to take hold of Patricia. In it she held the small, cloth-covered bundle the young woman had been handing her as she entered the room. Sharon peeled back the cloth, and a chunk of hard bread was revealed in the dim light of the corridor. A pang of regret at her own actions passed through her as Sharon realized Patricia's intent.

Resignation followed as she also remembered her need to understand whatever was happening to her here.

"Patricia?" she whispered again, this time from the other side of the door. "I'll be back as soon as I can."

"Mistress Reynolds? Please let me out. Lady Randall will punish me if you run away." The girl's voice trembled as she spoke, increasing Sharon's guilt.

"I promise not to run away. I just need to find out . . . find someone downstairs."

"Please, mistress. I will be turned out if Lady Randall finds I let you go."

Guilt made Sharon wince at the words she heard. Of course, she tried to tell herself, this was all some sort of play anyway and Patricia was keeping to her part, an excellent actress cast in the role of the young servant girl. But a feeling of great unease was settling over her, and Sharon was afraid there was more to the situation than her first assumptions.

"I will return in a short while, Patricia. Keep quiet in there and no one will know I've left."

With those last words, Sharon crept to the stairs and looked for witnesses. Seeing no one, she picked up her skirts and walked down the stairs, following the lights and sounds. Two long flights below, Sharon stood and unabashedly stared at the sights before her.

The halls were aglow with hundreds of candles and people were everywhere. Glittery jewels reflected the light of the candles. Sharon looked for the disco ball hanging from the ceiling that could really cause that kind of flashing. It was nowhere to be seen. Then she saw the dresses.

Every kind of fabric and style on every shape of body; she saw velvets and silks and wool and a few materials she didn't recognize at this distance. The men strutted like peacocks as well, in their short, rolled trunks with matching or contrasting hose and fancy doublets. Heavily decorated jackets and capes and headpieces completed the outfits on both sexes. But even the workmanship she could see from her place on the stairs was remarkable. This was much more accurate than any Renaissance fair she'd ever attended.

Sharon reached for her glasses so she could examine the costumes more carefully and then stopped herself as she realized what she was doing. She decided to try to get a closer look at the spectacle in case there were any clues to what was really going on. As she reached the bottom step, a stomach-turning wave of heat and odors rushed over her—the scent of unwashed bodies, mingled with food smells, was so strong she nearly gagged.

This definitely didn't feel right. RenFaire people took extremely good care of their costumes. As she watched, one staggering man spilled a cup of wine on another without so much as an "excuse me." A laughing woman stepped on the hem of the woman next to her, tearing it. No reaction.

Definitely not right.

Sharon stumbled down the hall, moving toward the huge reception room she'd seen earlier when she first arrived at the manor. The hall was crowded and her progress was slowed by the partygoers. Finally, she made her way to the doors of the room. Now she would find out the extent of this masquerade.

Her mouth fell open and she gaped at the change in the room. It was lavishly decorated and hundreds of candles shone from around the perimeter. On a small raised stage in one corner, musicians—all in costume—sat tuning and testing what looked like period instruments. Tables around the room were jammed with more participants—all in costume. Waiters and waitresses poured into the room in large numbers, carrying trays of steaming food—and all were in costume. The sheer size and reality of this ball shocked her senses. This was not a reenactment. . . . Could this be *real?*

Real?

Although she knew with a scientist's logic that the evidence in front of her had to be fake, she found it impossible to ignore the insiduous voice in her mind insisting strongly that it was all real. These people were not acting—they were truly from England's past. A past she apparently was now in!

Sweat broke out on her forehead and waves of nausea passed through her. Her knees threatened to give out, so she stumbled back to the nearby wall. Pressing herself up against the solid support, she took a few deep breaths, trying to regain control. It almost worked; her ragged breathing began to slow and quiet. It was then the call came.

"Make way. Make way," a man's loud voice cried out from down the hallway. "Make way for Her Most Glorious Majesty, Elizabeth, queen of England, Ireland, and France."

Men and women crowded around Sharon, pushing her harder against the wall and opening a space in the corridor. A group of tall men, all wearing deep red damask doublets and carrying long poleaxes, strode toward the ballroom doors. Several took up positions in front of the doors, several backed up against the people lining the hall, and the rest paused and waited before entering.

The man with the loud voice was now directly in front

of her and he repeated his announcement. Sharon peered past him to the woman he led in procession. She'd seen the woman's face in countless portraits, she'd even examined a dress believed to be hers, but nothing could have prepared Sharon for the moment of seeing her in the flesh.

Her Majesty, Elizabeth Tudor, queen, by God, of England, Ireland, and France. And, covering most of the red hair that would become her trademark, she wore the cloth-of-gold headdress Sharon had repaired earlier.

Not possible, not possible, Sharon thought. Words and phrases and scenes exploded in her head. She could not be in the past. It was simply not possible. Shaking her head, Sharon glanced at those near her and realized she was the only one still standing. Her knees finally gave out and she dropped into something that passed for a curtsey. Wiping her brow and peeking up slightly, Sharon noticed that the procession had stopped right in front of her. Sharon lifted her head and looked right into the face of the queen.

"You there, what is your name?" Elizabeth demanded as their gazes held.

"Uh . . . Sharon Reynolds . . . Your Majesty," Sharon stammered. Elizabeth nodded and touched her headdress briefly.

"Lady Randall and your aunt have spoken to me of your spirit and your skill, mistress."

"Uh . . . yes . . . Your Majesty," Sharon stuttered once again, not sure what to say.

"Randall will tire of one quickly without the other, so make certain she sees more of the skill and less of the spirit."

Without pause or another word, the queen pivoted and walked into the reception room with her entourage at her heels. Cheers and applause roared as she walked through the room, greeting those around her with a tilt of her head and an occasional smile. She reached a large carved chair and sat, tugging her gloves off and handing them to one of the women standing beside her. The crowd around Sharon moved forward into the room, blocking anything further from her view.

The air became stiflingly hot and close and Sharon knew

she had to get out. Standing on tiptoes, she saw the corridor that led to the back door and she pushed her way through the courtiers until she reached it. *A few more steps, a few more steps,* she chanted under her breath. Focusing on escape helped to keep her from passing out or surrendering to the urge to scream.

Once through the back door, she paused and looked around. Gone were nearly all of the dozens of carriages and their grooms that had been there this afternoon. A few soft nickers from a nearby horse were the only sounds carried by the evening air. She gathered her skirts up and ran past a few waiting carriages and toward the road that she'd driven in on today. Weaving through the attendants and their horses and carefully avoiding the reminders both left behind, Sharon at last reached the exit from the stable yards. It was then she noticed. No lights . . . no driveway . . . no paved road leading to town.

The stable yard was very dimly lit by several torches but the direction where the road lay was in complete blackness. The streetlights that lined the road to the estate were gone. The moonlight was the only light. A few minutes of searching convinced Sharon that she was not where she started. The driveway and garage that had been adjacent to the house this afternoon were gone. And so were the cars.

She had traveled through time.

She was in Elizabethan England.

It was time to panic.

Running down the dirt road, she refused to stop. Surely, all the normal things were here. Surely, just a few more steps and she would find them. After a few minutes of desperate jogging, she stopped in the center of the road and looked around. Nothing. She didn't recognize one landmark around her.

Her breath hitched in her chest as the fear began to sink in. Everything, everyone she knew was gone. She had traveled back to fifteen-something England and just met Queen Elizabeth the First. Oh, right, this was really happening.

Glancing off to one side, she saw a large boulder just off the road and decided that this might be a good time to sit down. The night had cooled and the air carried a slight chill for an August evening. Even through the layers of clothing she wore, Sharon could feel the lowering temperatures and dampness. Reaching the knee-high rock, she tucked her skirts around her legs and sank down onto its large flat surface.

Traveling through time would explain a lot. It would explain the accuracy of the costumes, the changes in the manor house, and the appearance of all these people. If time travel were possible. But it wasn't, was it?

She shook her head and tried to retrace her steps through the day. Thinking back, Sharon remembered her conversation with Mo and her examination of the dress in the trunk. And she remembered finding the parchment package that seemed to prove another heir, a male one, to Henry the Eighth's throne. She tapped her pocket lightly, making certain the package was still there. The last thing she remembered thinking was about how unfair it was to this heir never to have known.

Oh, dear God! Was that it? Had she traveled back to find him? She laughed out loud at the thought of it. She felt her control slipping and knew she needed to . . . what? She pushed the loose hair out of her face and looked around. What could she do?

Well, the first thing would be to get back to the room where she first "landed" and try to find the way out. She was not equipped to find a missing heir and turn over the proof of his legitimacy to him. Then what? Poof, and she would return to her own time? No, the room was the key, if only she could find the latch to open the panel.

The sounds of rough laughter echoed up the road to her. She peered through the dark and tried to see who was coming. Movements in the dim moonlight caught her attention. It looked like three men, three drunken men from the way they staggered as they walked. And they were walking right toward her.

"I doubt it not that she came this way," the first one said.

"And I think that she did leave with someone else," answered the second.

"Come, gents, there were many a wench to be had back at the queen's dinner," said a third.

"I am telling you both, she came this way."

She froze, afraid that any movement she made would get their attention. It didn't help—at that moment one of them pointed at her.

"Aha! I was right. There she is."

The three men staggered toward her. Sharon, deciding it would be better to meet these men on her feet, scrambled off the boulder and put it between her and the approaching men.

"See, Will, she does have spirit." The first man reached out and tried to touch her arm but she stepped back before he could. Edging her way around the boulder, she thought she might have to make a run for it. As long as they stayed together and were as drunk as she thought they were, she had a chance.

"Come, mistress, no harm will be done to you." The younger man, the one named Will, stepped over to block her way.

"Then what is it you want?" Sharon asked. Her path to the road was now blocked. A shiver of fear coursed through her. Three drunken men were more than she could handle even on a good night.

"We heard the queen speak to you and we did not recognize you from court. We were just curious," the first man explained.

"I am not from court."

"Where are you from?"

She saw the men exchange nods. Clearly this was not something new to them. Will reached out and grabbed her arm while the other two crowded in on her, making escape impossible. Fear now tore through her, and she pulled as hard as she could but could not free herself from their grasp.

"Mistress Reynolds is from Lancaster, though lately of the queen's wardrobe. And, gentlemen, you know the queen holds no love for knaves who would treat those of her house with less than the esteem they deserve."

Richard Granville's voice broke through her fear. In the moon's light, she saw him standing a few yards away, near the road, the frown and displeasure as clear on his face as was the hand he placed on the hilt of the sword at his side. Dressed more elegantly than when they'd met earlier, he definitely looked the role of courtier rather than horsemaster now.

"Richard, 'tis you?" one of the men asked.

"Aye, 'tis me." Richard strode over to them and even in the dim light of the moon his glare was obvious to all of them.

"Well, then, we had best be going," Will said as he released Sharon's arm. Muttering under their breath, all three of them let go of her and stumbled to the road. She pushed her hair back from her face and glared at them as they left, hoping to appear more confident than she felt inside.

She didn't quite understand what had just happened but Richard Granville had saved her once more.

Chapter 4

HE MATCHED HIS longer strides to hers, keeping pace as she headed farther away from the manor house that should have been their destination. Her confident demeanor and the thrust of her chin did not hide the fear in her eyes or the way her fists clenched at her sides. As bold as he knew her reputation already to be, three drunken men were unfair odds for any woman.

"I do think that the least you owe me is an explanation," he began. Placing his hand lightly on her shoulder, he slowed his steps. She stopped but would not face him.

"Thank you, sir. I can find my way back to the house now."

The woman stepped away from him as though to continue in the mistaken direction she followed. He blocked her way.

"You are mistaken, Mistress Reynolds, if you believe I would allow you to wander through the countryside in the dark of night."

"I am not wandering, milord. I know where I am going." Her chin trembled and he knew that if he looked into those warm brown he'd see tears. She still would not face him.

Studying her, he saw that she shivered in the night's dampness.

He tugged at the cord holding his cape over his shoulder and loosened it. He swept it around her shoulders, wrapping her in its warm length. Mistress Reynolds accepted his gift quietly.

"And, Mistress Reynolds of Lancaster, to where do you go on a cool evening such as this one?" He purposely flirted, trying to bring a smile to her face and to alleviate her trepidation. Mayhap he was losing his touch? He'd had many successes with town and country misses but this one seemed more a challenge.

"I . . ." She hesitated, turning in one direction then the other. She pulled his cape around her shoulders tightly and let out a loud, slow breath. For a moment he wished his arms were that cape, surrounding her, protecting her from the coolness in the air. "I guess I am lost," she whispered, not meeting his gaze.

"Well, lost I can fix, Mistress Reynolds," he said, stepping closer and putting his arm around her shoulders. Nodding his head in the direction of the manor house, he drew her along at his side. "The manor house is this way."

"Thank you, milord," she mumbled, mistaking his rank once more. Could she be the only one within miles who did not know his sad story? She was fresh from the country, although *fresh,* if her aunt's servants had the right of it, was probably not a good word to describe her.

"Richard. You may call me Richard."

She paused and let her gaze roam over him from head to toe. Even in the dim light, he saw the intensity of it, felt the scrutiny move over his legs, his stomach, his chest and face.

"You're dressed as a nobleman. Your clothing is obviously costly and of very good quality."

Costly . . . nobleman . . . quality . . .

It always came back to that, did it? Richard felt his guard rise in the face of this woman's—this stranger's—slight. She had not said he *was* a nobleman, just that he dressed as one. The old cuts still burned.

"I'm sorry if I used the wrong title, Richard. I am new to the ways of court." His name came out as a breathy whisper that floated up to him, and her hand on his forearm drew his attention.

He relaxed a bit as he realized she was new to court and probably overwhelmed by the pomp and circumstance of working in proximity of the queen. He remembered his first days among his father's court and knew how thunderstruck he'd appeared in that early time. He'd swept his hat off and shown quite a leg to the lowliest of the housekeeping maids but stood boldly upright before the highest of Queen Catherine's ladies-in-waiting. 'Twas many a week before he learned the hierarchy of those attending the sovereign.

"Your apology is accepted, Mistress Reynolds. I was new at court once and know how confusing it can be. Too many 'my lords' and 'my ladies' to keep straight in anyone's mind."

"Sharon," she said and he could hear a slight lifting in her voice; she was not so fearful now. He wondered if her eyes had turned that remarkable warm shade of brown he'd seen earlier. How would they look in the low light of a candlelit room? Or in the throes of passion, with her head flung back on his pillow and that hair spread out around and over them both.

The lower part of his body reacted with remarkable speed to agree with his wayward thoughts. By God's blood! He had saved her from the unsavory attentions of Will and his comrades only to subject her to his own lust.

"Sharon it is. Come, let us make haste, for the dark and damp are upon us."

He picked up the pace of their steps, hoping that the cool air moving over said body parts would work to calm them down. He was considerably more comfortable when the manor house came into view in front of them. Sharon, however, stopped abruptly in the center of the road and let go of the arm she'd held a moment before.

"I can't," she said in such a mournful tone that he wanted to take her into his arms and comfort her. He slid his finger beneath her chin and lifted her face to his.

"Can't?" he repeated in the strange accent she affected. Must be a country dialect from her own area in Lancashire. She blinked several times quickly and stuttered out a reply.

"I . . . cannot go back there, Richard." She pointed at the building now ablaze with torches outside and candles within. "I don't . . . do not belong there." With her head still shaking from side to side, she looked like a lost child instead of the alluring young woman he'd pulled from harm's way earlier this day.

"The court can be intimidating but you will be fine," he began. "Even though your duties in the queen's wardrobe will take up most of your time, you shall see a bit more of England than if you were still at home."

His words did not have the desired effect, for he could see her pale. He would talk to Lady Randall's maid more on the morrow and find out the extent of the "difficulties" that Mistress Reynolds had been involved in before she arrived here at Tenby Manor in Sussex. Mayhap that information would give him insight into her fears.

Mentally shaking himself, Richard was amazed at the path of his thoughts. Why did he care if she were afraid? And, other than for gossip's sake, why did he want to know more of her past, shady or otherwise? The women in his life provided great distractions for him but he did not allow his feelings to go any further than that. In the last ten and two years since Elizabeth took the throne, his precarious position as bastard of the old king, and a Catholic one at that, had not changed. His future was in no way certain, in spite of the queen's obvious affection for him. He would not open his heart until his future could be secured.

Yet, standing here with this frightened woman, he felt his heart soften at her plight. A stranger, one with a reputation to prove or disprove, she waited for his words. He took in a deep breath of the night's chill air and looked at her once more.

"Come, Sharon, let me take you into the warmth of the hall. The morn and good Queen Bess's departure will come swiftly."

"Departure?" she asked in a whisper. "She's, I mean, the

queen is leaving in the morning? How do you know?" Sharon pulled his cape around her shoulders once more and faced him more boldly this time.

"I am in charge of the queen's stables—the order came down earlier this even from Dudley himself to ready the carriages and wagons at dawn."

"Dudley? Robert Dudley? But what year is this?"

" 'Tis fifteen hundred and seventy, and the twelfth year in the reign of Elizabeth, as you must know."

Her eyes widened first then fluttered shut. She swayed, just a slight tilt, but he saw her faint coming before she did. And he caught her before she hit the ground.

Dear God, he thought, she couldn't be involved with Dudley, could she? The queen would never have permitted her into her personal staff if a hint of involvement with her favorite existed. And why did she ask him about the year? The wench was clearly confused, but her faint had to be caused by something else.

He slipped an arm beneath her knees and lifted her into his arms. Debating for only a few moments on his destination, he left the road and skirted the fencing surrounding the stable yard. Walking through a small gate, he carried her swiftly to the room he used over one end of the stables. It wasn't his but he'd found its location very advantageous for various assignations during the last sennight of the queen's stay here at Tenby Manor. Sometimes 'twas better to have privacy than an honored place in the hall.

She was warm and comfortable, that much she knew. Or rather, that much she felt. Earthy odors surrounded her, not unpleasant, just different. The warmth was a welcome change from the dampness of the night's air. Her dress was not enough covering to withstand England's changeable evening weather. She snuggled deeper into her cocoon of comfort. It was the very male chuckle that grabbed her attention.

Sharon opened her eyes and looked around. She didn't know how she got here—wherever here was. Searching through her jumbled thoughts, the last thing she could remember was talking with Richard on the way back to the manor house. Then he'd mentioned Robert Dudley.

Dear God! *The* Robert Dudley? The reality of where and when she was hit her again. How could she accept this?

"Will you wake or do you plan to spend the night here?"

Pushing off the blankets that covered her, Sharon shifted her position and sat up. She lay on a mattress of hay that had been covered with a sheet. The fragrant smell told her it was fresh hay.

"Are these the stables?" she asked as she straightened her skirt around her legs before tossing the blankets completely.

"Yes, this room is over the back end of the stables," Richard answered quietly from his seat a few feet away. He sat on a low bench, his elbows resting on his knees, his chin resting in his hands.

"Is this your room? Do you sleep here?" The room was actually cozy in a rustic sort of way. Other than the bench on which he sat, the only furniture was a small table and this mattress.

"No, I do not *sleep* here." His wicked grin, one that started on his lips and slowly moved to his eyes, and the inflection on the word *sleep* were her answers about what he did do here.

"How did I get here?"

"I brought you here when you fainted. It seemed a better idea than leaving you in the road where you lay." A hint of laughter laced his deep voice. She started to get to her feet but he stopped her.

"Lean back for just a few more minutes; your color is still too pale to let you up and run." He paused and reached for a goblet nearby. "Here, sip this until you feel stronger."

He'd saved her twice already in one day, so Sharon allowed his smooth-as-honey voice to lull her into obedience. Honestly, she was too tired to fight any of this. She reached for the cup but he retained his hold, sliding off his seat and down on his knees next to her. Taking hold of the cup, she felt his warm hand cover hers as he brought it to her lips.

His other hand supported her shoulders as she leaned forward.

The wine slipped over her tongue and down her throat, spreading more warmth as she swallowed one sip and then another. Before she could take more, he lifted the cup away.

"Ah . . . here now. A small sip will do. Too much on an empty stomach and your head will feel much worse for the wear."

Startled by his knowledge and reminded of how empty her stomach truly was, Sharon shook her head.

"How did you know I hadn't eaten?"

"I am familiar with Lady Randall's means of punishment. First she takes away food, then, if the hunger hasn't tamed her target, she moves on to the appropriate beatings."

She gasped. Was that what awaited her back in the manor house? Or worse yet, was that the fate of Patricia, who had unknowingly participated in her escape? Sharon struggled to her feet, unable to waste any more time here.

"I doubt that she'll do that to you on your first day."

"I'm not worried about me—I left Patricia locked in the room where Lady Randall left me. If she returns from the queen's dinner and I'm not there . . ."

"Here now, let me help you."

He grasped her hand and pulled her to her feet and into closer contact with his body. Still holding onto her hand, he reached up with the other and put it behind her head. Oh, God, was he going to kiss her? She watched as he leaned closer and then quickly pulled some pieces of hay from her braid. Sharon let out the breath she didn't know she was holding and waited for him to finish.

"That's better now. What would Randall say if she saw that in your hair?" He released her hand and turned her head to get a better look.

"I have to go, really." She glanced around the room, looking for the door. Sharon could see no way out.

"Come, this way," he said, taking hold of her hand once more and pulling her toward a darkened corner. He bent down and pushed against a section of the wall and it opened onto a narrow flight of wooden steps. With his guidance, she walked carefully down the stairs and soon was on solid ground at the rear of the stables. He continued to lead her around the building and toward a door in the back of the manor house she'd not seen before.

"Another servants' entrance," he said before she could ask. "I'll get you back to your room without Randall seeing you."

She stopped for a moment, wondering how he knew where her room was located within the huge house with its many floors and chambers. He tugged her hand and they stepped into what looked to be a small storage chamber off the kitchen.

He grinned over his shoulder at her, nodded his head, and pulled her along as they turned through many rooms on the lower floor. Servants, busy carrying platters of food and pitchers of ale and wine, moved past them with hardly a look. Loud rumbles emanated from her stomach as she caught whiffs of the cooked meats and breads. Clutching her free hand to her belly, she tried to cover the embarrassing noises. Without looking back, Richard laughed out loud when he heard them.

They entered a small alcove and Sharon gasped at the huge trays of meats, beef, and some type of small poultry, all of which were well seasoned and well cooked, judging from the aromas. Another platter, this one laden with loaves of bread and wheels of cheeses, caught her attention, too. The rumbling in her stomach grew louder and more insistent. Richard looked over at her and they both laughed this time.

"Do not worry, Mistress Reynolds. I have a plan." He winked at her and she couldn't help but smile back at him. He was flirting outrageously with her; she suspected he flirted with anything in a skirt.

Richard picked up a linen square from one of the tables and proceeded to gather food in it—a small cooked bird, a loaf of steaming bread, a wedge of cheese, and more. Gathering the corners together, he tied them in a knot and handed it to her to carry. He grabbed her free hand and again led her through hallways and up stairs until at last they stood before the small chamber she'd been locked in some hours ago.

"How did you know this was my room?" she asked in a whisper.

"I found out many things about you, Mistress Reynolds, not the least of which was the location of your room." He did that strangely attractive wink again and she forgot to breathe. Each time she looked at him she was struck by his blatant male sensuality. It was in the way he walked, the way he talked, and definitely in the way he winked. And, damn the man, he knew it!

Sharon felt the heat of a blush creep into her face. He couldn't possibly have found out anything about *her* and yet she felt as if he knew her deepest, darkest secrets. She would have to watch her step with him while she was here.

The momentary realization of where and when she was brought her back very quickly. She needed to focus on why and how she was there and how to get home and not on this gorgeous specimen of Elizabethan manhood and his flirtatious manner. But her curiosity about the woman she was being mistaken for won out.

"What else did you find out, Master Granville?" She leaned closer to him to hear his whispered answer. That was her first mistake.

"I was told that your aunt, Lady Seagrave, has despaired of ever bringing you under control and that she fears your wayward tendencies will bring further disgrace to her family's name."

"All that?" she asked in a whisper made huskier by his nearness and the game she tried to play. She realized she played against a master, and thinking she could beat him at his own game was her second mistake.

He took a step closer and leaned over nearer; his warm breath tickled her ear as he continued his answers.

"There are tales of lewd behavior and the granting of favors, but I could not believe but half of all I was told. No one"—he moved closer to her ear—"could possibly do all those things and survive more than one night."

She swore he touched her ear with the warm, wet tip of

his tongue. Shivers raced through her, uncontrollable tremors that pulsed to her very core. And then she made her third mistake—she turned to look at the wonderful, stirring smile she heard in his voice. His lips met hers and she tasted that smile and all it promised.

The kiss at once deepened, lips touched and melted, tongues danced and stroked. Oh, he was a master at this. Without using any other weapon, he completely conquered her with that kiss. She forgot that she was impossibly in another century. She forgot about not eating all day and the bundle of savory food in her hand. She forgot about Lady Randall and all the threats and possibilities of her wrath.

The kiss was the only thing on her mind.

He tasted of some wild and hot flavor she didn't recognize, except she knew it was his alone. He slid his tongue deeper into her mouth and moved it in an imitation of another movement—one that her body recognized. She ached for his hands to touch her, for his body to join to hers. She hungered for more. . . .

Richard placed his hands on her shoulders and moved back a step from her. Her breathing was ragged and her palms sweaty. And he didn't look affected at all.

"I do wonder if any of the stories are true, then, Mistress Reynolds. But, alas, the morning comes in a short few hours and 'twill be a most busy day for all of the queen's loyal servants. Mayhap we will have time to spend *discussing* the truth to such rumors on another night?"

He took another step away and, presenting a wonderful leg to her, bowed as though she were royalty. Then with another wink, he turned and ran down the stairs across from her room. Sharon leaned back against the door and tried to calm herself. She felt as though a tornado had run right over her and she tried to examine her responses to this man.

Sounds from inside the room reminded her that she did not have the time to stand around thinking. She reached in her pocket for the key and slid it into the lock as quietly as she could. Turning the knob, she hoped to find Patricia asleep. The young woman sat in one corner, warily watching her enter the room. Sharon held out her bundle as a peace offering.

Eat, sleep, and then find out what was going on—that sounded like a logical plan to Sharon. But where did Master Richard Granville fit in, logically speaking? She'd think about that tomorrow.

Chapter 5

TRUE TO RICHARD'S words, the chaos of the queen's departure greeted Sharon early the next morning. She woke to a loud banging on her door just as the sun started to rise in the sky.

"Make haste, make haste, mistress. The queen leaves for London this morn," Lady Randall called out as she pushed Sharon's door open. "Pack your things and make your farewells to your lady aunt. We must be on our way quickly to keep up with the queen."

Sharon stretched her tired muscles for a moment and climbed to her feet. Peeking out of the opened door, she saw that the household was already awake. Servants and the nobles they served filled the hallway and stairs, preparing to leave. Patricia appeared in the midst of it all carrying a large leather satchel. Without meeting her gaze, the young woman walked into the room and began gathering some of the clothing from the cupboard and the chest. Sharon watched the efficiency with which Patricia chose and folded and packed the clothes, apparently for her.

"Here, Patricia, let me do that," Sharon said. She picked up one of the skirts and began to fold it.

"Nay, mistress, please let me do this. You should change

those clothes, and be certain to wear your boots. You will need something sturdy for the trip."

"I will?" Sharon asked, not quite sure of the details of the excursion ahead. She'd hoped to wake and find herself in the large feather bed at the cozy bed-and-breakfast where she slept the night before. She'd hoped to wake and find this all some strange dream brought on by the stress of the last few months at work. Instead, she found herself in an impossible location and time, and in the household of Elizabeth Tudor, queen of England.

"Aye, mistress, you will. The rest will follow us in the baggage carts. Take this as well." Patricia took a long cape from the wardrobe and handed it to Sharon. "The day will warm, but you will need this before we reach London tonight."

"Tonight?" she asked as she laid the cloak next to her on the pallet. "But it only took an hour to get here from London."

"An hour?" An expression of complete disbelief met her when she glanced at the woman. "That's not possible, mistress. And I was told you came from Lancashire, not London."

Silence filled the room—Sharon wasn't sure what she should say or even if she should try to explain her words. If she found it difficult to accept the possibility of traveling through time, how would this servant girl from the sixteenth century react to such a story? Then she remembered Richard's words about "her" reputation. She would use that and keep her suspicions and knowledge to herself.

"You are correct, Patricia, I *did* come from Lancaster, *not* London." Sharon emphasized the words, making it sound as though she was just agreeing with Patricia's words, not really telling her the truth. As she'd hoped, Patricia blushed and looked away. Now even she would believe the wild stories about Lady Seagrave's niece from the country. It should give Sharon some camouflage for any mistakes or behaviors that didn't quite match the time and place. At least until she figured out a way to get back to her own.

Sharon finished putting on her own boots and picked up the cloak. Patricia made short work of packing and stood by the door waiting for Sharon. She took one last look around the room. She really needed to check for a latch that would open the hidden panel in the wall. It may be her only way home.

"I will take this down to the baggage wagon, mistress. Your lady aunt said to tell you she will await you in the foyer to bid you farewell."

She must have choked, because the younger woman was at her side immediately. Coughing to clear her throat, she tried to think of a way out of this situation.

"My aunt? In the foyer?" she whispered in a voice hoarse from coughing.

Patricia gave her a look of complete and utter sympathy and, putting the bag down next to her, patted Sharon on the shoulder.

"Here now, mistress. I doubt not that your aunt would give you a fond farewell in sending you to court. She thinks enough of you to secure your place within the queen's household."

"You don't understand, Patricia, Lady Seagrave—"

"Can be as stern as Lady Randall?" Patricia smiled and nodded. "I understand more than you think, mistress. I will tell Lady Seagrave that you have already left on one of the earlier wagons, if that is what you wish. You will want to leave by the back stairway." Picking up the bag, she turned and left the room, never noticing Sharon's stunned expression.

Not wasting a second of her reprieve, Sharon dropped the cloak on the chair and went first to the wardrobe. If she were to carry that parchment packet with her, it needed more protection than her pocket offered. She'd not seen anyone with a purse but that's what she needed—for the documents and for her glasses. She found a small rectangular leather bag in the bottom of the wardrobe that was perfect for her needs. Taking a thin belt as well, she threaded it through some holes in the edge of the pouch. Tied around her waist under her skirt, it would hang in the front, between layers of clothing. Taking the documents from her pocket, she placed them inside the bag, and after wrapping her eyeglasses in a handkerchief, she put them inside, too. Securing it closed with a thin leather lace, she positioned it where it would be safe and straightened her skirts around it.

Then, she walked over to the wall opposite the door. With only the light from the hall to brighten the room, she could see no differences in the wood grain or find an uneven border. Gliding her hands over the surface, Sharon tried to find the edge she knew must be there. She could find nothing. She tried tapping to see if it were hollow in places, but she could detect nothing different as she listened to the echoes of her knocks.

It had to be here. This was really a doorway not a wall. Sighing, she leaned against it, frustrated at her inability to find what she knew must be there. A noise caught her attention and she glanced out of her room.

Richard stood in the hallway watching her, his eyes darkened with worry and something else she couldn't identify. Fear? Guilt? Without a word, he turned and walked away. Grabbing her cloak, she tried to follow but the stairs and hall were so crowded she was unsuccessful. They were both going in the same direction—London with the queen—so she would catch up with him later and ask the questions that had plagued her all night long.

She followed the moving crowd down the back stairs and into the kitchen area. Trays of bread, fruit, and cheese filled one large table in the kitchen and people took what they wanted as they passed. This was the Elizabethan answer to "drive-thru" fast food. Obviously there was no time for sitting down for breakfast so this was eat-on-the-run food.

Taking a hint from Richard last night, she took a cloth napkin, filled it with some bread, cheese, and apples, and tied it closed. Again following the flow, she exited the house and found herself in the stable yard once more.

In the light of day, it looked much the same as it had yesterday. Carriages and wagons, filled with people or baggage, lined the yard. The chaos of the house spilled out here and grooms fought for control over their mounts and their teams. Stepping carefully this time, Sharon searched for Patricia and found her standing next to one of the wagons. Patricia saw her at the same time and waved her over.

"This is where you will ride, mistress. I've secured cushions and a blanket for you for the journey." Patricia pointed out a place in the back of the wagon.

Sharon blinked and looked once more at the vehicle in front of her. The large open wagon looked like something she'd been in during an autumn hayride—benches were set around the perimeter and the middle left empty. It was hitched to a team of six huge horses. A driver sat at the ready in the front and a pair of grooms stood at the back to assist people in boarding.

Stumbling up the tall step, Sharon waited for Patricia to follow. She sat down on the cushions but noticed that the younger woman had nothing but her cloak to protect her from the bumps and rough ride ahead.

"Here, Patricia," she said, pulling one of the flat cushions from underneath her. "You should use one of these. The ride will be hard on you, too."

"Why, thank you, Mistress Reynolds." Tucking the pillow under her, Patricia took her place next to Sharon on the bench seat.

"I am grateful for your help in this confusing time for me," Sharon added. This girl had been a great help so far, easing her way this morning and in not causing trouble after Sharon's sojourn into the night. "But I don't understand why you're being so nice to me."

Lowering her voice, Patricia answered, "Because you did not leave me alone last night to face Lady Randall's wrath. You came back as you said you would."

Another pang of guilt moved through her as she thought of how close to running away she really had been last night. It wasn't for lack of effort or want that she found herself still there this morning. Sharon smiled at the girl and settled in for the ride.

The wagon filled quickly with many of the same women she'd seen in the sewing room yesterday and a few others she didn't recognize. Everyone tried to make themselves comfortable on the hard wood benches and soon the driver shook the reins to get the horses moving. With a lurch and turn, the wagon was off to London.

After hours of rocking, swaying, and bumping in and over every deep groove and rut in the road's surface, Sharon was certain that she was black-and-blue everywhere on her legs and bottom and spine. This was unlike any ride she'd ever been on in her life. The cushions so thoughtfully provided did little to blunt the rough thoroughfare's effects on her body. She pulled herself up to the side of the wagon and looked at the others traveling in their procession. Most of the women servants and staff traveled in wagons in front of or behind her own. She could see very few fancy carriages along the length of the dusty road. There were, however, a number of men and women riding horses in small groups throughout the line of wagons.

Her hands itched with the desire to touch the clothing they wore. The scientist awakened in her as she gazed at the riding habits the obviously wealthy noblewomen wore. Nothing in the chest she'd examined came close to the exquisite workmanship that she saw as the riders would canter past her slower conveyance. Actually, she'd even like to take a closer look at the clothing in her bag, but that would probably look very suspicious. There would be time in London.

They were going to Windsor Castle, Patricia had told her. Some royal business had drawn the queen's attention and interrupted the schedule of the next few weeks. Although the queen had a wardrobe stored at each of her residences, Patricia also informed her, the household moved with her so that she could be assured of a certain level of comfort and care. The seamstresses were kept constantly busy with no lapse in their duties of maintaining the queen's extensive collection of clothing.

Sharon longed for a break from the slow and lurching pace; she really needed a chance to stretch and walk. So did most of the occupants, who groaned loudly at each bump. Soon they entered a small forest and a rider passed swiftly by, calling out a command to the drivers. From the reaction of her wagon-mates, she knew a stop was being called.

As soon as the wagon came to a stop, the women started pushing their way out. Manners were clearly not useful when nature called after several hours on the road. Sharon followed Patricia's lead and, after unkinking the muscles of her legs and back with several minutes of stretching and after a visit to some bushes away from the wagon, she felt like a new woman. As she heard the call to load up once more, she saw him.

He moved as one with his horse—his hands barely moving as he controlled the huge gelding's movements. Dressed as the horse-master once more, Richard's dark hair flowed out behind him in the wind. His shirt was open, exposing his chest to the sun and to all who looked. And she noticed, many looked. And many made comments.

When one of the drivers called out to him, he turned his horse and approached her wagon. After answering the man's question, Richard began to turn the horse back to his path and then stopped and looked directly at her. Touching his heels to the horse's sides, he walked it over to where she stood. The sun's glare made it difficult for her to see his face until she shielded her eyes with one hand above them.

"Good morrow, Mistress Reynolds," he said cheerfully.

"And good morrow to you, Master Granville." She mimicked his tone and nodded her head toward him in greeting.

"How do you fare on this beautiful morning?"

He flirted still, always. She smiled.

"I do well. Will Goliath be jealous to know you're riding another horse?" She noticed this one, although nearly as big as Goliath, was not a stallion. Years of those riding lessons her parents provided for her had paid off—finally!

"Ah, you noticed? So you have some knowledge of horseflesh?" He reached over and patted the horse's neck.

"Not nearly so much as you do, but I can tell horses apart from one another. He is beautiful, but not so temperamental as Goliath, I think." She stepped closer to touch the mount's nose. The horse snorted and bumped her hand. Richard smiled now.

The loud call to load up broke into their conversation and Richard tugged the reins back, moving his horse a step away from her so she could pass.

"I must go now, mistress. Mayhap I will see you again on the day's journey?"

"Richard?" she called out before he could turn completely away from her. "I saw you outside my room this morning. Were you looking for me or did you need something else there?" The question that had bothered her all morning since she saw the look on his face just burst out. She'd had no intention of asking him.

And from the look he gave her, he had no intention of answering her question. He smiled and raised his eyebrow but his smile didn't quite make it to his eyes. His warm and flirtatious demeanor toward her suddenly cooled.

"You must be mistaken, Mistress Reynolds. I have been about the queen's business all morning. Mayhap 'twas someone else?"

The silence around her told her that others were watching and listening to their conversation. She needed a graceful and quick way to end this until they could speak in private. He had been in the hall, watching her search the walls, there was no doubt in her mind of that. But for now . . .

"Master Granville, I do believe I was mistaken. I am, as you know, new to the court and the household and mistook another for you. I beg your pardon." She lowered her gaze from his and waited for his reaction.

"Have no fear, you will become accustomed to us and our ways, Mistress Reynolds. Good day to you now."

Without another word, he turned the horse, kicked his heels against its sides, and galloped off away from her and her questions. Sharon lost no more time climbing into the wagon and taking her seat. The rest of the day passed quickly in a blur of a rocking wagon ride, the warming and cooling of the day's temperatures, and Patricia's friendly attempt to tell her the name of everyone in the queen's current household.

When they passed through the gates to Windsor Castle, Sharon was too worn out to take notice of anything. Even knowing she would regret not looking, she waited until the wagon stopped in one of the many courtyards and then trudged behind the other women, who were obviously as tired as she. Without a word, she allowed Patricia to guide her to a room on the third floor of one of the many wings of the massive stone keep. Too exhausted to do anything at all but sleep, she wrapped one of the blankets she carried from the wagon around her shoulders and dropped onto the small feather bed in one corner.

Two days had passed and she was no closer to understanding what had happened to her than when she first tumbled through the wall in Tenby Manor. Two days of not knowing what to say or who to say it to. Not knowing who was friend or who was foe. Not knowing if she'd wake up in this time or in her own time. Her thoughts and fears jumbled together as she felt her body give out. Tomorrow . . . this would all be clearer in the morning's light.

Chapter 6

IF THE FIRST two days of her adventure had passed slowly, the next two weeks moved at a caterpillar's pace. Dragged into the daily routine of the women working by her side and still suffering from a kind of shock, Sharon had worked from dawn until dusk repairing, cutting, and sewing garments for the queen. She spoke very little to those around her, even those whose quarters she shared at night, for fear of slipping up and revealing more than would be safe. She knew that Tenby Manor held the secrets to her traveling through time, but she'd had no opportunity and no help to return and seek out the truth.

Her nights were her own to explore the many hallways and rooms of Windsor Castle. She'd visited it many times during her previous trips to England, but in no way did the modern-day palace resemble the building as it appeared before her now. The furniture, draperies, and tapestries were very different from those of the palace of her time. Even the structure itself was different, changes having been made by several monarchs between this Elizabeth and the present-day queen. And this Elizabeth had yet to begin her renovations and additions, ones which would add significantly to the northeastern section of the castle.

She tried to convince herself that her tours of the castle were to explore the history and architecture of it, that she searched for fabrics and weaving styles that had not survived until her own time. Deep inside she knew that she always carried with her a seed of hope that the next turn in the corridor would lead to Richard.

She had seen him across one of the crowded eating halls, but she doubted he'd noticed her since the day they arrived. She thought about seeking him out and asking for his assistance in returning to Tenby Manor. He knew about the secret panel—his cryptic expression and his later reticence about even speaking about being there convinced her that he knew more than he would admit. Maybe if she asked him in private, he would agree to help her.

No, she thought, being with him in private would cause more harm than good. The gossip in the sewing room convinced her of that. Another young woman in the queen's service had been found with one of the queen's guardsmen and had been turned out from the position in shame. The only thing that was keeping Sharon alive right now in this distant time was the charade she played of being Lady Seagrave's niece. And, with that young woman's present reputation as she knew it, one misstep could lead to disaster. So she would wait until she saw Richard in public and try to speak to him then.

Then, as if her words had conjured him up, he stood at the end of the hallway. His long, rolled trunks and cape were of dark blue velvet, making him look very much the courtier. A white shirt, though designed to be loose-fitting, hugged his chest and arms, displaying his well-muscled form to perfection. High black leather boots covered his legs up to his thighs. He wore no hat; his long black hair hung loose around his face and down over his shoulders. Sharon shivered at the male sensuality he exuded without any attempt to do so.

Richard was speaking quietly to someone standing off to one side of the corridor, his hushed tone barely carrying down the empty hall to her. She stood still, not knowing whether to interrupt or to try to leave without being seen.

Sharon suddenly had the distinct feeling that this was not a conversation he would want known. Maybe it was in the way he turned to keep the other person hidden. Maybe it was in the way he bent down closer and continued to use that hushed voice. Whatever it was, Sharon knew she had to leave before he saw her.

Turning quietly and feeling grateful that she wore soft shoes this evening, she took a few steps back and started down another corridor that would lead back to her room. Hoping not to attract his attention now, she found herself holding her breath as she moved quickly and quietly away from the furtive conversation. She'd not made it far when she heard footsteps behind her. Turning, she watched as Richard and a man she'd seen before but whose identity she didn't know walked past the junction of the two halls. As they moved on, she saw Richard glance in her direction without slowing or acknowledging her presence.

Something tugged at her memory—that man looked very familiar. Although she had some knowledge of Elizabethan history, she could only remember a few of the more notable names and the positions they held. She'd already seen William Cecil, Lord Burleigh, and Robert Dudley, the Earl of Leicester, when they'd attended the queen in her chambers. But this swarthy-faced man with glossy black hair made her uneasy.

Maybe he was one of the household? No, he carried himself as though he were above all those around him, even Richard. He must be some level of noble. She would ask Patricia about him—Miss Prescott was a veritable font of knowledge when it came to names within the household and those visiting from the various courts of Europe. The girl would have been a natural for the society column of any major newspaper or gossip magazine if she lived in Sharon's time.

So, Richard was a man of secrets. She guessed it would be difficult for someone living so close to the queen not to be involved in some level of intrigue. People were always congregating in small groups in the eating hall and all throughout the palace—whispering behind their hands, with heads tilted to hear the hushed words better. Courtiers, ambassadors, guards, and messengers rushed in and out of the private apartments all day and a good part of each night since they'd arrived two weeks before. Politics. She'd left it behind in her world to be thrown into an even deeper mire of it here.

Sharon turned down a familiar hallway and made her way back to the tiny room she shared with four of the other seamstresses. Yawning, she fought off her exhaustion. She had to find a way to convince Richard to return her to Tenby Manor. She had to find a way back to her own time. As attractive as he was, Richard was not reason enough to stay here without trying to get home.

"Methinks thou doth walk on the edge, nigh to safety but nigher even to danger."

Richard bit into the crispy salted skin of the pigeon in front of him, tore off a piece, and chewed it several times before even raising his glance to his dinner partner.

"Methinks *thou* doth tread where *thou* is not welcomed . . . or needed." With a quick nod of his head, he looked across the table at the father of his groom, John. Robert Calder was the captain of one of the palace detachments of the queen's yeomen of the guard and one of very few he could call friend. But, friend or not, 'twas best that Robbie stay out of his private affairs. Picking up his goblet, he washed down the hot food with a large swallow of ale.

"In faith, Richard, you made no secret that you spoke with that Spaniard Ramirez. All in the hall saw you enter with him, still conversing—about what, they can only speculate."

Now it was Rob's turn to attack his own food and Richard knew that his avid attention to his meal was caused by his consternation over Richard's probably foolish behavior.

"Rob, there is nothing for them to speculate about—Ramirez and I share a mutual acquaintance from our own days in the nursery. That is all. No more, no less."

Rob snorted his reply.

"I assure you, Rob. Read no more into our conversation

than that." Richard dipped a chunk of bread into the juices pooled on his trencher and bit into it, purposely ignoring Rob's look of disbelief.

The conversation this evening with Miguel Ramirez—*Father* Miguel Ramirez—had been innocent in nature. But, with the many rumors of impending Spanish and papal actions against Elizabeth, meeting him here and now was not the most intelligent thing Richard had done lately. As part of the Spanish contingent, Ramirez's actions were scrutinized by a variety of Elizabeth's ministers.

"Then be you not stupid and flaunt it where you know Elizabeth will hear of it . . . has most likely heard of it already." Rob's words lowered to a grumble.

"Come now, friend. Good Queen Bess knows the love I bear for her is true. I am no threat to her." Richard knew differently, but kept that to himself. No use putting Rob or the others involved in any more danger than they already were.

The Spaniard had brought news of a strong alliance between Catholics in Spain and England to raise a Catholic monarch to the throne. His name had been bandied about by too many. He feared that his most secret desire, to sit on his father's throne, had been unmasked and this alliance sought to make him their pawn king.

He did want to be king. He wanted that final, unattainable level of acceptance among his father's children to be his. He had been educated with them, fed with them, clothed with them. His father had given him some measure of affection, as was due him as Henry the Eighth's natural son. But the bastard label that had been removed from both Mary and Elizabeth by an act of Parliament had never been lifted from him. Of course, Henry *had* married their mothers and not his.

Elizabeth was entrenched on the throne and was, in his own opinion, good for England. Better than the years of strife caused by their older sister or the uncertainty of the short reign of their younger brother, Edward. And the people loved her. Certainly she moved now more and more openly and harshly against Catholics. But there were those who still practiced their faith in secret.

Such as Lord and Lady Granville of Tenby Manor.

His mother's parents had raised him with tender and loving care until his father discovered him. They had him baptized in secret after his mother died in childbirth and had taught him about his faith in his early years. His mother had died from Henry's attentions and his robust desire for a son. Unfortunately, Henry was still married to Elizabeth's mother at the time, so neither marriage nor legitimacy was a possibility.

Thoughts of his grandparents reminded him of his discovery on the morning they left for London. He'd gone to see Sharon to apologize for his outrageous behavior the night before: for lying to her about what he'd heard of her reputation and bad behaviors. He'd heard only a hint of mistakes, common to any spirited young woman, and not the lewdness he told her about. The look in her eyes, fiery flashes of passion and desire had urged him on . . . to both the teasing and the kiss.

The kiss made him dream of the things he hinted at with her. He dreamed of her nightly, even now, even fearing that she knew the truth about the panel in the wall. The truth that, if revealed to the wrong person, could get his grandparents executed.

There was a priesthole at Tenby Manor.

And now she had witnessed his meeting with Ramirez. He had best watch his step with this enigmatic young woman of secrets. Pretty or not, she wasn't worth his head on a pike. Shaking from his reverie, he found he'd almost finished his meal and so had Rob. And Rob was ready to argue.

"That faraway look in your eyes usually means a woman is involved."

Richard laughed and pushed the remainders of his food away. Wiping his hands on a cloth, he removed the stains and grease of the meal.

"Alas, you know me too well, friend. 'Tis a woman that

causes me to lose sleep and bemoan my fate to God and to my friends."

" 'Tis always a woman, Richard," Rob chuckled as he answered. "Mayhap 'tis time to pick just one of them and settle down—'twill end the constant bickering over you and your bed."

"Marriage? Nay, not for me. I still have many things to accomplish before I marry."

Rob leaned over and lowered his voice so none but Richard would hear. "And many of those things will put you in the Tower or be your death, Richard. Think well on my words, friend. Marry and let the rest go. Let the rest go." Rob reached over and clasped Richard's hand in his, squeezing it firmly to emphasize his warning. "Well, I must go. My duty begins once more."

"My thanks for sharing the meal." Too many warnings and bits of wisdom offered by friends and possible foes filled these last days. Richard released Rob's hand and stood up.

"And you will ignore the rest?" Rob stood up from the bench and replaced his black bonnet.

"Nay, Rob, never think that. I will consider your words carefully, for it may mean my life to do otherwise."

With a nod, the captain of the yeomen guard strode off to take his place behind the queen in the great hall. Richard stood and watched him walk away, knowing once more that this man was one of his very few true friends.

Musicians began once more to play a lively tune and Richard glanced around the room at those still remaining. More than one woman invited him closer with her eyes and a teasing turn of a shoulder or leg. Any of them would be good for a quick bout of pleasure. But marriage was another matter. Bastard or not, Elizabeth would have something to say about his choice of wife.

Their father had promised him a bit of land in his will. Mayhap Rob was right? Was it time to find a wife and remove himself from the intrigue that swirled around him? The plotting and secrets that always surrounded the royal family grew even stronger with the influence of the Spanish and the Pope. Mayhap it was time to leave it behind and make a life for himself?

His heart ached and yearned for what could not be—he would never sit on the throne of his father. How could he ever be satisfied with a life other than that? Reaching back for the goblet he'd left on the table, he lifted it to his mouth and drank the ale down. Filling it again, he drank that cupful in several swallows. Knowing that the ale alone would not bring the comfort he sought, Richard winked at one of the comely women at the table next to him and offered his arm to her.

With a laugh and a broad smile, she jumped up from her seat and wrapped her arm around his. Pulling her along, he walked quickly from the hall and into the residence area of one of the wings. He knew of an unused room not far from his own quarters where he could seek comfort in this woman's ample bosom and welcoming arms.

The ale began to affect his balance and they swayed a bit as they made their way down a corridor. Almost to his destination, he shushed his companion when her giggling became too loud. Most of the household were already in their beds and it would not do to waken or disturb them.

Unfortunately, he tripped and bumped against a door as they rushed to their liaison. Staggering for a step or two, he gathered his companion closer, ready to leave. But the sound of the door swinging open stopped him.

She stood there, with only a thin nightgown covering her and with her hair long and loose around her shoulders. Her mahogany-brown eyes widened in recognition as she looked at him. Seeing he was not alone, she tugged at the door. Holding it like a shield before him, she didn't say a word. She didn't have to—her eyes said it all.

Anger . . . disappointment . . . pain? He read it there in her expression even though his thoughts were not very clear. Damn! Why should this stranger's reaction to him matter so much? He had a lively wench in his arms, a promise of a night's romp and some soothing and comfort, and yet the haunted glance of Mistress Sharon Reynolds gave him pause.

After a moment, she closed the door. He stood still for a minute more before turning his attention back to his companion. A long dark night awaited him—one made much more tolerable by the warm touch and feel of a woman. He pulled her along into the dark hallway and toward the room he knew stood unused at the end of it.

Chapter 7

"HE DID INQUIRE about you once more."

"He did? I'm surprised he remembers who I am."

Sharon blew out the breath she didn't know she was holding. Pushing the thick needle through the layers of purple satin, she ignored Patricia's gaze. The skirt for the queen's newest gown was almost complete. Lady Randall insisted that it be finished in time for the formal banquet planned later this week. Sharon had spent every waking moment working on the intricate design of the overskirt and the matching sleeves. She'd been promised a day of rest once the gown was done and Sharon wanted that day to herself more than anything.

When she returned to her own time, she would never again underestimate the importance of a sewing machine! Her fingers ached from the repetition of the small stitches required in hand sewing. Actually, she thought, when she returned to her own time, she would never sew again.

"Well, mistress? Would you not like to know what he asked?"

Sharon shook the cramp out of her hand and looked at the young woman. Pushing the loosened strands of hair that always seemed to fly about her face back behind her ears, Sharon repositioned the needle once more.

"Why should I care what he asked? I do not know him and he does not know me." Sharon tried to remember not to use too many contractions. Other than the more flowery flow of their words, that was the biggest difference she noticed between their speech patterns and hers. She could rearrange her words into their style of speaking, but she found giving up contractions more difficult.

"Come now, you must confess to being at least curious." Patricia smiled at her and waited. The girl could be a pain in the neck, but she was Sharon's only friend in this time . . . and the only one who seemed interested in Sharon's well-being.

"Oh, tell me then, since it seems you will not be satisfied until you do!" Sharon leaned back against the chair and rested the costly gown on her lap.

"He asked me to find out your most favorite flower and color!" Patricia's eyes lit with excitement as she revealed her knowledge. "And, he asked if Lady Randall would give you leave soon."

"And this means something to you, Patricia?"

All Sharon could remember was the sight outside her door that night last week. A drunken Richard wrapped around a voluptuous woman, staggering down the hallway in the dark. That had told her pretty clearly where she stood in his regard. She only wondered if his bumping into her doorway had been his way of telling her more about himself than she wanted to know.

"Of course, Mistress Reynolds, of course! He plans to give you flowers. And he plans to seek out your company on the day you have no duties here. Is not that wonderful?" Patricia reached over and patted her hand, smiling happily.

"And why should I waste my time off with him? He obviously prefers the company of other women to mine."

A picture of the buxom blond in Richard's arms flashed through her mind once more. A twinge of jealousy and anger confused her even more—there was nothing between them but some harmless flirting and Richard's help on her first day here . . . and now. She had no claim to his time or his affections. So why the jealousy, she wondered.

"He is handsome, is he not?" Patricia asked.

"In his own way, I suppose that he is," she grumbled. She really didn't want Patricia to know how attractive she thought he was. How her knees went weak when he approached. No man had ever affected her this way. Of course, she'd been so focused on her career and her present job that she hadn't really spent much time with men lately. Other than Jasper, that is, who made her skin crawl and her stomach turn.

"More work and less chatter, Mistress Reynolds, if you please." Lady Randall's raised voice cut through the room, silencing all others.

Without looking up from her work, Sharon nodded in response. One of these times she was going to lose control and tell the old bat off. For now, she bit her tongue and kept quiet.

" 'Tis sorry I am, Mistress Reynolds," Patricia whispered a moment later. "I did not seek to cause you trouble with Lady Randall." The younger woman's voice trembled.

"Do not worry yourself, Patricia. All is well."

Sharon bent down to take a closer look at the embroidery on the sleeve. Slipping her glasses from her pocket and putting them on, she examined it to ensure that it matched the other one. She used to embroider for relaxation at home—another pastime she would give up once she returned . . . if she returned.

No, she wouldn't allow herself to think anything but positive thoughts about getting home. First, though, she needed to figure out how and why she'd been brought to this time and place. There must be a reason, something she had to do or someone she had to meet? And the packet of parchment, the midwife's confession, had to be the key.

Not wanting anyone to get a close look at her non-Elizabethan glasses, she removed them as soon as she finished checking the sleeve. Then, surreptitiously, she felt her skirt for the leather bag holding the documents. She didn't dare leave it behind in the room she shared with the others.

Until she found out if this son of Henry VIII and Anne Boleyn even existed or still lived, the packet stayed with her.

One thing was certain—she had to get back to Tenby Manor to return home. And, to do that, she would need a horse. And, to get access to a horse here in the queen's household, she would need . . . Richard. So, maybe, it wouldn't be such a bad idea to encourage his friendship. Then, once she'd found this Henry Tudor and given him the proof of the circumstances surrounding his birth, she could get back to Tenby and find that hidden panel and her way back to the future.

"Pink roses," she whispered without looking at Patricia.

"You have my thanks, Mistress Prescott." Richard added a wink at the girl as he smiled. "You are certain she did say pink and not red?"

"Oh, no, sir," the girl stuttered and would not meet his gaze. " 'Twere pink roses, of that I am sure."

Richard stood off to one side of the queen's guard chamber, waiting to see Elizabeth about his own business. Finding Sharon's maid was a stroke of luck, and mayhap a sign of good things to come.

"And Lady Randall has said she will give her leave on the day of the banquet for the French ambassador?" he asked, not taking his eyes off that very person as he stood with his own courtiers also awaiting the pleasure of the queen.

"Aye, sir. She has promised her that as reward for the excellent work she does on Her Majesty's gowns."

He took the girl's hand in his and raised it to his mouth, brushing his lips lightly over her knuckles. She blushed deeply, her pale cheeks filling with color as she tried to pull from his grasp. "I am forever in your debt, mistress."

Without replying, Patricia freed her hand and dashed from the room, never looking back. Richard smiled as he thought about the information she'd presented to him. Sharon would be free of her duties for an entire day and her favorite flowers were pink roses. The urge to apologize to her filled him. Her stricken look as he stumbled off with the wench from the dining hall still haunted him, over a week later.

He'd been too full of ale to accomplish anything amorous and the urge to bury himself in said wench had left him at the sight of Sharon's distressed expression. Mayhap she was only confused and frightened by his late-night interruption, but he could not wipe the memory of the pain in her eyes from his mind.

A few more days and, with the aid of some specially chosen pink roses, he would make his apology in person. And that would be followed, hopefully, with another such kiss as they had shared the first night at Tenby Manor. Or mayhap two of those kisses. As his thoughts drifted back to the feel of her lips sliding against his, her tongue tasting and touching his, her breasts pressed against his chest, he felt himself harden. Shifting his stance and rearranging his trunks, Richard shook from his reverie at the call of his name. There would be plenty of time to engage in woolgathering later, but for now, the queen awaited him.

The day dawned bright and clear in answer to her prayers of the days before. The inhabitants of Windsor and Eton and nearby Clewer stirred early and began their daily routines, all oblivious of the specialness of the day. It was hers . . . finally hers. Pulling on her sturdy walking boots and gathering her cloak, she made her way to the queen's dressing area to check the gown once more. Lady Randall would arrive there soon.

The heavily embroidered overskirt and sleeves lay on top of the ornate bodice and coordinated underskirt of pale purple satin. A newly made headpiece sat on a form, ready to be placed on the queen's head when her hair had been dressed appropriately. Sharon ran her fingers lightly over the pattern on the satin, enjoying the slippery texture. She was proud of her work, even if no one would ever know she'd done it. And, as far as she could remember, there was no painting of Elizabeth in this gown on file or display anywhere.

"I doubt it not that you are proud of the work you have done for our queen."

Startled from her thoughts, Sharon looked up and noticed that Lady Randall had entered the room.

"I am that, my lady," she answered, still sliding her fingers over the trim on the sleeves.

"You have chafed under my rules this last week, Mistress Reynolds. 'Tis not difficult to see past your downcast glances and hear the quiet whispers you exchange with your maid." Lady Randall circled the table where the gown lay and took a step closer. Sharon backed up a step at her approach.

"Your lady aunt did beg me to use my sternest demeanor and control to scare you from your wanton and destructive path. Lady Seagrave believes, as I do, that living within the queen's household will place you among women who live solid, chaste, and obedient lives. A life you should strive to emulate, perhaps?"

Sharon did not dare raise her glance to meet Lady Randall's. She wasn't sure if she'd be able to keep a straight face at such a lecture. In her own life, Sharon did live as this woman was suggesting. Whether or not by conscious choice, solid, chaste, and obedient pretty much described her lifestyle in Chicago.

But, apparently, Lady Seagrave's niece did not follow the rules and was sent here to learn some self-control. If even a small part of what Richard had alluded to was true, this niece lived a fast and furious life, filled with wanton behavior and lots of men.

And, this niece was still missing. Sharon wondered if the young woman had left of her own choice, and hoped that she had. What could have made the "real" Sharon give up this opportunity at court? A man? Love? Those were probably the choices available to the sixteenth-century Sharon. Of course, this meant that the other woman could return to court and to her aunt at any time. A shiver of apprehension inched its way down her spine as she turned her attention back to Lady Randall's instructions.

"However, at Her Majesty's suggestion, you are to be

freed from your duties this day. Lest you seek out those behaviors that your lady aunt and I find so abhorrent, you will not be permitted to go about alone."

Sharon did look up then. A chaperone? Or a guard?

"Your maid will accompany you at all times or you will be restricted to the royal apartments where I can watch you closely. Do you understand?" Lady Randall crossed her arms and tapped her foot, waiting for Sharon's response.

It wasn't the way she wanted it to be, but Sharon could accept Patricia's presence for now. She would find a way to lose the girl or leave her behind when it was necessary. For now, she would abide by the rules.

"I understand, my lady," she replied in a voice as respectful as she could make it. She was almost free.

"Your propensity to become acquainted with the most inappropriate of men has been revealed to me by your aunt. I do hope that your behavior here under the queen's very eye will not bring any more shame to Lady Seagrave. 'Twould distress not only your aunt but also Her Majesty, who doth call your aunt friend, to hear rumors of wantonness or lewdness."

"I understand, my lady," Sharon repeated, dipping into a slight curtsey. Just another minute or two of lecturing and she would be free. Free to investigate, free to search, free to explore.

"Now that we have a clear understanding of my expectations of you, you may seek out your maid and go. Return you none the later than supper this eve."

Sharon turned to leave. She knew Patricia would be in one of the sewing rooms, so it wouldn't take long to find her, grab a quick bite to eat, and be off and out of the confines of the queen's chambers and hallways.

Lady Randall called to her as she left the room. Returning to see what the woman wanted, she was surprised when the woman handed her a small leather bag.

"Lest you think I am completely heartless, I give you this purse. Your lady aunt did give me coins for your use while here or in Londontown. Not a large amount, but surely enough for you to use as you will on your tour of the nearby village."

Sharon was shocked. Generosity was the last thing she expected. The money was also a surprise—she hadn't thought about where to get any for use in her escape back to Tenby Manor. Lady Randall dropped the small bag in her palm and turned away. As she walked through the door leading to the queen's dressing room, she added a warning.

"Be thou careful of the cutpurses and other miscreants about when the queen's court is at Windsor. And," she added without turning back, "avoid the alehouses."

Sharon lost a moment or two waiting for her astonishment to pass. Lady Seagrave's niece must be a wild young woman, judging from the sound of the gossip. She opened the purse and poured the coins into her hand. Not much, but it would help. Placing the money back in the bag and then securing the purse inside her skirt pocket, Sharon walked quickly through the halls until she reached the largest of the sewing rooms. Patricia was inside, along with several of the other servants, straightening up the piles of fabrics and spools of thread, preparing for the day's work.

"Patricia, I have been given leave as promised. Lady Randall said you must join me or else I cannot go."

The girl's face brightened at her words. A day off was uncommon, especially when the queen's own schedule was so full and varied. Within minutes, Patricia had found her cloak and was ready to leave. They left the queen's apartments and walked through the great quadrangle and toward one of the many gates leaving the castle grounds. The sun peeked through the fluffy high clouds and shone its warming rays on the ground around them. It would be a perfect day to walk around Windsor and its village.

Chapter 8

"THEY COME NOW! Are you certain you understand your role, boy?" he asked as the two women approached on the path to St. George's Gate.

"Aye."

"Have you questions or doubts about the day's plans?" he asked once more, probing for any hesitation on the younger man's part.

"Nay, Richard. I have no questions about this, save one. Is she pretty?"

Richard smiled at the boy and, reaching over, patted the boy's back.

"Aye, that she is, John. She is a pretty one—fair-haired and blue-eyed. And with a smile kissed by the sun."

John stood a bit straighter and taller and adjusted his cap. Richard tried not to laugh at the young man's obvious primping. It would not hurt to have him believe there was a chance with Mistress Reynolds's young maid, Patricia. 'Twould make the day's activities that much easier.

Sharon and her maid walked swiftly toward the gateway, chatting and laughing, never taking note of his presence. Her hair was loose this day, flowing in waves over her shoulders and down her back. What he would not give to wrap her hair around his fist and draw her close to him. He shook himself from these thoughts—had he been so long without a woman that the mere sight of this one walking in the sunlight with her flowing hair entranced him so?

Motioning to John to follow, he moved forward and stood in the women's path in a few short steps. Holding up his hand, he called out to them.

"Good day to you both. Where do you go in your travels this day?" He bowed to them, pulling his hat from his head as he did. Throwing a meaningful look at John, he watched as the young man followed his example.

"Richard," Sharon said, in that breathy whisper he heard in his dreams. "I did not expect to see you today." She paused and nodded at his bow. Ignoring her surprise and wondering at the frown she wore at his appearance, he pointed to John.

"Mistress Reynolds, you have met my young groom, John Calder. May I make him known to your companion?"

"I'm sorry," she replied, blushing with but a hint of embarrassment at her lack of manners. "John, this is Patricia. Excuse me, I meant to say Mistress Patricia Prescott, Master John Calder."

The two younger people glanced at each other and quickly averted their eyes, stammering out their greeting in low voices. This would be perfect! John would occupy Patricia and he would have Mistress Reynolds to himself. 'Twould not be difficult to separate the young maid from her mistress in the busy streets of Windsor village.

"Mayhap since we are all of an age, we might call each other by our given names and so become more comfortable in each other's company?" Richard said. He knew John would not slip up in their conversations, but he could not be sure how Patricia would speak to him, or of his circumstances, in front of Sharon. Perhaps this would prevent the disclosure he hoped would not occur.

"Certainly," Sharon replied.

"I could not," Mistress Prescott exclaimed. "You, sir, are of such a standing that I could not address you—"

"You have my leave, *Patricia*—indeed, my request—to call me by my name."

"Patricia, Richard has said it is o—fine with him. Do not fear it." Sharon reached over and took the girl's hand, patting it to reassure her. After a moment, the girl acquiesced to his request.

" 'Tis well. Now, John and I were about to exercise our mounts and ride down to the village. Would you grant us the pleasure of your company?" Richard pointed to the two horses, saddled and ready.

"Actually, that's where we are headed, but there are only two horses," Sharon said. "Where will we ride?"

"Come now, surely Samson can carry both of us the short distance. And John can take Patricia up before him on his horse."

Richard took Sharon's hand and placed it on his arm, guiding her toward the nearby horses. Reaching the place where the horses stood grazing, Richard released her and mounted. Once in the saddle, he reached down for her hand once more. She shook her head at him.

"I cannot ride sidesaddle." She backed away when he would have lifted her onto his lap. She turned to look at the younger couple and watched as John lifted Patricia onto his lap and secured her with his arms. Although Patricia blushed, she did not argue or shift in her seat on the sturdy horse John rode. Richard awaited her reaction.

Sharon looked at him and her expression was one of complete confusion. He, in turn, was baffled by her lack of riding experience. She lived in the country and must ride. But she seemed to be lacking in the knowledge of how to mount and ride with another. He jumped from his mount to the ground.

"How do you ride? Astride?"

"The last time I rode a horse, yes, I rode astride. But I did not have these skirts to contend with." Sharon swept her hand over the dark brown skirt she wore and the cloak that hung open around it. She did not have skirts to contend with? In God's holy name, what did she wear then? When he would have asked her to explain, she waved him off.

God's blood, but he would love an explanation of her words!

He held Samson steady as she slipped her foot into the stirrup and pulled up against the saddle. She lifted her leg over the horse's back and smoothed her skirts in one motion. Settling onto the front rise of the seat, she motioned to him to join her. He stepped into the stirrup and mounted behind her, fitting more snugly than he had planned against her. He felt her settle back against his thighs and groin and he sucked in a breath. His mind reeled at the lewd thoughts racing through it. All from the innocent contact of sharing a horse's back.

Sliding his arms under hers and securing his hold on the reins, Richard touched his heels to the horse's sides and guided him onto the path. Glancing behind them, he saw John do the same with his mount. A few minutes later they had passed through the gate and past the guards and were on their way into Windsor village. Keeping his horse to a steady trot, he leaned forward to speak. Her words were still ringing in his mind about no skirts to contend with and he could hold the question in no longer.

"If not skirts, then what did you wear?" he asked, almost hoping the answer would be "Nothing." An image of her, naked and riding a horse, with her hair floating around her as she moved through the wind, filled his mind and body. A ludicrous idea but an arousing one nonetheless. He shifted slightly and waited for her answer.

"Why, Richard, I wore trunks, hose, and boots, just as you do."

He could not respond because he could not breathe. The wench had rendered him speechless. He, one of the biggest flirts of the queen's court, and she had unmanned him with naught but her words.

She wanted to laugh out loud at him. She could hardly resist answering him as she had; his flirting question deserved no less than a similarly flirting response. She had not, however, expected this reaction from him.

She peered back over her shoulder and thought she saw

his mouth working but heard nothing. He coughed and then cleared his throat once and then again.

"Mayhap you will show me this riding habit one day?" His voice had taken on a huskier tone.

"Mayhap," she answered. Turning her attention to the scenery around them, she focused on the road they took and the buildings on either side. As they neared the village proper, the houses and storefronts grew closer together and the streets more narrow.

Soon Richard slowed the horse to a walk and John guided his to Richard's side. Patricia looked none the worse for her ride with a stranger. They came to a halt in front of a small inn. Richard slid off the saddle and then helped her down. John did the same for Patricia.

" 'Twould be easier if we walk through the village. We can leave our horses here at the stables until we return. John, George has seen us now."

With a wave and a shout, the man George came forward to greet them. He and Richard shook hands and George took the reins of both horses. Richard spoke to him for a few minutes, but his words were too quiet to be heard. Then they parted and Richard rejoined them.

"There now, our horses are cared for and we are free to seek the pleasures of the town." He offered her his arm and she placed her hand on it. She allowed him to guide her down one of the intersecting streets and toward the river Thames off in the distance.

Richard carried on a humorous commentary as they walked, and within a short time even John and Patricia joined in with their own explanations and points of interest. Sharon found she was the only one who had not enjoyed this Windsor before. Soon they argued over which merchant sold the best goods and which inn served the best food and drink.

They entered an area that featured many booths selling food, drink, and other goods. It reminded her of a county fair or even the most recent Renaissance fair she'd attended. Within a few minutes they were surrounded by crowds of people and she lost sight of Patricia and John. Standing on her toes, she could still not see them in the throngs in the market square.

"Wait, Richard. I must find Patricia." She knew she planned on losing the girl, but not until she was leaving to return to Tenby Manor. Until then she had to stay close or Lady Randall would hold her a virtual prisoner—and that would severely limit her chance of escape. Richard held onto her hand.

"John will not allow anything untoward to happen to her. You have my word on it." He gave her a very knowing look and she realized that this separation had been planned . . . and well executed. She didn't know if she should be worried or flattered.

"And will you make the same vow?" she asked, watching his sea-green eyes for evidence of his truthfulness.

"But of course, Mistress Reynolds. I vow, you do wound me and my honor by thinking I would do anything but protect you from anything untoward."

"I offer my sincere apology if I have insulted you, Master Granville," she teased. "I should only remember how you have saved my life twice before this day to convince myself of my safety in your presence."

That did it! Now he looked completely confused. He'd pledged to keep her safe and that would probably crimp his plans for their time alone.

"Can we go there?" She pointed to a booth that featured candles of different sizes and colors. She would purchase a few of her own with the coins in her purse.

A few hours later, with their various purchases wrapped and carried in a sack, Sharon and Richard arrived back at the inn. The morning, filled with teasing and lively conversation, had flown by and only Sharon's grumbling stomach and the sun rising high in the sky alerted her to how much time had passed. Again greeted by George, she soon found they were ushered into a private room. A fire was already burning in the hearth and a meal was set on a large table in the center of the room. No one else had arrived yet.

"You planned this well, Richard. How did you and John

decide the correct amount of time to keep Patricia and me apart?"

"Here, allow me to help you with your cloak," he said, easing the garment from her shoulders and hanging it on a wooden peg next to the door. He didn't answer her question.

"Will they be here soon?" she asked, shaking out the wrinkles in her skirts and pushing her hair back over her shoulders.

"We have some time before they arrive. Do you have some need I can fulfill?"

His teasing mouth moved into that wonderfully wicked smile and she ached to kiss him as she had that night at Tenby Manor. But a more pressing need presented itself. She leaned close to him and waited for him to tilt his head to hers.

"Where is the privy?" she whispered.

"Touché" he said, laughing out loud as he pointed to a door in the far wall. He was still laughing as she pulled the door shut behind her and found a closed-stool for her use in the small room.

If there was one thing she missed most in the past, it was her completely modern and spacious bathroom. As she used the sorely lacking facilities, she planned her first hours back in her own time. She would soak in her double-sized tub until there was no hot water left to use. She would use half of the bottle of her favorite shampoo and conditioner before drying her hair with her electric blow-dryer. And, most importantly, she would use that extra-soft toilet paper and no other.

Yes, she missed her creature comforts. And she missed variety and choices in her food. She would give everything she had for a huge Caesar salad. Or for broiled steak. Or for fresh vegetables. Or for a large mug of strong tea with lemon and sugar. How unfortunate to land in England before tea!

"Sharon? Our meal grows cold." Richard knocked on the door.

Realizing she'd been daydreaming, Sharon finished her task and joined Richard in the dining room.

"I did not mean to interrupt your . . . privacy, Sharon. I heard you mumbling and thought you spoke to me." He was not teasing her now.

"I must have been talking to myself."

He pulled out a chair and helped her sit down in it. Then he settled in one next to hers. Offering her the first choice from the platter of cooked meats, he slid his chair closer to hers.

"And what were you telling yourself?"

"How much I miss my . . . home," she answered, not willing to describe her bathroom to him. He wouldn't understand her need for indoor plumbing and a tub the size of a small pond. She wanted a tub filled with hot, clean water she was not expected to share with anyone else who may be interested in using it—that one aspect of bathing in this time and place had made her resort to sponge baths in her chamber.

"And what," he asked as he tore off two chunks of bread, "do you miss the most?" He moved a crock of butter and a small wheel of cheese to within her reach.

"A bath! A real honest-to-God, all-to-myself, steaming hot bath." She spoke without hesitation and then bit her lip, waiting for his reaction.

"You do not have such a bad odor about you. Are you not washing yourself and your clothes?" He bit into the heavily buttered piece of bread and looked at her as he chewed it slowly. She thought at first that he was teasing her but soon saw that he was serious. Well, at least the smell of her without deodorant bothered her alone.

"Of course. At least, as much as I can. Elizabeth, I mean Her Majesty, does not allow anyone with duties in her private chambers to be unclean. But I want more than that; I want my own bath."

He laughed again and the sound of it, rich and deep, moved through her. "And what else from your home do you miss? Pray tell, was there someone special for whom your heart doth ache?"

She met his gaze as she slowly took a bite of her own bread, chewing neither fast nor slow as she assessed his question. Although it had all the makings of his usual flirtatious ones, she sensed in his voice a sincerity not present before. Sharon swallowed the bread and took a mouthful of the cider he'd poured for her.

"Friends. Only for friends."

"Gossip has it that you left behind a certain man. . . ."

He let his words trail off and she wasn't quite certain how to answer him. She'd heard bits and pieces from Patricia about the rumors of Lady Seagrave's niece's unfortunate behavior. She decided to use her own background as the source of her answer to Richard's questions.

"And, pray thee, does the gossip mention that he was an unscrupulous one, who preyed on a young woman's uncertainty and inexperience?" She thought of Jasper Crenshaw and his actions over the past few months as she spoke. She could hear the disdain and mistrust in her own voice. Her words came too close for comfort to the truth of the matter.

"I beg pardon, I only meant to . . ." He stumbled over his words.

"Satisfy your own need for gossip and rumor to sow elsewhere?" She regretted the harshness of the words as soon as they were out. The frown that furrowed his brow and the downturn of those lips added to her remorse.

Richard took her hand in his and rubbed gently over her wrist and down her fingers. Her hand tingled under his attentions. He raised his other hand and, placing it under her chin, turned her face to his.

"You have no reason to believe my words, but I do harbor the hope that you will try. I have sensed within you a feeling familiar to my own. You are an outsider here and an unhappy one at that."

Oh, gosh, if he only knew the truth. Of course he never would, never could, but his attempt to offer her comfort touched her heart.

"I want you to know that you may call on me if you have need of anything during your time with the queen.

When I think back on my own first days at court, I remember well how disconcerting a time 'twas. I would spare you from that, and I would discourage any information that was not true from spreading further among those I know."

She wanted to believe they could be friends. But she was never quite sure if he was telling her the truth or building up to the big seduction scene. His voice never lost its flirting tone, his eyes still sparkled, his mouth still looked so inviting. Maybe that was just . . . Richard?

"I do thank you for your offer, Richard," she said.

"But . . . ? You fear that I play the pursuer even now? That I seek to lull you from your guard? You disbelieve that I can be honest in my feelings or in revealing them to you?" He sat back a bit and his glance roamed over her. Sharon wanted to say exactly that but waited for him to continue.

"Well, then, let me be as bold as you would seem to want. I do not seduce women, nay, not even those whose beauty and womanly form call to me as yours does. I do but invite them," he explained, leaning toward her, his voice warm and low. "I would invite you to passion's play with me if you were willing. But never, never will I force or make you uncomfortable with my advances. I may tease and cajole you, I pray thee not to ask me to give up those small pleasures. But you are safe with me, even within my arms, Mistress Reynolds, until you give the word to abandon those restrictions."

She couldn't breathe. Heat pooled in her belly at his words and she longed to ask him, no, to beg him to invite her to wickedness. She reached over and picked up her goblet with a shaky hand, hoping that the cider within would cool her, since the room had become several degrees hotter with his words. She peered over the rim of the cup at him. His face was unreadable, giving no hint of how she should proceed.

"I can accept your words, your offer, in the good faith in which you made it, Richard."

" 'Tis well, then. Hear now, let us seal our understanding

with a friendly kiss," he said as he stood, leaned forward, and touched his lips to hers.

She waited for him to deepen the kiss but he didn't. He sat back in his chair, pulled it in closer to the table, and reached for the platter of meat. The commotion outside the door drew her attention from Richard and the kiss she truly wanted.

Chapter 9

"THERE NOW! DOST thou see with thine own eyes that thy mistress is safe?" John's exasperation was clear, as his voice bordered on whining.

Patricia pushed past him and into the private parlor. She stopped and glanced around the room, taking in the two of them sitting by a fire, with plates of food and goblets of drink.

"Art well, mistress?" Her face was red with exertion and worry and Sharon was touched by her concern. And, poor John, his morning must have been a trying one, from the looks of it. He stood in the doorway with his arms crossed over his chest and glared at Richard.

Sharon rose and walked over to the girl. Pulling her over to the table, she guided her into a chair and poured her some cider from the pitcher on the sideboard. Holding it out to her, Sharon waited until Patricia had taken a few sips before speaking.

"I am well, Patricia, and sorry that you spent this beautiful morning worrying about me. Richard saw to my safety when we were separated." She smiled and winked at him as he picked up on her use of the word *safety*.

"First, he tripped over his own feet and when he had

regained them, you were gone." Patricia scowled across the room to where John still stood. "Then he would not quicken his steps when I did see you across the square and then once more on a different street."

"I am certain that John tried his best. John, join us and share our meal," Richard called out. After a moment of consideration, the offer of food and drink won out over the young man's displeasure with Patricia. Sharon held out the loaf of bread to them. They both reached for it together and then both dropped their hands as the other touched it. Sharon would have laughed if not for Richard's giving her a stern warning shake of the head.

Finally, after a few awkward minutes, they were all eating the luncheon fare. She caught a few of the furtive glances that passed between the two teenagers and smiled over them. They were trying very hard not to like each other. The rest of the meal passed in silence.

Richard stood first and asked John to see to the horses. Sharon wiped her hands and stood, motioning to Patricia.

"Richard, Patricia and I would walk back to the castle now that we have eaten. Thank you for the enjoyable morning," she said gathering her cloak from its peg and walking to the door.

"Would you not wish to ride back? 'Tis a long distance to walk," he argued quietly. Obviously he had more planned for them. But it was important that she look around and make certain she knew how to leave Windsor. And Richard's presence would make that impossible.

"No, and again I thank you for such a pleasant morning. Patricia?" Sharon opened the door and let Patricia pass through first. They made their way through the public room of the inn and were met by the owner, George. Richard shook his hand and assured him that the fare was well appreciated. Soon, she and Patricia were on their way back to the castle by themselves . . . or so she thought until Richard and John rode up behind them.

"Come, Sharon, a large troop of soldiers heads this way," Richard said as he leaned over in the saddle and pulled her onto his lap with a thump. " 'Twill be safer if we take a different path back to the castle."

"But, Patricia . . ." she started to say.

"Will be seen to by John."

Richard guided the horse off the main road and onto a smaller one that took them into the woods. Although it was definitely not comfortable on his lap, it was not as precarious a position as she once thought. He slipped his arms around her waist and gathered the reins in.

She should be upset by his predisposition to take care of her, but she realized that men and women dealt differently with each other in this time. And, although he promised protection, she wondered when he would get around to the invitation he so clearly meant to offer.

They rode in silence for a few minutes and then Richard brought the mount to a stop by a small stream. A cool breeze floated through the thick trees surrounding them. The sunlight flickered through the branches, throwing speckled rays on the ground. Sharon leaned her head back and drew in the fragrant air. Although she'd heard terrible things about the smells of London, apparently Windsor was far enough in the country to be spared the worst of it.

The air was one of the first things she'd noticed after coming here. The smells of the pines and other trees and plants, the odors of the castle, both human and animal, and the clarity of the sky and clouds told her she was living before industrial pollution. And the multitude of stars visible in the night sky told her she was living before the glow of electric lights.

She walked a few paces to the edge of the stream and watched the sunbeams touch the rippled surface of it as it moved off through the forest. Bending over, she dipped her fingers into the water and shivered at the coldness. She took her still-dripping hand and spread the cool water over her face, allowing its temperature to freshen her skin.

She was so caught up in enjoying the outdoors after being in the castle's domain for two weeks that she forgot about Richard's presence and his probable reason for this stopover. He didn't let her ignore him for long.

He watched as she shook her hair loose of her cloak, its length spreading down her back. He would ask her to wear it down like this when they were together. All that was needed was for him to wrap his hand in it and pull that tempting mouth of hers to his. His feet moved before he even knew of his intentions.

She intrigued him, this young stranger from the country. He'd observed her more times than she knew over the last two weeks. Oh, he'd seen her in the hallway the night he'd spoken to Ramirez. And he often took his own looks into the queen's sewing rooms just to see her bending over some task assigned her. The expression in her eyes that night when he drunkenly staggered into her door still haunted him. 'Twas that lost look that spurred him on to his plan to befriend her.

Sharon stood by the stream, her eyes closed, just letting the breezes flow around her. God-a-mercy, what would she be like in his bed? She fought to control her passion but 'twould be a wondrous thing to see unleashed. Was she a virgin still? The pain of her experience with the man she left behind was clear in her words, in the vehemence of her response to his question. He thought not a virgin, but clearly not too familiar to loveplay.

He stood now just behind her, not knowing whether she knew he was there or not. He was just reaching to place his hands on her shoulders when she spoke.

"So, Richard, is this the next part of your plan, to separate me once more from my maid?" She turned to face him. "You should know that Lady Randall required me to bring Patricia with me. If she sees us apart, I will be restricted to only the royal apartments for the rest of my stay here at Windsor."

"She will not see you apart, since you will arrive back at the castle together, as you left it." He stepped closer, waiting to see if she backed away. Of course, with the stream so close at her back, she would not have room to maneuver away from him. He smiled as she stood her ground and lifted her chin to look at him.

It gave him the opportunity he sought and he took it at

once. Tilting down, he touched his lips to hers and then engaged her more firmly in a kiss. At first it was just their lips and then she opened to him and he touched his tongue to hers. A shiver passed through her and he drew her into his embrace. Not stopping to allow reason to guide her, he lavished one kiss after another until they both were breathless. Mayhap his plan was working too well?

He felt her hands encircle his waist and she grabbed his shirt and held on to him as they continued this mating of their mouths. His cock hardened as she was caught up in passion and gave as well as took. Mayhap she was more practiced than he thought, after all?

He lifted his mouth from hers and saw how swollen it was from his attention. Her eyes, those wonderfully expressive eyes, were glazed with passion . . . for him. Richard untied the cords holding her cloak in place and slipped it from her shoulders. Dropping it onto the ground next to them, he tugged at his own and it joined hers. Stepping closer once more, he wrapped his arms around her and took her mouth.

Without conscious thought of his actions, he found they were soon lying together on the cloaks, his body stretched out next to hers as the kisses grew longer and even more passionate. 'Twas a moan from deep within her throat that sent him over the boundary of his control. With her head cradled in one of his arms, he moved to touch her with his free hand and to taste her with his mouth.

Releasing her mouth, he kissed over her chin and onto her neck, nipping his way down to the place where her blouse tied. She panted in short breaths as he pulled gently at the laces, exposing her shoulders and the swell of her breasts to his gaze. She closed her eyes once more, as she had when she'd stood feeling the wind. When she did not naysay him he leaned down and kissed the creamy skin of her shoulders and then, with just the tip of his tongue, he traced a path onto her breasts.

By God's heart, she was sweet! Her skin was like that of no other woman he'd seen or touched. Noblewomen would clamor for her secret if they knew of it. She grasped his head and held him close and then moved restlessly against him. He slid his leg over hers to get closer and to rub that part of him that was now throbbing to life against her. The blood thundered through his veins, heating every inch of him, making him more ready than he thought possible.

Richard lifted his head and moved back up to kiss her mouth, his hand now sliding over her skirts onto her thighs. Grasping inch by inch of the layers, he pulled them out of his way and finally touched her skin. Smooth there too. He slipped his hand higher and higher until he reached for the curls between her legs. He was stopped by some kind of cloth, silky and smooth, but a barrier to his quest.

She tugged on his hair, pulling him from her mouth and she grabbed at his hand with her other one, stopping him from finding out what she wore beneath her skirts. At first he thought it was just her reticence coming into play, but then he heard John's voice calling from the path. Why had he told the boy where he'd be? He'd had to, since his time was not his own when traveling with Elizabeth. He sighed, looking at Sharon, whose eyes still carried the glimmer of passion within them.

He sat up on his knees, effectively blocking her from the boy's view as she pulled her blouse back into place and straightened her skirts. She said not a word but he could tell from the set of her mouth that she was angry. He pushed his hair out of his face and took a deep breath. Passion interrupted was not passion cooled. He ached for more of her. And, curiously, not just to touch her body and mate with her, but also to share his dreams and spend time laughing with her. This was not his usual reaction to coupling and he was confused. Mayhap he had been drugged somehow by her kisses.

"Sharon, I apologize for the interruption," he began.

"There is no need to, Richard. Apparently John is familiar with the places you use to extend your 'invitations' to your lady friends. He found us quickly enough."

"He needed to know where I would be, for if the queen summons, I must go."

"And he did find you, didn't he?" she replied. "I wonder how many invitations he must rescue you from if he knows your secret hideaways?"

Seeking refuge in his usual court behavior, Richard answered, "Not as many as some would have you believe and not as many as others might wish." He winked at her and nodded his head at her.

She bent over and picked up her cloak, tossing his on the ground at his feet. Shaking hers out, she threw it around her shoulders and strode off down the path where John had come. She offered not another word to him and he thought that might be best.

"Richard, 'tis sorry I am, but the queen summons you to the hunt," John said.

"Nay, boy, be not sorry for carrying out the queen's commands. 'Twas my own folly that led me further than 'twas prudent to go." Richard looked at the boy as he shook his own cape out and put it in place over one shoulder. "And you John, how did you fare with Mistress Prescott?"

The boy's face flamed before he answered and then his words were muffled. "Tolerably well, sir."

"Tolerably well, was it? Then your day has turned out better than mine, John. Better than mine." Richard untied the reins of his horse from the tree and gained his seat in one step. Reaching down for his young groom, he pulled him up behind him. "See to the ladies' safe return to Windsor."

"Aye, Richard."

Richard urged the horse into a trot and soon Sharon came into view on the path ahead. He stopped while John slid to the ground, ready to escort the women back to Windsor. She never even looked in his direction.

Mayhap he had wrought more damage than good this day with her? He'd thought to apologize for his drunken behavior, but any words regarding that would now be worthless. He felt as he did once when learning a new dance—he'd taken one step forward only to take three steps back.

Aye, three steps back.

Chapter 10

Do not look, *do not look!* She repeated the words over and over in her mind, trying to convince herself that looking at him as he passed by was the very worst thing she could do.

No, actually she'd already done the worst thing—accepting his damn invitation by the side of the stream, under the speckled rays of sun as the breeze cooled everything he heated within her. His mouth and his hands invited her, seduced her, cajoled her into proceeding further and faster than was prudent. Her body still thrummed with the heat and the wanting he had conjured with his magical actions and her faced burned as she remembered her own fevered reactions.

Strumpet? Was that what they called wanton women here and now? She was quickly living up to the reputation of Lady Seagrave's niece without ever having met the woman in question. Doubts attacked her. She'd held on to her virginity this long—and now to face losing it to the "first pretty face" who wooed her? How would she ever face him now?

Sharon looked back and saw that in her haste to escape the scene of her humiliation she'd outwalked both Patricia and Richard's young groom. They meandered in the distance as she continued at her faster pace toward the castle.

He'd told her what his intention was during their meal. She shouldn't be surprised by what followed. Her own arousal after his kisses was probably as clear to him as the scent of a mare in heat to a stallion. No mention of a wife or a fiancée had been made, although he was quickly approaching Elizabethan middle age. Just great. She was involved with a Renaissance rake.

The only good that could come of today's embarrassment was that he might consider helping her get back to Tenby Manor. He had offered any help he could to her. He was certainly willing to play his game, so maybe she would look at this as her game plan.

Well, with his help or without it, she would return to the place where she arrived once she found out if Henry's bastard still lived. Stopping on the road, she waited a few minutes for Patricia and John to catch up. If John showed her around the stables, it would at least make her feel that the day was a success.

The two teenagers walked side by side, each one maneuvering so that they never touched. John led his horse along behind him. When they reached her, she walked just behind them. From there she could see their frequent glances at each other, again each timed carefully to avoid actual eye contact. She fought not to let the laughter inside her escape. These two would actually make a cute couple. They were about the same social status, as far as she could tell and remember about the mores of the time.

Richard's words were true—it took much longer to walk back to Windsor Castle than riding back would have taken. About thirty minutes later, they passed through the gate and back into the castle's grounds. John took the lead after Sharon told him how much she'd like to see the stables. From his puzzled expression, he must have thought she wanted to see if Richard had arrived before them. Letting him believe it, she gained a quick tour of the stables and he even pointed out the "ladies' mounts" as opposed to the men's. That information would help her—with her limited riding experience, a calmer mount would be exactly what she needed for the ride back to Sussex.

Once she and Patricia were alone on the final leg of their journey back to the section of the palace housing the royal apartments, Sharon knew she had to speak about the day's activities. And she had to make certain that the girl had not been overly upset by her part in Richard's plans.

"I would speak to you before we get back to our rooms." She touched the girl's arm to stop her.

"Yes, mistress?" Patricia looked at her, but still would not meet her eyes. A bad sign.

"Patricia," she began then stopped. "Please look at me." She waited for the girl to meet her glance. "I did not know of Richard's plan to separate us today."

"I know, mistress." Patricia answered in a whisper.

"You do? How?"

"John told me on the walk back. He also said that Richard's plans did not go the way he wished today."

"Really?" Of course they hadn't. The summons from the queen arrived just in time to prevent her from accepting his invitation to the full extent he planned.

"John said you never saw the pink roses that Richard had at the inn."

Sharon blushed; she could feel the heat move into her cheeks as she misunderstood Patricia's words.

"He said we rushed off before Richard could give them to you. Mayhap he'll give them to you on another day?" The girl looked away and Sharon wondered if there were more plans being made that she didn't know about.

"Mayhap. . . ."

Or maybe Richard would just ignore her now that he had the answer he wanted—now that he knew she would believe his words and fall under the spell of his magical caresses.

"Patricia, nothing happened to you today? With John?" She would hate it if the girl had been hurt because of her.

"Oh, nay, mistress," she said, her face gradually transformed by a smile. " 'Twas a wondrous day."

Sharon turned and looked at her. "Wondrous?"

"Well, not at first. I was frightened when I could find you not. John stumbled and held me back when I would have followed you. Then he did repeat it when we saw you once more in the next square. Truth be told, I was most angered by what he did."

"When did 'wondrous' happen?"

"I was overcome with worry—about both you and me if Lady Randall should find we parted and were in the company of men," she whispered. "I found I could do nothing but cry. John," she said with a sigh, "did but offer me comfort in my moment of need."

Sharon wanted to laugh once more at the antics of these two teenagers. Patricia had already learned the value of tears when facing young men. This one would get what she wanted.

"I would warn you about men and their pretty words, Patricia. Be careful in dealing with John."

"You mistake my words, mistress. John did nothing untoward during our time together. He was most kind in his behavior, filled with all caring and concern. Truly." Patricia nodded her head as she proclaimed the young man's honorable behavior.

"I am glad for you, then. It was a wondrous day."

Sharon could feel a question nagging at her—it had been there most of the day. Something Patricia had said that she'd wanted to ask about at the time . . . but she'd forgotten then and could just barely remember now. Ah, now she remembered.

"Patricia, this morning you said something I did not understand. I am still new to the queen's household and court and am not sure who holds which rank and position."

"What did I say that has you puzzled so?"

"When I was introducing you to John, you mentioned something to Richard about his standing being above yours. Isn't his standing about the same as yours within the household?"

She watched as the color left the girl's face. Patricia took a breath and looked at her and took another. Blowing out, she looked around the yard where they stood and then back at her—all without meeting her eyes.

"Oh, mistress, I forgot that I carried your bag. John did give it to me when we met you on the road. Did you make purchases this day in town?"

Sharon knew a distraction when she heard one and this was a doozy. Rather than forcing the issue now, she would bide her time. She would find out when she needed to. Taking the offered sack, she told Patricia about her new candles and some soaps she'd purchased. They made their way back to their section of the royal apartments. "Royal apartments" sounded so lavish to her—better than small cubbyhole on the fourth floor without heat or windows. Nonetheless, it was home for now. For now.

Once there, Sharon opened the bag to take out her treasures. The candles would extend the light in this room and the soap would make it easier to keep her and her few meager undergarments clean. Something else still remained at the bottom of the sack. Reaching in and lifting them out carefully, Sharon was overwhelmed to find three perfectly formed, fully bloomed pink rosebuds.

She couldn't help the smile that found its way onto her face or the slightest little tug that pulled on her heart. Rake or not, he'd found her favorite flowers.

Tension was building around the queen. It had been growing stronger and more intense since their return to Windsor but Sharon was not privy to the whys and hows of the court. She heard rumors; indeed, anyone working within the household heard the rumors. The exasperated yelling of Elizabeth from her private quarters and the angry huffing and stomping of ministers like Cecil, Dudley, and Hatton as they left made it clear to everyone that matters of state were clearly heating up.

Sharon wracked her brain trying to remember the historical details of the time. She knew that Queen Mary of Scotland was a prisoner already in England and she remembered that some plots to rebel or overthrow Elizabeth occurred at the end of the queen's first decade in power.

If you had asked her when silk was first imported into England or when English weavers began making their own velvets, she could have answered down to the month. But her view of history was slanted toward the cloth and clothing styles and not the politics of the day. The irony of the importance of politics was not lost on her even now so far away from her own fiasco.

She barely saw Richard during the next weeks. A brief sighting of him in the dining hall and once in the queen's own room as she delivered a new farthingale to one of the women closest to Elizabeth. He caught her glance and offered a tentative smile but there was no time or opportunity for anything more.

Once, Elizabeth and her advisors left for a short trip to London and Sharon thought it might be the perfect time to try to travel back to Sussex and Tenby Manor. Unfortunately, Richard accompanied the entourage and so she lost the person who might help her the most.

She thought many times about her behavior with him and of his touching gift of roses. Obviously, if he'd wanted to pursue her he would have. He must be one of those people who love the thrill of the chase and then lose interest. And she'd fallen for it. Patricia never brought up his name, although that didn't stop her from regaling her with the details of every encounter with young John Calder. In a way, Sharon was pleased that if she left, *when she left,* Patricia would have someone who seemed genuinely interested in her.

Not a devilish rogue like Master Richard Granville.

The whispering in the hall outside the room she shared with three other women drew her attention. A lighter woman's tone blended with a man's deeper one until her curiosity got the better of her. She wrapped the underwear she was washing out in a linen towel, placed it on the table and walked quietly over to the door. Opening it ever so slightly, she saw the teenage duo, heads bent close, whispering.

"If you two are trying to keep a secret, you are failing," she advised them in a voice louder than theirs.

The two bumped heads and then turned to face her. Both wore the same guilty expression.

"You can tell me what is going on now, Patricia." Looking from one to the other, she saw that neither looked ready to divulge any information to her. A bit embarrassed now at having interrupted an obviously private moment, she stepped back away from the door. "I will be inside if you have need of me."

"Please wait, mistress," Patricia said. "John has come to see you."

"He has?" she asked, looking at the boy. "You have?" She opened the door further and invited them inside.

"If you can spare a short while, Richard has asked me to show you something."

"Richard has? What are you to show me, John?"

The boy looked at Patricia and even Sharon could see the urging in his glance. He wanted Patricia to do the dirty work.

"Mistress, if you will follow John, I will come in but a few moments."

Curiosity won over her own desire to argue. What could he be up to this time? Somehow she didn't think it would be anything dangerous to her or her reputation if he was involving the young people. Nodding, she walked into the hall and motioned with her hand that John should lead her.

They walked down the stairs and a hallway and into another one of the towers. They passed a number of rooms that she had not seem before and stopped in front of one near the end of the corridor. The kitchens were not far, for she could smell the aroma of meat cooking somewhere nearby.

"Richard bade me to say these words to you. He is still your true friend and apologizes for any false impressions given or discomfort caused on your day of leave in the village. This"—he pointed at the door—"is his gift to his friend."

Sharon was confused by the words of Richard's message. Friend? What in the world had he given her? What could be on the other side of this door. The fear that he would be inside and the anticipation of finding out made her stomach feel like thousands of butterflies had been let loose within it. Her heart pounded as she took hold of the knob and, turning it, pushed the door open.

Chapter 11

STEAM FILLED THE room, making it difficult to see anything but the flickering light of several candles. As her vision became accustomed to the dark, she saw the large wooden tub in the center of the room, with several more buckets sitting off to one side of it. The scent of roses drifted through the heavy air and she smiled as she inhaled the heady fumes.

Stepping into the room, she walked over and dipped her hand into the water and winced at the hot feel of it. Sharon looked around and saw some small bowls of soap and then noticed the long piece of linen that lined the bottom of the tub. John cleared his throat in the doorway, gaining her attention.

"Richard said 'tis yours alone to enjoy."

Sharon laughed at this turn of events. He had arranged this for her? She thought back to her words at the inn that day. *A real honest-to-God, all-to-myself, steaming hot bath.* And Richard had granted her wish.

"Oh, I will enjoy it, I assure you." She began to close the door but John stopped her.

"You are pleased with this?" He looked very, very doubtful as he glanced from her to the tub and back to her once more.

"Yes, John, very pleased. Tell Richard he has my gratitude."

"He is in the stables—I go there now and will tell him that you are pleased"—John's brow wrinkled in disbelief—"with this bath."

Nodding, the young man pulled the door closed. Sharon checked the knob for a lock but there was none there. At this point, lock or none would not stop her. The heated water called to her after so many weeks of sponging herself clean in the various garderobes and privies of the palace.

Peeling off the layers of clothing, she tested the water once more with the tip of her toe. Shivers passed through her and she stepped carefully into the tub, gingerly sliding down to sit on the cloth lining. Dipping her hands into it, she splashed the rose-scented water over her shoulders and onto her neck and face. Shifting lower into the water, she let the water cover her head. It felt almost better than she'd imagined.

Sitting once more, she reached over the side and picked up one of the bowls of soap. Sniffing it, she smiled at more of the rose scent. He'd thought of everything to make this a wonderful gift. Whether his words and motives were genuine or one more "move," she didn't know. But she would seek him out and try to assess this gesture more closely. And, at the very least, she would have to thank him for fulfilling her one wish.

A soft knock at the door roused her from her heat-induced lethargy. Patricia opened the door and crept inside, carrying clothing over her arm. Sharon pushed herself up to sit once more.

"I have come to help you with your hair if you have finished your bath?"

"That would be lovely, Patricia," she said as she covered as much of herself as possible with the small washcloth. Having someone act as a servant, as a maid, was a difficult enough concept, but to have said maid be part of bathing was harder still to accept. She tried to think of it as a trip to the hair salon and when Patricia guided her back and shoulders to the edge of the tub so her hair would hang over the side of it, it was easier to imagine that. Within a few minutes, her hair and scalp felt as well-scrubbed as the rest of her.

After rinsing and getting out of the tub, Sharon sat by the fire wrapped in several drying linens while Patricia dried and brushed her hair. Wave after wave of the smell of roses spread through the room with every stroke. Sharon found herself drifting off in her thoughts once more.

These last weeks she had lived in a kind of stupor, just moving through the days and nights, not questioning or trying to understand what had happened to her. Or how she had come to be in this distant time and place. She guessed it was her usually rational mind's way of protecting her from overload. The thought of traveling through time still overwhelmed her—the possibility of it, the how and why of it.

But, unless she focused on the apparent reason for her trip—finding the son born of Henry and Anne and giving him the proof of his birthright—she had the feeling that she would remain here. Planning her approach to the problem, she realized that Patricia would be the best place to begin. As she'd noticed from their first meetings, the girl was a veritable keeper of the who's who list of the court.

"Patricia, I need to find someone who may be here at court. You might be able to help me find him," she began.

"A man, mistress? Was it not a man who was at the center of the troubles that brought you to your exile here at court?"

Sharon wanted to laugh. The disapproval in the girl's voice was clear. Using her own experiences, she answered. It had been her flight from her problems at work with Jasper Crenshaw that had brought her to England and indirectly to this time.

"Yes, Patricia, my naive confidence in an unscrupulous man's word brought me to this disgrace. But I am not looking for a man like that. I am simply curious over some gossip I heard and wanted to clarify it one way or the other."

"Gossip, mistress?" The long strokes continued uninterrupted but Sharon knew she'd touched on Patricia's favorite topic other than Master John Calder.

"Is it true that Elizabeth has a half-brother still alive?" She tried to keep her voice even and not show her true interest. When Patricia abruptly stopped brushing her hair, Sharon thought she was on to something.

"A half-brother? Nay, Elizabeth is the last royal child of the old king." The brush moved once more through her hair but in jerky, pulling movements. Patricia knew more than she was saying.

"I mean . . . are there any illegitimate children of the old king still alive?" Sharon held her breath and waited; her goal could be in sight.

"I would have to ask one of the older women, mistress." She stammered out her words. "I have heard of but one bastard who King Henry recognized and he died years ago, before Elizabeth even drew a breath."

Sharon's hopes of a quick answer to her puzzle died. She did remember one son who was granted some title, duke of somewhere or other. Damn! Well, where and who now? Maybe the boy had perished in the rough life of sixteenth-century England. Even if he had lived past childhood and into adulthood, as the midwife's letter seem to indicate, there was no guarantee that he still existed.

Patricia stepped away and gathered up the dirty clothes from the floor. Sharon nodded to her and the girl left the room. Standing and stretching, Sharon enjoyed the feeling of being clean, completely clean, for the first time since her arrival here. And she had Richard to thank for making the arrangements for this.

She pulled on her stockings, shoes, chemise, and skirt and wrapped a woolen shawl around her shoulders for warmth. Her underwear was still back in the room, probably dry by now. She could stop there on her way to the stables. It took only a few minutes to retrieve and put on her undergarments before she proceeded through the living accommodations, heading for the stables. About fifteen minutes of brisk walking took her to the side door.

Pulling the door open a crack, she listened for any activity. Hearing and seeing none, Sharon was about to leave, thinking he'd finished his work while she was bathing. Then, quietly at first, she could hear singing from somewhere inside the building. A man's deep voice echoed through the stables. She pulled the door open further and followed the voice to its source.

He knelt on the floor, amid piles of hay and straw, at the side of a mare obviously in labor. Holding the horse's head, he stroked it as he crooned a soft lullaby to calm her during her ordeal. Sharon didn't know the words, didn't have to, but the emotion and caring in his voice and song tugged once more at her heart as she watched him soothe this animal in need. She stood back, not eager to disturb this scene.

He was dressed in the same kind of clothing he always wore but these trunks and shirt were coarser, and a long leather apron was tied over them. His long black hair was pulled back and tied with a lace. He was a stable-master ready to work.

"Now, lass, I know you are fearful but I will be with you through this. I promise," he said softly to the mare as she tensed, awaiting the next stage of the birth. "You and this foal will be the beginning of my own fortune. Come now, do not fear. 'Twill be fine and by morning you will have a beautiful new colt or filly to fuss over."

The mare answered with a huff and nuzzled Richard's hand. Sharon was mesmerized by his voice and his calm demeanor as the mare was caught up in the move toward birthing this new life.

"You are to be the first part of my dream, lass. I will not let you fail. Your get will start my own stables, if the queen so wills it. Yours will be the first of many."

Sharon stood in the shadows, guiltily listening as he spilled out his dreams to the mare. Stables of his own? Being sponsored by the queen?

"My stables will be known throughout the country. Your

line will live and improve and it will stock the best horse farms in the land. And tonight we start it." He swept his hand down her head in long strokes, then onto her neck and shoulders. He moved from her head around to the other end. "Tonight is yours."

Sharon gasped and then covered her mouth as she watched him reach deep inside the mare. She saw his forearm disappear and then come out, covered in slippery goo.

"Not quite ready then?" he asked. "We have the whole night if you need it." He leaned back on his heels but stayed at that end of the horse. Apparently, the birth would commence soon.

Sharon stood silently by as he continued to hum the song once more. Every few minutes, he would stroke the horse and then check it again. She couldn't stand here the whole night, so she would have to interrupt sooner or later. Before she could speak, he did.

"So, has the country girl come to help us with the birth?"

He knew within moments of her approach that she stood there in the shadows. The light scent of roses floated around her now, and drifted to him where he knelt next to the mare. He wanted to turn and look at her but the horse needed his full attention now.

She stepped forward and into the low light thrown by the lanterns hung around the stall. By God's eyes, she was a beauty! Her hair was loose and freshly washed and brushed, from the look of it. It rippled over her shoulders and down her back as she walked closer to them. This was the first time he had seen her up close since their interrupted afternoon in the park. She positively glowed with freshness and smelled wonderful, especially considering the odors around them. She cleared her throat and smiled at him. With one hand on the mare, he smiled back.

"I would thank you, Richard. I truly appreciated the bath." She pushed the hair off her shoulders and more waves of rose-scented air moved to him.

" 'Twas the least I could do, Mistress Reynolds, to apologize for my appalling behavior." Make a bold move, he thought, apologize and move on.

"Which appalling behavior do you speak of, sir?" She raised her eyebrow at him and just a hint of a smile threatened at the corners of her mouth. "There were so many."

He was about to offer his retort when the mare began to struggle. Without thought, he moved into position to help the foal pass into the birth canal. A few minutes later, he realized that she stood silently as he and the mare worked together. He looked up to see her staring at them—the mare grunting in labor and he wearing all manner of stains and smells, but Sharon fresh from her bath and looking like an angel. He wanted to laugh.

"What can I do to help?" she asked. Her expression was one of hopeful anticipation, but he thought she hoped he would not answer by assigning her some task.

"Can you hold her head? Steady her as I work here?" Richard nodded since both of his hands were already engaged in pulling the foal free. Sharon answered nervously and stepped across the stall to the mare. She knelt where he had been and placed her legs under the horse's head. Speaking in low, quiet tones, she spoke to the horse as he had—murmuring encouraging words as the birth became imminent.

Soon he had no time to spare on Sharon, for the foal came quickly after a slow start and the ensuing minutes were filled with the birth and first steps of the new colt. He laughed at the shaky start and was filled with hope for this new life and for his own plans. Molly and her colt would be a fitting beginning to his thoroughbreds.

"I should leave." Sharon stood and moved away from the horses as the new mother and babe learned each other. He started to reach over to help her out of the corner and then caught sight of his hands. Walking to the large barrel outside the stall, he splashed water on his hands and arms and scrubbed them quickly. Untying the belt of the apron, he lifted it over his head and hung it over the low wooden wall next to him. Sharon was there as he finished.

"Wait. Give me but a few minutes more and I will escort you back to your room." He needed to clean and check the mare before he could be certain that all was well.

She nodded. "I will wait for you outside." Adjusting her shawl until it was once more around her shoulders, she walked away, down the center of the stables and out the side door. And, again, she left the scent of roses in her wake.

Richard took the time necessary and, when convinced that Molly and her colt were fine, he washed again to remove all traces of the birth and left the building to find Sharon. As promised, she was outside, sitting on a bench in the cool night's air. He pulled on his leather jacket against the cold and drew her up from her seat and into his arms. Surprisingly, she did not resist.

"Come, let us walk. We can keep the night's cold breath away by staying close." He turned her under his arm and held her about the shoulders. They headed in the direction of the private apartments.

"Richard, I did not mean to eavesdrop in the stables but I heard you say you are starting your own breeding farm?"

So, she had been there longer than he first thought. Long enough to hear his dreams vocalized. Well, at least she heard the safer of his dreams mentioned. The other one festered just below the skin and out of view. 'Twas the one that would come to naught and he had been fighting it of late. He had almost convinced himself to let it go, as Robert Calder had urged. Thoughts of a home and a family and a future grew in his heart and mind and almost obliterated the other hopeless desire.

To be king.

'Twas God's own truth that he was a faithful servant of Her Majesty, his half-sister. But a kernel of disloyalty remained buried deep within him—a single unspoken desire that he should sit on the throne instead. However, he would never take action to make it happen. In spite of all the rumors and innuendoes that flew about the court, there was no legitimate Catholic male heir to Henry's, now Elizabeth's, throne. No matter how the Catholics of England and their supporters in Spain and Italy hoped and prayed, his own birth could never be legitimized now that his father was long dead.

So he turned his longings away from that which could not be his to something more attainable, something more tangible. If Elizabeth agreed, the land and farm that his—their—father had bequeathed in his will would be Richard's own. If Elizabeth's cooperation could be arranged.

His efforts in this direction were looking very promising—until this recent round of political intrigue and plotting. He truly could not believe the turn of events that had made Windsor, and every place around the queen, into a fortress—the Pope had issued a bull excommunicating Elizabeth from the Catholic Church.

Although it had been issued several months before and the existence of it was being officially ignored, the tension caused by this action and its possible repercussions had heightened the queen's normal level of security. This could be a death warrant for Elizabeth, since Catholics in England were now being urged to rid themselves of this illegal monarch. The Pope had even gone so far as to offer the reward of Heaven to any Catholic who succeeded in assassinating her.

And, as word spread of the order, the queen's temperament understandably grew more strained; audiences were canceled, and requests ignored. His own desire for the granting of a charter for his farm must wait upon the pleasure of the queen. Once more, he could be ignored because of his lack of status within the royal family and the court.

"From your mouth to Her Majesty's ears. I but await the granting of the charter now," he answered as they walked.

"Where will your farm be?" Sharon swept the loose tendrils of hair from her face. 'Twas cold walking across the quadrangle at night. Soon they would be inside and warmer.

"Not far from Tenby Manor. 'Tis not large nor extravagant but will give me the chance to raise fine bloods."

"Tenby Manor?" she asked, stopping and forcing him to do so as well. "In Sussex?" Her eyes flashed and her pale cheeks flushed with some excitement he could not explain.

"Aye. The same. Why does this interest you? Do you know someone there?" Could that be it? Did she have some connection of which he knew not in Sussex?

"No, ah, I know no one there," she stuttered. "I left something valuable there and wish to retrieve it if we are not returning."

She would not meet his gaze as she offered this mean excuse of an answer to his inquiry. His misgivings over her search of the wall in her chamber at Tenby returned. He could see in his mind's eye her hands gliding over the wood, her fingers searching for the latch. He knew that was the object of her investigation. But why? Did she know of the priesthole hidden there? Did others know or suspect? Were his grandparents in danger?

"If you tell me what and where it is, I will attempt to have it returned to you. I can send a messenger there with word—if you so desire?"

He watched as confusion and then some other emotion moved over her face. He could see she was trying to come up with an answer for him and that she had not an idea of what to say. Disappointment filled him at the realization that she was about to lie to him.

"No, Richard, but I thank you for your kind offer."

"Are you certain? 'Twould be no trouble." He felt a bit of guilt as he pressed her to see her reaction. Not enough to stop his probing to find her secrets, though.

"You have done enough for me, Richard. Truly. The bath was more than I could have asked for. I am certain that you had to use many favors to make those arrangements and I would ask no more of you." She smiled at him, but her eyes were still filled with that other look and he finally recognized it for what it was—guilt. He should know—he wore that look often enough himself.

They had reached the gateway that would lead to her wing and room within the apartments. Richard opened the door for her and she walked inside. When he tried to adjust her shawl, she pulled it tighter around her shoulders, shivering.

"Still cold? The hall will be warmer." They began walking down one corridor and up another.

"I still cannot get used to the cooler weather here," she started. "It was much warmer . . ." She didn't finish.

"Warmer where? I thought you came from the north of England. I doubt not that 'tis colder there than here." He watched her struggle for an answer once more. Another of the woman's secrets.

"You are right, Richard. I am chilled, most probably by going about in the night's air after the wonderful heat of the bath. Well," she said, "here is my room." She paused in front of the doorway.

When she would have turned to open her door, Richard blocked her by resting his hand on the wall. She looked up at him and later he would swear it was the smell of roses that bewitched him into kissing her. He leaned closer and touched his lips to hers, promising himself that it was just a kiss. His body took over control and it became so much more.

He wrapped his arm around her and kept her close to him, moving his other hand into her long hair. As he slid his fingers through it, visions of her covered in naught but pink rose petals filled his mind. The smell of it was intoxicating. Nay, she was intoxicating—he felt drunk with the longing to make her his own and to remove from her any memory of unscrupulous men and their betrayals.

His mouth moved over hers, his tongue finding her and touching, tasting, mating. He would have stopped had she not moaned in reaction. He could have forced his mouth and hands from her. But her moan freed his desire and he pressed her against the wall even as he more deeply moved within her mouth. His erection grew and hardened until he knew she must notice it.

Sharon reached up behind his head and loosened his hair. Tangling her fingers within it, she pulled him down to her. Her response threatened to overwhelm him and he eased back from her mouth, her hands, her heat. If they did not cease, he would take her right there on the floor outside of her chamber. And his doubts and questions be damned!

"I did arrange for the bath to apologize for my past behaviors," he whispered, kissing her once more. "Now you would spur me onto more actions and more apologies."

"Should I apologize to you then?" she asked with a hint

of laughter in her soft voice. "I must go in, Richard. Thank you once more."

She had almost entered the room when he whispered her name. "Sharon?" She paused in her movement and looked at him expectantly.

"My plan, until Molly called me away at last moment, was to join you in that bath."

Her eyes widened and a most attractive blush crept up her neck and face. She opened her mouth to say something but words never came. He just smiled, pulled the door closed for her, and stepped away. Let her think on that while he figured out a way to discover all of the secrets she held so closely.

Chapter 12

LIKE A MOTH to a flame, Sharon found herself drawn time and time again to seek him out. She tried to deny the attraction to herself but after that night, "the night of the bath," as she called it in her own mind, she couldn't fight it. His words inflamed her, his hands and mouth inflamed her, he inflamed her. As someone who had made it to the ripe old age of twenty-nine and still remained a virgin, she was completely confused by her physical reaction to him.

She'd dated and been seriously involved with men in her life but none had had such a devastating effect on her self-control. Sharon wondered if it was the surreal life she lived at the moment that kept her so off-balance with Richard. Maybe subconsciously she didn't believe any of this was real, so where was the harm in enjoying herself?

She also rationalized quite thoroughly to herself that, since Richard was about the same age as Elizabeth, he might have information about this missing heir. She had just not built up the courage or found the right approach yet to ask him such indelicate questions about the queen and her family. Since Richard obviously had an open door to the queen's presence, he might have heard something during the years he'd spent in Elizabeth's court and household. One day she might even ask him what gave him his position and his expectations of the queen's support in his plan for a horse-breeding farm.

So, as she waited and watched for an opportunity and a possible source of knowledge about the royal family's history, Sharon enjoyed every moment of working within the queen's wardrobe and the exposure to the life and times of England's greatest queen.

"Mistress Reynolds and Mistress Prescott, will you share our meal this evening?"

His voice sent shivers down her spine each time she heard it. Not sure if it was anticipation or arousal, Sharon took a deep breath before pausing on their way to supper.

"Master Granville! And a good evening to you and your friend, as well." Sharon didn't know the man sitting with Richard but by his uniform of red she knew he served in the queen's guard. And he looked very familiar to her. She studied his face as the men stood and bowed slightly to her and Patricia.

"May I make my friend Robert Calder known to you? He is a member of the queen's yeomen but presently off-duty. Robert, Mistress Reynolds and Mistress *Prescott*." Sharon noticed the emphasis Richard placed on Patricia's name and watched as Robert noticed it too.

"You must be related to John?" Sharon asked as she sat down on a stool across from Richard. She had not planned to walk past him but she and Patricia had been so engrossed in conversation that she didn't realize he was so close until he called out her name.

"I am the lad's father. Mistress Prescott, I have heard much about you from John." Robert smiled warmly at them both. Patricia blushed furiously and tilted her head down, not meeting anyone's gaze. "As a matter of fact, the lad dines just over there." Standing, Robert offered his arm to Patricia. "Shall we join him for a bit?"

Patricia looked at her with a panic-stricken expression and Sharon was just about to step in and rescue her when Richard butted in himself.

"There, Mistress Prescott. John is waving at you now."

"If you do not mind, mistress? May I go?"

Sharon had not become comfortable with having someone always around her at her beck and call since the first day. Although she chose to look at Patricia as a young companion, the girl was completely at ease in the relationship as established by Lady Randall . . . and just as untroubled at asking permission.

"I do not mind at all, Patricia. Go. Enjoy yourself this evening, since we have no other duties. I will see you in the morning." Smiling at the girl and nodding at Robert, Sharon watched as they walked through the crowded room to where young John stood waiting. Then she turned back to Richard.

"Well, I commend you once more on your maneuvering, Richard."

He laughed loudly and theatrically thumped his chest with his fist. She answered with her own chuckle and smiled back at him.

"Mea culpa, mea culpa, mistress." He offered her the platter of cheeses and bread. As she made her choice, he added, " 'Twas at John and Robert's request that I did so stage that introduction. 'Twould seem my young apprentice is quite taken with the young lady and wishes to pursue something more than just a casual dalliance. I did but what he asked."

"Marriage? He seeks her hand in marriage? But she's—they're so young," Sharon answered.

Richard laughed again and then looked at her. "Not so young and not as old as we. Some would say a perfect age for entering that holy estate."

She looked at him and raised both eyebrows in dismay. "Old am I? And I thought you a courtier, much learned and practiced in the ways of compliments and soft words. I guess I was wrong again." She raised a goblet and he filled it from a nearby pitcher. Swallowing deeply, she choked and sputtered as the ale hit her stomach. Coughing several times, Sharon finally cleared her throat and then wiped at her tear-filled eyes.

" 'Tis only ale, lass. Surely, you have drunk your fill of that?" He held up a napkin to her and she used it to dab her eyes.

"No, I avoid ale whenever possible. It does not like me."

" 'Tis a funny way of putting it—the ale does not like you? But it does tell the tale, does it not? Here," he said, pouring from another pitcher, "here is the cider you favored at the inn."

Sharon drank a few mouthfuls of the cool cider, letting its fruity aroma and flavor soothe her irritated throat. She would definitely avoid ale. If it was anything like beer, her tolerance of it would be very low. Memories of a few wild parties at college reminded her of why she did not drink beer.

"Tell me what thoughts are going through your mind right now. Your eyes did take on a most interesting look for a brief moment." His voice was low and incredibly sexy. Did this man do anything but exude sex appeal and personal magnetism? He could probably charm a squirrel out of her winter's supply of nuts!

"I did but think of a time when ale made me even more foolish than I thought I was. It loosened my tongue and my control."

"Would that I was there to witness such a night!"

"Oh, Richard, you are so funny," she said, patting his hand. 'It was not a pretty sight, I assure you. I heaped insults on those around me and, after one too many, the ale did not stay quietly in my stomach." She grimaced as she remembered swearing off drinking after the experience.

"Still I would like to have seen you."

Richard passed her the meats and stewed vegetables, such as they were. Boiled leeks, spinach, and artichokes had only so much appeal after seeing them served at so many meals. What she wouldn't give for a broiled hamburger and potatoes and a large ice-cold iced tea . . . with lemon and sugar.

"What do you do now that the queen has moved to London? I was surprised that you did not accompany her."

"So, you do keep track of my person! I dared not hope

that 'twas true." His eyes gleamed with pleasure as he bit into a piece of poultry. She watched as his tongue swept over his lips, capturing the juices before they ran down his chin. She ignored his attempt to flirt and refused to fall for his tricks.

"Everyone at court interests me, especially those I would call friend. Do you usually go with Her Majesty when she travels to London?" She lifted a spoonful of spinach to her mouth.

He finished chewing and swallowed before answering. "I carry out the same duties whether the queen is present or not. I am not needed at Whitehall, so I remain here. And I prefer it here to the company I would keep there."

"And speaking of such company, how is Molly's colt?" Sharon had seen the mare and colt in one of the yards near the stables, but she'd been on an errand to the laundry and not able to linger and watch.

" 'Tis well. He grows and strengthens with each day." His enthusiasm was contagious. He seemed completely comfortable in his role as stable-master. Would she ever find herself feeling that good about her job? She'd thought that her position at the museum would bring her all she desired: professional standing and respect, enough money to enjoy life, and the opportunity to be challenged both in her field and within her administrative duties.

Things had gone badly very quickly and almost without warning. Purchase orders had been changed. Her signature had been copied and misused. Errors in displaying objects and in keeping the records of the museum had been discovered. Oh, she knew she was ultimately responsible but it hurt to have all of Jasper's accusations come true. And to know that it was her youth and inexperience that contributed to her own downfall. Funny thing was, here in Elizabethan England she was considered old at twenty-nine. And as for the experience part, she would leave that for Lady Seagrave's niece.

"Would you like to see him now?" Richard's voice cut through her reverie.

"Now? But it's dark now."

"Not in the stables. There are lanterns aplenty to light them. And 'tis not so late that a trip there and back will cause you any problems."

He rose from his seat and held out his hand to her in invitation. Sharon looked at the hand he offered, knowing that it represented more than assistance in rising from her bench. She was sure that if asked, he would not even bother to deny that this was another attempt to get her alone. She licked her suddenly Sahara-like lips with the tip of her tongue before looking at him. Going with him now was a step for her, for them, and she thought about whether or not she was ready and willing to take that step. It took only a moment to decide.

"I would love to see the horses, Richard."

A few minutes of brisk walking brought them to the stables. Both had hurried along the hallways and then paths, neither speaking a word until they reached their destination. Richard had then excused himself briefly when they entered the building. A few minutes later, he returned carrying two steaming mugs of some liquid. Although she was a bit suspicious and sniffed at it before tasting it, it was a wonderful raspberry drink, similar to a modern-day wine cooler. The heat of it warmed her from the inside out.

Richard took her by her free hand and led her to a large stall in another part of the huge building. There Molly and her colt stood quietly in the darkened corner. Soft nickers and neighs were carried on the still air and echoed through the stables. Richard nudged her arm and pointed like a proud papa at the recently born horse, who was still all legs and not much bulk.

"He has fine lines already, Sharon, and his form shows great promise. He will make an auspicious beginning to my own stock."

"Has the queen consented, then?"

"Not yet, but I am hopeful that word will come soon." She could hear the hope that permeated his words and she could see it in his eyes.

"Tell me about your own breeding establishment," she

said, anxious to learn more about him by his hopes and dreams.

" 'Tis not overly large but the size and location are perfect for my needs and wants. I have already chosen most of the mares needed to start and I still seek a few more stallions with the right bloodlines." He lifted his drink to his mouth and swallowed deeply from it before continuing. "And, it will be mine."

The issue of sole possession was important to him. She sipped more of her own drink before asking her next question. She started to speak but he reached over and took her cup from her. In a flash he was gone and back again and the cup was filled to the brim with the steaming liquid. Light alcohol content or not, she would have to be careful of this brew. It tasted too sweet and fruity and felt too smooth going down to ignore the possibility of getting drunk on it.

"And what else do you wish for, Richard? Is love not important to you?" That wasn't how she planned to ask the question but the words spilled out.

"Love? Oh, nay, not that." He laughed and drank more. Pointing to her face, he touched the tip of her nose and laughed once more.

"What was that for?" Was he making fun of her?

"You did but take on such a disgruntled expression I thought you were asking personally for my love."

She swatted his hand away. "Never that, Richard. You can be assured. I simply meant do marriage and family figure into your plans?" She lifted the cup to her lips once more and swallowed, insulted by his laughter at her expense. She would be damned before she ever asked him to love her.

Now where the heck did that come from? It must be the drink making her think these strange thoughts about him. She liked him, she admired his work and his dreams, but want him to love her? Not a chance! This Renaissance Romeo would "love" too many women in his life—damn it, *had* loved too many women already for her to ever want a relationship with him.

Tipping the cup back, she drank the last of it and looked at him. Okay, so he was good-looking. She shook her head as she then immediately disagreed with her own assessment. If the truth was told, the man was built like the Greek god Adonis without so much as an ounce of excess fat on his well-muscled form. His long, dark hair and sometimes hazel, sometimes green-gold eyes, reminded her of that actor who played on a television series about an immortal Scotsman. She looked at his eyes, trying to remember the actor's name, but all she could think of was Duncan MacLeod. She knew that was the character's name but she just couldn't seem to think of the guy's real name.

"Pardon?" he asked. "I do not believe I know any Duncan MacLeod. He is, of course, Scottish?"

"Never mind," she said, waving his question off and not remembering saying Duncan's name out loud. "What of a family?"

Before he answered, he disappeared once more. She had only closed her eyes for a split second to blink and he was gone. Then she saw the outline of his body edged by the flickering light of one of the hanging lanterns as he walked away from her once more.

"Damn, how does he do that?" she whispered to no one in particular. Sharon tilted her head and squinted into the shadows and soon observed his return. His long legs, well-muscled thighs, and hips were definitely worth watching and she remembered the feel of them behind and under her as they rode the horse together. Every step taken by the horse over the uneven ground that day brought her in more and more intimate contact with those legs, those thighs. Gosh, if those damn skirts hadn't been in the way, it would have been so much more enjoyable. She fanned her face as she felt the heat growing in it. There must be a fire lit somewhere close, for the temperature was much warmer now than when she arrived. He handed her the cup and, feeling that this one was not heated like the first one . . . or was that two . . . she took a sip to try to cool off a bit.

"Of course I will seek out a bride once the farm is established. A family will be important."

He answered without asking her to repeat her question, which was good because she had already forgotten what it was she'd asked. Especially as she watched those long, powerful legs of his move closer and closer to where she stood.

"Do you have someone in mind already? I'm sure with all the women you've . . ." She clapped her hand over her mouth to keep the words from coming out. "I mean . . . with all your contacts in the court . . ." Then realizing that every version would be worse than the one before, she just stopped asking and laughed.

The laughter went on and on until she spilled some of her drink. She took the last mouthfuls remaining in the cup and handed it back to Richard.

"Would you like more?"

From the silky smooth tone of his voice, she wasn't quite sure if he meant something else—was this another *invitation?* But wait, if he was making wedding plans with someone else, she was in no danger from him. Was that right? She pushed her hair back from her face and touched her heated cheeks. Every time she tried to focus on his face, he kept moving. Reaching out, Sharon placed her hands on his cheeks to hold his head still. His face wasn't hot to the touch like hers. This didn't make any sense.

"Where are you getting this from? You keep disappearing and coming back before I realize you're gone."

"I am here, Sharon. Truly. Can you not feel me next to you?" His smile grew wider as her hands moved down from his face, onto his shoulders and then down onto his chest. He took a step closer, which was good because he was starting to sway on his feet. She held him steady with her hands on his waist. Now, there it was! He was hotter there than on his face. Noticing that the laces of his shirt were loosened at his neck, she pulled it open to test his chest. Running her hands over the finely formed muscles, she felt the heat once more.

What they needed was a central heating system. These hot and cold zones were really very strange. He never moved beneath her hands except to come another step closer. He was being quite polite, since it made it easier for her to touch him. The crisp chest hairs tickled her palms and she giggled at the sensation. Without thought she rubbed her cheek against his chest, wanting to feel that too. She was jolted by his quick move then and stumbled back away from him. She would have landed in the straw if he had not grabbed her and pulled her back.

"Mayhap you should sit down a bit? Let me show you where I keep the wine." He wrapped his arm around her waist and guided her away from Molly's stall and away from the lights. She tried to watch but all she could focus on was his chest. Turning in toward him, she slipped one hand inside his shirt and just touched his skin. He laughed once more and she realized he must be ticklish.

Soon—or was it a few minutes later?—they entered a small room off one of the stalls and she heard the door close behind them. He walked her over to a bale of straw and she sat down on it.

"This is like your room at Tenby Manor. How nice to have one here too."

It was a tiny room, no bigger than her bedroom's walk-in closet at home, but it was cozy and warm. Blinking and trying to focus, she saw some clothes hanging on a peg by the door, a low table with a lantern, and a bench next to it. A makeshift bed lay in the corner next to a small brazier.

"So you remember the room in the stables there?"

She watched as he swayed over to the table, refilled their cups, and came back to hand hers to her. If she tilted her head just so, the room didn't move much at all as she stared at those legs. Finally realizing that she would be more secure sitting lower, she slid off the block of straw and sat on the floor, pulling her skirts up so she could sit yoga-style more comfortably.

"Do you bring all your women here?" she asked him.

She must remember not to drink any more of this fruit-cooler. She had no tolerance for real wine and thank goodness this wasn't the real stuff or she'd be pretty drunk by now!

He looked for a moment like he was choking on his own

drink, so she pulled him down next to her and patted him on the back to help him clear his throat. She was glad when he stayed at her side.

"Would it disappoint you greatly to find that I truly do not keep a *harim* of women to tup at my beck and call?"

"You don't?" she asked, realizing she used a contraction and completely unable to correct it. "But you flirt with so many—I've seen you in action."

"As do you. Do you tup with every man with whom you flirt? There are those rumors. . . ." His voice drifted lower and then off. He was talking about the real Lady Seagrave's niece and didn't even know it. She laughed.

"Not quite all of them."

"How many of them? One? Two? Five?" His tone became more insistent—how should she answer him? Oh, gosh, she wished she could form a coherent thought. She rubbed her brow and was about to answer him when he helped her out.

"Did you tup the one you mentioned at the inn?"

"Jasper Crenshaw? Are you kidding me? I wouldn't sleep with him if he paid me to." Still holding her goblet, she crossed her arms over her chest, glad that she'd made her point about the scumbag.

"Jasper Crenshaw is the knave who dishonored you? The one who passed rumors of your scandalous behaviors to your aunt?"

Now he understood, but of course, the rumors had been told to her supervisor. Jasper had asked her to sleep with him; he'd promised to help her straighten out all the problems recently plaguing her department if she did. Shivers pulsed through her at just the thought of his offer.

Richard moved closer and put his arm around her shoulders. He thought she was cold! Oh, well, the feel of his arm and his body so close did feel quite wonderful, so she wouldn't correct him yet. He took her cup from her and lifted it to her lips for one more drink. Luckily it wasn't pure wine or she would have to stop drinking it now. Any more and she'd be really, really drunk.

"And you, Sharon, do you want marriage and a family?"

She would have answered him, but when he placed his lips so near to her ear that his moist hot breath tickled it when he whispered, she lost track of all thought. The heat of his breath, the heat of his body, the heat within her own body all made her melt inside. She sighed, trying to concentrate on his words.

"A family? I do want one, but there is plenty of time for that."

"Is there? Most men will not want so aged a wife. Bearing children is a dangerous task in even a young woman." He touched his mouth to her ear and she closed her eyes, enjoying the shivering sensations his action sent down her spine. She should stop him. Shouldn't she?

"I am not . . . old! Twenty . . . nine . . . is . . . not . . . old!"

"I did not say it, but some would. Twenty and nine sounds just fine to me."

"Richard, could we stop talking? I am getting so confused trying to think about your questions."

"You are?" She could hear the laughter in his voice.

"I am truly. And I cannot tell you everything, so please . . . stop talking?" She looked up at him and couldn't remember when he'd moved so close. His face was right there, his chest was right there, and his lips were so close.

"Richard, please kiss me. Just shut up and kiss me."

Chapter 13

AND HE DID as she asked.

He could not refuse her, even knowing that the amount of wine she had drunk had much to do with her breathy request. He heard her desire and it piqued his own. Wrapping her in his arms, he touched his lips to hers and waited for her response. Not long in coming, she tossed her goblet and tangled her hands in his hair. Tilting his head, he pressed against her lips until she opened to him. With her moans spurring him on, he swept his tongue into her mouth and gently teased hers. Turning her body to his, he slipped one hand down onto her throat and caressed her neck, looking for the sensitive spots on her flesh. Drawing his mouth away, he followed his fingers' journey, down onto her neck, and licked below her ear, nipping at the tip of it as he passed.

She writhed against him, her feet sliding in the straw as she turned and tried to fit their bodies closer together. He obliged her by pushing them down until they lay on the floor, then he covered her legs with one of his. It had been all he could do earlier not to reach up her skirts when she exposed her legs to him. Sitting in that outrageous position before him, all he could think of was touching her . . . *there*.

"Kiss my mouth, Richard. My mouth . . ." she said. Apparently he was not doing an adequate job of it because she rolled him to his back and climbed on top of him. Leaning down to his face, her hair formed a curtain around them. The scent of roses surrounded them as Sharon touched his mouth once and then again. Now it was his turn to live one of his fantasies—he wrapped his hands in her hair, twirling them over and over in its length until he held her close. Their mouths met once more and she led the kiss.

By God's blood, she was wondrous in her kissing. His body was inflamed by her actions, his flesh aroused and ready by the touch of her tongue on his. Freeing one hand, he pulled at her laces until her blouse opened to his touch. Her moans grew deeper and longer into his mouth as he slid his fingers over her breast. Flicking his thumb over the nipple, he gained a new reaction from her—she sucked on his tongue. He quickened the action, teasing the tip of her breast into a tight bud, and she rewarded him with more moans and more suckling on his tongue.

He rocked his pelvis against her as he imagined her mouth on his cock. Her mouth did wonderful things and promised even more. With the hand in her hair, he tugged until, with a groan of refusal, she released his tongue. More than anything, right at this moment he wanted to taste her nipples and suckle on them. Tucking her legs around his waist, he sat up, bringing her with him. When she sat in his lap like this, it brought her own heat against his groin and put her breasts just in front of his mouth.

Pulling her blouse free, he used both hands to encircle and touch and massage her breasts. Her head fell back and she moaned out her enjoyment; the sounds echoed through the small room and incited him even more. He continued to touch and then lick and taste and tease her nipples. She began to move against him as he suckled and then again as he worried his teeth gently on the aroused tips. Soon he joined her in moaning as her movements caused more heat in that part of him that was screaming for release.

She leaned back and placed her hands on his thighs to

balance herself. Sharon seemed oblivious to everything but the wild feelings that must be pulsing through her even as they passed through him. He slipped his hands from her breasts and began to gather up the layers of her skirt. He had to touch her heat. Finally reaching under and finding the top of her naked thigh, he slid his hands toward the curls at the top. And found the same strange cloth there again.

But the flimsy, silky cloth was no barrier to his quest or to her moist response. His hand felt the wetness there and it increased as he continued to slide across the material over and over again. He wanted to get inside this strange garment and inside her heated core. He lifted her from his lap and placed her against the bale of straw. She protested but he kissed her breathless and then lifted her skirts to look at this barrier to his pleasure.

"What in God's holy name is this?" He had never seen anything like it. This garment hugged her hips and covered her private parts, and yet was light enough in color and weight that it did not prevent him from seeing the dark curls underneath. He was intrigued by the tight fit and slipped his fingers inside the front and ran them around the edges.

"Panties. They're called panties." She whispered, answering his question. "They are from . . . France."

He looked at her and waited for her permission. At her nod, he pulled the *panties* down and off, sliding them down the length of her legs and then rubbing them between his fingers to feel the silkiness of them. Now she was naked *there* to his sight. She made such an alluring picture with only her stockings covering her legs to just below her knees and her legs spread, ready for his caress.

She sat leaning back, arms spread over the bale behind her with her skirts around her hips. Her blouse lay open, showing him her pale pink nipples on the tips of breasts swollen from his caresses. Kneeling between her legs, he drew her feet up slightly, opening her even more to his view and to his touch. The folds of skin between her legs glistened with moisture and he moved his fingers against them to gain more. Her head fell back and she panted as he spread the wetness from inside out and over the engorged nether lips. Bending forward, he took her mouth as his hand mimicked his tongue's actions. Suckling her harder, he spread the folds and entered her tight passage with one finger and then two. In truth, 'twas much tighter than he expected.

Caught up in the excitement, she returned his fevered movements with her own as she arched over and over against his hand between her thighs. His body urged him to take her, to move inside her and to make her beg for more. To make her come.

He needed to make her his own so she would forget those who had had her before him. His cock grew larger and harder until he swore his seed would burst. She must have known, because her hand slid down his body, searching, until she rubbed against it. She molded her palm to his length and caressed him as he touched her.

Richard pulled himself out of her grasp and lowered himself between her legs. Lifting them over his shoulders, he placed his mouth at her heat and kissed her there. He could feel the tension building within her; she twisted against him and her breathless moans grew louder and louder. He licked and tasted the salty muskiness of her sex as her own peak approached. Sucking the sensitive bud that sat high in the folds of skin between his teeth, he pushed her over the edge to her release.

A high, keening sound filled the room as she moaned out her excitement. The sounds aroused him even further and, instead of stopping, he continued his gentle assault between her thighs. She moaned out his name as she was overwhelmed with her fulfillment, her wetness flowing as he released her from his mouth's intimate kiss. He pressed his hand against her core until the waves and pulses that traveled from inside out and outside in stopped. Then he knelt up to see how she looked when satisfied. Of course, he had hopes that his own needs would be seen to before the night was done.

Sharon was asleep. Sound asleep.

Too much wine had been his downfall this night. He

knew the *raspes* was much stronger than she'd thought it was, but it did not make him tell her so. She made a lovely drunk as she'd begun to feel the effects of it—first swaying on her feet and then flushing with heat. Mayhap he was a scoundrel and a knave and no better than her Jasper Crenshaw to let her drink more and more just to see if she would join him in love's play.

Nay! A true rogue would have pressed himself into her even as she slept, replete with her own satisfaction. A dastard would have taken her whether she knew it or not, making her his and taking his own release on her. Especially when she would not or could not naysay him about it.

And it would have felt wondrous to be inside her tight heat. He'd felt her own release when it came upon her—the contractions pulsing on his mouth and then his hand as he continued to draw it out for her. He was even now still aroused from her touches and kisses and sounds. 'Twould take some time to calm down.

Richard gently turned her on her side, adjusted her clothes as best he could, and tucked himself up against her back. Realizing she would have to sleep here and return to her own room in the morning, he pulled a blanket over both of them to ward off the night's chill. He could not carry her unnoticed to her room at this time of night, and explanations would be worthless. He settled behind her and picked some of the straw out of her hair. Smoothing it down, he placed his arm around her and over the blanket.

"Thank you," she murmured in her sleep.

Thank you? She thanked him for his near debauchery of her? She must be very drunk—or accustomed to being used in this manner? He shushed her and closed his eyes. More likely, she had no idea of what she said.

"Thank you for keeping me safe, Richard. I knew I could trust you." Her words, whispered with some thought, tugged at his heart. She trusted him. Did she know him better than he knew himself? His intent that night had been to seduce her and yet her words seem to indicate that she believed otherwise.

"I would always keep you safe, Sharon." He surprised

himself—he meant the words. She had secrets, and those mysterious *panties,* and yet he wanted to be responsible for keeping her safe. If she trusted him with her body and reputation, would she also trust him with her secrets now? A twinge of guilt assailed him as he thought to probe her with questions. He may have been able to control his own bodily desires but the power of knowing someone's secrets was something different.

"Why do you seek to return to Tenby Manor?" he whispered in her ear. She shifted against him and he thought she was deeper asleep than before. Just when he was about to drift off to sleep himself, she answered.

"Tenby Manor is my only way home."

"Your way home? Tell me what you mean." He moved slightly back from her and tucked his hand beneath his head. "Do you want to go home and face the disgrace you left behind?"

"I have to make things work there. Face the rumors . . . answer the questions."

"But what about Jasper?" Mayhap it would be best for her to find someone here at court instead and not in the place where her reputation was shattered.

"Can't go home until I find the bastard and tell him . . ." She followed him across the distance between them and snuggled against him once more.

"Tell him what, Sharon? What could help your cause?"

"That he is not a bastard. He needs to know, then I can go home."

Tell the bastard that he is not a bastard? What could she mean by that? Was he there now at court, this Jasper Crenshaw? Did she mean to absolve him of his part in her ruination, of his betrayal of her hopes and dreams? Was this some cleric's instructions to her to gain God's forgiveness?

He would seek out knowledge of this man for himself through his own sources. He promised her that he would keep her safe and he would. Then, once her honor was restored, he would ask her about the future, their future. For more and more each day, he pictured her beside him in all things. She would work with him once the queen granted his charter, she would lie with him at night, fully his equal in passion's play, and she would bear him the children he craved. He knew that he would have to reveal his own secrets to her even as he sought hers.

But, for now, he would hold her close and enjoy the quiet warmth of her body next to his.

Chapter 14

WHY HAD SHE stood so close to the amplifiers on the stage? Her head buzzed and pounded inside, just like all the other times when she went to a loud concert. She tried to open her eyes but they refused to obey. Her eyelids felt swollen and locked in place. Finally, she made one give a slight bit and then forced it to open more. Peering around the room with just one eye, waves and waves of dizziness flowed through her. Her stomach began to churn and she closed that one eye to fight off the terrible nausea.

Sharon reached up and pushed her hair out of her face. Then, feeling more brave than sick, she opened both eyes at once. The room spun around her faster and faster until she clasped her hands over them, closing them once more.

Dear God, what had she done? There had been no rock concert. There had only been Richard . . . and his damned raspberry wine coolers! But, as her stomach and head now told her, there was more wine than cooler in the drinks he had given her last night.

Last night? Oh, no! She had spent the night with him? The roughness of the straw on the floor beneath her and the pungent odors of horses and their by-products nearby convinced her of her location—the stable room Richard kept for just this purpose. Visions of the scene that Lady Randall would throw when she found out flashed through Sharon's mind, making her sicker than before. Where would she go? If she returned to Lady Seagrave, she would be exposed as a fake. What would happen to her then?

What had happened to her last night with him? She lifted the coarse blanket and slipped her hands underneath to check on what she wore. Her blouse was undone, her skirts twisted around her thighs, and, worse yet, her panties were gone! No, the worst part was that she didn't remember how she came to be undressed and under this blanket.

Knowing only that she had to get back to her room and come up with some explanation for her absence, Sharon sat up, clutching the blanket to her chest. A moment later, her belly did as it threatened—she barely made it onto her knees over a bucket before the retching began. Somewhere in the middle of her stomach's rebellion, she felt an arm supporting her and a damp cloth cooling her forehead. Since she couldn't fight what her body was doing, she gave up her struggle and prayed for a swift death instead. A few minutes later she sat back on the ground, trying to catch her breath.

That was when she saw Richard. He knelt beside her, holding the cool cloth on her head, but he stared lower than that. Following the direction of his gaze, she saw that her blouse was completely open, leaving her breasts naked to him. Apparently he had not looked his fill the night before. She grabbed the ends of her blouse and pulled them closed, glaring at him for his audacity.

"I would ask your pardon but they are a fair sight to see." He smiled, giving her an I-know-what-we-did-last-night smile. "And were fairer still to touch and taste."

His words, uttered in a madly sexy tone, did her in. Her body responded even if she didn't want it to and those "fair" breasts tingled and the nipples tightened until she shivered from it. The contemptible knave just laughed at her.

After reaching down and tying her blouse's laces, she pushed her skirts down around her legs and decided that her best course of action would be to leave, *now,* as quickly as she could. Dropping the blanket and scrambling to her feet, she pulled herself together and prepared to leave. Her cloak hung on the peg next to the door. She grabbed it, threw it around her shoulders, and tugged on the door's handle. She had almost made a wordless escape, so proud that she had not even given in to the urge to ask him what they'd done in the night, when he cleared his throat and she was forced to look at him.

Her panties dangled from his outstretched hand.

She covered the space between them in one or two hurried steps, grabbed her underwear without touching his hand, and forced herself to walk, not run, from his lair. His laughter made it very difficult not to scream. Sharon was pulling the door closed when he called her name quietly.

" 'Tis early and dark enough that you will not be seen returning to your room. Go quietly and carefully and none will know of our time together."

His expression was serious, his warning and advice well meant. She would never figure him out.

She could not have been asleep for more than a minute when the others in the room began to rouse for the day. Waking for the second time felt even worse than the first, if that were possible. Pain tightened around her brow like a vise and the slightest noise reverberated through her head, increasing the throbbing to nearly unbearable.

This was why she never drank more than a glass of wine.

Maybe a few more minutes prone on the straw-filled mattress would make the rest of this hangover go away? Sharon doubted very much that employers allowed sick days in Elizabethan England. And how would she explain her absence to Lady Randall? *Oh, milady, I was up drinking with Richard Granville until all hours of the night and didn't get much sleep. I'll just take the day off.*

Not in this lifetime and especially not with the reputation that she allegedly had as Lady Seagrave's niece. She was still trying to come up with a plan that did not involve her lifting her head from her makeshift pillow when the door opened once more.

"Mistress?" Even Patricia's whispering voice sounded like the wild screams of the *banshee* echoing across the empty room.

"Shhhhhhh . . ." she begged, covering her ears.

"Are you ill, then, mistress? Your face has lost most of its color and that which remains is rather ghastly." Patricia leaned down closer and touched Sharon's face. "Praise be! At least you have not the fever."

"Patricia, I am sick. What will Lady Randall say?"

"I will go and tell her now. Stay here and I will come back to take care of you."

"Will she be angry?" Sharon tried once more to open her eyes and focus on the room around her. This time she managed for a few seconds before her surroundings started to move around her instead.

"Oh, nay, mistress. The queen likes no one near her who is ill. 'Twould be Lady Randall's duty to keep you from Her Majesty's rooms for fear that you would carry the seeds of illness there."

Patricia's footsteps sounded like booming cannons as she moved across the room, intent on leaving.

"Shall I bring anything for you?"

"Patricia, truly I would like nothing more than to lie here in the quiet and try to sleep."

The younger woman quietly closed the door without further discussion and Sharon was left in the darkened room. If she lay completely still with her eyes closed, her stomach settled down to an almost bearable level of churning. She swore to herself that she would never again drink anything Richard offered her when he had that simultaneously dangerous and attractive sparkle in his gaze. She would never trust him again.

Or would she?

For all of her doubts, she knew deep inside that Richard had done nothing to harm or abuse her during their hours together. As a matter of fact, she had the distinct feeling that he had somehow protected her through the night.

How was that possible? She'd woken up half-dressed, *with no underwear on,* in his secret room, still reeling from the amount of wine he'd served her himself for the purpose of seducing her. Sharon knew they had shared something of a sexual nature—her body had that languid feeling that came with satisfaction.

She rubbed her brow and tried to ignore the obvious question that would not let her rest. What had they done? That question would have to wait until she could at least raise her head. Still pondering how she could find out the truth from Richard with the least amount of further humiliation, she was assailed by another wave of nausea. She was once more over a bucket in the corner, when the door opened. From her crouching position she could see only a woman's skirts. It was a few minutes before she could lift her head to see who was the witness to her hangover.

"So, I see that Patricia has the right of it. You are ill and your presence is not suitable for the queen's rooms this day."

"Aye, milady," she groaned as her stomach tried to empty itself rather forcefully. Mercifully, Lady Randall did not say anything else. Not that Sharon could have answered her at this point anyway.

Her belly finally settled, Sharon was preparing herself for the approaching battle with the imperious woman when a cup of water was pushed into her grasp.

"Rinse."

Sharon followed the order, not having the strength to fight anything at this point. Swishing and spitting out the water, her mouth at least felt clean. Pushing her hair out of her face, she sat back on her heels to regain her balance before attempting to go back to her pallet. And Lady Randall surprised her once again.

With a hand under her arm, Lady Randall helped Sharon to her feet and guided her across the room. Sinking down onto the lumpy surface, Sharon remained sitting, even though her head begged to be lowered onto the pillow next to her.

"I thank you, milady," she murmured, truly grateful for

the help. She wasn't sure that her legs would have made it there unassisted.

Lady Randall touched the back of her hand to Sharon's cheek and nodded, apparently satisfied that no fever was present. Stepping back away, the woman walked wordlessly to the door. Reaching it, she grasped the handle and began to pull it closed.

"Remain here for the day, Mistress Reynolds. I will send Patricia to you later this morn to aid you in your illness."

"Aye, milady."

"And avoid drinking *raspes,* since it clearly does not suit you." The door close, leaving Sharon sitting with her mouth dropped open in surprise. Did the woman miss nothing?

Richard strode down the corridor, pausing for no one or nothing. This meeting was distasteful to him but necessary, so he would follow the instructions he'd received. Coming to an intersection of hallways, he peered into the darkness and looked for the signal. Ah, there it was. A light flickered and then disappeared as he watched. He followed that hall and soon came to the room as it was described in the note.

Taking a deep breath to still his nerves, he knocked twice and then once more, as the note had said. The door opened slowly and despite his unease and discomfort he stepped inside. By attending, he was taking a step against Elizabeth, at least in his own mind. Torn between his long-held belief in her rightness as queen and his own deeply felt desire for legitimacy, Richard decided to give these men their say. There was no harm in listening, was there?

Richard crossed the threshold and the door was closed immediately and silently behind him by an unseen hand. He waited until he was beckoned, moving slowly across the room, recognizing some faces and not others. Icy tremors moved up his spine, making him wonder whether his were just foolish hopes or dangerous dreams.

Finally, Miguel stepped from one of the shadowy corners and, reaching out for his hand, drew him close.

"Richard, I was not certain if you would come," Father

Ramirez said in his quiet, accented voice. "But I am glad you did."

"And I am not certain why I came here either, Miguel."

"Ah, but Richard, I think we both know why you are here."

Richard raised one eyebrow in question, crossing his arms over his chest. "Why do you think, Miguel?"

"In service to His Holiness, of course. As faithful servants in the one true Church, we must try to follow His directives."

Richard leaned in closer and lowered his voice, determined that Miguel understand his position once and for all.

"I will not be a party to anything that harms her. Be clear on that, man. I came only for the truth," he whispered. "Once and for all, I would know the truth."

Father Ramirez stepped back and smiled at him. Taking his arm, his old family friend led him to a different part of the large room, one less crowded though no more private with the number of other gentlemen in it.

"I have received a report just this morning. 'Twould seem that our old nurse did indeed make her last confession before she died."

Richard gasped. He was so close to finding out the truth. He had lived with innuendo and rumor all of his life. This one had been heard before but he knew not if it was truth or lies. A deathbed confession was held sacred—no dying soul would lie, knowing judgment was at hand.

He knew Miguel dragged this out for his own reasons. Of course they wanted his cooperation in their plans against Elizabeth. If there were a Catholic male heir to England's throne, their plots could succeed. The people would want someone legitimate, a man, to lead them. Could it be him?

"I thought that a confession was between the penitent, their priest, and God Almighty."

"A Pope's dispensation can ease the way, Richard. It has eased the way."

Richard waited, not daring to breathe, not daring to hope. He closed his eyes and forced himself not to ask for this uncovered truth.

"Maria told her priest that she was present for the birth of Anne Boleyn's son."

Richard waved him off with his hand. "We knew that already, Miguel. That is not news to us."

"Maria confessed that she stole the babe when he was thought to be dead. And that she gave him to a Catholic family to be raised in the true faith."

"And I am supposed to believe that the babe was me?—is me?" Richard laughed roughly and looked around the room. 'Twas obvious the others here had heard this story. And, judging from some of their expressions, some already believed it to be the truth.

"Who else could it be? You were raised by the Granvilles. . . ."

"My grandparents, Miguel—they are my mother's parents."

"Maria worked for them when you were born. . . ."

"Aye, a faithful Spanish midwife whose queen had died and who married an Englishman. She had nowhere to go and no one back in Spain to return to," Richard argued. This rumor was not any different than the last time Miguel had come seeking his cooperation. It all boiled down to a lack of credible proof.

He had confronted his grandparents with this information the first time Miguel and his cohorts had approached him with it. Lord and Lady Granville swore that he was their daughter's son, born out of an illicit affair with the king. They had lost their only child but swore to her as she stepped through death's door that they would not abandon the child she left behind.

Their guilt over their treatment of their only child and her subsequent death during childbirth weighed heavily on their souls. They even fought the king's desire to have Richard raised under his control—in spite of the danger to themselves and to their rather tenuous position at court. 'Twas only their long history of support for the king that saved their lives in the dispute. Without proof, how could he allow himself to believe it?

Richard sighed and turned back to Father Ramirez. "And, your proof of this confession?"

"Proof? We have no need of proof! Her confessor has sworn to the Pope that it is God's truth."

"There is the rub, then. I need proof before I will act against Her Majesty."

"We have the confession and we have the papal bull to give us the right, Richard. You can take your rightful place on the throne and lead the loyal English subjects back to the true faith and the true Church." Miguel reached out and placed his hand on Richard's forearm, keeping him close.

"And I tell you again—until proof is laid in my hand and seen with my own eyes, I will take no action!"

Richard pulled free, turned away, and walked to the door. The room was as silent as a tomb after his loud exclamation. Well, at least no one would misunderstand his position on this.

The rest of the men in the room stood dumbfounded as they watched Richard leave. Miguel shook his head, disbelieving himself how the man could throw away the perfect opportunity to gain the one thing he knew Richard had always coveted. Well, the two things—legitimacy and the throne of England.

Certainly no written proof was in hand but he had faith in the Church and in the Holy Father and knew this confession was the truth. The others in the room had believed, they were ready to act—to free Mary Stuart from imprisonment, to remove the Whore's Bastard from her unlawful seat, and to place a Catholic monarch on the throne. Richard was to be that monarch.

And, with Queen Mary Stuart or another appropriately royal and Catholic princess at Richard's side, England would return to the Mother Church for all time.

Miguel walked to the hearth at one side of the room and faced the fire, signaling quite clearly that he did not wish to speak to anyone. He did not care whether or not Richard was truly Henry and Anne's son. He did believe that Richard was being used as God's own tool in this endeavor. And, if Richard needed proof to finally accept his place in this, he would find the proof.

If it existed, he would find it.

Chapter 15

SO, WHAT DID someone with a hangover in Elizabethan England do to get rid of it? She had no aspirin or acetaminophen to help with the intense pain of the headache that still made her dizzy. She had no seltzer water or any of the thick pink stuff to help calm her raging stomach. The only thing she could do was to tough it out and hope she lived long enough to feel better.

Patricia arrived as promised later in the morning and brought some warm water and cloths for her to use to wash. As difficult as it was to keep her head still while she moved the washcloth, she did it. Soon, at least the stench of her previous bouts of upset stomach were gone and she relaxed in a fresh chemise and shawl. From Patricia's strange looks, she knew she was not behaving like a good sick person should in this day and time. But, for her, survival and comfort were the two priorities.

After convincing the young woman that sitting in a chair was really what would make her feel better, Sharon sent her on an errand to find some broth and crusts of bread. They would probably go down easiest on her troubled stomach and she was beginning to feel hungry. What she really needed was some sunlight and fresh air. After Patricia returned, Sharon would attempt getting dressed and taking a short walk to clear her head.

Then she would regain her strength, find Richard, and kill him. Or maybe she would get him drunk, learn his secrets, and then seduce him? Oh, no. She couldn't even let her thoughts go in that direction. And, wait, she thought—what had she told him during her drunken stupor anyway?

Oh, God help her! She searched her mind for some clue to what she might have said to him last night. Didn't they talk about his plans for his horse farm? And didn't they talk about Jasper?

She rubbed her temples and tried to concentrate. Why did the image of that Highlander guy and Richard keep melding together in her mind's eye? Richard did look like him, a little anyway. Had she told him that, too?

Words, she could almost hear words she'd spoken to him . . . *Shut up and kiss me.*

She would have to find him and kill him now. In spite of the fact that she had been the instrument of her own downfall, Sharon would have to do something or confront constant humiliation every time their paths crossed. Her face felt on fire now as she thought of how shameless her actions must have seemed to him—a few drinks of wine and she had begged him to kiss her.

She moaned out loud as she contemplated whatever else she must have said to him that had her ending up in his bed without her panties on. Her cheeks felt very hot and she fanned herself as she hoped that a kiss was all she'd asked of him.

"Mistress?" Patricia entered the room carrying a tray with a few covered bowls on it. "I did tell you 'twas a foolish thought indeed to sit on this chair when you are so very ill."

After placing the tray on a nearby table, she came over and tried to get Sharon to follow her back to the pallet. Sharon resisted, knowing that upright was the position she needed to be in at this moment, even if her brain was urging her to curl up in a ball and hide for the next month. Finally, the short battle of wills was over and Sharon claimed victory.

Patricia moved the table in front of her and lifted the covers from the bowls and plates on the tray. There was one short mug of liquid, but honestly, Sharon didn't have to courage to try it. There was a wide, deep bowl of some kind of steaming broth and the crusts of bread she'd asked for. Some kind of porridge sat in another bowl, looking completely unappetizing to her at the moment. Tearing off a small piece of crust, she chewed it slowly and swallowed, awaiting her stomach's acceptance or rebellion. When it seemed to be staying down, she tried more.

Soon, most of the bread was gone and half of the broth as well. She felt much better with something in her belly, improved enough to try that short walk to get some fresh air. Of course she hadn't counted on Patricia being so overwhelming in her opposition to her taking that walk. They reached a compromise—Sharon would rest for a while longer and they would try the walk later in the afternoon.

After getting settled down on her pallet, Sharon couldn't believe that she let herself be ordered around by some teenager. But, as sleep pulled her down, she realized the girl knew what she was about. A little nap would give her strength and then maybe her headache would be gone. A little nap would do her good.

He'd ridden hard and fast and wild, trying to burn out the anger and self-loathing and the longing that bubbled up from deep inside him. Samson held up well under his demands, as both the pace and the distance increased. Reaching the Thames, Richard steered the horse along the banks, following the river's course for several miles. Sweat poured over both of them as he became one with his mount, leaning over and urging the horse on. When the wind stung his eyes and each breath he took burned, he knew he'd had enough.

Easing up on the horse, he slowed from an all-out gallop to a trot and then, a few minutes later, to a walk. Jumping from the saddle, he tugged the reins and continued to walk alongside his horse. Samson was blowing hard and perspiration covered his shoulders, withers, and back. Richard kept moving until they were both breathing easier.

Soon he caught sight of a familiar bend in the river and a growth of trees. Speaking words of encouragement, he led Samson to the shallow stream that fed into the river some yards downstream and let him drink his fill. Once the horse's thirst was satisfied, Richard took him a few paces away from the edge, where some grass grew, and tied him to a branch to keep him from wandering too far.

Going back to the river's edge, Richard knelt and splashed large amounts of water in his face and on his hair and neck. Then, cupping his hands, he drank of the cold water. Once refreshed, he stood and walked back to the shady glade. He dropped to the ground and leaned against a tree, resting his head back and closing his eyes.

With each meeting he attended, Richard could feel the noose around his neck tighten. In his more lucid moments of contemplation over his involvement, he knew that he had no intention of going forward with anything that would harm Elizabeth. They had shared too many times filled with fear about their futures as each of their siblings had taken the throne.

He admired the control she'd exercised over her own actions when, from time to time, her behavior had been questioned and her own involvement in possible plots against the throne had been suggested. She had a backbone of the strongest steel and lived with the clear conviction that she would one day be queen.

Richard had not shared such a clear vision of his path in those days, first at the various royal country houses and later in the Tower. He'd lived in fear that one less royal bastard would be one less possible provocateur in the family and that his very existence would be snuffed out. And he'd lived with the fear that no one would care.

He did not doubt that his mother's parents held some affection for him. But he knew that at the heart of it they cared for him out of a sense of missed duty to their lost daughter rather than a sense of true love and familial devotion. For when Henry's push came to shove, they stood aside and did not fight for him. Not as they would have for a legitimate child of their family.

Richard shifted against the tree, reached back, and twisted his hair, wringing out more of the water. Running his fingers through it then, he loosened it so it would dry faster in the breeze that flowed off the river. Bending his legs once more, he crossed his arms and rested them on his knees. He sat for a few minutes just watching the rushing waters of the Thames as it moved through the park and toward London in the east.

He felt at times that he was trapped on a rushing river, a current carrying him along that was so strong he could not resist it. Miguel and the others were like that current, irresistible and still growing with each passing day and each new convert. He did nothing to get out, to remove himself from their plans. Oh, he had raised his objections and stated his terms, but he was not fool enough to believe that they would stand in the face of the Catholic cause.

He sensed that a time was coming, and coming swiftly toward him, when he would have one final chance to step off this uncontrolled path upon which his feet seemed to be set. Although proof of his old nurse's confession would answer his questions and fulfill his lifelong dreams, he had little hope that 'twould be found. Even if it was, Richard would be faced with the same decision that had faced the Granvilles—would he give up Elizabeth to those who would have her under their control? Would he have the strength to fight for his half-sister—nay, she was fully his sister, if the rumors were true.

Or would his first act as rightful king of England be to order her death to protect his place on the throne, the one he had coveted for so long? Could he do it, knowing they had sworn oaths to each other in the dark of the night when the fears were the worst? How would those childish promises fare when held up against the wants and demands of those who had helped him gain the throne and wanted Elizabeth dead?

A breeze carried the light scent of roses on it and he

inhaled, enjoying the fragrance. And there was the other side of his problem.

Sharon Reynolds.

His actions last night weighed heavily on his conscience. And his desire to have her as his own confused all the other issues at stake. As much as he wanted his rightful inheritance, a part of him sought none of it. A part of him wanted only a good life, far from the court and its intrigues and plots and dangers. With Sharon. Away from the fakery and insincerity of those whose very livelihoods depend on the whim and fancy of the monarch.

Mayhap it was the too many years he'd been living in that way that made it so distasteful to him now? Mayhap he was tired of being torn in two by the conflicting desires within him? Others within the cause believed he pursued Henry's gift to him as a cover to keep suspicion from his hidden actions. Was that the real reason he pursued it now, pressing Elizabeth at every possible time to grant him the charter? Did a part of him also hope that if she denied him that which should be his by his father's will and decree, 'twould give him another reason to seek redress by taking the throne from her?

Richard rubbed his eyes with the heels of his hands, tired of all the subterfuge in his life. And into this he had dragged young Mistress Reynolds. Mistress Reynolds, who smelled of roses and who had her own secrets to keep, battles to fight, and wars of honor to wage. Why did he chase her now?

Oh, aye, he surely did want her, of that there was no doubt. His body's quick reaction to the scent of roses she wore, even here, far afield from her, made his feelings clear to him. And his thoughts as he held her in his arms as she slept were of their future together. Shaking his head, he realized he would have to make a choice. If he sought his place on the throne, he was less a man than that bastard Crenshaw in using her for his body's desires and then leaving her alone to bear the shame afterwards. He would not take advantage of her while the possibility existed that he would not be there to take responsibility for his actions toward her.

If he remained within Ramirez's group, if the proof were found, *if he were king,* she would have no place in his life. Somehow he knew she would not be satisfied as his mistress, and that would be all he could offer her. As king, his first duty would be to marry, undoubtedly some well-placed and Catholic noblewoman, and to provide heirs to protect his throne.

And Sharon could never be that woman, that wife, that mother to his children. Not if he were king.

Richard stumbled to his feet and brushed the dirt and dust from his trunks and hose. This conjecture was getting him nowhere. And yet he knew that this duality within him was tearing him apart. Soon. Soon he would be forced to decide his fate, to take charge of it for himself.

For now he thought it best if he kept some distance between Sharon and himself. He truly did not want to pull her closer only to involve her in something that could be the death of her. But the thought of pushing her away was just as repugnant to him.

By God's eyes, it had been easier to ignore the longing within him before Miguel had promised proof! He had all but given up on his desire for the throne; only a tiny flicker of unsubstantiated hope still lived in his heart. That would remain a part of him regardless of what followed, of how he lived his life or of which path he chose. Then, the slight hope had ignited into a much stronger flame with the priest's words.

This confusion could not continue for much longer. With a strong sense of certainty, he also knew that Sharon was someone different, someone special. And if he had a chance of a normal life he knew in his heart that he wanted her in it.

Walking over to Samson, he tugged on the reins, freeing them from the branch. Holding on to the saddle and the reins, he boosted himself into his seat and positioned his feet in the stirrups. Turning the horse, he guided it back toward Windsor.

He knew what he would do—he would give Miguel a deadline for producing the proof. If it was not forthcoming, he would put an end to his involvement, gain his inheritance, and move from court. The priest would not like his ultimatum, but Ramirez and his group needed him to continue in their cause.

Elizabeth was not due to return to Windsor for several weeks. He would tell the conspirators that the proof would be his by that time or his involvement was over. He could surely resist his desires for Sharon for that short time? Then, his course would be clear and he would move forward in one direction or the other, with Sharon by his side or not. 'Twould only be a few short weeks.

Chapter 16

SHE WATCHED FROM her seat on a bench near the gate built by the late king. It was much farther from her room than she'd expected to walk and she rested to regain her strength for the way back. Still, exhausted by the distance covered or not, Sharon was very glad that she'd fought her avid nursemaid's attempts to keep her in her room. Now, the late afternoon sun dipped below the top of the wall around the castle.

The breezes turned cool, no longer warmed by the rays of the setting sun, and Sharon gathered her cloak around her shoulders. Not quite ready to surrender to the lingering effects of the hangover, she closed her eyes and turned her face into the gentle wind and let it soothe her frazzled nerves.

Patricia had promised her an hour only in the fresh air and she was determined to take every moment of that time. The sound of hooves disturbed the quiet area. Sharon opened her eyes and looked toward the swiftly moving horse.

Again he was one with his mount, moving in tandem with its every movement across the green in the direction of the stables. But there was something different about him today. Anger blazed from his eyes; indeed, it was obvious to her in his every move. Samson was affected as well, snorting as they galloped by her into the shadows thrown by the high walls around them.

She watched them race past, never breaking their stride as they wove around some guardsmen in their path. She held her breath at his daring moves through the yard. It was clear to her that he was preoccupied and riding the horse on automatic pilot, oblivious to everything around him.

Sharon stood and slowly walked toward the stables, curious about the cause of his dark look and mood. One thing she knew was that he never misused his animals; no one who helped deliver a colt with as much passion as he had, would. And yet his manner as he passed her bordered on brutal.

He had stopped and dismounted by the time she reached the fence surrounding one of the stable yards. Barking out orders to his left and right, he strode into the main building as the various workers sped off to do his bidding. Should she follow him? She debated the wisdom of interrupting him when he was so focused on something else. Before she could decide, Patricia caught up with her.

"Mistress, you do overtax your strength by walking all this way. I thought to find you over by the gate."

"I saw Richard come this way," she began. "I wanted to ask him a question." Just as she sensed that Patricia would resist her efforts to stay, the girl leaned against the fence in front of them and let out a loud sigh. Fighting not to let out the laugh that threatened, Sharon followed Patricia's gaze to its target—John Calder.

Patricia's dreamy smile turned to a frown as they watched John across the yard. They heard Richard before they saw him. John had just caught sight of them when they saw him cringe at Richard's yelling insult. John shrugged and turned away from them, walking toward his supervisor. Sharon was stunned at this new side to Richard that she'd not only not seen but had also never heard about before.

The women spoke of his funny, sexy manner, how he teased and flirted with them whenever the opportunity arose. The men she'd overheard spoke of his easy manner and competence in his position overseeing the day-to-day workings in the queen's stables. He ate with them, drank with them, and worked with them, and no one said a negative thing about him. She wondered if any had seen this side of him before.

Richard's gaze followed John's to them and then, without acknowledging her, he looked away and motioned to John to accompany him. The younger man lifted his hand in greeting and then complied with the order.

Patricia sighed once more, a very dramatic one that made Sharon smile. Young love. And it must have started that day in Windsor when she and Richard were separated from Patricia and John. Sharon stood back from the fence and rewrapped her cloak around her. It was clear Richard was having a bad day and this was not the time to approach him.

"Come, Patricia, it is getting too cold to stand out here in the open. Let's go back to the room."

They'd walked a few yards when Sharon decided to find out how serious this attraction was between the two young people.

"So tell me. How did your dinner and talk go with John's parents? Is this serious?" The girl turned many shades of pink and then red before answering.

"The talk at supper went well. Did I tell you that I met his mother today? Mayhap I did not mention it earlier when you were ill?"

Sharon smiled and nodded. Even through the dullness left by her hangover, she heard Patricia mention being introduced to John's mother several times.

"Both of his parents are so warm and welcoming. 'Twould be a good match for me." A very contented smile filled the girl's face. The first meeting with her future mother-in-law must have been a positive one.

"And is it a match? Do you have to ask permission for

this marriage?" Sharon knew that Elizabeth had been adamantly opposed to some of her higher-ranking noblewomen's marriages but she didn't think that the queen became embroiled in every romance.

"I am not high enough to catch Her Majesty's eye in this. As long as his parents and mine agree, the marriage can go forward." Patricia's eyes twinkled merrily, demonstrating her hopes quite clearly to Sharon. She prayed for a moment that nothing would stand in the way of this match.

"And tell me, Patricia, would I be high enough? To catch her attention?" She wasn't sure why the question came up. Maybe just an attempt to understand the royal court better. The woman she was charading as was of questionable character.

They reached the doors leading to the staircase near her room. Sharon stopped to catch her breath for a moment.

"Well, mistress, I should not think so. You do not carry a title and are not an heiress of any measure. The only quality that would bring Her Majesty's regard to bear would be the love the queen has for your lady aunt."

"You think so? I would not be free to marry where I would?" Sharon wondered if the real niece wasn't already off and married. That would explain many things about her disappearance.

Patricia paused and looked at her. Her hesitation spoke of some bad or upsetting news about to be shared, so Sharon prepared herself before the girl shared her knowledge of the situation.

"I thought your aunt had contacted you already about their efforts on your behalf?"

Sharon shook her head in response and waited, now nervous about the impending news.

"I have heard that your aunt and your uncle have made a match for you and await a proper time to have your return home for it."

"I did not know this, Patricia," she answered, at a loss to say more that that. Sharon turned away and lifted her skirts to climb the steps in front of her.

Could that be true? She would really be between a rock and a hard place now. If this match had been made and her time at court was looked at as a cooling-down period, it could end at any time.

Sharon started up the stairs, thinking about the pressure that was building inside of her. She sensed very strongly that time was now her enemy. She needed to move more quickly in trying to find the missing son, if he lived, and giving him the proof that would be his birthright. What he did with it didn't concern her. She also felt that once the proof was in his hands, her way home would be opened.

If she could reach Tenby Manor.

That's where Richard came in. Although right now she wouldn't ask him the time of day, she would need him and his help to get back there. Sharon wasn't certain how she could convince him to cooperate, but she would have to think of something when the time came.

Maybe the truth? Could she share the truth of her real home and time with him? Would that be against the rules of this extraordinary game? And what would he think? She thought of some of the everyday things in her time that would be so foreign and unworldly to his—planes, trains, and even cars, for starters. Just about everything would be unexplainable to him.

Would he think she was a witch or some other practitioner of the black arts? Witchcraft trials did take place even in the Elizabethan era, although not with the vehemence that would follow later, in the seventeenth century. Still, she would need a very down-to-earth reason for him to help her. She would think about it and be ready when the time came.

Tomorrow. Once the rest of the hangover's effects left her, she would begin in earnest to find this son of Henry and Anne. She could not allow Richard to divert her from her task anymore. And, after seeing him today in this mood, she knew that he had more going on in his own life, too.

Rounding the last landing and then reaching their floor, Sharon walked quietly down the hall toward her room. It was still early and her roommates would not return from supper until later. She decided to reexamine the documents to see if she could come up with any more clues about who and where this son might be.

"Mistress?" Patricia asked as they reached her door. "Would you mind if I took my supper in the hall this evening after I bring you a tray?"

"That is fine, Patricia. I plan on going to bed very early tonight. Maybe the . . . sickness will wear off much quicker that way."

"I did tell you that you should stay abed today for just that reason."

Sharon smiled and nodded at her. That had been Patricia's advice but Sharon knew that fresh air was the one thing she needed to clear her head of the alcohol's influence. And the stale musty odor that sometimes filled the rooms would have made her stomach churn again. So, out of doors was the only place for her today.

"I will return anon with your tray," the girl said as Sharon opened her door and entered the room.

Sharon took off her cloak, hung it on a wooden peg near the door, and gathered the leather pouch from inside her straw mattress. Opening the storage trunk at the foot of her bed, she found the sack of candles she'd purchased in the village and took out the costliest ones. They would burn the brightest and clearest and she would need them to examine the parchment pages. She'd only looked at them once more since she arrived in this time and would reread them until something important could be gleaned from their words.

Patricia completed her errand and with very little encouragement was gone from the room and on the way to the dining hall in a few minutes. Since her stomach grumbled with hunger for the first time that day, Sharon helped herself to the light fare on her dinner tray. Once done, she washed and dried her hands and then did the same to the tabletop so that the surface would not damage the priceless papers she needed to read.

Lighting the candles, she spread out the pages before her on the small table. First she read the confession once more, feeling some guilt at her invasion of this woman's innermost thoughts. But this information was vital if she was to find the boy or man who should be king. The year stated at the beginning of the confession was 1560—almost ten years prior to now, and two years after Elizabeth gained the throne. The baby, however, had been born closer to Elizabeth's own birth, about thirty-five years before.

If this midwife thought she could successfully pass this baby off as one of Henry's bastards, then there must be, or must have been, more than one. Darn it, she wished she had paid more attention to her Tudor history. At least if she had some idea of the number of "natural" children Henry had had, she could try to eliminate each one and come up with the one she was looking for.

Once again, she came back to the realization that she needed help. She needed to ask someone from this time who was familiar with the court and with the royal family and especially with Henry's sowing of wild oats. Richard seemed about the right age, maybe he would know? But how did you politely ask about bastard sons of the former king?

She turned her attention back to the documents and read through the section about the baby's birth and his escape from death's grip. She could almost feel the despair and the devastating grief that must have existed in the birthing chamber. Anne Boleyn's inability to produce a male heir and Henry's displeasure over it were well reported and it was that inability that caused Anne's downfall from power and eventually her death. Not many scholars believed that she had committed adultery or treason, but convicting her of those crimes was Henry's way of ridding himself of a recalcitrant queen. That much she remembered. And, that Henry already had turned his glance elsewhere for a new queen and breeder.

The midwife had given the baby to a Catholic family to raise. Asking about that would be very difficult and probably dangerous at this time. She'd heard the rumors of the threats and the plot to overthrow Elizabeth the previous year in the name of the Catholic cause. And added to that was Mary Stuart of Scotland's presence here in England. No, asking about Catholics who might have adopted a bastard of Henry's was not the way to do this.

Deciding to look over the physician's statement, Sharon folded the confession and carefully replaced it back into the pouch. Unfolding the doctor's letter, she pulled out her glasses to help her see the ornately scribed words. This writing was much more difficult to follow but gradually she became more familiar with how the words blended together and how certain letters curled at the beginnings and ends. Soon, the story of the babe became clear.

He was born prematurely to the queen after a long and painful labor. When finally born, he did not take a breath. No measures were taken to help him since they did not know even basic life-saving techniques or rescue-breathing. Having declared the baby dead, the physician made his statement to a secretary, who transcribed the words. The desolate queen was left to her women and midwives and Henry, without offering a word of comfort to his wife, escaped the chamber, with the doctor following swiftly behind him.

Sharon felt the tears flow as she continued to read, catching them with her hand before they could land on the precious parchment. Leaning back, she let a few sobs out before regaining control. Wiping her eyes dry, she couldn't believe the waves of emotion passing through her—grief, despair, loss, and anger. Anger at this midwife who could have changed the course of history then, when it happened. This Maria could have saved Anne's life by giving her back her son.

With a surety she had not felt before, Sharon knew this was the reason she was sent back in time. No, her actions couldn't save Anne now, but if things worked out maybe Anne's son would sit on the throne that should have been his in the first place. She leaned back over the documents, searching for the physical description of the baby. With any luck there would be something that she could use to find this man.

Scanning that area of the physician's words, the only

things noted about his appearance were his hair and eyes and the mention of the Boleyn birthmark. Of course, since many babies had coarse black hair and bluish eyes at birth, those colorings would not be of much help. The birthmark was something different.

It was located on the back of the baby's left hip, almost on his buttocks, and diamondlike in shape. When the doctor reported it, the queen's women exclaimed that it was the same as the one on the queen's body and one which they said was also present on the queen's sister and father as well as other Boleyns.

So now all she had to do was find the man with this birthmark and explain that she came from the future with proof of his legitimacy. Oh, sure. When pigs fly, she thought.

Men didn't exactly go around in the body-exposing bathing suits or briefs that they wore in her own time. Give her a decent beach and the correct suit and she'd find him quickly. Elizabethan England, with its trunks and hose that covered from toes to waist, would not make this easy. Well, at least now she knew what she was looking for and where to find it.

Voices and footsteps in the hallway leading to her room alerted her to how much time had passed. Folding the papers together, she tucked them with the confession into the leather pouch and walked over to her pallet to hide them inside once more. She straightened her belongings, then blew out the candles and replaced them in the sack. Then, after securing her glasses in her trunk, she began to undress for sleep. Pulling on a chemise she reserved for nighttime, Sharon climbed under the covers and drew them up close to her neck.

What would this man's reaction be to her news? Did he have any inkling that he should sit on the throne of England? What position, if any, did he hold now? Was the family who raised him still alive? Was he?

She rubbed her forehead as too many questions raced through her brain. This was the same what-if game she'd played momentarily in the cubbyhole before falling through to this time. There would be no answers until she found him and then the decision would be his. Then the thought struck her.

What about Elizabeth?

Everything she did know about the queen told her quite clearly that Elizabeth would never give up the throne without a fight, and a fierce one at that. She had weathered many storms as she grew up and even more since taking the throne. Even now she fended off the efforts of the Pope and other Catholics to remove her. Yet her position on that royal seat solidified with each passing day and year.

This son, this brother, had a tremendous task before him if he wanted to use the proof to take the crown from Elizabeth's head. Maybe he wouldn't use it? If he didn't know who he was, maybe there was no ambition to be king? Sharon shook her head, answering her own question. Anyone presented with this kind of evidence of the circumstances of his birth would develop some appetite for the power, prestige, and wealth that went along with being king of England.

Turning onto her side and facing away from the door, Sharon feigned sleep when the three women who shared the room with her entered. Whispering quietly among themselves, it was not long before they were in their own beds and sleeping. Thoughts about the power struggle to come filled her mind, preventing her from drifting off to sleep herself.

If he did want to be king, there would be bloodshed, no doubt about it. Someone—many people—would die on both sides. If he had been raised Catholic, it would turn into another religious war as the old faith tried to raise itself once more. She cringed at the death and devastation that would ensue and the damage to England in its wake. The world as she knew it would no longer exist. Elizabeth would not be there to guide, cajole, threaten, and bribe England and her people to their zenith as a world power.

Would the king? Which one of the two would survive the war and would there even be enough of England left to withstand the challenges of the foreign monarchs on the

Continent who would come looking for easy pickings in the confusion and desolation?

Oh, dear God, what a mess!

Sharon sat up in the darkness and listened to the soft snores in the room, trying to calm her raging thoughts and new fears. Maybe it would be best if she never found him? She knew what Elizabeth was capable of, what she would do for England. Should she keep the evidence or give it to him when she found him and then try to convince him not to use it? For if she changed the world now, with the proof she held, what would become of her own time? And, once history was changed, could she ever go home again?

Fear inched its way up and down her spine with icy fingers as the ramifications of her actions finally became real to her. She was in more danger here and now than she'd first realized. Even being discovered as a fraud did not compare to being the one responsible for the destruction of the world as she knew it.

What could she do? Rocking back and forth with her arms wrapped around her knees, Sharon thought of her options. Obviously some very powerful force wanted this man to have his chance. Something wanted her to find him and give him the packet that had been hidden for centuries—nothing else could explain her presence here in the past. And she did not want to resist anything so powerful. Truly, this force would have its way.

So, for now, she would continue—no, she would step up her efforts to find this missing heir. And God help them all when she found him and he found his destiny.

God help them all.

Chapter 17

THE QUEEN HAD still not returned to Windsor a few days later when Lady Randall confronted Sharon in the hallway outside her room.

"Get your cloak and come with me, Mistress Reynolds."

By her words and manner, Sharon knew this was not a request. She returned to her room, grabbed her cloak from the peg on the wall, and met the woman at the top of the stairs. Following her swift and sure steps down the three flights, Sharon emerged behind Lady Randall outside the royal apartments. The woman continued away from the buildings and toward the northern wall of the castle. She turned and faced Sharon, who was literally holding her breath in anticipation of being found out.

"Do not look so fearful, Mistress Reynolds. I but wanted some measure of privacy for our words."

Sharon swallowed several times before the words would come out. "Privacy, milady? Words with me?"

"Aye, 'twould seem at times that the very walls of Windsor have ears and I wanted to speak to you without being overheard." Pointing at a nearby bench, she motioned Sharon to it. "Sit."

Once they were seated, Sharon thought about her words.

What could Lady Randall want to talk to her about that required privacy? Her curiosity began to overcome her initial fear. If Lady Randall knew the truth, that she was not Katherine Seagrave's niece, she would probably be on the way to the dungeon, or wherever they took prisoners.

"You are not the young woman I thought you to be," Lady Randall began. Sharon fought the swirling panic that grew around her. *Wait, wait. Listen, listen,* she told herself.

"Your lady aunt led me to believe that you were a frivolous girl, unmindful of anything but her own desires. You are not that girl," Margaret Randall continued, and Sharon tried to focus on her words. The woman's tone had changed; it had softened somehow; its usual harshness was gone and replaced with a conciliatory one.

"I have watched you as you work and as you go about your life within Windsor and, other than the unfortunate incident with the *raspes* last week, you have lived with a certain dignity and respect I did not expect in one so troubled."

Sharon raised her head, now feeling more confident about the direction of this conversation. She was just different from what Lady Randall had expected. No matter how skilled she was at charades, she would never be able to masquerade successfully forever as the wayward niece.

"You have followed my instructions, and your work on Her Majesty's clothing is nothing short of superb. You do not join in with the others as they gossip their way through the day. I am more pleased with you and your demeanor than I truly ever expected to be. Mayhap you have grown to appreciate the seriousness of your circumstances?"

Sharon smiled, relief now coursing through her. "I have thought on my mistakes, milady." She was not lying—not a day went by without thoughts and plans of how she would correct things when she returned home. Watching the politics here at Windsor and around the queen had given her some insights into the politics of her own precarious situation.

"I also believe that you hold Patricia in some esteem?"

"Patricia Prescott? My maid?" Sharon wondered where this was leading.

"Aye, the young woman I assigned to you when you arrived at Tenby Manor. She also comes from a good family and is here by the grace of the queen."

"She has been wonderful to me since I arrived. She has shown me around and smoothed my path in many ways." Sharon couldn't tell where this was going. She had never treated the girl with other than the respect any person deserved and they had grown very comfortable with each other during the last few weeks.

"That is how I saw it as well. Now, I would ask for your help." Lady Randall paused in her words and Sharon found herself astounded by this turn of events.

"My help? How?"

"I would see Patricia happy in the match being considered for her, as I truly want you to be in yours. The parents have given their permission for the young man to court her while arrangements are made. I would ask you to serve as chaperone during this time." Lady Randall, done with her request, folded her hands in her lap and waited for Sharon to speak.

The words would not come as she considered the information that had been shared with her in Lady Randall's request. Lady Randall did have some stake in this match. Lady Randall wasn't the total fire-breathing dragon she tried to be. And, more importantly, Lady Randall knew about the marriage plans for Lady Seagrave's niece.

" 'Twould not infringe greatly on the duties you carry now. They are to be permitted to have their supper together and some walks, no more than that at this time. The final arrangements will await the queen's permission once she returns to Windsor. So, what say you?"

"I would be pleased to do this for Patricia—if you think it wise. Many will question your decision to have me fulfill this duty." Kind of like having the old fox guarding the henhouse!

"Not many will question it to my face, though, will they?" Lady Randall stood, laughing at her own jest. She obviously did not underestimate her effect on people.

"I suppose not." Sharon stood as well, the conversation drawing to a close.

"Be aware of something, Mistress Reynolds." Lady Randall fixed a serious glare on her. Sharon straightened and met the woman's gaze. "This is also a test for you, of your growing maturity and what I sense is your God-given natural intelligence. Fail me not in this."

Lady Randall nodded and Sharon offered a quick curtsey as the woman turned to leave. But she had not told Sharon anything at all about the marriage plans for her—or, rather, for the woman she pretended to be.

"Milady?" she asked. "You did mention my own marriage. Have you any news of such a match made for me?"

"Oh, aye, I did have news for you from your lady aunt," the woman began, and the churning in Sharon's stomach started to build. That powerful feeling—that time was turning against her—returned, stronger now with these words. She waited for the worst of it.

"Your aunt and uncle sent word that a suitable match for you has been found and the betrothal documents are being drawn up even now. They have told me he is from an old noble family and is himself the fourth son in that line. Once the arrangements are acceptable, you will be called home for the wedding."

The tension and fear tightened around her, making it impossible to draw in a breath. Not much time left to find this heir before her own bluff would be called. Sharon turned away and tried to calm herself. Maybe this was fate's way of kicking her in the butt to get her moving. Nothing got her creative juices flowing more than an approaching deadline. Still, if this didn't work out as planned, her neck—and the missing heir's—might be in a noose.

"Come now, mistress, surely you do not fear marriage? 'Tis a woman's rightful place and duty in life. And you have been raised to know that your aunt and uncle will seek a man whose temperament is like your own. Come now"—Lady Randall reached over and rubbed her cheeks—

"where is that backbone that brought you to your place with us? Do not lose it now."

Let her think she was scared at the upcoming marriage. Sharon had other things, much more important and pressing things, to worry about now—like her own life, her existence in the future, and England's existence, too. What would happen when the queen returned to Windsor?

"Come, let us return to our duties now. You will begin with tonight's supper?"

"Yes, milady," she answered, still thinking of her real problem.

She walked back to their workroom and took up the task she'd left behind before having lunch. Luckily she could sew without paying much attention to it, because her mind was racing the whole afternoon. How to find him, who to ask, where to begin . . . she only hoped that whatever had the power to send her back here and now also had the power to find someone to help her. And soon.

He had hoped to avoid her, a plain and simple plan and one that was doomed to fail, given their duties and their positions within the queen's household. But it became worse when she stole his friends. From his place by the door, he watched them laughing and enjoying some snippet of conversation as they ate. He fought the urge to join them and enter into the teasing and laughter.

He could use some laughter in his life. The past week, since his last meeting with Ramirez, he had been filled with a sense of foreboding. His mood and behavior had reflected that. He had snarled and barked at people around him like a mad dog. And, when time and time again he felt the urge to seek out her company, her smile, her difference, he stopped himself. No, he had decided to allow Ramirez until Elizabeth's return and so he vowed to follow his plan and not put Sharon in any danger. He would not seek her company, not seek to engage her in conversation, and definitely not seek to seduce her again.

The last part was causing him the most trouble because it seemed as if his body had a mind of its own. His dreams were filled with visions of her in his room, sitting before him in that most provocative of poses. His fingers and mouth itched to touch and taste her once more and more fully at that.

But it was for naught. He had committed himself to this plan of the Spanish priest and would not, could not, let her become involved. And, as always, he felt torn in two by his own dreams. Part of him almost hoped the priest would fail in his efforts to find the proof he demanded for his cooperation. Then he could let go of the sometimes overwhelming and hopeless dream of sitting on his father's throne and go about making a life of his own. And, maybe, Sharon Reynolds would be part of that life.

He smiled as she laughed once more at something Robert said to her and he found himself standing in the aisle next to their table without any recollection of walking there.

"Richard! Come, join us at table," Robert called out to him as he motioned for all of them to shift and make a place for him. "Have you eaten yet?"

"No, I have yet to eat my fill or"—he filled an empty mug with ale as he spoke—"quench my thirst from my long day of work in the yard." He was swallowing his first mouthful when she spoke.

"You would seem no worse for wear from a good day's work, Master Granville. Mayhap you should do it more often?"

The sarcasm made everyone in their group, not only him, wince. Sharon's voice did not have the lightness of tone to be mistaken for a teasing comment. It was an insult, nothing more or less. And it was directed squarely at him.

"Are you saying, mistress, that I shirk my duties?" He drank once more from his cup as he watched the anger flash in her eyes.

"I would never say that, sir."

"Then what would you say?" He looked at her and waited for her reply. Robert interrupted first.

"Richard, have you heard the news of John and Patricia's betrothal?" Leave it to Robert to try to divert his attention.

"I have heard. And I have yet to offer my felicitations

on your happy event." He lifted his cup and nodded at the young man currently under his tutelage and the lovely young woman seated next to him. "May you both find happiness in your life together. John, may you seek to make Patricia happy all your days and may she seek to do the same for you."

"Here, here," Robert added as they lifted their cups as well. He noticed that Sharon sipped from her cup but had not lifted it in the toast.

"Mistress Reynolds, do you not share in our hopes for this young couple? Is not this match to your liking?" Her anger goaded him. 'Twas obvious that she was spoiling for a fight with him and he wanted to know why. Or maybe he should just let her have her ire and use that to keep her away from him?

"I am quite happy for Patricia and John. I believe she has found that one rare man among men to be her husband. It is a good match for both of them." She raised her cup to the young people but gifted him with a look of such irony that he could not stop himself.

"And just what is it that makes him such a rarity, in your own opinion, Mistress Reynolds?"

He recognized that the level of discomfort was rising at the table. The others knew there was something more going on here than a toast to the happy couple. And he wanted to know what was at the bottom of it.

"He appears to be a *constant* young man, of good upbringing and a sensible nature. And he does not *drink to excess*." He heard her stress the words. Everyone there did and he fought not to laugh as Robert and John abruptly put down their mugs of ale.

It was time to put an end to this in public and take it up in private with her. He stood, walked around behind her, and slipped his arms under hers. Lifting her from her seat, he took hold of her arm and pulled her away.

"Come, Mistress Reynolds, we shall discuss young *men* and their *constancy,* since you seem to be so very concerned with it."

He tugged her along, her resistance continued quiet but

firm, until they reached the corridor leading to the outside of the dining hall. He shoved open the door and walked into the brisk night's air. Without relaxing his grasp on her arm, he headed for a nearby bench and pushed her onto it. When she would have darted from it, he blocked her way by leaning over her and trapping her with his hands next to her shoulders.

She was the picture of righteous indignation as she sat with her arms crossed over her chest and her lips pressed tightly closed. He took a breath and tried to control his own anger.

"Come now," he began in a low voice, "tell me truly—do you think all men are inconstant?" He purposely used the word she had chosen as her insult.

After a few moments' delay, she answered through her gritted teeth. "No, not all men, I am sure. Just the ones I seem to have the misfortune of meeting."

"You speak of me, then?"

"If the shoe fits . . ."

"I am not inconstant," he argued.

"No? Then you must be one of those men who is interested only in the chase and who loses interest when their goal is achieved?" She glared at him, her anger-filled eyes gazing up unabashedly into his own.

"Nay. I deny that. And I did not attain that which I desired from you." So this was where the problem lay? with what happened, and what did not, in the dimness of that drunken night?

"You didn't? You did not?" she repeated, seemingly surprised at his response.

"Nay, I did not."

Her lower lip trembled and her eyes lost some of their anger; now a look of confusion filled them. She did not know.

She did not know!

He moved to her side and sat next to her. Placing his arm around her shoulders, he slid closer to her. She was angry because she thought he had obtained what his physical desire had sought from her and then had discarded her as if she was no better than a round-heeled kitchen maid.

"Did the wine we drank that night cloud your memory of what we did together?" He whispered the words to her, teasing her once more and trying to entice her at the same time.

"Oh, yes! All right? The wine made my judgment that night and my memories of whatever we did disappear. Just tell me and get it over with—what happened between us?"

He noticed she closed her eyes. This must be her way of steeling herself for the bad news she anticipated. He felt a pang of sympathy for her over her confusion. She'd awoken in his makeshift bed of straw and hay, in his private room in the stable, with her clothes and self in a state of dishabille and her *panties* in his hand. They'd not spoken much at all and he'd not thought about whether or not she remembered her passion-filled kisses or the tasting and touching . . . before she fell asleep in his arms.

"You truly do not remember?" He laughed out loud at this turn of events. Her expression, filled with guilt, remorse, and some measure of pain, stopped him. "I am sorry at my behavior toward your distress, mistress, but I had never considered that the reason for your anger at me."

She looked at him and said nothing. She waited as he decided how to tell her. No, he would not dance about this with her—he owed her at least that much for causing her drunken stupor. And he wanted the truth to stand between them while it still could.

"I do truly and completely confess that my full and devious intention was to ply you with wine and have my way with you." He stopped and smiled at her, a genuine one and not the flirting curve of lips and eyes that he usually offered. He did not remember the last time he had admitted to trying to seduce someone. She did not move at all; no smile lit her face.

"I have not been dishonest in my feelings toward you or my desire for you, Sharon. And when you accepted my hand and accompanied me back to the stables . . ." He let the words trail off. 'Twas clear in his own mind what he thought and how he assessed the situation leading up to their arrival at the stables that night. He was curious about how she viewed her actions.

"You thought I was saying yes?" Her face was still blank; he could read nothing there—not her earlier anger nor confusion.

"Oh, aye, I did. I offered the wine to warm you. I had not the foresight to see that you were so unused to its effects. I expected some results but truly not to the extent that you experienced." Was that an apology? The words sounded suspiciously like one as they left his mouth.

"And to what extent was that, Richard? Please be clear, for I would know the depths to which I sunk that night." Her voice trembled just a bit but the fleeting look of vulnerability in her eyes stopped him from teasing her again.

"We touched and kissed. I tasted every part of you. You received some measure of satisfaction from our encounter." He paused and smiled once more before continuing. "Then you fell asleep."

"You're kidding me?" she asked, and her face, once pale, now filled with the deepening color of a blush. He frowned at the unfamiliar words. "Surely you jest?" she asked this time.

"I would not take such things lightly, Mistress Reynolds," he answered. "I assure you this has not happened many times in my experiences to date. As a matter of fact, this is the first time in my memory that I have put a woman to sleep with my lovemaking skills."

She laughed out loud and it was a lovely sound to hear. A wide smile brightened her face and she clapped her hands with glee. This was not his usual effect on women, especially his paramours. They generally celebrated what he did with them, not what he did not do! Sharon finally looked at him and stopped laughing.

"I have insulted you now, haven't I? And this time I was not trying to."

"I thought that it was what you wanted, what we wanted, when I asked you to walk with me. Was I wrong then? Did I misinterpret your actions, your own desires?"

Her look turned serious then and he knew she was considering how to answer him.

"No, Richard, you did not misunderstand. I did accept your *invitation,*" her voice grew husky as she whispered the word. "I came, er . . . I accompanied you willingly and knew what you planned that night. I guess the wine got in the way."

That was not the answer he expected. It was the answer he had wished for that night—for her to be a willing partner in passion. But he was no fool. The moment, the night had passed and with it, her willingness. Or had it?

"And now where does this take us? I would know your mind in this."

"Actually, Richard, my mind has little to do with this. It would seem that my body and my heart outweigh the sensible approach that my mind is urging."

He could not believe his ears. Now? Now, when he had made the decision to stand away from her? When he wanted not to soil her with this plot that could go wrong at any time? Now she tells him of her desires for him. By God's heart, what kind of jest was this? He leaned over and rested his elbows on his legs, rubbing his eyes with the heels of his hands. Nothing went as he planned or wanted. 'Twas as if some unseen, yet irresistible force was moving him as a pawn in a chess game.

He did not notice her touch at first but then he felt her fingers ruffle the hair at his neck. With gentle caresses she rubbed his neck and then shoulders. She was trying to calm him? to comfort him? And all he could think of was taking her in his arms and kissing her breathless and senseless. She was more dangerous to his resolve than anyone he had ever encountered. She made him want for things, for a life and for a future that he did not know yet was to be his.

"Richard? I must return to the hall and Patricia. Will you be all right? I mean, are you well?"

"I do not think I will be well for some time, Mistress Reynolds. I fear there is too much on my mind to be well." A strong urge to tell her the whole of it grew inside of him until he fought to keep it in. He would be resolute in his decision, at least for now.

"I can see that I am part of your problems, Richard. I will not inflict myself on you again." The hurt and anger crept back into her voice.

"You are the best of my trouble, Sharon," he said, taking her hand in his. Raising it to his mouth, he turned it and touched the inside of her wrist with his lips. "Never doubt it."

She gasped and shivered as his tongue made contact with her skin, but she did not pull from his grasp. He wanted more, she wanted it too, but it was not to be this night. He smiled, let go of her hand, and stood.

"Go now. The night is too cold to sit without your cloak. And I am certain that Patricia will seek us out soon to be assured that I have not harmed you."

"Good night, then, Richard." She walked away from him toward the doors that would lead back to the dining hall. A few steps away, she stopped and looked at him. Her gaze was one of serious regard and he thought for a moment she would turn back. "I would like to discuss something with you, Richard, but not here and not now. Can you spare me some time on the morrow or the next day?"

"Certainly. Find me when you are done with your duties."

He was concerned over her serious approach and then realized she must need his help. Had that good-for-naught Crenshaw shown his face to her here? Was he pressuring her into something? His own efforts to find this man were as yet unsuccessful. Maybe she would know where to find him?

"Thank you, again, Richard."

"You thank me for what?" he asked.

"You did not take advantage of me when you could have that night. I am grateful for that." She nodded and walked away, this time not looking back or stopping.

"But I wanted to, Sharon. I truly wanted to," he whispered under his breath.

Chapter 18

The Tower of London

THE PRISONER'S ANGUISHED cries still echoed through the chamber as the door opened for the queen to enter. Lifting her skirts, she trod cautiously down the damp steps. Approaching the small group of men, she called a halt to their torture.

"I would rather have him alive and talking than dead and silent. Cecil, what has he revealed?"

"Nothing yet, Your Grace." The older man nodded as he spoke to her.

She moved closer to the man tied to the rack. Leaning over, she examined him and found him still breathing. His legs and arms were pulled tightly by the ropes. His back was arched and only his faint wheezing breaths bespoke of the faint bit of life in him yet.

"Give him some time to recover, then begin anew. I would have names."

"Your Grace," the commander of the prison's dungeon began, "we have the names we need. Bring them to me and I will have the truth out of them for you."

Elizabeth looked at the hulking form and knew not many

would resist his torture. But she wanted proof before she would take action. Especially against her own kin.

"Your Grace, we know he is involved. Allow me to arrest him and we will have a confession from him," her most trusted minister urged.

"No, my lord, I want more than a confession at the urging of our loyal dungeon-master there."

"But it will stand in court, I assure you," William Cecil continued.

"But it will not stand before me, my lord. I require more than that to send my own blood to the executioner's block." She turned away, unable to contain the fury inside.

"He is but a bastard and one with strong Catholic ties, Your Grace. He is trying to bring down your throne. Think you he and his cohorts will spare your life if given the power to end it?"

She gasped at Cecil's words. She and Richard had vowed their faith and loyalty in this very prison. So many nights they had fallen asleep listening to the cries of the tortured and hopeless. So many times in those early years they'd had only each other for comfort—both of them motherless bastards. She had, however, risen to her present station by the grace of God while he remained below her, never recognized officially by their father. Elizabeth held out her hand to silence further argument.

"In this I am resolved, my lord. I need proof in hand before I will act against him. He has sworn oaths to me and I am wont to believe them."

"Your Grace . . ." Cecil began, but she would not hear him now.

"I am not opposed to applying a bit of pressure to see if he continues to act in good faith with me."

"I understand, Your Grace." Cecil bowed and stepped back, clearing her way to the door.

"I will send word that his request for the inheritance left to him has been denied. Let us watch to see if this makes him turn away from our oaths." She lifted her skirts once more and carefully walked up the stairs. "You see, Cecil, an innocent man will simply become angry and loud about being denied that which is his. A traitor will seek revenge and use this as his reason to move forward with his plot."

"I see, Your Grace." Cecil followed her through the doorway and they watched as the guard closed the door with a loud bang.

Stepping over to the bars, she called out to those still inside. "Have a care, Master Smith. Alive and talking. Alive and talking."

Then, following the guards, Elizabeth left the Tower.

Chapter 19

SAMSON STOOD SADDLED by the fence and Richard led a smaller but sturdy-looking gelding from the stables. Sharon watched as Richard talked to the horse as they walked through the yard. A moment later, he tied the gelding near Samson and then caught sight of her. A puzzled expression crossed his face then disappeared in an instant. She waited for him to approach her, not sure how he would act toward her after last night's discussion.

"Good day, Mistress Reynolds. How do you fare?" His tone was light and teasing. She was confused now.

"I am well, sir. And you?" She nodded at his greeting and waited for his assessment.

"Truly I was intrigued by your request made last evening. Shall we talk?" He motioned with his hand to a small bench off to one side of the yard.

She wasn't sure that this was the best place for her questions. Looking around, she saw guards on their patrol of the grounds, various men and women carrying out their duties in the stables or the nearby buildings. There would be no privacy here.

The stables caught her eye but she'd never suggest that to him. Maybe they could walk around the grounds? No, she needed a place where they could speak openly. But that meant being alone with him. She shivered, chills running through her at the very thought of it.

Part of the problem was that, even after tossing through the night over her task, she still had not decided how much or what to tell him. Or how to ask him the most important question. But the certainty that she was dawdling too long and not moving toward her task brought her here today in spite of her own doubts. He must have sensed her indecision, for he pulled his hand back and waited for her to make up her mind.

"Are you having second thoughts about involving me in your problem?" He smiled at her as she considered his words.

"Well, without being rude, I am."

"Honesty I can appreciate, since I find it so infrequently among the court. If you have changed your mind on this, I will not press you." Richard took a step back and away from her and leaned up against the fencing that surrounded the yard.

"I have no one I call friend here, Richard, and I hesitate to burden you with this. You said last night that—"

"I would claim exhaustion and confusion as my reasons for the sharpness of last night's words, Sharon. I am ready to listen if you have need of me."

She looked at him for a moment and realized he was the only one she would be able to ask. It was now or never. And her time grew short, she could feel it. She nodded her assent at him and looked once more around the yard for a better place.

"Do you have duties this afternoon?" he asked as he lifted a pair of leather gloves from their place in his belt and tugged them on his hands.

"I am done my duties until Patricia needs me at supper."

"There is a farm nearby that I need to visit. I had thought to do it after our talk but it seems to me that it would give us some measure of privacy if we speak on the way. Will you accompany me there? Now?" He held out a hand to her, repeating the same words and gesture as the night they ended up in the stables. She hesitated, thinking about the propriety of such a ride together.

"You may ride your own mount if it will make you feel more in control. If I become overzealous in my attentions or inappropriate in my actions, you will have your own means to return here at any time."

Since she could ride somewhat competently, this seemed to be the answer. She smiled and nodded her agreement and was met with his own wide smile.

"Come then, the ride is not too long and another horse awaits my inspection."

He called out to one of the grooms, who brought the horse next to Samson over to her and held it as Richard assisted her into the saddle. It was awkward going for a few minutes, as she rearranged her skirts to allow her to sit astride. Making sure that her legs were covered, she gathered the reins in her hand and guided the horse in the direction of the gate. Richard was mounted in a moment and she followed him through the yards and toward an exit from the castle grounds.

A few minutes later they were cantering down a road away from Windsor and back in the direction of Tenby Manor, though that place was miles away. Her horse was spirited but not difficult to control—a good thing, since she hadn't ridden in a while. The skirts tucked around her legs served as some cushioning for the ride.

Sharon pushed her hood back and let the afternoon sunshine warm her face. The cool air swirled around her, refreshing her spirit and giving her some courage to move ahead with her plan. She would wait for the perfect moment and then ask him if any bastards of the old king still lived. If there were any, any sons, she would find out if he knew them and if he could help her find them. Simple enough.

Richard called to her, pointing out one thing and then another in the woods around them or off in the distance. Her own Elizabethan tour guide, she laughed at his humor and enjoyed listening to his explanations about the park around them and the local noble families who held land and titles near Windsor. Eton was already there across the

Thames but not, of course, in the form that she was familiar with from her own time.

They rode silently for some time and then Richard pointed out a path leading off the main road. Following him onto this path, they entered a wooded area and then came out near a large manor house. This was not the size of Tenby Manor, but with its many surrounding smaller buildings it represented a well-sized and established estate. They entered through a gate in a stone wall that encircled the property and Richard greeted many of the people as he rode past them toward the stables in the back.

Two grooms came forward and took hold of their horses. Richard was off first and came to assist her in her dismount. He held her around the waist as she freed her foot from the stirrups and slid down from the saddle. If her slide down brought her into too close contact with him and if his hands lingered on her waist or brushed against her breasts as he released her, she did not comment to him. He stepped away as he was hailed by an approaching man.

"Richard!" the man called out. "You are here at last to see them?" The tall man smacked Richard on the back and then pulled him into an affectionate bearhug. She laughed as Richard made a face over the man's shoulder at her. It was obvious that they were friends.

"Matt," Richard said, freeing himself and turning both of them toward her. "May I make Mistress Sharon Reynolds known to you? She hails from Lancashire and is now part of Her Majesty's household."

"Mistress Reynolds, this is Matthew Christopher, horse-breeder extraordinaire."

Matthew reached over, took her hand, and bowed to her, just lightly touching her knuckles to his lips. "It is my pleasure, Mistress Reynolds. But, tell me, how did this incorrigible rake meet someone as obviously refined as you?"

Richard swung and hit Matthew in the back of his head. The two then flung headlong into a brawl right at her feet. She blinked rapidly, finding it difficult to believe how this friendly introduction had dissolved into a fight before her. Turning over and over in the dirt, the men stirred up so much dust that she had to wave her hand in front of her face to breathe. Coughing once and then again, she gingerly backed away as Richard and Matthew pounded each other into the ground.

Looking around for someone to help, she saw a woman come running toward them. The woman paused by a trough, filled a bucket with water, and continued on with a determined look in her eyes. Sharon closed her own eyes, knowing what was coming. The screams of the two wrestling men as the cold water hit them told her this woman had a great aim. Opening her eyes, she saw that Richard and Matthew had separated and were both wearing matching angry expressions. The woman was the target of their glares.

"Ah, Nelly, why did you do that? I had him! I finally had him," Matthew whined in a loud voice.

Nelly looked unaffected. She stood with her fists on her hips, looking from one to the other as the men climbed to their feet and dusted off some of the muck that now covered them.

"Sweet Nell, this was my favorite doublet and now you have ruined it," Richard added as he wrung out some of the water she'd thrown at him. "Is this any way to treat someone you care about?"

He stretched out his arms and walked directly for her, intent on hugging her. Sharon winced at the squishing sounds from his soaking wet clothes as he grabbed Nell and wrapped his arms around her. Nell stood completely still in his embrace but Sharon saw that her eyes were on Matthew. Wife? Probably, judging from the warm gaze that Matthew cast back at her.

"Here, now, Richard. You have held my wife quite long enough. Release her now and I will let you live out the day."

Richard did not seem worried about the threat and kept Nell in his arms but Sharon noticed the two of them whispered words back and forth. She just waited for someone to notice her. It was Nell that spoke to her first.

"You have brought a guest to my home and treated her

such? Richard, I know you have more manners than that!" Nell walked toward her and smiled as she got closer. The smile did not hide the frank appraisal that also was accomplished during those seconds.

"I do offer my humblest apologies to you, Lady Christopher, and to you, Mistress Reynolds, for my lapse in attending to the social proprieties. I was rudely attacked before I could—" Richard began his false apology but was interrupted as Matthew tried to tackle him again.

Nell took Sharon by the arm and led her away from the mayhem. "This will go on for some time. Can I offer you some refreshments in the house?" At Sharon's nod, the women left the yard and entered the house. The men never paused in their mock battle.

A short time later, Sharon was ensconced in a large, cushioned chair and sipped freshly pressed cider from the estate's own orchards. A tray of small cakes and pastries was offered to her every few minutes by a young maid. Nell waited until she had finished a few of the sweet snacks before proceeding with conversation.

"Do you require anything else, Mistress Reynolds? More cider, perhaps?" Nell pointed to her cup and the maid was there instantly refilling her drink.

"Thank you, milady." She looked around the bright room as she took another mouthful of the sweet drink. Where could Richard be? The fight was a sham, she knew, so why didn't they finish and come in? Sharon looked at the door of the room and listened for any sounds that might indicate the men's approach.

"They will finish rolling around in the dirt, go to the stables, talk about the horses as though they were children, and then remember that we exist."

"In that order, milady?" Sharon smiled at her hostess and the clear understanding she had of the two men.

"In that exact order. And please call me Nell."

"I do not think that would be appropriate, milady."

"We do things a bit differently in my household, if you please?"

"Fine, then. Nell it is. And you must call me Sharon."

Sharon settled in for a chat and found out that Richard visited often, the men always behaved that way when together, and that they never behaved that way in front of company. Nell's raised eyebrow alerted Sharon to the fact that Richard's informality with her did not go unnoticed. As Nell moved to a chair closer to hers, Sharon heard the deep voices of the men coming down the hall.

Matthew and Richard entered, their laughter loud and warm, looking much better than when she'd seen them last. Richard's damp hair was pulled back and he wore a snowy white shirt but no doublet. Matthew was also dressed in trunks, hose, and shirt. And they presented such a picture of sensual masculinity that she had trouble breathing. Their coloring was almost opposite—Richard had long dark hair and hazel eyes and Matthew had short, curly blond hair and blue eyes. They were both the same height and both muscularly built. And very pleasant to behold.

Nell apparently thought the same thing, for she walked over and kissed Matthew with some affection. Then, Nell took two goblets from the servant's tray and handed them to the men.

"Well, Richard, are they not everything Matthew promised they would be?" Nell asked as she stood by her husband's side.

"Oh, aye, true beauties they are, Nell. I find myself filled with anticipation of taking them home."

"These horses are for your farm?" Sharon asked, walking closer to where the others stood.

"Yes. Two more mares and one filly. Along with the others I have acquired, they will be a promising start to my breeding program."

"Too promising, if you ask my opinion," Matthew added. "Your stock will rival my own."

Richard moved closer to Sharon and whispered loudly, "Lord Christopher is a renown breeder in this part of England. He provides many fine horses for Her Majesty's stables."

"An honor that Richard hopes will be his shortly," Matthew added.

"From your mouth to good Queen Bess's ears," Richard said, raising his drink in a mock toast.

"She still delays in granting you your rights?" Matthew looked surprised.

"I will press the issue when she returns to Windsor. A few more weeks at the most." Richard held out his cup and a servant took it from him. "The hour grows late and I must return Mistress Reynolds to her duties."

"You cannot stay for dinner, then?" Nell asked, obviously not content with the short visit.

"Nay, mayhap another time?"

Sharon put her goblet down and allowed Matthew to assist her on with her cloak. Richard kissed Nell once more and then offered Sharon his arm. The four of them walked out together to where the grooms held their horses for them. This time Matthew aided her in mounting while Richard gained his own seat.

"Sharon, make certain that Richard brings you back when you can spend more time with us," Nell called out.

Sharon nodded at the couple and wondered if she would be in this time and place long enough to return for another visit. Once she found the man she was looking for, she would make her escape to Tenby Manor and try to return to her own time.

Richard guided her past one of the enclosed yards and pointed out the three horses he'd come to see. Pride and longing filled his voice as he spoke about their importance in his breeding plans. Soon they left the Christophers' property and were on their way back to Windsor. They took a slightly different route that brought them closer to the river as it twisted along west of the castle and town.

He said nothing else along the way and, other than occasionally pointing to something along the banks, they made their way silently back to Windsor. Sharon could feel the tension rise with each passing minute. She was trying to figure out the right things to say and he was giving her a chance to ask her questions. Finally, she took a deep breath and just said the words she'd practiced to herself for days.

"Do any of Henry's bastards still live?"

Chapter 20

NOT ONLY DID silence greet her question but he reined in his horse to a stop. His face was like stone and she knew immediately that she had made a mistake in how she'd phrased her words.

"I mean, I have heard that he had a bastard son and I wondered if . . ." His expression never changed, even as she struggled with her words. This must be a sore subject within the queen's household. She felt like kicking herself as she realized how inappropriate her even asking about something like this was.

"And what do you want with the old king's bastard?"

"Is there one?" she pressed. His words seemed to indicate that there was some hope, though the cold look in his eyes made her want to turn and run.

"I ask again—what business have you with a royal by-blow?" He pulled on the reins and positioned his horse in front of hers, blocking her path. Icy beads of sweat trickled down her back and she knew this was not going well. Richard's reaction puzzled her, but in this time of political tension, she guessed he was being protective of the queen.

"I . . . uh . . . have something to talk to him about, but I am not certain if he even still lives."

"Oh, he lives."

"He does?" she asked, her mind reeling and her thoughts jumbling together as she finally got her first clue about the mystery man she sought. Why hadn't she asked Richard before? But wait, would this man even know of his connection to the royal family? The one Richard knew of might not be the right person.

"Does he live nearby or in another part of England?" Her horse sensed her excitement and became skittish. Sharon gathered the reins and tried to control it. Calming the horse down, she looked back at Richard, surprised that he had not attempted to help her with the horse. He looked immobilized and although Samson stamped and snorted, Richard sat like a statue before her.

Suddenly, scenes and words passed before her in a rush, like a fast-forwarding videotape. She closed her eyes and saw with such clarity that she thought she was having a dream. But she was awake and everything she saw and heard made her want to scream in frustration.

How could she have been so stupid? How did she miss all the clues, all the information around her in the actions and words of others that told her quite clearly who she sought.

It was Richard. Richard was Henry's bastard son.

" 'Tis you?"

So, it was out there now for him to see. She was just like the others—seeking the bastard Tudor for what she could gain. He wanted to look away, but the changing expressions on her face kept his attention. One after another flashed across her expressive eyes and he hardly knew what to say. He tried not to let her see the disappointment he felt. It tore at his insides, burning through his stomach and his heart. She'd seemed so different from the other women at court and in the queen's household. But, once again, a woman was drawn to him for what she could gain by his connections.

Her country accent, her unfamiliarity with the personalities and procedures at court, her lively wit and freshness all managed to fool him. She sought the old king's bastard.

"You did not answer my question. Why do you seek him?"

"I have . . . I must . . . talk with him. That is all. I need to talk with him, with you." She was watching him with a barely suppressed smile. She was pleased that she had found her quarry. "Henry was your father?"

"Aye, Henry was my father." He would make her work for the information she sought. Part of him just wanted to turn and ride away, away from Windsor, away from her deception and questions. But the stronger part of him wanted to know why.

"And your mother?" She gave off the air of voyeurism as she was clearly excited about her questions. Why? What could her motive be? And why, after countless times of seeing this happen and steeling himself for just this reaction, did this hurt so much?

"I fear my dam is long dead, mistress. She gave her life giving birth to me." As he watched, her gaze stared out past him as she obviously prepared another question.

"What?" he asked. "Your gossips did not give you the whole story about Henry's bastard son? The one he allowed to be raised with his own legitimate children but would never give recognition to?" Anger and bitterness built inside him and soon he needed to let it out. Well, she had asked the question.

"Do you know who she was, Richard?"

"Oh, aye, mistress. Everyone in England knows who she was. A proper Catholic girl who had not the foresight nor the courage of spirit to resist Henry as Elizabeth's mother had." He took a breath and looked at her as she sat on her horse with a look of puzzlement on her face. "He went after her, before Anne Boleyn was even out of his life. He went looking for someone else to bear him the son that Anne denied him and his kingdom, and my mother was his target."

His rage poured out even as he knew it was not Sharon's fault. Too long this had been denied and skirted. Too long.

"Richard, I . . ." she began but he waved off her words with a slash of his hand.

"You asked the question, Mistress Reynolds. Now hear the answer you sought. To all outsiders, the king and queen still pursued the same goals—a male heir for England. But within the court, nobles lined up their daughters for his consideration. Rebecca Granville gave up her virtue to him, however, against her parents' wishes and long before charges were even considered against Anne."

Richard patted Samson's neck, trying to calm him. The horse knew his master's mood and danced under him. Gathering in the reins a bit tighter, he quieted the stallion.

"Through her pregnancy, she waited and waited for Anne to be divorced and for her own betrothal to be announced as Henry had promised it would be. Then it happened. The queen made an announcement of her own—she was pregnant once more. Margaret was left out in the cold. Pregnant, Catholic, and abandoned by her own family. She gave birth God-knows-where and died in that same place. She bled to death because of me."

Richard felt the tears burning in his eyes and his throat tightened. He had never known his mother but lived with the fact that he had been the cause of her death, a lonely, terror-filled death, away from the comfort of family.

"I did not know, truly, Richard."

She held out her hand in supplication, but he was far too angry at her for choosing to seek him out for some nefarious reason, angry at his father for pursuing his own desires at any cost, and even angry at his mother for giving in to the king's demands. In this, even as in most other things in his life, his illegitimacy tore him and his feelings in two.

"I was presented to her parents and they raised me, keeping me hidden from the king. They had lost a daughter and, to their credit, they were shamed by their behavior toward her. They promised to care for me and see me raised well. When I was almost nine, the king found me and took me to his own household."

"He claimed you?" Her eyes were wide in surprise.

"Even though you were . . ." She mouthed the word but didn't say it.

"Even though I was base-born."

"I would not say that, Richard. Your mother and her family held some title?"

"Titles do not matter if your mother and father are not married and he is king. You are a bastard and live in some condition between accepted and rejected. Since all of Henry's children were called bastard at one time or another, save for Edward, God rest his soul, we lived together at different times under the care of various nurses and tutors."

"Then that is where you were educated?"

"Aye. I had the very best of teachers the kingdom could offer until Henry and then Edward died. When the two sisters rose to the throne, I was caught between. Favored when Mary held it, due to my dam's Catholic stock, and in question when Elizabeth first sat there, due to the same."

"But you have a position here with Elizabeth and she seems to hold you in some esteem."

"Bess and I shared some rough times together as children. In spite of my beginnings and the somewhat shaky start to her own reign, she knows that, although I am a king's bastard, I am the queen's man in all things. She has my oath from . . ." He stopped, unable and unwilling to speak of the terror-filled days and nights he and Elizabeth spent as prisoners in the Tower. "I am her man."

Richard laughed then—what a liar he was. Even as he claimed faith with the queen, he plotted, half-heartedly though it may be, to overthrow her and take her seat. He raked his fingers through his hair, loosening it into the wind's control. He must not do this thing. It was wrong and he knew that Elizabeth deserved the throne. He must back away and seek out his own life, his own destiny, and not seek to steal hers.

"I am sorry for prying into your personal life, Richard," she said softly. Her face wore a look that mingled concern with disappointment, understanding, and some measure of pity. He read it in her eyes. He would not take pity from anyone.

"I need not your pity, Mistress Reynolds, so do not give it here." He guided the horse to move next to her and faced the direction back to Windsor. "And now, I have answered your question but you have not answered mine. Why do you seek Henry's bastard?"

Her mouth opened and closed several times. Although his first inclination was to believe she was making up her lie, he felt that she was completely unnerved by what he had shared and was looking for the words to say. Finally she spoke.

"You are not the man I sought, Richard. I was mistaken." Her eyes darted to him and then away. Her voice lost its intensity as she spoke. "If there is no one else who was born out of wedlock to Henry, I was simply mistaken."

"I am the only one who still lives. His earlier children are all dead save Elizabeth and I."

"Well, then, this is where the matter and my unseemly curiosity ends," she said, looking down the road toward the castle. "The hour grows late and Lady Randall will be looking for me. Are you ready?" She nodded at their destination.

"I fear I am not ready to return yet, Mistress Reynolds. If you will but follow this road, you will arrive safely at Windsor's gate."

"Richard, I am sorry for prying."

"As am I that you did, Sharon."

Without another look or word, she tapped her horse's sides with her heels and took off in a trot down the road. His path was a different one, toward the river and a slight hill where the whole of Windsor, Eton, and the river spread out before him. Dismounting and tying his horse to a tree, Richard walked to the banks of the Thames and stared at the rippling water as it passed him.

He could not live in this constant state of indecision. He could not allow everything in his life to be thrust upon him by others. It was time to make a choice and follow one path only. But, by God's heart, he knew not which one to take.

• • •

She pressed against the horse, increasing their speed as she rode toward the castle. And she cried. Tears poured from her eyes and clogged her throat. For him, for her, for the whole situation. She could feel his anger and his bitterness, but it was his own pain, always there and always denied, that tore her heart in two.

She thought at first that she had found the right person, but as he spilled out his story to her, she knew that this could not be the man she was searching for. He was Henry's bastard but his mother was very much known to him. He'd not been adopted by some unrelated Catholic family; he'd been raised by his own maternal grandparents, the Granvilles. And if, as he'd said, he was the last remaining natural child of the old king, her task was an impossible one.

What were her options now? There was no king-in-waiting. Then it struck her—maybe she should turn this evidence over to Elizabeth? Maybe it would further secure the queen in her place and prevent false claims from being legitimized with documents of this kind.

Was that what she was supposed to do? Maybe her focus wasn't supposed to be on the son but on the daughter, whose hold on power was still precarious? Maybe fate or whatever power sent her back had intended that she give this proof to the queen?

She would have to think on this. She had some days before the queen was expected back. If she did decide to do this, she would make her arrangements to leave and then have the package delivered when she was on her way to Tenby Manor and, hopefully, home.

This new possibility lifted her spirits a bit, but not enough to erase the memory of the pain and longing she'd seen in Richard's face. That would take some time to fade. And she knew that whatever was between them had changed now with her questions. She cared for him, more than she should, more than he knew. But the stony look on his face as she'd asked about Henry's son told her that she had crossed some line with him. And she didn't know how to make things go back to what they were.

She only knew she wanted the teasing, flirting Richard back.

Richard was summoned to the queen's chamber the next day as the sun began to drop behind the walls of Windsor. Since Elizabeth remained in London, he was not certain what this was about, but when William Cecil called for you, you attended him. Walking quickly, he took the stairs and then followed the long corridor past the queen's private apartments and down to the presence hall, where Cecil was holding his own audiences.

A quarter hour and more passed before Richard was recognized and invited into another chamber to wait his turn. Familiar with these strategies, Richard found a chair and bided his time wondering what this could be about. The only thing pending was his request that Elizabeth release his inheritance to him. With a desperation that frightened him, he clung to the hope that she would. For if she granted him the land and money, he knew he would walk, nay run, from the other like the madness it was.

Standing, he walked over and peered out one of the floor-to-ceiling windows. Gazing out at the Quadrangle, he watched the many workers and visitors to Windsor as they made their way about, doing their duties. It was much quieter without the queen in residence but still it took many people to keep a castle and armory in its peak working condition.

And it took many to keep the household running smoothly. Of course that thought led him directly to where he did not want to go—Sharon Reynolds. Well, truth be told, he did want to go there. He'd tossed and turned through the night, thinking about her questions yesterday. She had not revealed to him why she sought a bastard of Henry's, just that she did. And for some reason, again not revealed in their conversation, he was not the one she looked for.

He had gone over and over this through the night and came to many conclusions, but one was more troubling than the rest. She was involved in the same plot as he but through different contacts from his own. If this was so, she was certainly not very good at keeping her involvement a secret. He had spoken only to Father Ramirez and to no one else. Yet, she had approached him with her questions.

If she were connected to this plot and had come with information, would not her contacts have given her instructions about who to seek if she needed help? But she came to him. Why?

He stepped away from the windows and paced around the perimeter of the large chamber. Cecil liked to be waited upon and there were dozens of others also milling about the room, waiting their turn. His thoughts turned back to her.

If she were part of the plot, she was the most inept spy he had the misfortune to meet. She boldly asked him her questions, trusting him not to speak of it to others.

Trusting him? That was it: she did trust him. His heart warmed as he thought of the many times she had put herself at his mercy. Even now he could be exposing her search and yet she had turned to him for answers when she needed them.

Women did not make sense! They trusted where it was unwise to trust. They put their noses in business that was not their own to meddle in. And they loved where they should not love.

Not in this instance, of course, but women in general, he meant. Sharon trusted him, no more and no less. But how could she? After her experiences with the ignoble Jasper Crenshaw, how could she have placed her trust in him so quickly? Their relationship to date had been a series of chance meetings, passionate exchanges, and social situations. He enjoyed her company, her wit, and her differences from other women at court. She seemed unable to be false or pretend, even when it would benefit her to do so.

Was there more going on here than either of them realized or would admit? Where did it lead from here? Now that she had admitted she came to court with a mission, would she tell him the rest of it? He would seek her out after his audience with Cecil and make her tell him the whole of it.

The door to the inner chamber opened and everyone in the room stopped their conversations and waited to see who would be called. The messenger approached Richard and beckoned him in to see Cecil. Following the man, he entered and found Cecil seated at a table signing documents while a clerk sanded and sealed them. Cecil looked up briefly, acknowledged him with a nod, and motioned him closer.

"Her Majesty bade me to give you this, Richard," he said as he held out a scroll of parchment to him. "She said to assure you that this does not mean she loves you not, just that the timing is not good."

"The timing?" he asked. He did not realize he was holding his breath until the buzzing started in his ears. He grasped the scroll and unrolled it, his gaze following the words until the message within was clear. He was not to have his inheritance. She denied him the only birthright he had from his—from their—father. She could not do this to him.

"She cannot do this!" he yelled at the queen's highest ranking advisor.

"She cannot?" Cecil asked, lowering his voice but raising an eyebrow in question and challenge.

"My father's will . . ."

"Your father's will doth state that it is within the full power and rights of Her Majesty to continue to keep the grant in her control."

Richard held out the parchment in front of him, scarcely believing that his request was being denied. How could Elizabeth do this to him? Had he not kept faith with her? Had he not faithfully served her during her reign? Now he wanted only what was rightly his and *she said no?*

He spun away from the table and Cecil and bolted for the entrance of the chamber. Pulling open the door with such force that it bounced against one of the walls, Richard paused there and turned back to face Cecil.

"This . . . this maneuver reeks of your touch, Cecil. I will speak to Bess myself when she returns. I will not stand for this."

Waving the scroll, he walked briskly through the outer chamber and down the hall.

"This is not the end by far," he yelled back to those in his wake. "Not by far."

Chapter 21

GOSSIP SWIRLED THROUGH the dining hall during supper. Sharon heard many versions but none of them eased her sense of impending danger. Richard's request had been turned down by the queen and his reaction had been swift and loud rather than measured and private. The many witnesses in the audience chamber and along the hallway all reported their opinions to any who would listen.

Richard had threatened William Cecil. Elizabeth refused his grant of land. Richard made no secret of his displeasure, calling it out so all could hear. Sharon listened as Patricia repeated what she'd heard from the other women and shook her head. He must be devastated by this turn of events. All he hoped for and worked for and it was not to be.

"Where is he, Patricia? Does anyone know?"

"Nay, Sharon," the girl started hesitantly. Sharon had insisted that they call each other by their given names, but Patricia was still not comfortable with it.

"Has John spoken of this to you? Or his father?"

"I have not seen either of them yet today. I am certain they will know the truth of what happened and then we need not rely on this gossip." Patricia paused and looked around the room. Her frown deepened when she couldn't find either man.

"Let us finish our meal and then we can find John or his father and find out where Richard is."

After pushing the food around in front of her for some minutes, Sharon gave up the fight. The stewed turnips and leeks and the boiled mutton quickly lost whatever appeal they may have had when hot. She shoved herself up from the table and picked up her cloak.

"Come, Patricia. I can wait no longer. Do you stay here or will you come with me?"

The girl swallowed her mouthful of food and stood as well. They weaved through the crowded hall and Sharon led her companion outside for an easier and quicker walk to the stables. She fought the urge to take off in a run to get there faster.

"Sharon, I must ask you a question."

"What is it?"

"Should you do this? I mean, should you seek out Richard and his attention and his concerns when you are about to be betrothed to another?"

She came to a halt abruptly and Patricia walked several paces past her before she realized she had. The real niece would definitely not do this. This outward expression of interest would get the real one further and deeper into trouble with her family and the queen. But she was concerned. Richard had been a friend and more to her. He had saved her twice from danger and, in spite of yesterday's tension, Sharon needed to know that he was safe.

And, as someone whose own dreams had been crushed, she thought she could help him. At the least she could offer him some consolation. At the most? Maybe she could repair the damage done by her prying questions and they could continue as friends for as long as she was there. Or maybe more?

She shook her head at that thought. More than friends? This was not the first time she'd thought about giving in to his amorous advances. She loved to watch his long legs as he walked by, or his arms and shoulders and back muscles ripple as he worked with the horses. He was incredibly attractive, she could freely admit that to herself. And there wasn't one time that she watched him speak that she didn't think about kissing that mouth of his. Or think about the hot chills that spread through her that day by the stream. Oh, she wanted him, that much she knew. But should she allow it to proceed when she knew, or rather she hoped, that her time here was limited?

Patricia was waiting for an answer. How could she explain this interest of hers to someone who was very much caught up in the strictures of the day and knew her only as the role she played?

"I am but his friend, Patricia. Can a friend not worry about another?"

"You and I both know he wants you not as a friend but as something more than that. His actions in the past show that clearly."

Her mouth dropped open at Patricia's words. Clearly the quiet girl missed nothing.

"And he has mentioned your name to John more than once in passing." Patricia gasped and covered her mouth with her hand, obviously having spoken of something she'd heard in confidence from her betrothed.

"Really? I mean truly?"

"I was not to share any part of this and most probably should not tell you this, but, aye, he has talked of you to John. And—" She paused and Sharon knew something important was coming. "He has said how much he wishes you were part of the plans he has for his life."

She couldn't breathe. She tried to force air in but the shock of those words made it impossible. He wanted more than just a quick encounter with her? He'd actually spoken of her as part of his future? This was more complicated than she'd ever imagined. She needed to find him now and straighten this out.

"I must find him, Patricia. I must make certain he knows how it stands between us."

The girl nodded and they walked again. Sharon realized that Patricia took one meaning from her words when she wasn't even sure herself of how to take them. What would she say to him when she did find him? Her thoughts were interrupted when they reached the stables. Asking one of the grooms for John, they waited at the door for him. John and his father met them minutes later.

"Is he here, Robert?" she asked straight-out. No use mincing words now.

"Aye, Mistress Reynolds, he is." Robert eyed her with open suspicion.

"I would speak to him."

"He is not fit for a woman's company at this time, mistress. Mayhap on the morrow?" Robert stood taller and John shifted uncomfortably next to him.

"Nay, Robert, tomorrow won't do. I would see him now." She crossed her arms over her chest and tapped her foot. She was not leaving without seeing him.

"Truly, Sharon, you should leave him be for now."

"He's drunk, then?"

Robert looked at John and then back at her before answering. He sighed and ran his hand through his hair.

"He is well on his way to drunk."

"I want to see him."

All three of them challenged her, all arguing their points against her seeing him now, but none were successful. In her heart, she knew he was hurting and from her own experience she knew that she could help him through this. And she wanted to be there for him. She waited for them to realize she was not joining in the argument.

"John, would you please see Patricia back to her room? It grows both late and cold." John opened and shut his mouth several times before looking at Patricia and then nodding his agreement.

"Robert, would you escort me to Richard?" Robert would not be as easy to intimidate as his son. He drew himself up and prepared for another battle. "Please, Robert? I can help him."

"I fear for you, Sharon."

"He would not hurt me. Surely you do not believe him capable of harming a woman?" Even from her short time with him, she knew Richard would never do anything but protect her.

"Not physically, Sharon. But his words are full of venom this day."

She leaned over and touched his arm. "Please, Robert. Let me help him."

She watched as the battle raged within him for a few seconds and then saw capitulation on his face. He nodded. After a few words to John and Patricia, she followed him inside the building. It was no surprise to her to end up at the door to the room where she had gotten drunk with Richard. The door was barred from the outside.

"You locked him in?" She was shocked.

"He was out of control, Sharon. For his own safety I felt it best to keep him here until he regained that control."

"Is he awake?" She leaned her head toward the door and listened for any sounds within. "Is he well?"

"He threw himself around a bit when he first went in, shouting and tossing things. Then he stopped his shouting a few minutes ago."

"Can you get me a jug of water and some linens? He will need to clean up." Robert nodded and left her. He returned carrying a basket with the items she asked for and a few more. Taking it from him, she stepped to the door and waited.

Robert lifted the bar and opened the door slowly, as though he expected Richard to leap through at any moment. When no movements were heard, she entered and, after placing another bucket of water on the floor, Robert shut the door quickly behind her. She jumped as she heard the bar slide down.

The room was in near-total darkness. The dim glow of a lantern hung above her head barely lit the room . . . and its occupant. Drunk or not, Richard had placed and left the lantern high and out of danger of being knocked over. She smiled as she realized that he was in control of his actions enough not to endanger the stables or the horses by doing anything stupid.

She squinted into the darkness and finally found him. He

sat with his back against one of the walls, knees drawn up and head tilted back. Reaching up, she adjusted the wick of the lantern to get more light and then she could see better. His arms rested on his knees and she noticed the skin on his knuckles was torn and bleeding. A wineskin sat next to him in the straw. With his eyes closed, she didn't know if he was sleeping or not. His shirt was loose from his trunks and no longer its usual white. Covered in sweat and some wine, the shirt added its own particularly pungent odor to the whole scene.

Looking around, she located the small table she remembered from before and straightened it so she could put the basket down. Then she tiptoed over to take a closer look at him. She yearned to smooth the hair out of his face but did not want to disturb him if he slept. There would be time for him to clean up when he awoke. His opened eyes and direct gaze startled her and she stumbled back, landing in the straw.

"So, do you come to witness the bastard's comeuppance?"

She sat up and settled her skirts around her before answering. She took a deep breath and looked at him. For all his bluster, the pain was there in his eyes for her to see. She wondered if he knew how much he gave away in his gaze.

"What have I ever done to you, Richard, other than my prying questions yesterday, that would make you think I would find joy in your misery?" There. Throw it right back at him.

"I do offer my humblest apologies for thinking ill of you, Mistress Reynolds." She winced at the sarcasm in his voice.

"I would rather have your honest anger than your false apologies. Are you drunk?"

"Aye, drunk, but not enough, I fear, for my purposes. And I do not think you would ask for my anger had you been here when Robert locked me in." He flexed his hands and she saw that the raw abrasions still bled. "How did you convince him to allow you into my prison?"

Sharon climbed to her feet and walked to the basket of

supplies. Carrying a small bowl and a linen square, she dipped into the bucket of water by the door and went back to where he sat. Then, crossing her legs, she dropped back down onto the floor.

"I told him the truth, Richard. I could help you."

"So," he said with that daunting raise of his eyebrow, "you would comfort me in my time of need."

"As one who has suffered that which you suffer now, yes, I offer you comfort." She saw so many emotions passing over his face—anger and longing and hope and loss and more.

"You? You have suffered the loss of your life's dream?" He rubbed his hands over his face and pushed his hair back. He laughed out roughly and looked at her. "Surely not?"

"Is it because I am a woman or because I am young that you think I have not suffered the same thing you do now?" It always came back to those two attributes, even here and now. Her own dreams, of success and of a future, were shattered because of them as well. Things hadn't changed much in the relationships between men and women over the centuries.

"If you would suspend your disbelief, I would tell you a story. Mayhap then you will understand."

He nodded and she thought of how and where to start. She wanted him to know the story but not the details. Leaning over, she took the cloth and dipped it into the water. Taking one of his hands in hers, she squeezed the water out so that it dripped over his injured fingers and then she slowly cleaned his torn skin.

"In a place far, far away, there lived a woman." Luckily he didn't know about movies from George Lucas or he would have laughed right then. "This woman was put in charge of a huge project for a . . . college."

His laughter stopped her. "A woman? In charge at a college? Women are not even permitted in such a place!"

"Richard, if my story is going to help you, you must open your mind to a broader view of women and what they can do."

He looked as if he would argue with her, but then just

nodded, giving her an enigmatic look before he leaned his head back once more.

"This woman was also young, but she was the best person for the task of overseeing this project." At his snort, she was tempted to clean his bruised knuckles a bit more brusquely but didn't let herself sink to his level. "This was something she had wanted to do for most of her life and she had many ideas about how to succeed in her endeavors."

She finished one hand and lifted the other as she spoke. She wet and squeezed the cloth once and then again to remove the blood from his hand. He winced a few times as she cleaned.

"But, there was a man who wanted the position of authority she was given."

"Of course . . ." he interrupted.

"Richard! I ask for your cooperation and for you to listen to the whole story before you ridicule it." At his nod, she continued. "Because the position was hers, he sought out ways to undermine and destroy her credibility. He turned those who worked for her and those who supported giving her the opportunity in the first place, against her. With doubts and questions growing, she was removed from her position and the man replaced her."

"This knave won then?" He looked at her with interest. "Did she not tell them of his subterfuge?"

"Come now, Richard, political intrigue exists at all levels of power whether here in Elizabeth's court or in other institutions. The right person does not always win out."

"And her dreams? Her plans?"

"Dashed quite well by all involved. She fears to hope for a brighter outcome. Her reputation is in shambles and her word is doubted by all who know her."

"But if they know her, will they not stand by her?"

"It is not always possible to stand and fight. But her dreams will not die easily. She will try other means and methods and maybe something else will work."

"And if this is your way of comparing this woman to me, then I should not give up?"

"Tell me what happened, Richard. Mayhap we can make sense of it together?"

He stood and walked to the other side of the small room. Looking back, his gaze became unfocused as he told her what had happened.

"Cecil called for me and he delivered the queen's message. She will not grant the charter for my land and give to me the only thing my father left me."

Now his expectation of a grant of land made sense to her. As a half-brother to the queen, he had some measure of standing in Elizabeth's court and household. Many things she'd seen and heard made sense to her now.

"Did she give a reason? Did Cecil say anything that gives you insight into her decision?"

"Only that the timing is not right. That is her only reason and that is not one to my liking or understanding."

She walked to his side and looked up at him. "Have you asked before? Maybe this isn't a final answer?"

"I have discussed and asked informally and prodded in this direction. This is the first time I had put it into a formal written request for her to honor the terms of my father's will."

"Why now? Would it hurt to wait and ask again?"

"You mean beg once more? Aye, it would hurt. Even bastards have some measure of pride. And I am well past the age when I should seek a bride and settle into married life. I stand at a crossroads in my life with two choices. This grant would be a sign to me of which way to turn. 'Tis out of my hands now, I fear."

His expression became cloudy and she felt that he was keeping something from her. Considering her own secrets, she wondered if he would tell her about his other choice. He paused and stared off at the far wall, not speaking for a few minutes. In watching his face, she noticed a few more cuts on his face and forehead. She may as well tend to those while she was here.

"Your face is bleeding. Sit and let me take care of it."

She tugged on his hand to get his attention and pointed at the bale of hay in the corner. Once he was seated, she used a dampened cloth to push his hair from his face and wipe his forehead of the blood that dried there. A small cut was revealed above his brow and she cleaned it carefully. She wet the linen square once more and washed the rest of his face. He closed his eyes and allowed her to minister to his injuries.

"How did you get these?" she asked as she found two more puncture wounds on his cheek. She fought the urge to kiss those spots. Heck, with him this close, she was fighting all kinds of urges!

"I threw a mug at the wall and it shattered. The pieces must have struck my face. Tell me, Mistress Reynolds, will my beauty be marred by the cuts?" He peeked from beneath one eyelid at her.

"You have the devil's own luck, sirrah. The cuts are minor and should heal without much notice."

She placed her hand beneath his chin and lifted his face into the light to check one more time. She felt his own hand slide up to rest on her hip. Shifting her feet, he then put his other hand on her other hip, effectively trapping her between his legs. He then opened both eyes and gazed at her.

"You have my thanks for your attentions to my injuries."

"You are most welcome." Her voice trembled; even she heard it, as a wave of overwhelming desire passed through her. Giving in to it, she leaned down and touched her lips gently to his. "Most welcome," she whispered again.

"Should you not go now that you have offered your comfort?" he asked as he reached up to her and touched his lips to hers again.

The next thing she knew, his hands were in her hair, pulling her down to meet his mouth. Soon he was kissing her, his tongue touching hers and his hands holding her close. He shifted on the bale and brought her down into his lap. She could hardly breathe as wave after wave of heat passed through her. Every inch of skin tingled and her breasts ached for his touch. Her body responded to his kisses and wanted for more.

"Truly, I am well now. If it is your wish to leave, now

would be the time to do so." His kisses didn't stop, though; he continued to press their lips together over and over again.

She wrapped her arms around his neck and enjoyed the cascade of sensations moving through her. He did this to her with his touch. And she wanted more. Abruptly, he withdrew from her, leaning his head back and untangling her hands and his. Lifting her off his lap, he stood and faced her.

"I am not so drunk that your kisses have no effect. If you are going, do it now, for I cannot withstand the urges I have within me for you much longer."

"I would stay," she said, now certain of what she wanted to happen with him.

He looked at her with passion-filled eyes and walked to the door. Knocking on it lightly, he called out to his friend. Sharon heard the bar scrape upward and the door swung open. Robert looked in and nodded to her.

"Come now, Robert. You would not have let her enter if you were truly in fear of my actions. And you knew better than that, did you not?"

"Are you in control now, Richard? You know I did this to prevent you from . . ." He ended without finishing his words, but Richard obviously understood his meaning, for they grasped hands and shook them.

"I thank you, my friend, for all you have done. Now, you may go. I will see Sharon safely to her room."

Robert looked to her for confirmation and she nodded to him and smiled. Richard motioned to her for a moment of time with Robert and they both left the room talking.

It was actually a few minutes later when he returned, but from the look and smell of him, he had put that time to good use. His hair and skin were damp and he wore a clean shirt now. The smell coming from him was definitely more pleasant than before. He stepped inside, picked up a piece of wood, and dropped it into the holders on each side of the door. They now had privacy.

She just stood and stared at him—the shirt hugged his chest and shoulders and she could see his form quite clearly. He met her gaze and for a moment neither one of them moved or spoke. Her mouth went dry at the thought of making love to him, with him. Her nipples tightened and moisture gathered between her thighs as she considered the night ahead.

"I want you here for all the wrong reasons." He stood before her, his hands fisted on his hips, an erection apparent to her even through the layers of clothing.

"I want to be here with you for all the right ones. Comfort, caring, desire," she answered.

"Those are my same reasons, but I thought you would do this only for love." He was challenging her to go; this was her out.

"Who says I do not do it for that, too?"

"I cannot offer you that."

"Because no one has ever loved you, Richard? Do you not know what it feels like to love another?"

She knew from the look on his face that she had touched a tender subject with her words. He'd grown up a motherless bastard, raised first by grandparents doing their duty and then in the household of a self-absorbed king who moved from wife to wife looking only for a son, a legitimate son. Then, he was surrounded by people who wanted him only for his close position to the royal family. No wonder he had hidden his real feelings under the guise of playfulness and flirting . . . and never married.

"Love, Mistress Reynolds? 'Tis an overrated emotion, I fear, much less reliable and less understood than plain old lust and desire."

"Then let's begin with those and see where we end up." She smiled at him, knowing full well where they would end up and wanting it more with each passing second.

He took the first step and in a moment had her backed up against the wall, pinned between his hardness and the boards behind her. Richard grasped her hands in one of his and lifted them over her head as his mouth took possession of hers. His knee insinuated itself between her legs and she pressed against it.

His lips left hers and Richard trailed wet, hot kisses down

her neck and onto her shoulders. With his free hand, he unlaced her bodice and then her chemise. Pulling on the laces, he opened her clothing and continued to kiss and lick his way down onto her breasts. Her nipples, already tightened into small buds, drew his attentions and she could not stop the moans that came from deep within her. Pulsations moved through her, shivers caused by the touch of his mouth and teeth on those sensitive tips, more tremors moved to her core and then emanated outward. Her skin felt hot and cold at the same time.

With his free hand, he rubbed and teased her relentlessly, making her other breast ready and aching for his mouth's attention. She could do nothing but enjoy it—held in that position by him, her body was open to him and the sensations he made her feel. He brought his mouth back to hers while his hand moved down her skirts, searching for the end of them.

"Look at me," he urged while his mouth still tasted hers. She opened her eyes and their gazes met even as they still kissed deeply. His hand had found the bottom of her skirts and he now tugged them from between her legs and slid his hand underneath. The cooler air on her legs did nothing to stop the heat between them. His fingers moved up on her thighs closer and closer to the cleft of her legs and she waited, now not even breathing, as he approached the place that throbbed in anticipation of his intimate touch.

Their eyes still gazing at each other, his fingers found her panties in place and she saw him smile at first contact with the silky barrier. He leaned back from her mouth and released her hands. Placing them on his shoulders, she held on as he slipped the panties down her legs and dropped them at her feet. He startled her as he bent down and, still holding her skirts out of the way, kissed her belly and onto her mons. Her legs threatened to give out as he moved his mouth through the curls there and parted her thighs.

Kneeling before her, he used his hands and mouth to make magical sensations move through her. She clutched at his shoulders and her moans echoed through the small room. Soon she felt the waves building and building within her. The tension grew as he touched and tasted and rubbed and pinched until her moans became louder and louder and her peak was upon her. Her legs tensed, she could feel the contractions moving throughout her core and into her lower belly. He continued to play until, weak with satisfaction, she slid down the wall and sat before him.

He leaned back on his heels and stared at her with such a look of ravenous hunger that shivers moved up and down her spine. She pushed the hair from her face and took a deep breath. Once more he had seen to her satisfaction before his own. But the expression on his face said not for long.

"And, that, Mistress Reynolds, is lust and desire. What say you now?"

He knew as soon as the words left his mouth that it was a challenge to her. He saw her eyes light up even where a moment before they wore the sated look he had put there. He stood up and stepped back, helping her to her feet when she reached out her hand to him. He watched and waited, curious and yet hopeful that her actions would prove his skepticism wrong.

She reached behind her and unhooked her skirts and let them fall to the ground as he watched. Then she freed herself from the loosened bodice and other clothing until she stood before him in her chemise and her stockings. Her hair was rumpled and her cheeks flushed and he wanted to taste every inch of her again and again. His erection grew and became like steel as he saw her nipples were once more tight little buds under that chemise that hid nothing from his view.

She walked over to him and then around behind him, smiling as she moved closer and closer. He felt her movements there and waited to see what she would do next. Her hands reached around and pulled his shirt up and then over his head. It dropped on the floor next to them. Then he felt her skin, her naked skin on his back and her breasts pressed up against him. He closed his eyes and waited.

Her hands slipped around him and rubbed lightly over his chest and his own nipples. Her fingers caressed his skin and moved in ever-lowering circles that approached, then moved away from his breeches. His hardness surged within those breeches, waiting for her touch. He stood breathless, awaiting her next move.

She found the laces that tied his breeches around his waist and untied them, loosening them until she could slip them down and over his hips. They slid down his legs and he stepped out of them. Then he felt her arms encircle him again and begin their seduction of him.

Her hands and fingers traced his waist and then his hip-bones and tickled his thighs. His back was heated, very heated by her body leaning on it, rubbing against it, even her mouth tasted him from behind, licking and biting as she explored his nether parts. He was panting by the time her fingers actually touched him, touched the hardness, and it responded with a lurch of its own in her hand.

Her soft laughter tickled his back and when he could stand no more, he pulled her around in front of him and kissed her mouth. Wrapping her in his arms, their bodies touching from chest to thighs, he slanted his head to taste her more deeply. His tongue thrust into her mouth and his hardness thrust against her belly. 'Twas then he felt her pushing against him, trying to separate them.

She took him by the hand and led him to the rough bed in the corner. Backed up against it, he tumbled down onto it with a push from her. Sharon followed him down, kneeling on the side of it over him. He could almost feel her touch as her gaze moved over him from his head to his toes and he prayed that she would hurry with her attentions.

She did not keep him waiting long.

She began to spread kisses, light, teasing kisses on his brow, then down his nose and over his mouth and chin. Her tongue traced a path down his neck onto his chest. He barely breathed, waiting for the next touch. Her tongue made its way down his chest, onto his belly, and closer and closer to his manhood. He closed his eyes and waited.

She did not disappoint him. Her warm, wet tongue traced circles around the head of it, while her hands massaged and lifted him from underneath. Soon she took him fully into her mouth and he was the one whose moans filled the room. His muscles tensed and he grew even harder while she sucked and licked him. Time passed slowly but he knew he approached his release soon. Taking her by the arms and lifting her off him, he turned over, pulling her beneath him as he went.

Cradled between her legs, his body urged him to enter her, to become one with her. She entangled their legs and opened to him as he pushed against her swollen, wet outer lips. Into her tightness he slid a bit at a time, her gasps and his moans filling the room even as he filled her. He knew he was stretching her, that she was extremely tight, but he gloried in the sensations as he moved deeper and deeper within her woman's passage. Then he was one with her, in as far as he could go, and he began to move out and in, out and in, spreading the wetness he found there and easing her tightness as they became accustomed to each other.

Soon, only their straining breaths and moans could be heard as his loins clenched and readied itself for release. Her body moved against his, slick with sweat and as heated as his. Her own cries grew louder and more intense and he knew her satisfaction was upon her. He kissed her, one long breathless kiss, as she reached her peak and then he followed with his own.

It was like none he had ever experienced—not better nor longer nor more intense. But there was something about becoming one with her in this act that was like nothing or no one that had gone before her. It was only as his breathing was slowing down that he realized he'd never removed himself from her in time.

She held him inside her even as he recovered, and she tried to keep her legs entwined with his. He untangled their legs, turned on his side, and pulled her close to him. Reaching to the floor, he grabbed a sheet that had fallen there and covered them with it. She made no sound for several minutes and he thought she slept. Then her whisper filled the room.

"And that, Master Granville, is love."

Chapter 22

HE COULD NOT sleep, not in this state of complete confusion. His body was sated, she had seen to that, but even that added to the questions spinning through his mind. The wine he had consumed did not help either, for as his body relaxed, his mind had difficulty staying awake.

She was a virgin. Well, no longer one, thanks to him, but she had come to him and given herself for the first time. Obviously her reputation was not deserved. By God's heart, a virgin! It had been years since a virginal woman gave herself to him but he remembered the feel of being the first and he'd felt it once more tonight with her. He could not remember, however, spilling his seed into any woman. He had made the decision early on that he would not make bastards of his own, not like his father had. The only sons he would have would be sons on his wife . . . when the time came for it.

He pushed the hair back out of his face and looked at her. She lay in his embrace, her head on his arm, asleep with the most untroubled look on her face. He had spilled his seed in her, been her first lover, and she slept on. She was truly different than any he had met before. And more determined than anyone, too.

How she had convinced Robert to let her in, he could not imagine, but he wished he had witnessed it. Robert did not bend and sway to anyone's demands. At least not until Mistress Reynolds.

Leaning over, he smoothed her hair and pulled the sheet up higher on her shoulders. He pressed his lips against her skin there and breathed in her scent. His body reacted to her closeness and he wanted her again, even now as she slept.

No, 'twould not be right to take her again when they could not be together. When each time would increase the risk of putting a babe inside her. When each time would simply make the ending more difficult for both of them. She shifted in her sleep, rolling against him and fitting more tightly against his legs and groin. He felt his resolve slip even as his body readied itself for her.

He tried to lean away, but she followed his movements with one of her own. Then he heard her quiet chuckle and knew she slept no longer. She turned her face to look at him.

"You are courting more danger than you know, Mistress Reynolds."

"So we are still being formal, Master Granville?"

She placed her bum up against his erection and had the audacity to smile at him. No, he would not let his control slip when there could be a steep price to pay for it.

"I would think that what we just did would make us close enough to call each other by our given names?" Her breathy whisper and reference to what they had done made the urge to kiss her almost overwhelming. Until he thought momentarily about the consequences.

"If you mean that I was your first lover, then indeed, I should call you Sharon."

The smile left her face and she would not meet his gaze. After a moment, she spoke.

"I suppose I should explain. . . ."

"Please do, for I have questions about your reputation and the impossibility of what I know of it."

"Richard, I . . . ah . . . am not the person you think I am."

His breath caught in his throat. Then who was she? What was she? a spy? Her questions came to mind—asking him about bastard sons of a dead king and being disappointed when he did not seem to fit the description of one she sought. So much intrigue swirled around the throne and at times it was nigh to impossible to keep the players straight. But, hold! Mayhap it was the suspicion that made him interpret her words differently from what she meant them to be. Let her explain.

"Then, tell me, who are you?"

She lifted his hand and entwined their fingers, staring at it instead of looking at him as she spoke.

"I am a woman undeserving of the words spoken against me. I am a stranger in a strange land. I am—" She paused and took in and let out a deep, slow breath before finishing the words. "I am a woman who loves where she should not."

More puzzles. Her words were vague enough to be interpreted and misinterpreted easily.

"Like the woman in your story?"

"Just so."

"Then there is no Jasper Crenshaw? This was some farce to escape your lady aunt's custody?"

"There is a Jasper Crenshaw."

"And you loved him and he proved false?" He needed to hear it from her own lips.

"I never loved him, Richard. I spoke of you."

He closed his eyes and let her words wash over him. She had touched on the one thing he hungered for more in his life than anything else, more than the damned throne of his father. He wanted to be loved. He longed to have someone who cared for him. He wanted it so badly that he was willing to look past the bad choices they had both made and hope for a future together.

Such a future was not to be—Patricia had already told him that a betrothal had been made for Sharon and that she would be called home soon to fulfill that promise. And even his future was uncertain, although he had come to some sense of it during the hours spent in this room today. After his anger drained away, he saw the two paths he could travel and had decided which one he would take. And, as much as he wanted her as part of it, there were no guarantees that any of it would work out the way he wanted it to.

"Sharon, I would ask the queen for your hand in marriage if you give the word."

There. The words were out. He had thought them often enough in the last few weeks and now he had said them. He waited for her answer, although, from the grim look on her face, he thought he knew what it might be.

"Oh, Richard. You cannot do that."

"Marrying the fourth son of an earl is more acceptable than marrying the bastard half-brother of the queen?" Those words were also out before he could stop them. The old hurts raised themselves once more. It always came back to that—he was never quite good enough.

She turned in his arms until she faced him. An angry frown marred her brow and her mouth was set in a thin line. The softness was gone.

"Did I not just give myself to the bastard? How can you ask such infuriating . . . stupid questions?" Without warning, she balled her fist and thumped him on the chest. At this close range, her blow did not hurt, but it did demonstrate how upset she was.

"I beg your pardon, I did not mean—"

"Yes, you did," she interrupted. "You are so used to being treated that way that you wait for me to do it too." She took a breath and then rubbed the spot she had just punched. She was such a confusing, enticing woman—one moment all-caring and tenderness and the next full of spit and fire. But, still not his.

"I meant that my life is not my own. I do not control how long I am here or when I will leave."

"I will beg the queen. I have already decided to submit my petition once more for her consent after the furor over her excommunication has calmed down."

"You have?"

"Aye. I think 'tis the intrigue and danger around her that

clouds her judgment in this matter and I am willing to give her time to make the correct decision."

"I was beginning to think you were involved in something dangerous. . . ." The ire left her face and concern replaced it. "Your words the other day frightened me."

"My words?" He thought back to what he may have said in explaining the sad circumstances of his birth and could think not of anything that would alarm her.

"You spoke of being at a crossroads and of making a choice. It was not the words you used but the tone of your voice that made me think you were planning something foolish."

He did not remember revealing that much to her at all. He'd stood at the point of no return that day, and did still. The difference was that he knew he could follow but one path and he now knew which one that would be. And he could still not speak of it to anyone.

"Fear not, I have my wits about me now. You have not answered my question, Sharon. You have not told me your desires in this." He leaned forward and kissed her forehead and then the tip of her nose. "Would you have me to husband?"

"I will return home soon and have many things to attend to then . . . er, there. I cannot accept your offer knowing that I cannot stay. If things were different, I would be honored to be your wife, Richard."

Tears filled her eyes and her lower lip trembled. He reached over and touched his thumb to her mouth, rubbing her lip even as more tears threatened to spill. Pulling her into his embrace, he slanted his head and covered her mouth. Kissing her deeply, he wrapped his leg over her hip and brought her closer still.

He tasted the saltiness of her tears as they reached her mouth and felt her gasping sobs as he kissed her once and then again and again. Soon, the tears stopped flowing and she became passionate in the meeting of their mouths. She reached out and took him by the shoulders, holding him closer still.

"Love me, Richard," she whispered, a certain desperation

filling her voice. She slid her leg over his and pressed her hips forward, rubbing his now-hardened member against her belly.

"Hold a moment, Sharon. 'Tis too soon—I will hurt you if we do this now."

She responded by rolling under him and trapping him with her hands wrapped in his hair. He answered her passion-filled kisses with some of his own and when she begged him once more, he surrendered to their desire.

And he answered her call twice more before morning showed itself to the world.

She ached from head to toe and every place in between. As she slipped from his embrace and edged her way off the pallet, he mumbled something in his sleep and rolled over on her side of the bedding. She took advantage of the opportunity and moved out of his grasp.

Stretching her arms over her head, Sharon worked some of the kinks out of her muscles and looked for her clothes. Dawn's faint light inched into the room from under the door and she turned the lantern up just a bit so she could see her way around the room. She desperately wanted to bathe but that wasn't possible right now so she made do with a quick wash using the cold water left in the bucket from the night before. Shivering, she pulled on her panties and stockings and then her chemise to cover most of her.

The air was crisp in the room, the brazier long extinguished, and Sharon longed to climb back into Richard's warm embrace and sleep a few more hours. But even Lady Randall's departure yesterday for Richmond, to join the queen, didn't change Sharon's work schedule appreciably. So she stood and pulled the bodice over her chemise and relaced it snugly. Using her fingers as a rough comb, she untangled her hair as much as possible and pulled it back into a loose braid.

Ready to leave, she slid her feet into her shoes and pulled her cloak around her shoulders. Turning to look at him once more, she smiled at the innocent expression he wore in sleep. With one arm thrown over his head and his mouth open slightly, he looked much younger and much more carefree than he did awake. She couldn't resist the urge to touch him once more before she left so she walked quietly over to the pallet. Leaning forward, she brushed some hair out of his face and touched his lips with her finger.

He'd been so gentle with her during the night. Once he'd realized she was a virgin, he had slowed down their pace and made sure she was well loved. She sighed, remembering him taking the time to help her wash away the small amount of blood on her thighs after their lovemaking. If only . . .

If only they could be together. . . . If only they could stay together. . . . If only she knew how this would all turn out.

But they couldn't, they wouldn't, and she didn't. And no amount of wishing would make it happen. Once she'd finished her task here and delivered the documents, she would go home. At least she hoped to go home. If fate had brought her here, fate would take her home. And Richard would stay in sixteenth-century England.

So, she'd traveled through time, met the man she could love, gave herself to him in a night of passion, and that was it? She'd thought that when she finally did decide to give up her virginity it would be to someone who was and would be a big part of her life. Richard had certainly been an important part of her life in the past few weeks and months. But she could not see a future with him.

Standing, she turned and walked to the door, knowing that the night would never be repeated. A fleeting sense of regret and sadness was replaced by acceptance as she lifted the bar from its holders.

"You would leave without a farewell, Mistress Reynolds? Fie on you, then!"

He sat up on the pallet with the sheet tucked around his waist. He stretched as she had and the sight of muscles rippling those arms and that chest made her body respond on its own. She had to leave . . . now.

"Good day, Master Granville. I must leave before the day is upon us fully." She nodded to him, intending to leave on that note. But when he stood on the pallet and the sheet fell at his feet, all thoughts of leaving, all thoughts of anything sensible left her head. Her mouth went dry and the palms of her hands dampened with sweat. She had to leave, she had to . . .

"Leave. I mean, I must leave now, Richard." She backed away from him, sliding her feet along the floor to find her way without looking, since she couldn't take her eyes from his. Finally her back hit the door and she grasped its wood bar in her hand. He reached her at the same time.

Smiling a wicked smile, he leaned down and touched his lips to hers. When she would've opened to him, he drew back and winked at her.

" 'Twas all I wanted, Sharon. A kiss before leaving."

He placed his hand over hers and started to lift the bar. Realizing his nakedness would be seen by anyone near the door in the stables, she tugged his hand off hers and pushed him back.

"Richard! You will be seen."

"Aye. So? Many have seen me thus."

It must be a guy thing to walk around comfortably naked. Still, she didn't want word of their night together to spread throughout the queen's household.

"Richard, please move back?"

Laughing at her discomfort, he nodded and stepped back. She opened the door and started to leave the room. At just that moment, strong rays of sunlight pierced through the gray clouds and shone through the small window overhead in the stable's roof. Just as Richard turned to walk away from her, those same rays of light brightened the small room for a brief moment. Richard bent down to pick up the clothes that were strewn across the floor.

There on the back of his left hip, almost on his bottom, was a small, diamond-shaped birthmark.

The birthmark of the Boleyns.

The birthmark of the rightful king of England.

Chapter 23

SHE STAGGERED BACK from the door, her breaths coming quick and shallow and her head beginning to swim. Grabbing on to the wall, she stumbled outside and barely made it to the side of the yard before the heaving began. Though her stomach was empty, it continued to convulse until she could hardly breathe at all. Finally, it stopped long enough for her to lift her head from the dirt.

She was lucky that most of the grooms who worked in the stables had not yet arrived or were not in the area where she was, because she knew her legs would not support her if she tried to stand. She knelt there for some time before her breathing became calmer and she regained her balance. She had to get out of there and find someplace quiet to think. She needed to think.

The chapel. The chapel of St. George.

Standing on wobbly legs, she took one step, then another, slowly making her way across the yard, along the path to one of the side entrances to the chapel. Trying the doors, she found one unlocked and eased it open. Stepping quickly and quietly into the darkened hall, she looked around for anyone. Seeing no one, she crept in and found a bench facing a side altar. Sharon sank onto it, grateful for its hard and sturdy surface.

Richard Granville should be king. The thought ran through her mind, over and over again. He had the birthmark, the physical sign of his link to his mother, Anne Boleyn. His father was already known and never doubted. She rubbed her eyes and her forehead. What now? What should she do?

Taking a few deep breaths and trying to calm herself down, Sharon focused on the evidence before her. She'd been an observer since her arrival here, now, and hadn't used many of the skills she'd developed as a scientist. Oh, she'd taken note of fabrics and designs, but her investigative skills were in some kind of holding pattern and she needed them now.

Okay, first, assuming that the documentation she'd found was factual and accurate, there was a living male heir. Next, again based on the documentation, he was raised by a Catholic family. Then, his real parentage was a secret to them and to him. And, he had the birthmark to show his connection to the Boleyn family.

Richard fit most of the criteria but he knew who his mother was. Could he be mistaken? If a nobleman's daughter were pregnant with the king's child and the king knew of it, surely some kind of arrangements would be made for her "lying-in." Henry had wanted a male heir too much not to take some precautions about the birth of a potential heir. So, if the woman that Richard thought was his mother had died in childbirth, what could have happened to her baby? Could it have died and Richard been passed off as hers so that her family would raise him?

It seemed too neat—but a midwife would have had access to both mothers and babies. And, if she were driven by vengeance, what better way than to have Anne's son raised by the family of one of Henry's lovers? And a Catholic one at that.

She was engaging in a lot of supposition, but she felt strongly that she was going along the correct path. Richard would think, did think, that he was raised by his mother's family and, as a bastard, was prevented from taking the throne. Of course, as Maria Morales carried out her plan, she had no way of knowing that it would be Anne's daughter who would eventually sit on that throne. So her vengeance against Anne was for naught. But it was her vengeance against Henry that prevented Richard from becoming the king he should have been.

So, now what? Sharon shifted on the hard seat and looked around. The sunlight grew stronger and she knew that she would be missed if she didn't get to the sewing rooms soon. How could she get through the day now, knowing what she knew?

Giving the proof to the rightful heir and then returning home had seemed so much easier when he was a stranger to her. All the ramifications of carrying out this deed made her mind reel. She knew what Elizabeth would do as queen. Could Richard ever come close? Could he seize the throne and take power? Her head ached as the endless possibilities flooded her thoughts.

Just when the confusion was almost overwhelming, Sharon heard the door open. Startled from her reverie by the squeaking wood and by the sunlight streaming in, she was surprised to see Patricia standing in the doorway. The girl spotted her and waved her over. Sharon walked to where she stood.

"Come, Sharon, 'tis time for us to be about the day's business."

"What are you doing here?"

"I thought that since you wished to go to early prayers this morn, I would join you."

"Early prayers? I did not go to . . ."

"You came early to observe prayers. Lady Cranford was most impressed that I planned to join you here this morn."

Lady Cranford? Prayers? Sharon closed her eyes and offered up a prayer of thanksgiving at that moment—Patricia was covering for her absence. At least fate had blessed her with someone with a good heart to be her companion in this day and time. She would not have survived this well without the girl's help along the way.

"Patricia, you have my sincerest thanks for your help. Come, let us make our way to the sewing rooms now."

Sharon followed her out of the church and down the path toward and past the Round Tower and into the royal apartments. They were almost there when Patricia whispered to her.

"Were you praying for God's forgiveness, then?"

"Forgiveness? For what?" Sharon wondered what she meant.

"For . . . being . . . with Richard all night." The girl stuttered the accusation, obviously not comfortable with the subject matter.

"I prayed for many things, Patricia. Forgiveness was not one of them."

"I did warn you that you should not seek him out."

"Yes, you did. And I think I should have listened to you."

If she had, Sharon never would have seen the birthmark and could have ignorantly given Elizabeth the documents in her possession. That may have been the easier way out for her. Now, Richard's and England's destinies lay in her hands and she wasn't certain she was up to the task of making the right decisions about them both.

"So he did seduce you? What will happen now?"

Sharon knew she was referring to the upcoming wedding that was planned for Lady Seagrave's niece, but Sharon was thinking about everything else.

"I guess what was meant to be will be."

"Come, then," Patricia said, as she took hold of Sharon's hand and pulled her into the door leading to the royal apartments. "You will simply not see him again between now and when you leave for home."

"That sounds like a good idea. Avoidance."

"Would you like to break your fast?" They stopped near the entrance to the dining hall. Sharon could smell the aromas of freshly baked bread and some porridge cooking nearby. Unfortunately, her stomach was not yet recovered from its recent upheavals, so she shook her head and walked on by the room. Soon they arrived where they should be and Sharon took her seat near the window. Picking up her current assignment, she was soon lost in her thoughts.

Avoid him? Was that the way? No. She needed to make a decision about whether or not to give the papers to Richard. How would she explain them? How would she tell him? *Hello, Richard, and, by the way, did you know you should be king of England?* And then what? She would just walk away and hope that the doorway through time would let her pass back to her own century?

There was another problem that she hesitated to acknowledge, for even thinking it was going to make it unavoidable. Maybe she could ignore it for now and deal with it when she was far, far away from here, in her own time and place.

She was in love with the man who should be king. She was in love with the man who could be king if she turned over the evidence she had to him. Feeling as she did about him, how could she just walk away? But if she stayed, the choices were not any better for her. If she held on to the evidence while remaining there, she and Richard could have a life together. He had already asked if she would marry him. Maybe the best course of action would be to hold on to the evidence and try to find the passageway back home. If she couldn't return to her own time, she knew that a part of her would be very happy with Richard here.

There was also a part of her that wondered what would happen if he ever found out the truth and knew that she'd kept it from him. Whether she stayed or returned to her own time, Richard would feel as betrayed by her actions as he now felt by Elizabeth's denial of his petition.

So, what could she do?

The day passed and, as she worked on a new bodice and matching sleeves for a gown, she turned the problem over and over, examining all of her options and all of the possible ways this could go. She came to only one conclusion by the end of the day—it would have been easier if she'd never fallen in love with Richard and if she'd never found out the truth about him. She could have turned over the proof and left. He'd have been somewhat disappointed by her disappearance; she didn't fool herself by trying to believe that he shared her feelings. The man was a good-hearted flirt and she'd fallen for him.

The isolation she saw in his eyes softened her heart toward him. Seeing him look out for young John and watching him yearn for family and a future had pulled her in even deeper. And then to understand his pain, to know that he walked many of the same isolated paths as she did in her own life, well, that just sealed her fate. The passion they shared in the night was a confirmation from Sharon's own soul that it was love.

In the past, when the moment had come to commit physically to a man, she'd found herself unable to do it. She'd only had a few, very few, relationships serious enough to contemplate becoming lovers with someone. Yet, last night, she knew from the bottom of her soul that it was the right time, the right reason, and the right man. Obviously, living over four centuries in the past, charading as someone else, and loving a man who should be king didn't matter to her soul.

There was another possibility that she didn't want to examine. If Richard became king and she was trapped here, they would not have a life together. He would have to marry to secure his own line and to hold on to the throne. An unknown woman, with no family or background—for that's who she'd be once her charade as Lady Seagrave's niece was exposed—could not be a queen to his king. They could be lovers but never share the joys of marriage and family. Sharon knew that she could not live that life. Richard had been clear about creating bastards—he would not, and so that life might be filled with passion, but she would never know the fulfillment of husband and family.

She stood to stretch her legs and arms after sitting for a long time. Walking to the window, she gazed out at the quadrangle and watched the people there hurrying about their business and duties. She pushed open the one pane and breathed in the damp air, enjoying the freshness of it. Clouds now covered the sunny sky of earlier and a fine, misting rain filled the air. The gray day somehow soothed her senses. With such tumultuous feelings inside, the cool, dreary weather comforted her.

They would stop for a short time soon and the afternoon loomed ahead, long and troubled. Although Lady Randall was at Richmond Palace with the queen, the work here never ceased. Things slowed a bit and some of the excitement of the queen's presence was gone, but their tasks were assigned and expected to be completed on time. Lady Cranford was one of Elizabeth's inner circle of "gentlewomen of the privy chamber" and stood in Margaret Randall's stead when she traveled with the queen or when the household moved to another residence for any time.

Sharon had just finished one of the elaborate sleeves of purple and gold velvet when a commotion was heard in the outer chamber. Lady Cranford's voice rose in argument, but a man's lower tones could be heard, too. She looked across the room at the doorway and there he stood. She fought the urge that welled inside her to run to him or to break out in tears.

A few months ago, neither of those choices would have suited her. She snickered as she thought, *Look at me now.* The talk behind her back from other staff members at the museum was that she had no feelings about anything that wasn't a piece of fabric from the Middle Ages. Her all-work-and-no-play attitude came off as arrogant instead of professional, as she'd hoped. Actually nothing she did came off as she wanted from the time she arrived and took over control of the collection. Now, here she was, a bundle of mixed emotions and nerves—and facing the man she loved and would probably lose.

"A word, Mistress Reynolds, if you please?"

His voice rang out in the stunned quiet of the room. Not many men visited here, unless accompanying Elizabeth, and that did not happen often. Sharon looked around and almost laughed out loud at the ping-ponging effect on the women in the room. Back and forth they turned, and their mouths dropped open farther and farther with each turn of their heads. Richard smiled unabashedly at her, seeming to enjoy the reaction they were causing.

She stood and carefully laid the fragile materials on the workbench next to her. Then, without meeting anyone's gaze and especially not Patricia's, she walked to the doorway and followed Richard from the chamber. They passed by an astonished Lady Cranford and took a few steps into the hall.

"My thanks once again, Lady Cranford. The young people will thank you." He doffed his hat and then offered his arm to Sharon. He guided her down the corridor to a small alcove.

"Richard? What is—" she started, only to be interrupted by his signal; a finger to the lips warned her not to argue.

He stepped into the secluded niche and pulled her in behind him. One moment she was stumbling in and in the next he wrapped her in his embrace and captured her mouth in a breathtaking kiss. And, that fast, it was over. Sharon felt as if she were caught in a whirlwind.

"I depart for Richmond this day and wanted to speak to you before I took my leave."

"You go to speak to Elizabeth?"

"Aye, to ask for my father's bequest and for your hand in marriage." He looked at her with sparkling eyes, waiting for her response. She could tell just by the playful expression that he was prepared for any argument she would raise. And she had many she could bring up to him, not the least of which was that fate seemed set against them.

"Richard, please do not ruin your chances of getting your grant from the queen by bringing me into the mix." There, that was the tack she would take.

"I fear you are in the mix, Mistress Reynolds. I will offer Elizabeth the opportunity to rid herself of two troublesome subjects at one time."

A chill ripped through her at his words and she shook at the intensity of it. This was not going to work out, she knew it now through her entire being. This did not bode well for either of them.

"Come now, fear not. I will protect your reputation even as I gain her permission. None will know how we passed the night." He leaned toward her and whispered, "But I cannot forget."

"I am not afraid of my reputation being soiled, Richard. I am afraid for you." She placed her hand on his arm. "Something is going on and I have a very bad feeling about the outcome of it."

If she hadn't been watching his face closely, she would have missed the slight furrow of his brow and suspicious glance he threw her way. She did see it and wondered even more about what distressed him during those dark days earlier this week. What other trouble was swirling around waiting to settle on them?

Then, he pulled her close again and kissed her. Just when she was about to join in the kiss, he released her and stepped back.

"I shall be gone about one week. I will send you word of Elizabeth's answer."

"Richard, I—" He stopped her words with a finger on her lips.

"Fear not, Mistress Reynolds, I will have a care until I see you next."

Before she could say anything else, he turned and strode down the hall, away from her. She offered up a quick and silent prayer that God would protect a fool and returned to the sewing room.

Her faced burned and she was sure that everyone in the room, all the women who now looked at her in open speculation, suspected what passed between her and Richard. His excuse of speaking of John and Patricia was about as transparent as the air around them. Now everyone in the room wondered about her connection to the royal bastard. The embarrassment lasted through most of the day, as she overheard bits and pieces of their conversations.

It was later, much later, as she tossed and turned in her rough bed, that the worst-case scenario came to her. What if she gave Richard the documents, he made a bid for the throne, and Elizabeth prevailed? And, if she couldn't travel back through the doorway to her own time, what would happen to her? Richard would face certain execution as a traitor, if he survived the attempt to take power. Would she face the same fate once it was discovered that she was not Lady Seagrave's niece?

If she could escape, maybe she could find some small town to hide in and make her living as a seamstress. The future loomed before her, shrouded in darkness, and she had no way of knowing which of the scenarios would come to pass. But, as she finally sank into the arms of a fitful sleep, Sharon realized that she had to take the first step and give the documents to either Richard or Elizabeth. Did she love him enough from their short time together to hand them over to him or did she love him too much to put him in the middle of danger and probable death?

How could she decide his fate?

Chapter 24

RICHARD SIGHED IN relief at the note in his hand. Ramirez was ready to see him. He had spent three days waiting for an audience with Elizabeth and a meeting with the Spanish priest. Now, in the space of one morning, both would happen. By tomorrow at this time, he could be back at Windsor . . . and with Sharon.

In just a short time he would be freed of this plot and ready to seek Elizabeth's permission for marriage and his grant. He had never been completely comfortable with his participation and now saw it as a half-hearted attempt to fight the injustice of carrying the title of royal bastard. There would be no proof forthcoming from Ramirez and the others involved. As much as he would like to believe rumor and innuendo, he was and would be illegitimate.

Since meeting Sharon and even more so since their night of shared passion, he felt at ease about that. She was not affected by the truth of his parentage—she had given herself freely to him even knowing he was a bastard. He smiled as he thought back to her attempts to comfort him and the outrageous story she concocted to ease his pain. For the first time in his adult life, he wanted to leave the past behind and seek a new future. With her. Once he concluded this meeting with Ramirez, he would have his private audience with Elizabeth and his chance to make his plea.

He hummed a light tune as he walked down the halls of Richmond Palace looking for the appropriate room. Knocking as he was directed to do, he waited as the door swung open. Stepping in, he nodded at those in the room and approached Miguel.

"I did not expect to see you here, Richard," Miguel began. "I thought we had decided to meet once more at Windsor on the return of the queen?"

"The situation has changed. I needed to speak to you now."

"How so?" Ramirez took him by the arm and guided him to a private corner.

"I am withdrawing my involvement from this . . . situation," Richard answered.

"You think so? Many others are part of this. Your actions put their lives in danger." Miguel's face darkened in anger. "This is not some play we are acting here, Richard. You cannot simply walk on and walk off as you please."

"I will endanger no one any longer. I will not be a part of these plans you hatch against Elizabeth." His own anger grew—he was angry at himself for even becoming part of this and angry at his childhood friend for ever drawing him into it.

"That whore should not be queen!" Miguel's voice rose and the others in the room stopped their own conversations and turned to his.

"And this bastard should be king?" he asked, disregarding their audience.

"You are the rightful king, Richard. The proof is almost within our grasp. Then we will move."

"Nay," he said, holding out his hand toward the Spanish priest. "It ends here, now. There is no proof and I will not seek to remove Elizabeth from our father's seat. I am done."

In the speechless silence of the room, Richard turned and walked toward the door. It was opened for him and he left the room, feeling as though a thousand-pound weight had been lifted from his shoulders.

Now, to see Elizabeth and seek his and Sharon's future.

The antechamber of the presence room was crowded with petitioners and he moved through them and toward the clerk at the door. Nodding here and there to those he knew, Richard settled himself near the entrance so that he was ready. It was a few minutes later when his name was called. He walked into the inner room ready to beg, if necessary, for the right to his land and the right to marry Sharon.

The door closed behind him and the sound of two guardsmen startled him as they positioned themselves between him and the exit. Elizabeth sat before him at a large table with many documents spread out before her. Cecil stood, as always, off to one side behind her. She wore a grim expression before he even spoke his first words of greeting.

"I thought you at Windsor, Richard. What brings you here?" Her voice was as cold as a winter's morn and he noticed that her mouth was drawn in a tight line as she spoke. Fear tickled the back of his neck and crept down his back.

"I come to ask about the provisions of my—our—father's will."

"Do you? Did you never wonder why I refused your grant and sent Lord Cecil to speak to you?" She began to search through some papers as she asked.

"I did wonder, Elizabeth," he began and stopped as she raised her head and glared at his familiar use of her name. "Your Majesty, your pardon."

"Mayhap this will explain, better than any words I could choose, my reasons for denying your request."

She held out several sheets of parchment and he stepped forward to take them from her hand. Cecil also moved forward in what looked like a defensive position. This was truly very strange. He glanced at the words before him and felt his world begin to shatter.

His hands shook and the cold sweat of fear dripped down

his neck and back in an instant of recognizing the document. Unable to take a breath, he read in horror the accounts of his meetings with the Spanish priest and others involved in the plot. Exact conversations were there, as well as plans and names and dates. Richard fought to remain calm in the face of this damning evidence.

"What say you now, brother?"

He raised his gaze to hers and observed her in shocked silence. She knew everything. Whoever had written this was deeply integral to the plot and knew all the main characters, as well as other pertinent and incriminating information. How ironic to face these accusations on the very day when he left it behind him.

"Do you deny knowledge of this plot in your name? Can you deny that you sought to take the throne from me?" Her voice rose until it cracked. She took a deep breath, obviously trying to retain some semblance of a controlled demeanor.

"I deny that I meant you any harm," he began. How could he explain this? He was guilty of treason—of plotting and planning to remove her and take her place. But he never wanted her harmed. Never. Truly, though, how much did that matter? For he knew if he sat on the seat of power he would have to clear those who had a claim from his path.

"What then? Do you think your compatriots would let me live if your plot succeeded? Come now, Richard, bastard you may be, but stupid you are not."

He opened his mouth to deny it but stopped. 'Twas true and they both knew it—only one would survive this, the one on the throne.

"Take him to the Tower. Arrest those on this list"—she handed a paper to Cecil—"for treason against the Crown."

"Bess."

"Speak not to me and call me not by that name!" the queen yelled across the room at him. Cecil started forward but stopped next to her chair.

Richard walked the few steps that separated them. Cecil must have read his intent, for he motioned the guards forward. They took him by the arms just as he reached the table behind which she sat.

"Bess," he started. She would not meet his gaze and continued to look at the papers on the table. "I know you will not believe me now, but I left this plot because I could not live with the thoughts of what would happen to you. I came today to seek a new life, one away from court and this intrigue."

With a wave of her hand, she signaled for them to remove him. Numbed by this turn of events, he did not fight their hold. He allowed them to lead him from the chamber, down the halls and stairs, and out. His eyes would not focus and he fought to retain control as they led him onto a boat that would take him down the Thames to the Tower. Back to the Tower.

His only thought was that he was glad not to have mentioned Sharon. She would have been a suspect, despite her innocence in this, and he was pleased that no suspicion would fall on her. He would have to get word to her somehow. The future, the one that had looked so promising just this morn, was now as murky as the water beneath him.

"I want him held in the Bell Tower."

Cecil knew that the detachment in her voice now was simply her attempt to deal with the crushing pain over her half-brother's betrayal.

"And I want everyone who visits him questioned."

"As you wish, madam," he answered. If he was surprised that she would order him held where she herself had resided for some time, he would not show it. "We will begin questioning him on the morrow."

"Nay!" she yelled as she stood and pushed the papers off the desk and onto the floor. She took one breath and then another and looked at him. "Hold him, that is all."

"But, Your Majesty, he can tell us—"

"Nay, milord. You do not have my leave to do anything but hold him for now."

"As you wish, madam." He kept his own voice in a low monotone. Her mood would change once she saw the other evidence he had about Richard's involvement. There would be plenty of time for some creative questioning in the recesses of the Tower.

"Now, leave me, milord Cecil." She rose and walked to the door leading to her adjoining privy chamber. Turning the knob of the door, she opened it and allowed one of her women into the room. "Tell the clerk that I will see no one else this day. Send them all away."

Nodding, Cecil backed away from her. Turning at the last moment, he tugged open the door and, on his way through the antechamber, whispered something to the clerk. He'd let her have her day of mourning, for he recognized it for what it was. He would round up the rest of them and be done with these traitors who would harm her. By the time she decided what fate Richard would face, he would have everything he needed from him.

The door swung shut with a scraping that made him wince. It was a large room with a sleeping alcove and a window that let in the sun's light. The significance of being assigned to this room and tower was not lost on him. Elizabeth had been held here, during their sister's reign, when she was believed to be part of a plot to overthrow that monarch. Now this was to be his prison cell.

He walked to the window and looked outside. He could see into the outer bailey between the walls surrounding the fortress. At least this room was above the ground and away from most of the dampness of the river. It was, however, devoid of anything meant to make his stay more comfortable. Without the proper coins to smooth the way, it would be a cold, dark, disagreeable stay here.

Word would spread and those not arrested in the first day would make their escapes. Ramirez would seek protection in his connection to the Spanish ambassador and would simply leave England for the time being. Once again and as he always did as a child, Miguel would land on his feet, leaving others to suffer in his stead.

Try as he might, his thoughts returned over and over to Sharon. He had left her with the hope of a future together and now he faced execution. He offered up a prayer that their night together would not bear fruit. His unforgivable lapse in control might result in a babe and now she would have to carry that child and raise it alone. If he knew that to be the case, he would beg Elizabeth to allow him to marry Sharon and give her some protection. Mayhap his grandparents would help her.

He shook his head, trying to distract himself from such terrible thoughts. He needed to remain controlled and calm and assess his position. He faced very large challenges in the next few days and needed his wits about him. The very real possibility of torture loomed ahead of him as Elizabeth's ministers regrouped and sought answers about the width and depth of the plot. Being the linchpin made him a likely target for efforts to weed out more traitors. Did he have the strength to face this?

Rubbing his hands over his face, he wondered what Sharon's reaction would be to the charges. The rumors would quickly fly about the various households of the queen. How could he expect his few friends to stand by him when he was guilty of the crimes of which he was accused? If he were a true friend he would urge them to distance themselves in order to protect their own lives. Only time would tell how this would all turn out.

The idea struck while she walked along the Quadrangle. Her duties for the day were done and she had time before meeting Patricia and John for dinner. Walking around the perimeter of the grounds near the royal apartments relaxed her. Although procrastination was not usually her style, Sharon knew she was doing just that—putting off action by dragging out the decision-making part of it. The tension in the air and the frightening dreams that haunted her last night told her it was time.

There was one thing left to try before she turned the documents over to anyone. She would return to Tenby Manor and try the doorway. She would rather leave Richard behind not knowing the truth than make him face the danger that came with facing his true parentage. More than that—what to do if the doorway failed to work—she couldn't decide at this point.

Now she needed a way to get to Tenby Manor. A wagon or cart would take too long. The trek here had taken the better part of a day, but she did not have that much time to spare. A horse was what she needed. And an escort. The roads were probably not safe for a woman traveling alone. Could she ask John for his help in this? She needed an excuse for not waiting for Richard's return. Walking the length of one side of the building, she thought she might have it.

She'd left a family heirloom behind in her haste to pack and, since it was not in her trunk of clothing, she needed to retrieve it. Word was due any day now from Lady Seagrave about "her" impending marriage and she must find the brooch without delay. Richard would not return for at least four more days and that might be too late.

It was flimsy but if she acted distressed and she cried when telling John, he might believe her. The young man was extremely uncomfortable around a woman's tears. That much she knew from Patricia's words and from his actions the day they all spent outside the castle's walls.

She would speak to him at dinner and gain his agreement. They could set out tomorrow for Tenby Manor. That's when she realized something else she missed from her own time—weather forecasting. It was unnerving not knowing from day to day what to expect from the skies above. She smiled at the little things that bothered her about this time. The big things like lack of modern plumbing and modes of transportation and communication hit her within the first day of being here, but some other creature comforts were missed later. Zippers and underwear and broiled steaks and television and radio . . . and the list went on.

There were some nice things about being in Elizabethan England. She was lucky to be within the royal household and to observe the queen and the day-to-day life within a working palace. Handling and sewing some of the ancient fabrics she'd only heard or read about was another thrill for her. And to meet and see some of the historical figures whose lives changed history was an incredible experience.

But she was ready to go home now and face her problems head-on. No more letting Jasper spread his lies and innuendoes. No more turning away from the uncomfortable situations. She might be younger and less experienced than he, but she knew exactly where she wanted to take the museum's collection and how to improve its quality. At least some good would have come from her time here—she understood now, after watching and listening to the court and its politics, exactly what had happened to her in Chicago.

What was that saying? The more things change, the more they stay the same. Not even four centuries of change had affected the basics of how people worked within political situations, and she would use this newfound information to correct her mistakes and clear her reputation within the museum's own microcosm.

She heard her name being called and looked up to see Patricia approaching. From the expression she wore, Sharon could tell she was distraught.

"Patricia, are you unwell?"

"Nay, Sharon. I had to find you and tell you the news. Have you heard it?" The girl stepped up to her and took her by the arm. Sharon followed her to a nearby bench and sat down next to her.

"Nay, Patricia, I have spoken to no one since we left our rooms. Tell me quickly, what have you heard that is so upsetting?"

"Richard has been arrested."

Sharon shook her head, trying to clear her thoughts and her ears. This could not be correct—Patricia must have misunderstood what she'd heard.

"Aye, Sharon, 'tis true. Today at Richmond Palace. The queen had him arrested on charges of treason."

Treason? That couldn't be correct. Richard had gone to push her to release his land to him, but how could that be treasonous? She didn't realize she was shaking her head at Patricia until the girl nodded back at her.

"One of the grooms returned from there with word of it.

Richard has been charged with trying to overthrow Her Majesty. I cannot believe this, yet the source is reputable and reliable enough."

The world around her stopped; she couldn't hear the birds that had been chirping merrily a moment before or the people around her as they hurried about their duties. A buzzing started within her ears and grew louder, blocking out even Patricia's words. The light around her began to swirl and suddenly she felt as though she was being pulled backward, away from everyone and everything. She reached out to grasp Patricia's hand, but the girl appeared to be at the end of a long, dark tunnel. She couldn't reach her and couldn't even hear her. A moment later, she couldn't see her either. One second the world had been normal and then, one second later, normal disappeared. Sharon felt the blood rush out of her head and hoped someone would catch her as she fell.

Chapter 25

THE WHISPERS BROKE through her stupor first. Then a noxious smell made her nasal passages burn and itch and she sneezed in reaction to it. Opening her eyes, she recognized Patricia, John, and Robert. She reached up to rub her face and was assisted in sitting up on the bench. Patricia pressed a handkerchief into her hand and she used it to wipe her face.

"It can't . . . it cannot be true. You must all know that," she argued. Their faces said that they believed otherwise.

"Mistress Reynolds, I fear this is too serious not to be true," Robert answered.

"Robert, Master Calder, you are his friend. Surely you do not believe this?"

His guilty expression said he did. And she caught another look on his face. Knowledge. Robert knew more about this. He knew the charges were true.

"Tell me then the truth of it."

Robert looked as though he would argue and then nodded. Before speaking to her, he asked Patricia and John to go ahead of them into the dining hall. The two younger people looked as though they would refuse, but hesitated only a moment before complying.

"What know you of Richard's background?" He sat next to her and watched her closely.

"I know he is Henry the Eighth's son. Is that what you mean?"

"Aye. So you have heard the gossip, then?"

"Not gossip, Robert. Richard told me himself."

"I am glad you have spoken of it with him. That is the root of all his troubles." He leaned back against the bench.

She was confused. How did charges of treason arise from Richard being the king's illegitimate son? "How so, Robert?"

"There are some who believe he is more than a bastard son."

She gasped at his words. She looked over his shoulder, not daring to meet his gaze and give herself and her own knowledge away. Others believed him the rightful king?

"Who believes this? I still don't understand."

"There are those who are not satisfied with Elizabeth as queen. Some in the old faith wish to see it reestablished and rumors of a true son of Henry have swirled around the court for years. Lately, Richard has been listening too closely to those rumors."

"Is he? Is he the true heir to Henry's throne?" She held her breath as she waited for his answer.

"Some say so but no proof has been forthcoming. Richard has been torn between being faithful to Elizabeth and seeking proof of his legitimacy."

The world began to spin again and she swayed with dizziness. Robert grabbed her by her arm and shoved that horrible smelling vial under her nose again. One sniff and she felt her head begin to clear.

"Is this the treason, then? To seek proof of his true parentage?" she whispered to him. So many thoughts filled her mind. The undiscovered proof, the rumors, the documents she hid in her trunk. Fate, it seemed, was not willing to wait for her to make up her mind. It forced her hand now.

"Not to seek the truth, but to seek to overthrow Elizabeth is. 'Tis said that Cecil found much proof of Richard's complicity in a plot to remove his royal sister from her throne."

Robert stopped in his explanation and looked around them. A few others walked by and he waited for them to be alone before continuing.

"He is being held in the Tower of London to await questioning and a trial."

"I must go to him," she said, standing and turning to him. "Can you take me to him?"

Sharon knew what she had to do. Any doubts melted away as she realized the precarious position in which Richard found himself. He was a dead man without the documents she held. He might still not survive this, but at least with the proof of his legitimacy in his control, he had more to say about it than one of these shadowy conspirators. She could not take the chance and delay in turning over the packet—traveling back to Tenby Manor to try to find her way home was not an option any longer.

In that instant she'd found the answer to the question that had haunted her for days—she loved him enough to risk her return to her own world in order to at least try to save him in his.

Robert did not answer her so she pressed the point. "Will you take me to him, Robert?"

"Mistress Reynolds, I think it not a good and sensible idea to seek him out in the Tower."

"We—I—have no choice, Robert. I must see him as soon as possible. It is a matter of life and death and I cannot stand by and watch him face certain death. I ask you once more, as his friend, will you take me to him?" She clenched her jaws together, gritting her teeth as she waited for his answer. She thought he would refuse until she noticed a slight glimmer in his eyes.

"You would present yourself at the very gates of hell for him, would you not?"

"Mayhap not hell, Robert, but certainly the gates of the Tower."

He let out his breath and nodded at her. She smiled at his agreement, but he held up a hand to her.

"You cannot simply walk up to the guardhouse and ask to see him."

"I cannot?" she asked, wondering how it could be done.

"No, not Mistress Sharon Reynolds. But young John Calder, Richard's servant, could enter to see to his master's needs."

She frowned at him for a moment until his plan became clear to her. She would masquerade as Richard's servant and gain entry to his cell in the Tower. Then she could give him the papers to use as he wanted. Sharon stood and waited for Robert to rise. She would go and pack her things so they could leave.

"We will leave at first light in the morning. Meet me at the stables." Robert began to walk away before she said anything.

"I would like to go now. It is important that I reach him as soon as possible."

"Nay. If we leave now, there will be much speculation about our own involvement. Let those around us see us in the dining hall and about our business. We can go by boat in the morning down the Thames and reach the Tower late in the day."

She would have argued, but he ended the conversation by walking away. The men in this time did not give the same respect to women as in her day. Of course she already recognized that at some level, but Robert's manner, and Richard's for that matter, reflected the customs of the day—women should listen to and obey their men.

If obeying Robert got her in to see Richard, she would do it gladly. She just hoped they would be in time.

It wasn't, she decided, very bright at first light. Or warm, either. She wrapped her cloak tighter around her shoulders and hurried her pace toward the stables. Under her cape, she held a leather knapsack closely. She would need the valuable contents once she had the opportunity to speak to Richard. A dress, a packet of parchment sheets, her glasses, a few coins. All of them would be needed not only to save Richard's life but also to help her back home.

Reaching the stables, she looked around for Robert. Not finding him waiting outside, she tugged on the door and entered. The smells of horses and hay surrounded her as she made her way down one row of stalls. She heard a noise and spun around to see its source. Robert stood nearby, motioning for her to follow. She did and soon stood before the room where she and Richard had spent the night. She felt her cheeks and face heat up and caught sight of a faint smile on Robert's face. He waited for her to enter and closed the door behind them.

"Here, change quickly into these. John is readying some horses for us to use to get to the river." Robert handed her a small bundle and opened the door again. "We have not much time, so . . ." Even though he left his sentence unfinished, she got the point.

After removing her outer cloak and knapsack, she loosened the clothes and examined what was there. Robert had provided her with breeches, a shirt, a leather jacket, and a cap. Sharon untied her skirt and bodice and shrugged out of them. Leaving on her own chemise and stockings, she pulled on the breeches and found them a few sizes too big. The shirt and jacket were too large as well. Then she untied the end of her braid and ran her fingers through her hair. Bending over, she first gathered it on top of her head and then, standing up, she let some hang down. Tugging the cap as far down on her head as possible, she used its position to keep her hair in place. Her hand was on the knob when Robert knocked softly. His expression when she opened the door told her she'd been successful at hiding her identity.

"Whose clothes are these?" she asked as they left the building and headed for the yard.

"John's. And he is none too pleased about having a woman wear them." Robert's voice lightened and now carried a tone of amusement in it.

"Tell him I will make him a new set in exchange for these." The offer was made in good faith, but Sharon didn't know if she would ever return here to make good of it.

"Come now and try to walk like a man."

Robert led the way once more and soon they were back outside in the cool morning air. She shivered at the crisp-ness of it. She'd left her cloak behind, for it was clearly a woman's. Shifting the knapsack on her back, she lowered her head and followed.

John stood at the side of one yard checking the saddles and the tightness of the girth straps under the two horses he had readied. He did not speak when they approached; only a nod of his head denoted his recognition. He held the horses steady as they mounted and then waited for further instructions from his father.

"John, please give your cloak to Mistress Reynolds or she will freeze by the time we reach the river."

She was unable to control her shivering and was thankful for the heavy wool cape—even if it only reached her knees. Soon they were on their way out the gate and through the village to the Thames. After a few stops for provisions and by the time the sun had actually risen, they were boarding a boat that would take them down the river to London.

When Robert dipped into a pocket and took out a few coins, she started to reach for her sack. The purse that Lady Randall had given her all those weeks before was in it.

"Nay." Robert stopped her. "Save your coins. Richard will have need of them in the Tower."

"Richard will?" she asked as they took a place near the railing while the small barge prepared to leave the dock.

"Aye, to purchase small comforts and bribe the guards."

She blinked in surprise. Sharon remembered about prisoners buying supplies in order to survive in prisons in this time, but Robert's easy admission of corruption among the guards startled her.

"He will not be able to bribe them to allow his escape, but a few coins placed wisely will encourage them to look aside for visitors."

"Like me?"

"Nobles are permitted their servants. Other . . . visitors are admitted from time to time." Robert's face had turned a darker shade of red, so she knew from his discomfort exactly what kind of visitors he meant.

Women . . . prostitutes.

His embarrassment took a few minutes to pass and she

used the time to sightsee. The barge set off and soon Windsor Castle came into view to the south. Sharon couldn't take her eyes from it. The Thames turned and twisted and the hours passed by. The sun burned away the morning fog and still they journeyed on. Twice they ate from the foods and supplies that Robert carried in his own sack.

She was astounded, looking at the banks of the river. The changes that she'd observed before coming to this time and now were incredible. Without cars and powerboats along and in the river, the trip was quieter than she expected. The voices of the other passengers and the occasional calls from one barge to another were the most frequently heard sounds. The journey moved swiftly and the landscape began to transform from country to city.

Now, more boats and barges of different sizes crowded the river. Docks sprang out from both sides of the Thames. Buildings and roads came closer and closer to the banks. The air around them took on a hazy appearance and a smell that she'd not noticed before became stronger and stronger. Her face must have shown her confusion, for Robert laughed at her.

"You have not traveled to London before?" he asked, now staring at the city spreading out before them.

"I . . . no, I have not," she answered, after deciding that it was easier to come as a stranger to the city than try to explain how it had appeared when she was last there.

" 'Tis not quite as fragrant as near Windsor. Here now, shall I point out some of the places whose names you may recognize?" At her nod, he began. He showed her several palaces and royal residences along the river. The Thames turned to the right, or east, and not too far off in the distance stood London Bridge. Soon they were passing under it and Sharon was amazed to see dozens of houses along the bridge.

"Luck was with us. We caught the tide going out or we might have had to disembark and walk the bridge."

"May luck stay with us for the rest of the day, Master Calder."

He nodded and turned back to the river, watching as they

approached one of the docks just east of the bridge.

"Will you be in danger or trouble for doing this?"

"Bringing you to him?"

"Yes."

"Nay, I think not. I am on leave from my duties and gone to visit my ailing sister in London for a few days."

She just smiled at him and gathered her belongings together. During the trip, she'd managed to avoid thinking about what was to come. How Richard would react when she turned over the papers to him was the biggest question. But she had to come up with a way to tell him the truth first. Could she tell him where and when she came from? Or should she try another explanation? There wasn't much time to plan her approach, for she could see the Tower sitting east of the dock. A few blocks' walk and they would be there.

They left the barge and it wasn't long before her legs became accustomed to the solid surface beneath her feet. Robert took the lead and she lowered her face so that no one would look too closely at her. The late afternoon sun aided her, its light fading and throwing shadows across streets.

Robert did not walk in the direction of the prison, but led her north into the busy streets. When she tugged on his sleeve, he turned to her.

"We have a stop to make before we go to the Tower. Come along now."

She did not argue. Although the tension within her was building with each passing minute, she tried to be patient. Robert had proven himself Richard's friend. She would try it his way. Soon they stood before a pub, the Wild Boar, according to the sign swinging over its door. Robert opened that door and entered the main room. Without hesitating, he led her up a stairway and into a small room off to the side. Puzzled, she waited to hear his explanation.

"There is a privy through that door. I think you must have great need of it?"

"Thank you so much, Robert. I do, I do!"

"I will await you downstairs." He blushed again and left

the room, pulling the door securely closed behind him.

Sharon ran into the next room, loosening the breeches as she moved. She'd purposely not had much to drink because of the lack of privacy on the barge. There was a pot to use, but since she was dressed as a man, it would've looked strange for her to use it. The men simply turned their backs, opened their breeches, and used the flowing river as their urinal. That option was not for her either. Within a few minutes, she felt very relieved.

Adjusting her clothes and hat, she retraced her steps and found Robert sitting at a table near a large hearth. He waved her into a seat and pushed a bowl and plate in front of her. The enticing aromas made her mouth water. A day of eating only pieces of cheese, some hard bread, and some cider created a strong hunger in her. Without a word, she picked up the spoon and devoured the serving of stew, the hot loaf of bread, and the small roasted bird. She looked up into Robert's amused face.

"I did not realize how hungry I was." She lifted the cloth napkin and wiped the gravy from the corners of her mouth.

"You did not eat much during the trip; I thought you might have an appetite now."

"When do we go to the Tower?" she asked quietly.

"In another hour or so. The guards will change for the night and there will be less chance of an extended inspection at that time. Take your ease for now."

She leaned back and washed her meal down with some ale. She'd asked for water, but the horrified look on the serving woman's face warned her that something was wrong with that idea. Robert then told her of the dangers of drinking the water here in London. Although the ale did not taste too strong, she limited herself to one cup of it.

The hour passed quickly and Robert soon rose from his seat and tossed some coins down on the table. They left the pub and walked back toward the river. It was much darker now and a pervading dampness filled the air around them. The skin on the back of her neck was covered with goosebumps as they came closer and closer to the river and the prison.

"How do we enter?"

"We will enter through the Middle Tower."

"Do we walk in or take a boat?"

"Only prisoners and the queen use the Water Gate. Visitors walk in through the Middle Tower and over the moat."

Sharon kept looking at the impressive structure as they approached it. She'd visited it before. The Crown Jewels of England were kept there as well as some priceless tapestries, and she had attended a private showing of both. But the modern Tower of London and this one were very different—this one was a working prison, holding many unfortunates within its towers and cells. The one she was familiar with was a wonderful museum and housed a world-famous collection of artifacts from England's past eras.

Robert led her up to the guardhouse and waited in line behind some others. The flow of people did not seem to slow with the coming of night. Soon, it was their turn and she held her breath as Robert spoke to the guards.

"Who goes there?" the guard asked in a loud voice.

"I bring Master Granville's servant to tend to his needs."

"And this is?" The guard moved closer and looked her over from head to toe and back again. She lowered her eyes so their gazes would not meet and she slumped to make the clothes even baggier and her woman's figure less apparent.

"John Calder," she answered in a low, husky voice, still not raising her eyes to his.

"And what do you bring to your master? What is in the sack?" He moved to the side and started to lift the knapsack. She looked over at Robert for help. A woman's clothes would not be easy to explain. Robert reached into his pocket and drew out a few coins. Casually holding it out to the guard, he whispered, "Here is something for your trouble this night."

The guard paused and looked from her to Robert before opening his own palm and catching the money. He stepped back and ordered them to pass into the prison. Their encounter at the second guardpost went about the same, a bribe easing their way in. Passing through the Middle

Tower, over a drawbridge, and through the Byward Tower, they were soon escorted to the Bell Tower further in and to their left. It was difficult to stay calm in the oppressive atmosphere of the Tower.

She shook nervously as they walked on through the entrance to the Bell Tower and then up to its second floor. After pounding on it several times, another guard slid a large metal key into the lock on the only door in the narrow hallway. She jumped with each noise and she strained to see inside the cell from the hall.

"Your servant has arrived, Master Granville."

She waited, the tension becoming unbearable. Was he injured? Had he been tortured for information or for punishment? A moment passed and then another before she heard movements within the cell. She fought to control her emotions—it would be unseemly for a manservant to cry. That would endanger him even more, so she took a couple of deep breaths and tried to relax.

The guard unlocked the door and pushed it open. Motioning to her to enter, she nodded and took a step into the room. Robert stopped and exchanged a few words with the guard as she finally saw Richard for the first time.

His shirt was unlaced at his neck and pulled free of his breeches. His hair hung loose down his back and over his shoulders. He had not shaved in a few days and had a beard's shadow to prove it. And he looked wonderful to her. Fighting the urge to run and throw herself in his arms, she cleared her throat several times before speaking.

"Master Granville, art well?" Tears burned her eyes as she looked at him. At least she saw no blood or bruises or other evidence that he'd been mistreated while being held here. But Richard looked past her and at Robert.

"Robert, I did not request young . . ."

"John," Robert filled in the name.

"John. I did not request young John's services here. Take him back with you to Windsor."

"Richard, I fear I cannot do that. He wishes to serve you even here. Allow him a chance to fulfill your needs."

She was just beginning to hear the sarcastic humor in their voices when the guard interrupted.

"Are you both staying the night here or just the boy?"

"I leave now, Richard. I will return in the morning to see how the boy has carried out his duties." With a nod, Robert threw his sack at Richard and left the cell.

Richard closed his mouth and clenched his jaw. She could see the muscles in his neck and face tighten as Robert left the cell and the guard locked the door. Their footsteps echoed through the cell and only when the door at the bottom of the stairs slammed shut did he look at her.

"By God's eyes, Mistress Reynolds, what do you call this game?"

Chapter 26

HE WANTED TO throttle her and kiss her all at the same time. She stood before him dressed as a lad, a servant, and all he could see in her eyes was concern for him . . . and love, too. He watched as she looked him over once more, obviously searching for injuries. He balled his fists and let his arms hang at his sides as she inspected him. When her gaze turned from worried to something much more provocative, his body responded quickly.

He crossed the room in a few long strides and pulled her into his embrace. She gasped as he took her chin in his hand, leaned her head back, and took possession of her mouth. Over and over he kissed her, his tongue plunging into her warm mouth and tasting her. She swayed and he wrapped her firmly within his arms and continued the kiss. He could not, he would not ever get enough of this woman.

Pressing against her, he moved her back, step by step, until he reached his bed. Then, tugging off her cloak and pulling the ridiculous-looking cap from her head, he tangled his hands in her hair as it fell in waves around her shoulders. He leaned down once more, and this time, as he kissed her, he drew her down on top of him on the bed. It was when he tasted the saltiness of her tears that he finally reined in his desire for her.

She knelt straddling his hips, crying. The tears dripped onto his chest and stomach and soon soaked through his shirt. He sat up, took her in his embrace, and drew her down beside him, rubbing her back and whispering soothing words to calm her down. After a few minutes he could feel that she was not crying anymore.

"Are you well, Richard?" she asked in a voice roughened by her tears.

"I am well. I am also overwhelmed by your presence when I thought that I would never see you again."

"I had to come." She sniffled a few times and wiped her eyes to remove the remaining tears. "When I heard the news, I knew you could not be guilty of treason."

He wanted to laugh out loud at her belief in his innocence. The one thing he was guilty of and she thought him blameless.

He turned to face her and almost backed away from telling her the truth. She had risked much by coming here; he owed her at least an explanation of the situation. And, since he wanted her protected, she would have to leave here in the morning and never return.

"Sharon," he started, as he smoothed her hair back from her face. "I would like to tell you differently but 'tis the truth of it. I did conspire to take the throne from Elizabeth."

Her face lost all its color and if she had not been lying next to him, she would have fallen. Shock warred with disbelief as he watched her battle within herself to accept his words.

"But, treason, Richard? Why? How? You spoke of a future for yourself before you left. You wanted your inheritance and you were going to speak to Elizabeth about it. Did you threaten her somehow and they have misunderstood it?"

"There was no mistaking my actions. One man has been tortured already to prove my alliance with a plot to remove Elizabeth."

She sat up and moved back a bit, her gaze wary of his words.

"You plotted with others?" She dragged her hair behind her ears and pushed the mass of it behind her shoulders. Sitting in that cross-legged position that drove him mad with lust, she waited for his explanation.

"There are many who believe that she is not fit to rule. That the old church should be raised again. That a king is better for the realm than a queen."

He thought back to the story she had told him—the one with the woman in charge of part of a college. Ludicrous! Everyone knew, even the Church of England and the Roman Church, that men ruled over women, in every way and with complete power. From the disgruntled look on her face, he knew that Mistress Reynolds did not hold that belief.

"One of those who seeks a change is an old family friend who now works for the Spanish ambassador."

"Dark hair, dark eyes? Shifty-looking?"

"Father Ramirez would object to being described as 'shifty-looking.' "

"Father? He is a priest?"

"Yes, and I believed his promises and his assertions. I took rumors to heart and let myself believe that I was more than a royal bastard. I wanted to believe their words about proof of my legitimacy."

"He has proof?" she asked as her face became even paler than a moment before.

"He *promised* proof, but somehow the proof has never materialized. 'Twas my intent to seek the throne if the proof was presented to me."

She looked at him through horrified eyes as her mouth dropped open.

"I know what you must think. I am truly an ingrate to have chosen this path. Only a wretch would try to remove his own half-sister from her seat in power."

"What were you thinking?" she asked in a whisper, her voice straining and filled with some emotion.

He stood now and walked to the window, unable to meet

her haunted gaze. 'Twas obvious that she was disgusted by him now. She came here thinking him innocent of these charges and now he had confessed his guilt to her. Resting his hands on the bars across his window, he leaned his head there, too, and peered into the darkness outside.

So, he had lost it all. His longing to be recognized as a true son of Henry, his desire for his rightful place on the throne, and his contemptuous attempt to gain that seat had destroyed the possibilities of any happiness in his life. If he had a life a week from now.

And he had lost her. Sharon had come to him with love in her eyes, hoping to hear him proclaim his innocence. Instead, he had ravaged any of the plans he had talked to her about, had encouraged her to believe in. Even as he had planned a future with her at his side, he had been acting to block that same future.

What would she be left with if Elizabeth executed him as a traitor? He would send her to his grandparents. The irony of it made him smile, though without amusement. Just as they had raised the bastard son of their daughter, now he would ask them to raise any bastard he left behind.

Turning away from the window, he answered her question, repeating to her the same thoughts that had ruminated in his mind for weeks and months before becoming clear. The night spent together in the stables clarified much in his own mind. She sat motionless on the bed, not meeting his gaze.

"Have you ever wanted something so much that you would give anything to have it within your grasp?" She nodded at him and he continued. "All I ever wanted in this life was to be an equal with my other siblings. I wanted to be accepted as Henry's son. Not as a by-blow, but as someone worthy of their respect and attention. Instead, because of an incident over which my mother or I had no control, I was the bastard.

"I naively thought that, when he brought me to live and be educated and raised with his other children, I was one step away from that recognition. Since each of his daughters had at one time or another been labeled the same, I thought my time would come, too.

"At his death, I waited for his will to declare for me. I was older than Edward, I was just as educated and just as worthy. The bequest he made to me was generous for a bastard son, but I wanted more. I wanted his acceptance."

He looked at her. Dear God in heaven, she was crying. Tears ran silently down her cheeks from eyes filled with misery. Not pity—he would not have handled that very well. This was genuine sorrow for what would never be.

"I wish I was worthy of your tears, Sharon. I was more devastated by the provisions of his will than by his death, which says much for my own arrogance and self-seeking ways. Then, for many years, I forced myself to be satisfied with only the grant of land. I had always had a touch with the horses and decided to turn my talents to that. After a few shaky years, as the throne moved from sister to sister and from Catholic to Anglican, I settled into my position within the royal household. I was the real Master of the Horse for the House of Tudor."

He paused in his telling and walked over to the table near the hearth. Lifting a metal pitcher, he poured a cup of ale for himself. Looking in her direction, he saw her shake her head against any for her. Swallowing once and again, he let the cool liquid slide down his dry throat.

"And what changed that, Richard?" she asked, wiping her eyes with a small handkerchief she retrieved from her pocket.

"Father Miguel Ramirez. His assignment to the court when the Spanish ambassador arrived meant I would see an old friend." She frowned at his words, most likely trying to figure out how a Spaniard and Englishman could be friends of long-standing. "My nurse was from Spain; she came here with Katherine of Aragon. Maria also knew the Ramirez family as well from her work as a midwife. When Miguel arrived, he renewed that link with me even though Maria had died years ago."

If he had thought her pale before, her coloring faded even more now. Had he said anything, other than this whole sordid tale, to upset her? Mayhap she was overtired from her journey from Windsor. Mayhap she'd not eaten yet? Or mayhap she was just disgusted by his story of greed for power?

"Art well? You look nigh to fainting. Sharon?" He walked to her and offered his cup to her. "Drink this."

She did not refuse his offer, but drank it down in one long swallow. Wiping her mouth with the back of her hand, she gave him the cup back. He thought she did not like ale and so this easy acceptance puzzled him. Of course her arrival here had taken him completely by surprise so anything she did should not.

"When did he involve you in this plot?" She rose from the bed and walked to the window. Leaning her face close to the open bars, she breathed in deeply of the damp air that surrounded the Tower. He waited for her to turn to him, but she did not.

"A few months ago, he carefully mentioned the rumors of a legitimate male heir to Henry's throne. Once he had my attention, his intriguing and ambiguous words drew me in. His vague promises called to the one inside me who yearned to be that heir. I confronted my grandparents about this possibility and that is when they shared with me their own private hell. The guilt they felt over turning their daughter away when she needed them most was terrible indeed.

"In spite of the standing they would gain if I was recognized as legitimate, they assured me it could not be true and that any proof produced by Miguel would be tainted and untrue."

"And you believed them?" she asked, still not turning from her place at the window.

"I do. Miguel then increased the pressure. He promised the evidence would be delivered to my hands soon. I had begun to have many misgivings about proceeding in this. I was most bothered by the thought of what would happen to Elizabeth if, after the claim was substantiated, I prevailed and took the throne."

"Death?"

He shook his head. "Death. 'Twould be the only way to keep anyone loyal to her from seeking to raise her once more to it. When that finally sunk into my poor, confused brain, I knew I must disavow any participation in the plotting. And one more thing occurred to make me realize that I had dreams of my own to live for."

She looked at him and he smiled at her as he took one step then another toward her. When they were close enough to touch, he stopped.

"You, Mistress Reynolds. You came crashing into my life at Tenby Manor and there has been no stopping you since."

"Me? How did I make you change your mind about what Miguel promised you?"

"You were so fresh to the court, so new and unaffected. So . . . different. I had lost all appetite for setting up a household of my own with any of the women I knew from court. I wanted what Lord and Lady Christopher have, but until you appeared I had no hope of finding it."

She finally met his gaze. He reached out and took her hand in his, entwining their fingers. Lifting their joined hands to his lips, he pressed a kiss on her knuckles. The action pulled her closer to him.

"Theirs is a love match, made for all the wrong reasons, and yet, it has brought them the greatest of joy together. I hesitate to speak of it since you are already betrothed to another and since I have no say over my life or death. I find that I, too, would wish to marry the woman I love."

Her lip trembled and she looked as if she would cry again. He opened his arms to her and she stepped into his embrace.

"I would offer you my love. I fear I have nothing more to offer than that. I do not know what may come our way in the next days and weeks, but I would suffer what comes better knowing that I have pledged my love to you as you have to me."

She lifted her face to him and he pressed his lips to hers. Suddenly the need to join with her, the urge to be part of her even if for the last time, and the desire to celebrate their love in this physical way overwhelmed him.

"I want you now, Sharon. I want to be in you so deeply that I will feel your breathing and you mine. Please? Let me love you?"

"Oh, Richard," she whispered into his mouth, for he had not waited for an answer to his plea.

Their tongues mated even as his hands skimmed over the ill-disguised curves beneath a man's clothing. His desire was apparent quickly and her body responded to his touch. Reaching around behind her, he tugged on the laces that held the breeches tight at her waist. Once loosened, he pushed them down off her hips and let them slide to the floor. Then he made quick work of ridding her of the leather jacket, the shirt, and her boots. Soon she stood before him in just her stockings and chemise, and that was sheer enough that he could see the dark triangle of curls at the apex of her thighs and the tight buds on her breasts.

He bent down and lifted her into his arms. Walking to the bed, he laid her down among the pillows. As she watched, he removed his clothes. Her eyes moved boldly over him and his body strengthened in its response to the heated looks. By the time he was ready to lie next to her, his erection was blatant . . . and she never looked away. He knelt on the bed and leaned over her, taking her mouth in a ravishing kiss. She reached up to draw him closer and soon they writhed together in passion.

When he had finally teased and tempted and touched her to the brink of her peak, he knew that he would find true satisfaction for the first time in his life in this joining. As he thrust into her welcoming heat and heard her cries of arousal, he knew he was no longer alone. He had found his mate, the woman who would be the love of his life.

Unfortunately, it did not look to be a long life ahead of him.

Chapter 27

SHE WAS MAKING a complete fiasco out of this.

Sharon lay facing away from Richard in the bed, looking out the window toward the river and freedom. How had she let this get so far out of control?

She understood being overcome with emotion when Richard declared his love for her—those were words and a sentiment she'd waited too long to hear to not be moved by them. They made love then, and she experienced such a feeling of belonging together that it made her eyes burn with unshed tears. The second and third times, however, she could not explain rationally. Even knowing that they took no precautions to prevent conception did not give her the strength to refuse him.

Now she wanted to cry for all the time they would not have together. For, even if he made it out of this predicament alive, he would probably never want to see her again. Part of her still did not want to give him the evidence she brought back. She was being completely selfish in one way and completely protective in another.

If he took and used the documents, and lived, he was lost to her. And, since she still didn't know if she could return to her own time, she could be facing a life, stuck in the past, without him. If he used the proof to claim his throne, he would probably be killed. Elizabeth was far too entrenched and far too popular with the people for Richard to find it an easy path. So giving him the packet would be like giving him the means to his own destruction.

She thought she'd made this decision already, but when the deed was about to be done, it was much harder than she thought it would be. The one thing she did not want to face was his anger and disappointment when he found out that she really was here looking for the son of Henry. Sharon knew that many before her had been drawn to him for that alone, and the cynicism he showed to the world was the result of being an object and not a person.

Once she started her story, she doubted he would believe much of what she said anyway. She would tell him the whole truth about her presence here. In her satchel, she had some of the loose change she'd carried back in her pocket—the dates engraved on them might help convince him. She would show him her glasses. She'd let no one see them up close, since they too were unlike any that might be found here. The fine springs and hinges as well as the progressive bifocal lenses were too modern to pass off as the spectacles they had in this time.

Although those items may cause him to open his mind, he would believe her wild-and-crazy story only if he trusted her. And, she wasn't sure if their love, new and untested, could withstand something of this magnitude.

The sun's light grew stronger; rays of it cascaded through the bars and spread over them. She knew it was time. Slipping from his embrace, she collected her clothes from the other part of the room and dressed as Richard's servant once more. She opened the knapsack and took out the dress, glasses, coins, and the parchment sheets. Laying them on the small table next to the bed, she sat on the edge and thought about how to explain this to him. She was so wrapped up in her own thoughts she wasn't paying attention to him. His hand creeping up her thigh was the first indication that he was awake.

"You look as though you carry the weight of the world

on your shoulders," he said in a voice still roughened by sleep. "Come back to bed and I promise to help you forget whatever troubles you." His hand moved higher on her leg, sliding easily between since she wore the breeches and not the usual skirts of a woman.

She stood and moved out of his reach. If she did not do this now, she would lose her nerve and her chance to give him back his life.

"Richard, we must talk and then I must leave."

"You must leave today and not come back here, on that we agree."

She frowned at him, not understanding his meaning. "What do you mean?"

"I have thought this through and there is only one thing to do. You must seek out my grandparents and take refuge with them. They will protect you and"—he paused and cleared his throat before continuing—"if there is a child, they will help you raise it."

Her hand moved of its own volition to her stomach as if she would feel some proof there. A baby was possible, but she could not even contemplate all those problems now.

"I will ask Elizabeth to permit us to wed so that there will not be another Tudor bastard. I will also ask her to send you to Tenby Manor to live."

"Tenby Manor?"

"Aye. 'Tis my grandparents' estate. They will keep you safe there."

No wonder Richard was so familiar there—it was his boyhood home. How had she missed that little tidbit of information? And what else had she missed in this time travel–induced fog in which she'd lived since arriving here? This was getting more difficult by the minute. She needed to get moving.

"Richard, do you remember the day we went to Lord Christopher's estate and I asked you about Henry's son?" At his nod, she added, "And I told you I had made a mistake in asking about any living sons."

"Aye, I remember it. What has that to do with us making arrangements for your protection?"

"I could not tell you then, Richard—actually I did not know at that time that you were the son of Henry I sought."

His face began to harden as she watched. He sat upright in the bed and gazed at her with questioning eyes.

"For what reason, then, did you seek me out?" Even his voice grew cold. He was so accustomed to being used that he was preparing himself for the hurt already. Her heart ached for him and she knew it would get worse before she finished.

"I had information to give to the son of Henry who has a birthmark on his left hip." His hand went to that hip and she continued her story. "I'd been sent—"

"Who sent you?" he yelled, standing suddenly before her. "Do you spy for Spain or for the Pope?"

"I'm not certain how I came to be here, but I bring you proof of your true parentage, Richard. I have it here."

"How did you come by this proof you say you have? You let me spill out the whole story about Miguel and his plot last night—did you already know of it because you are party to it?"

"Wait, Richard. This is not coming out correctly."

"So you have your story confused—mayhap that is why women should never be spies? You lose your concentration after a night of vigorous bedplay? Your benefactors should have sent someone more practiced in the sexual arts."

She turned her back on him and walked a few steps away. She could not lose control and could not let his hurtful words wound her. But they did. He thought her a spy and a whore and accused her of sleeping with him to accomplish her assignment. A strong sense of déjà vu swept over her.

"The story I told you about the young woman who worked for the college was a true story about me, Richard. I am not Lady Seagrave's niece and I did not come from Lancaster in England." She allowed the soft British accent that she'd faked for so long slip now and her true voice came through.

"Then who are you and what is this about?" His voice was lower this time, but the softer volume of it did not denote any less anger. He stood, hands fisted at his sides and jaws clenched, waiting for her words.

"My name is Sharon Reynolds and I am from a city called Chicago. It is in the center of the place you probably call the 'New World.' " She looked at him and caught his gaze. "I work as a textile and fabric expert in the Museum of Chicago's Historical collection."

"Museum?" he asked.

"It is a place where artifacts are studied and displayed for the public. My job is—was—to oversee the collection."

"What kind of jest is this? You would have me believe you come from a place unknown to me in the center of the New World? 'Tis obviously a tale created by a spy who has been discovered."

"It is worse than that, Richard."

"How so?" He lifted one eyebrow in an arrogant challenge to her.

"I come from Chicago in the New World, but I live in the twenty-first century."

She waited for his reaction and it did not take long. He laughed out loud, a raucous, forced laughter that filled the room and jarred her nerves. He did not think this was funny. He just couldn't believe it was true.

"I was on vacation, on a visit, in England when a trunk of clothes were found during the renovation of a Tudor manor. Tenby Manor was the site of the work and I came to examine the find."

He'd stopped laughing and just stared at her with a blank look. This was too much for him to accept, but she must finish and get herself to the manor.

"I was looking at one of the dresses—this one." She pointed to the carefully folded dress on the table. "One of the seams was loose and when I tugged on the thread, a packet of parchment sheets came out." She lifted the documents that were still folded and wrapped as she'd found them. "I could not resist the pull to read them, even though, as a scientist, I knew they needed to be examined under better conditions than the priesthole."

He paled at her mention of the priesthole. His grandparents were responsible for that hidden room, she now realized, and he knew of its existence.

"Once I read these, I was overwhelmed with the unfair hand dealt to one son of Henry who thought he was a bastard, but was trueborn of Henry and his queen, Anne Boleyn."

"You are crueler than I thought possible, Mistress Reynolds. To have listened to my innermost thoughts and confessions last evening, and then to use them against me this morn. How like a woman!"

She tried to remember that he was overwhelmed now. Ignoring his mean words and understanding where they came from, she went on with her story.

"Richard, I will leave these with you to use as you please. I am sorry that I did not give them to you when I first realized who you were."

"You have known and not revealed this to me? For how long?"

"The morning after we made love the first time in the stables. I saw the birthmark as I left the room."

"Speaking of that night—you were a virgin. Is the real niece? Did you murder her so that you could take her place?"

She gasped, shocked that he thought her capable of such a thing.

"I have never met the real niece. When I fell through the wall of the priesthole, Lady Randall found me in that other room and assumed I was the one she sought. Luckily, I have some skill with sewing and was able to carry out the charade while I searched for . . ."

"Me?"

"Yes, Richard, you. Although, for all the time we spent together, I did not even suspect you. No one bothered to tell me about your position as royal bastard. If you will remember, you prevented Patricia from telling me during our day in the village. And no one else seemed to want to share anything with the already disreputable Lady Seagrave's niece."

Richard turned away for a moment and gazed at one wall

of the room. She knew he was struggling with this; she was struggling with it as well. Then he spun back and faced her, as angry as he'd been before.

"So you expect me to believe that you come from another world and another time? What was the date when you arrived at Tenby Manor?"

"August twenty-sixth, two thousand."

"With such talk, some may mistake you for a weak-minded fool or a witch. 'Twould be better to confess as a spy—the death is easier for that crime."

"Richard, I am not a spy. I ask you to believe me when I tell you—"

"That you have traveled through time to reach me?" he interrupted. "I would have less trouble believing that you spy for—" He stopped and stared at her with a wild look in his eyes. "Do you spy for Cecil, then?" He walked over to her and grabbed her by the shoulders. After shaking her, he demanded, "Is he your spymaster? Did you come here seeking my confession? Damme, I did provide it to you with little urging or work on your part." He released her and stepped back. "I hope you will be well paid by him for your part in this."

That was the last insult she could take. Her breathing increased and her heart pounded with her own anger. He was hurt, certainly, but that did not give him the right to carry on this way. And it especially made her mad that he was reacting this way when she was only there to help *him.*

"You know I am here to help you. There is no reason for you to behave like an ornery little boy." He frowned as her own anger became apparent. "I told you—I was sent here to find you and give you this." She walked to the table and picked up the parchment sheets. Turning, she handed them to him.

"I did not know when we met that you were the man I was looking for. I did not know when I fell in love with you, either. Now that I do, I have no other choice than to turn this over and try to return home. My only regret, well, not my only one, is that I did not give this to you a few days ago when it could have prevented your arrest."

"What is this?" He turned the packet over in his hands and examined it.

"This is the proof that Miguel seeks. This is the evidence that could allow you the chance to follow your destiny as the trueborn son of Henry the Eighth and Anne Boleyn. I must leave now and try to get back home, but you must read this for yourself and decide if and how to use it."

"What else lies there on the table?" His hand, she noticed, shook as he pointed to it.

"Some coins I brought with me from my own time and the eyeglasses I use in my work. I thought they might help convince you that I am telling you the truth," she said, laughing without humor. "The only way you can believe me is if you trust me. Do you trust me, Richard?"

He looked at her from where he stood; his eyes showed confusion and anger and loss. But trust and love were not there. She shouldn't be surprised—she expected such a reaction from him. Sharon could see the struggle that raged within him. This was so much to throw at him all at once.

She reached over and grabbed the man's cap from the bed. Tucking her hair up, she placed it low on her brow. She carefully placed the dress back in her knapsack and tied it closed. She would need to take that back with her . . . if she was able to return to the year 2000.

"Take some time to look over Maria's confession and the physician's statement. Think about all the possibilities ahead of you and plan well." Sharon walked to the door as Richard stood pale and silent near the hearth. Calling in a husky voice to the guard below, she slumped her shoulders and waited for him to release her.

The guard unlocked the door and pulled it open. Sharon stepped out and watched him close the door behind her. Then he called in to Richard.

"Will your servant be returning, Master Granville?"

"Nay," she heard Richard reply in a low voice.

Her throat tightened and she could hardly breathe as the tears filled her eyes. She fought them, since she would be watched on her way out of the Tower and the guards would know something was up. Blinking rapidly, she tried to clear them from her eyes. She swallowed deeply to clear her throat. The guard started down the steps ahead of her and she took a moment to look through the bars at Richard. He stood staring at the papers in his hands, still in the same place as when she walked out of the cell.

"Richard," she whispered.

He must have heard, for he raised his eyes to the door.

"Please remember that I love you." She waited for him to say something, but was hurried by the guard's angry bellow from the floor below.

"Good-bye, Master Richard Granville."

Then, not delaying her departure another second, she turned and followed the guard out.

Sharon kept her head bent forward as she and the guard retraced their route out of the Bell Tower, through the Byward Tower, to the Middle Tower. Only after passing the guardpost did she raise her head to look for Robert. Weaving through the crowd, she saw him off in the distance, standing and waiting for her. She waved and headed for him.

Suddenly, she was surrounded by guards from the Tower. Terrified at what this meant, she tried pushing by them, but one man grabbed her by the wrist to hold her. Looking around her, she noticed a crowd gathering and people pushing closer for a better look. She lost sight of Robert, which was probably best for him.

"What is this? Why am I held?" She tried to keep her voice lowered, but fear made it more a woman's and less a man's tone.

"You are held by the order of the queen. You will come with us now." His orders were clear and his own tone told her that escape or refusal were not options.

She nodded and walked with them back into the Tower. There were too many to fight and she needed to stay alive if she wanted to return to her own time. She would bide her time and watch for an opportunity to escape.

The guards led her back inside, but not to the Bell Tower. This time they took her to the Queen's House. Entering on the ground floor, she was escorted to a small room and pushed inside. The door closed quickly behind her and she heard the key turn in the lock, securing her own prison.

The room was furnished with a small table and bench. She took the knapsack from her shoulder and laid it on the table. The only good thing was that there was no evidence in that satchel to implicate her in any plot against the queen. No, that evidence was now in Richard's hands. God help him, she prayed as she sat on the bench, lowered her head onto her hands, and cried out the tears that had threatened for the last hour.

Chapter 28

RICHARD SHOOK HIS head, trying to clear his mind. The last hour had been the most incredible in his life and he was still not certain of what had actually happened. He looked once more at the documents in his hand and at the coins and spectacles Sharon left behind.

She traveled from a future time and place to this one? She searched for Henry and Anne's son? How could he believe these outrageous claims?

The only way you can believe me is if you trust me. Do you trust me, Richard?

Did he? Did he even want to? He rubbed his face and sat down on the bed. She told him to carefully consider all the possibilities these proofs would give him. He needed to read these papers and determine what those options were. He shivered, wondering if these could truly prove that he was the rightful heir to Henry. Richard walked to the table, poured a cup of ale from the pitcher, and sat down where the sun's light shone most brightly.

Opening the first letter, he read, line by line, the harrowing account of the birth and apparent death of Henry and Anne's son. Then of the revival of the babe and the placement of him with a Catholic family. By God's eyes, Miguel had been telling him the truth. His nurse, Maria Morales Browning, had taken the babe, had taken him, from the room. He read the notation about the babe having the birthmark of the Boleyn family and his hand touched that area on his hip.

'Twas him! This was what he had waited and longed for most of his life. Proof in his hand that he was legitimate and not a bastard born!

His hands shook and his eyes filled with tears. His mother was Anne Boleyn, not Rebecca Granville as he had grown up believing. His mind rebelled at this turn of events. Not able to hold the second document still in his trembling hands, he spread it out on the table before him to read.

This one, the physician's report, gave a narration of the baby's birth and condition. The babe was premature and his size and frailty were clearly the reasons for him not surviving the traumatic birth. The recounting ended with a description of the birthmark and mentioned the presence of such a mark on his mother's hip as well. His link to Anne Boleyn was established!

Richard wanted to scream out in joy, but this excitement had to be tempered with caution. He was, after all, a prisoner in the Tower, facing treason charges. He must tread carefully if he wanted to come out of this alive. And if he wanted an opportunity to use this evidence to establish his claim to the throne of England.

He then examined the last paper. It was a baptismal certificate from the Granville family priest. The baptism was performed in secret just days after Maria had given him into their care, making him a traitor to his father's new church.

His head reeled as all the truths upon which he based his life and his beliefs were revealed to be lies. The Granvilles were not kin to him; they had raised a royal prince as their grandson, never knowing what had truly happened to their daughter's baby. Would anyone ever know now, with Maria being long since dead?

And to find out that Maria did not place him with the

Granvilles out of concern for either their or his own good was disconcerting at the very least. She was bent on revenge, and, although she repented in this confession, she destroyed lives to accomplish her goals. His mother, his real birth mother, faced charges of treason and was executed a few months after his birth. All of that could have been avoided if his birth and survival had been known.

Damn her! Anger raged inside him and he threw his cup against the wall. The sound of it crashing and breaking made him feel much better. Then he thought back to the care Maria had lavished on him in his early years at Tenby Manor. She had cared for him on a daily basis, taught him the Catholic faith, and watched over his every move. Only after Henry discovered him and took him to live with his household, did she return to Spain and her work as a midwife for a number of years. When she was too old to continue, the Granvilles invited her back and that was where she died.

So, the story presented by these documents fit the intriguing bits of information that Miguel had used for months to keep him interested. He wondered if Father Ramirez had any idea of how close to the truth he was. He chuckled to himself, thinking about the priest's reaction to finding out that the proof truly existed. It was something he would probably never know.

Now, which way did he turn? The papers before him looked authentic. The physician's seal, bearing witness to his appointment by the king, was clear at the bottom of the page. 'Twould be an easy thing to verify the name and date. The baptismal certificate was also signed by his grandparents—by the Granvilles—and could be proven true or not. Although the confession was the weakest part of this chain of evidence, its most important use would be to explain how he had been removed from his lawful place as heir and fraudulently adopted by another family.

The birthmark proved the link physically—he had it and probably Elizabeth did as well. Mayhap others still alive in the Boleyn family carried it and could be called to compare them?

He contemplated his next move. Standing and walking over to the window, he stared out at the now cloudy and darkening skies and thought on what he would do next. Did he send word to Miguel and hope for a rescue? The Catholic contingent was his best hope for getting out of this alive.

Was that what he wanted? To escape, make his claim on the throne, and fight for his right to rule? A few weeks ago, he would have favored that path without hesitation, but the situation had changed. He did not want to fight for something that Elizabeth had clearly earned—not only by inheritance but also through her actions. She had been resolute in her commitment to rule England wisely, and part of him saw no reason why he should change that.

Could he do it? Could he rule England as its king? He could, but his claim would inevitably lead to civil war and a weakening of his country's position as a major power in Europe. And for what purpose? To right a wrong against him? To give him the opportunity that his birth demanded?

Although many would say any of those reasons were adequate, he knew that it would satisfy his longing but leave England in a dangerous position. How could he do that?

After spending months vacillating between wanting and not wanting, between longing for and then not, between expecting it as his right and then questioning those expectations, Richard had made his decision. He could not live torn between all those options—he needed a future of his own.

Of course, he had planned to share that future with Sharon, but that did not seem possible now. He was totally confused over her role in this intrigue. She had stood boldly before him and declared herself from a distant time and a place unknown in this day and age. The "boldly" part surprised him not. Sharon had proven herself quite bold during their times together. He smiled, remembering back to some of her outrageous moments.

Perusing them in his mind, Richard realized that she never had seemed to fit in here. Her language was sometimes phrased much differently from what he was used to hearing around the court. He'd dismissed this as being due to her country origins, but after hearing her speak in a very different accent when they talked earlier, he was not so sure.

One thing was certain to him, she had been a virgin when they had made love the first time. And that was completely at odds from what he had heard and discovered about the real niece. That one was loose and wild, and, if rumors were any indication of truth, she had taken more than one lover.

So, Sharon had given herself to him. Was she the whore he accused her of being? He shook his head, denying it even as he thought about it. Their first night and last night had been about caring and concern and love. She had felt the same as he did last night—he read the surrender and the love in her eyes even as she reached her peak. They joined in more than just a physical way during their love-making last evening.

Turning away from the window, he paced to the limits of the cell. If all she wanted to do was give him the documents, she could have sent them in with Robert. He would have felt betrayed, but she would have been safely away from here without having to face his anger. And she would never have had to concoct her wild and unbelievable story of how she came to have the proof in her possession.

So, if he believed the evidence was valid and if he believed that she came to him in love, did it matter where or when she found the documents? Talk of coming from another time and far-distant place could be signs of mental breakdown or confusion. But wait, he had not even looked at the coins or spectacles.

In a few strides, he was at the bedside table. He picked up a few of the coins and looked at them closely. They were like nothing he had seen before—different metals from that in the coins minted here in London. The designations and amounts were strange, too. There was a "quarter dollar," a "cent," and a "dime." Although there were some other English coins, these did not resemble the sixpence, shilling, or sovereigns he was familiar with. The various men and the one woman engraved on the face of the coins was also unknown to him. Then, when he looked closely at the minting dates, he was astounded. All of the dates, on the foreign coins and the English ones, were in the 1990s!

Impossible! Were these fakes? Where did she get them?

Let him look at the spectacles—they might give a clue to her true origins. Lifting them to the light, he peered through them. The glass was smooth and even, unlike any he had seen to date. And the frames were not made of metal, but of some strange material that could bend and not break. He brought them close to his eyes and looked through them. The strength of the lenses changed from top to bottom and yet he could see no difference in the glass itself.

Incredible! How could these be made? He'd seen nothing like this anywhere within the royal household. Elizabeth would be astounded by these.

He paced once more; the motion soothed his confused thoughts. What did this mean? Could he believe she came from another time and place? Were these objects artifacts from that time and place?

The only way you can believe me is if you trust me. Do you trust me, Richard?

He did trust her, but still was not certain if he could accept the story she told of coming through the priesthole at Tenby Manor.

Tenby Manor!

Hopefully she would head there. In a second, all the doubts and indecision about the right path to take cleared away and he saw what he must do. He would use the evidence and his knowledge of his true parentage to barter with Elizabeth for a safe conduct out of the country for him and Sharon. He would start his new life—it would just be in another country. Mayhap at some point, he could convince Sharon to reveal her origins to him and they could make their new life there? As long as there were horses to breed and raise, he could live elsewhere.

So, he thought out loud, he needed a final plan—one that ended with him finding and bringing Sharon back to him and convincing her that they should be together. And one in which he could convince Elizabeth to let them go. If not both of them, then he would barter his proof for Sharon's release.

He thought he knew at least where she was heading. Tenby Manor was an integral part of her story and her plans. Since he could find her there as soon as he was freed, he did not worry about her safety.

Sharon knew that hours had passed. She'd finished crying a long time ago and now paced around the small room waiting for whatever was to come. Footsteps moving toward and away from the door told her that many walked by during the time she was in there. From the shadows she could see move across the floor under the door, she thought a guard was posted out in the hall. And still she waited.

She continued to walk, since it was better than sitting. Over and over she tried to figure out why she was being held prisoner. Was it due to her visit to Richard? Maybe anyone who spoke to him was being interrogated for information about the plot. The ironic thing was that, although she knew the truth about Richard, she knew nothing of the conspiracy itself. Other than the name of Miguel Ramirez, she could give them no other details.

She forced herself to remain calm—panicking now would not help anyone, especially herself, to get out of this predicament. Sharon had almost succeeded when there was a commotion outside in the hallway. The door was pulled open and one of the guards entered first. With his short pike, he motioned her over to the wall. The ominous weapon aimed at her chest convinced her not to utter a word or gesture of refusal.

Once there, he stood next to her, holding his pike at the ready. Sharon looked to the door and was shocked to see Lady Randall enter with the queen, Lord Cecil, and another woman she didn't recognize, probably another of the queen's closest attendants. They all wore the same dark expression, glaring at her across the small chamber. She waited for someone to speak and then realized this was the queen of England. Dressed as she was, she bowed at the waist before the queen. She couldn't remove her hat or her hair would fall so she stayed low until she heard the queen's command to rise.

"So you still have some manners about you, then?" Elizabeth said brusquely. "Tell us, do you know this woman?" With a closed fan, the queen pointed to the unfamiliar woman.

Sharon studied her face and could not remember meeting or seeing her before. She shook her head, denying any knowledge.

"Speak up," the queen reprimanded sharply.

"No, Your Majesty, I do not know her," Sharon replied in a low voice.

"You can put off this charade, if you please. Although you wear a man's clothes, we know you are a woman. We are just not certain which woman you are."

Startled, Sharon looked directly at the queen and then Lady Randall. What could she say? The queen waved her hand and Sharon did not speak.

"This lady is my good and childhood friend, Lady Katherine Seagrave. She comes to us bearing the news that her niece, recently sent to our household to aid us in our wardrobe, has reappeared at their estate in Lancashire, married without permission and well advanced toward the birth of her first child."

Sharon could feel the blood rush away from her head. Swaying unsteadily, she leaned against the wall. This was Katherine Seagrave. The only good thought that came to mind was that the niece was found, safe and alive. Sharon had been plagued with concern ever since Richard had asked about her that morning. She wondered why the girl had never shown up in the months since her own arrival. Now she knew—the other Sharon Reynolds had eloped with someone and was just now returning. And returning very pregnant.

"So is Sharon Reynolds your true name or did you

choose it for your own nefarious reasons?" Lady Randall asked this question and stepped closer as she did.

"My name is Sharon Reynolds," she whispered.

"And to what purpose have you masqueraded as someone else within my household? Tell me now, Mistress Reynolds, as you say you are called. I lose my patience waiting for your answers."

The threat in Elizabeth's voice was clear.

Sharon could not make her mouth work. Words jumbled in her mind, but she lost the ability to put them in a coherent order. And, really, what could she say?

"Madam, if I may interrupt?" Lord Cecil spoke up from his place at the door. Elizabeth turned slightly to give him her attention.

"She can be given over to Master Smith's fine touch. He would cajole the truth from her lips."

" 'Tis not my wont to torture women, milord," Elizabeth began. "However, since I agree his work gains results, I will leave the decision up to her." Elizabeth turned her full gaze and royal regard on Sharon. "Which will it be, Mistress Reynolds? Do you speak of your own accord or does Master Smith ruin those finely trained fingers of yours one at a time to gain the truth?"

Sharon clenched her hands into fists and thrust them behind her back in a protective movement. Oh, Dear God! This was real, this was not a dream or make-pretend. The woman before her was Elizabeth Regina, queen of England, Ireland, and France, and she could have her tortured or killed at her command. The reality of this situation sunk into her consciousness and Sharon realized this was a life-or-death moment. Then her mind cleared and she saw the approach she must take—one that would possibly save herself, but at the least would protect Richard.

"I came seeking Master Granville, Your Majesty." Her voice trembled with real fear as she spoke.

The ladies other than the queen gasped. Elizabeth gave Lord Cecil a knowing look and then faced her once more.

"And for what purpose did you seek out Master Granville? Was it for his knowledge of horses or his knowledge of *riding*?"

Well, in for penny in for pound, she thought. The emphasis the queen placed on the last word gave Sharon an idea.

"For both, Your Majesty, though I confess more for the latter than the former."

She watched as Lady Seagrave's and Lady Randall's faces flushed a deep red with embarrassment over this crude comment. The others in the chamber looked to Elizabeth for her own reaction. It was not long in coming. The queen broke out into a raucous laughter that filled the chamber and flowed out into the hallway.

"And how did you come to step into the other Mistress Reynolds's place so effortlessly?" She saw the seriousness underneath the queen's smile. This woman was one of the most intelligent women ever to have lived and Sharon did not underestimate the danger she was in.

"I work as a seamstress near Tenby Manor. I came upon your niece, Lady Seagrave, on my way home one night. She and her escort were . . . involved and decided to stop on their way to the manor and her new place within the queen's household. She laughed about our shared name and that we both were skilled with the needle and thread."

Sharon paused and looked at the queen. Elizabeth was weighing each of her words as she spoke, listening intently.

"She shared with me her intent to escape the plans made for her and to seek her own happiness elsewhere. It was in our conversation that she mentioned that the one thing she was looking forward to in the queen's household and would miss by leaving was the opportunity to further her acquaintance with Master Granville. I had known Richard as a child, but had not seen him in some time and Sharon regaled me with tales of his prowess among women and his good looks and wit. I do confess that, once she left, I did conspire to take her place and meet him."

"Have you known him, then?" Elizabeth asked as she cast a sharp glance at Lady Randall. It was known that she did not like the women in her household to be loose or immoral.

"Yes, Your Majesty, I have." Sharon looked at the floor and could feel the heat of embarrassment moving up her cheeks.

"And were you a virgin when you cast yourself at him? Or had you shared your favors with others before him?" Silence filled the small chamber and she felt as though the walls were closing in around her.

"Yes, Your Majesty, I was."

The tapping of a foot was the only sound in the room. Elizabeth did not speak for a few moments and Sharon hoped her explanation would be accepted. Cecil broke the silence.

"Are you satisfied, madam?"

"I do not think Master Smith's skills will be necessary after all, milord. And this woman who thought to masquerade as her betters will need whatever skills she possesses when she is cast out."

Sharon let out the breath she held and waited to see what Elizabeth planned.

"Hold her here in an upstairs chamber until I have decided what to do with her."

"Certainly, madam," Cecil said, pointing to the guard to remove her.

The guard next to her nodded toward the door and Sharon walked to it. She offered a small curtsey as she passed the queen and then followed another guard who fell into place ahead of her.

Once they had gone, Elizabeth suggested that her two attendants meet her in the dining room for some supper. Soon the queen and her most important minister were left alone.

"You are not pleased by this turn of events, William?" He had been relentless in his pursuit of anyone who threatened her well-being or her reign.

"I would respectfully suggest that she be tried in the courts for crimes against Your Grace. Fraud, conspiracy, and robbery at the least."

"You are too harsh on this girl, William. A case could be made that, although she impersonated someone else, she was not fraudulent because she was called by her own name. She worked diligently in my wardrobe, shirking no duties as Lady Randall has reported, and was owed wages for what she did accomplish. And conspiracy? From the sound of her words, she conspired against my half-brother and not me."

Lord Cecil moved to the doorway and then turned back to her. "I sense you are not completely at ease with her. Do you have any reservations about her story?"

"Aye, just one," she answered, thinking of the one aspect of this woman's story that did not fit into what she knew of her half-brother's womanizing habits. "Richard has never been one to trifle with virgins. So, there is something very suspicious in that or she means something very special to him."

"Mayhap he was fooled as well, taking her offer while believing her to be the other one. As you know, madam, we had heard various and sundry rumors about that one's behaviors."

Elizabeth tapped the fan in her palm, thinking on his words. Richard had come to her at Richmond asking for his land. His petition also included a request for permission to marry. Was it to this girl? Did he know the truth of her identity and still seek to marry her?

She would have to speak to Richard about this. Her heart was still heavy with grief over his involvement in this plot. They shared many bonds made earlier in their lives and she hated the thought that he would betray her.

"Come, Lord Cecil, let us have supper now. We still have much to do here before our day is done."

Chapter 29

RICHARD BUNDLED UP the items and papers Sharon had given him and hid them in a safe place. He knew that once Elizabeth calmed down, she would seek him out. They were both like their father in having that quick, volatile temper that cooled just as quickly. He had considered his words and his plan carefully.

The call came just after he had finished his supper. The guard came to remove his tray and brought with him a large bucket of hot water and some clothes to use. The orders were to clean him up and bring him over to the Queen's House for questioning. Once Richard agreed to see to the cleaning himself, the guard said he would return shortly and left the cell.

Richard lifted the bag of provisions that Robert had tossed to him and opened it. Inside, he found several shirts, another pair of breeches, some stockings, and, at the very bottom, a smaller sack. He tugged the lace holding that smaller one closed and was surprised by the contents. Some candles, costly ones that would burn bright and clear, some soaps, and a purse with coins were inside. A faint scent of roses emanated from the bag and he realized whose this was.

Sharon had sent him the purchases she had made during their day together. This was the same bag where he had placed the pink roses she said were her favorite flower. He inhaled the scent and let it fill his senses with memories of her. Their first meeting when he had to save her from his own horse. The day they spent in Windsor and her acceptance of his flirting ways. He thought of her coming to the stables the night of her bath, surrounded with the scent of roses. And how she helped with the birthing of the colt that would now never be his.

He smiled thinking of how she turned into a little mother as she chaperoned Patricia and John in their courtship. John had shared stories with him about her quick wit and way of drawing him into conversation when he least wanted to participate.

And he thought of how she had turned his thoughts and desires to wife, family, and future and finally away from following a hopeless dream that would never be his—in spite of it being his birthright.

He inhaled once more and felt a hopelessness that he had never experienced before. For the dreams she inspired in him were within his grasp and were now lost to him. She was lost to him, for he knew that Bess would never allow his release, at least not alive. And, if the tables were turned, he probably would act in the same manner.

The sound of a guard returning made him hasten to wash and dress. He chose a less scented soap, removed his shirt, scrubbed away what grime he could, and rinsed. Pulling on a clean shirt, he tied the laces, tucked it into his trunks, and tugged on his leather jerkin. In a few short minutes he was ready, at least in appearance, to meet his sister.

The door swung open and three guards stood at the entrance; one held long shackles in his hands. At his questioning look, one said, "We have our orders, Master Granville."

"Who gave the order to shackle me?"

"My Lord Cecil did say that you should be secured in these before entering Her Majesty's presence. Will you allow them peacefully, or do we need to use force?" They stepped toward him together, making it clear what he would face if he chose to fight.

"By all means then, let us do Lord Cecil's bidding," he said as he held out his hands to them. They put the chains around his wrists and one of the guards knelt and locked them in place around his ankles. This was nothing more than an insult and Richard knew it. Noblemen held prisoner here would never have to bear this humiliation, but Cecil was making a point. It was much easier to bear this knowing the truth. There was no one higher in noble standing and blood in the whole of England than he.

He adjusted his strides to accommodate the length of the chain between his feet and followed the guards down the stairs and out of the Bell Tower. They crossed the green between the buildings and entered the Queen's House. He was led to a large gallery that was open up to the second floor. A balcony hugged the wall around the top story and a number of rooms opened on to it.

Then he saw her, seated on a chair on a raised dais at the front of the room. His guards' prodding made him realize that he had stopped walking once their gazes met. Elizabeth Tudor, the queen of England, his full-blooded sister, waited for him to approach. Her mouth dropped open as he did.

"What is this?" she yelled, pointing at the chains. "I did not order him shackled." She stood and started toward him. Cecil's arm stopped her.

"Madam, I am in charge of your safety and I ordered it." William Cecil stepped to the side of Bess's chair and guided her back into it, whispering words he could not hear.

"He is not a common criminal, milord," she argued louder.

"I beg to differ, madam, he is just that."

He could see the battle heating between them and wondered who would win. Most times, Cecil backed down if it was in public view. The guards shifted nervously at this demonstration of the queen's temper. Of *their* temper.

"For now, I will allow your order to stand, milord. And I thank you for so diligently carrying out your duties." She motioned to the guards on either side of Richard to bring him forward. Although her face remained void of any expression, he noticed her mouth tightened with every rattling noise the chains made as he walked toward her.

They stopped a few paces from her chair and he bowed low to her. Rising, he waited for her to speak. She did not keep him in anticipation for long.

"I have heard one traitor confess to his and your parts in this conspiracy. I have read the documents and seen the list of those involved. Now, I want to hear the words from your mouth. Tell me your reasons for turning against me, Richard."

He heard the hurt and betrayal in her voice; he recognized it in the rigid tilt of her head and in the way she twisted her handkerchief around her fingers. For a moment he was back in the Bell Tower with her as she waited for her fate. Accused as part of a plot against their half-sister Mary, they had spent weeks in the Tower. She had carried that same expression then.

"I will not speak of this before strangers, Elizabeth," he said, pausing as Cecil gasped at his use of her name in public. "Let them leave and I will speak the words you wish to hear." He crossed his arms over his chest and glared directly at Cecil.

"Clear this room. Now!" Elizabeth ordered. Cecil began to argue with her, but she would not listen this time. "My Lord Cecil, you may have the courtesy of waiting in my private chamber."

"Madam—" Her look cut him off and Cecil recognized the Tudor steel in that expression. She would not allow him to naysay her this time. He bowed to her and began to back toward that chamber.

"You there, guard. Remove those chains now." She crossed her arms over her chest and set her chin and he could see their father in her countenance.

The guard, not wanting to get between his queen and her minister, looked from one to the other and, when Cecil clamped his own mouth shut, did as she ordered. The chains dropped noisily to the floor. Elizabeth pointed to the door and the guard backed away, bowing in obeisance as he did. Soon they were alone.

"I have met your conditions, Richard. Speak." She sat down and focused her gaze on him.

How to begin? He had passed the words round and round in his thoughts, but when given the opportunity, he could not think of how to begin.

"For all of my life, I have wanted one thing. I wanted to be recognized as a son of Henry's. And, I confess, I wanted the right to sit on the throne you occupy. I have yearned for those for all the years I can remember, ever since Henry found me and brought me to his court."

"Richard, he did recognize you when he did that. What more could you have expected as a . . ." She paused and did not use the word.

"Bastard? I wanted more than that, Bess. You had been labeled that once—did you not want the stain of it removed from your name just as fervently as I do? Some still call you that—'the Great Whore's Bastard.' "

"Parliament named me legitimate years ago, you know that. Since your mother and our father were not wed, you cannot expect more than what he has granted you."

"Expect more? In truth, I did not expect more or even as much. But that did not stop me from yearning and wanting and desiring more." He walked toward her and stopped in front of her. "You know the pain of being looked at the way I am. It happened to you after your mother's death."

"I had no idea you felt this way, Richard. You seem always to be content with your position and with the opportunities being part of my court allows you."

"This raw and powerful desire is hard to hide at times, Bess, but it has lived within me since I found out Henry fathered me."

"And you let it turn you against me?" She still twisted the handkerchief once more.

"I had managed to turn my wants to the grant of land that our father willed to me. I decided some time ago that all my wanting would not change the truth or make what I sought happen. Someone made me see that I needed to make my own future, made me want to make my own future."

"Then you deny your involvement with these traitors?"

"Nay, I cannot. Although, by God's heart, I wish I had never listened to their enticements. I did plot to remove you from the throne. I wanted that seat of power for myself."

"You confess this freely to me?" She looked stunned. He knew this made his conviction and execution easy for her now.

"They came with soft words and offered me the one thing I had desired in the deepest part of my soul, Bess. To be king. How could I not listen? And when they promised me what I had always dreamed of, I was trapped."

He turned and walked a few steps away from her. Glancing over his shoulder at her, he felt a twinge of pity for her. She had never really known him, she had known only the side he revealed to the world. The depth of his hunger for the throne frightened her, or maybe it mirrored her own and that was what truly frightened her.

"But, Richard, by what right can you claim the throne? I am the lawful queen here, my claim supersedes all others."

"The Pope says—"

"Fie on that! The Pope does not rule in England! I do!" She stood and called out to him. "That man no longer rules the hearts or souls of good Englishmen. What say you now of a claim to my throne?"

"Only a trueborn son of your father and mother would have more right to that seat than you."

"And there are none! My mother tried three more times to bear our father a son and failed. Her death is a result of those failures and his relentless desire to make a son on a wife."

"One did survive. A trueborn son of the king and queen."

She walked to him and he saw her face pale as the consequences became real to her. She reached out a trembling hand to him. "None survived, Richard. I am the only issue of their marriage."

"Nay, Bess, not the only one. Just the only one known until now."

"What do you mean 'until now'?" She shook her head and studied his face.

"I held the proof in my hand and know the truth. I am your full brother, Bess. Not a bastard, but born of Anne Boleyn in January of the year 1536."

She began to tremble, shaking her head in denial as he spoke.

"Look you on this and then say I had not reason to pursue my claim to the throne."

He lifted his jerkin and loosened his trunks. Tugging the back down just far enough to expose the mark, he turned to her and let her see the mark that bound them both to Anne Boleyn.

"What say you now?"

She said nothing; her mouth moved a few times as she looked at the diamond-shaped birthmark, but no sounds came out. Then her eyes rolled back in her head and she fell forward into his arms. He guided her down gently to the floor, protecting her head in his lap.

"Cecil!" he bellowed. "To the queen, now!"

A moment later he found himself surrounded by the Yeomen Guards, all with weapons drawn and aimed at him.

Chapter 30

CHAOS ERUPTED WITHIN the gallery. Richard found himself dragged from under the queen, pulled into a corner, and roughly chained once more. Then, lifted to his feet, he was slammed and held against the wall.

He looked through the people who had flooded into the chamber and saw that Bess had awakened from her faint and was being tended to by some of her women. Cecil paced nervously in front of her.

Richard simply waited silently for calm to be restored. He knew there was more for him and Elizabeth to discuss, if not now then soon. He was willing to be patient now that he had gotten her attention.

A moment later, Cecil approached him. The guards held him firmly.

"You bastard! What did you do to her?"

"I did nothing, milord. We had only an exchange of words."

"Take him back to his cell," Cecil ordered.

"Hold there," Elizabeth called. "I am not finished with him yet."

She stood and shook off the women who clung to her.

Brushing them aside with a wave of her hand, she strode to where he was held.

"Release him. He did nothing to me. I but felt dizzy and he assisted me."

Cecil looked at her with open disbelief etched onto his face. He hesitated and then nodded his assent. The guards removed the shackles once more and he stood away from the wall. Cecil looked again at the queen and then, with a wave of his hand, cleared the room.

Richard gazed at her a few paces away from him. She was pale, so pale, but stood her ground with the experience and bearing of a queen.

"You should sit, Bess. There is no color left in your cheeks. Come," he said as he held out his arm to escort her back to the chair.

She did not resist and he knew she was still reeling from his revelation. Once seated, she looked at him with a different expression. Studying his face, she smiled.

"I have always seen the resemblance to our father, but I do now see something of our mother in the shape of your eyes and in your coloring."

Then, as he watched, her expression hardened. She sat straighter in her chair and became queen once more.

"So, Richard, where do we go from here? Although you would seem to have a claim to the throne, 'tis not my wont to simply give it up."

He laughed out loud at her words. "I seem to have a claim?"

" 'Twould depend on the strength of your evidence, and the cooperation of the courts . . . *my* courts."

"The evidence is strong or I would not raise it to you."

"That compelling, then?"

"Aye, that compelling." He crossed his arms and looked at her. He could see the struggle on her face.

"You understand that I can order you killed and no one would know of your claim."

"I know you would not do that, no matter how much you want the throne to stay in your control. I feel the same way—that is why I broke from the conspiracy. I could not stand the thought of you being harmed." He looked at her and saw the tears glistening in her eyes. "All I wanted was the bequest from my father's will and one more thing."

"What was that?" she asked.

"I wanted permission to marry someone. I have asked Mistress Reynolds of your wardrobe to wed with me."

"You have? Do you know that the woman working in my household is not the niece of Lady Seagrave?"

"She has told me her truth."

"Did you know she was an impostor?"

"Aye," he said, smiling at her. "Once I bedded her, I knew 'twas obviously not the niece we had heard about. But, the woman I would wed nonetheless."

"Richard, you may not survive this night and you would wed her?"

"I want no bastards left behind. At least I would give her the protection of marriage and send her to my grandparents . . . the Granvilles."

"Is she with child, then?" Elizabeth asked, shifting in her seat once more.

"If she is not, 'tis not for a lack of trying on our part." He chuckled then continued, "In all seriousness, Bess, I do not ask for my own life, but I would beg for hers. If you would promise to allow me to marry her and pledge her safe conduct to Tenby Manor, I will lay the evidence I have in your hands."

She was shocked by his offer. "And nothing for yourself?"

"I had truly accepted that the throne would not be mine and had decided to throw my energies into establishing my stables and breeding farm with Sharon at my side. If giving you the proof would make that happen, I would do it in an instant."

"I will have to think on this. I find myself quite overwhelmed by this conversation. Remain here and I will have Mistress Reynolds brought to you for a brief visit."

From the way his mouth dropped open she knew he had no idea that Sharon was still here. He had probably thought her safely on her way, but Elizabeth had her here all this time.

Elizabeth stood and walked across the gallery to the entrance to her own privy chamber, leaving Richard the one surprised now. His words had overwhelmed her, truly. 'Twould seem that he valued this woman above his claim to the throne.

She pushed open the door and William jumped back from his viewing place in the alcove behind the door.

"So, *milord* Cecil, what think you of my brother's claim and offer?"

She heard the guards moving in the hallway before the door opened. There had been so much activity in the building earlier, she wasn't sure if a guard remained in front of her door. The key turned in the lock and the door swung open. Motioning to her to follow, a guard led her out of the small chamber and down the maze of hallways until they walked down steps and reached the main floor.

She stood on her toes to try to see over the guard's shoulder. It didn't work. Neither did leaning around him, for his bulk took up nearly the whole width of the hall down which they walked. A few more minutes brought them to a doorway. The guard leaned over and opened the door for her. Then, standing aside, he let her pass inside.

At first she thought the room was empty. Then a movement further in drew her attention and she saw him. He stood alone in front of the chair meant for the queen. She walked quietly over to it, to him, not sure of how he felt about seeing her again. He never moved his gaze from the chair, but she somehow knew he was aware of her.

"It should be mine," he said quietly, still not looking at her. "But it will never be."

"You believed the documents?"

" 'Tis difficult to argue when the truth is there before you."

"Can you forgive me?"

"Have you done something which I must forgive? I see

you here, sharing the danger of the moment with me. What needs forgiveness?"

"I was selfish, Richard. I hesitated and look at what has happened."

He turned then and faced her. He reached over and took her hand, entwining his fingers in hers. "Tell me how you hesitated."

She took a deep breath and let it out slowly. She hadn't thought she'd have a chance to explain this to him.

"Part of me knew that if I gave you the proof, I would lose you. If you succeeded in making your claim, there would be no place in the king's life for me. You would have to marry and have children to secure your own line. A common woman might serve as your mistress, but not your wife." She looked at him, her eyes filling with tears as she spoke.

"Then I berated myself for feeling that way and decided that you should have the papers. When I had made that choice, all the dangers you would face came to mind and I found I was unwilling to give them to you. I played God and made the decision for you.

"That hesitation brought you to this now. Your life is in danger because I was jealous and overprotective. I am sorry I did not simply give you the information and trust you do use it the best way possible."

She felt the tears spill over and down her cheeks. She rubbed them away, for she was tired of crying. She needed to be strong for him, to help him face whatever came their way. It took a few moments for her to realize that he had wrapped his arms around her and was rubbing her back.

"How did you come to be here? I thought you left this morn," he said, stepping back to look at her.

"I was detained on my way out of the Tower—the guard said they were checking everyone at Elizabeth's order. So I thought it was because I had visited you, and in a way I was wrong."

"Then why?" he asked again.

"Lady Seagrave's niece turned up in Lancaster, married and pregnant, so they knew I was an impostor."

"What did you tell them to still be alive? You did not share your tale of being from another time?" Although his voice was light and teasing, she was miffed at his not taking her seriously.

"I cannot tell anyone else what I told you, Richard. No one else must know that I am not from this time. I told the queen that I was a seamstress from near Tenby Manor who had heard of your great prowess with women and sought you out."

"You did not tell her that! Surely you jest?" He laughed at her story.

"Well, I could not tell her I was from over four centuries in the future and had come back to right the wrong dealt to you, could I?"

"I confess, I am having a great deal of difficulty accepting that explanation of yours. I am trying, though."

"Thank you for at least trying. Did you look at the coins? or my eyeglasses? I thought those things would help convince you."

"Those were most interesting and most puzzling indeed. Tell me, in your future, did I become king?"

She paused, not knowing how to answer. Then she realized the truth was the best way.

"Nay, to my knowledge there was no attempt to take the throne from Elizabeth by someone claiming to be the rightful king. I am sorry."

He shook his head at her. "No need to be sorry—I asked the question. Tell me about Elizabeth's future."

Uneasy about revealing what she knew, she tried to keep her comments general. Since her knowledge of history was not as strong as her knowledge of fabrics from history, that should not be hard to do.

"She will be one of the longest-ruling and best-known monarchs of England. Your country will grow and become a world power under her leadership."

Clapping interrupted her words. She whirled around and found herself face-to-face with Elizabeth and William Cecil. And they had heard her words.

"Brava, Mistress Reynolds. Brava!" the queen said as she

walked toward them. "What other fortune-telling tricks can you perform for us this day?"

"You were listening?" Sharon asked, looking over at Richard.

"Of course I listened. I need to gather as much information as I can before making a decision on Richard's request. 'Twas interesting and gratifying indeed to hear that I will remain on the throne for some time. How long will my reign last, then?"

Sharon glanced at Richard and he nodded. He thought it best to tell what she knew.

"You will reign into the seventeenth century."

"And when and who will I marry?"

Sharon hesitated in answering this question—no answer could be the right one for Elizabeth to hear.

"You will not marry, Your Majesty. You will be called "the Virgin Queen" by history." She thought that would be enough for her, but Elizabeth whispered one more question.

"Who will succeed me on the throne? Richard?"

"No, Richard will not sit on the throne. Your cousin Mary Stuart's son James will be the first to rule over England and Scotland together."

Elizabeth reeled at her words, tripping back until Lord Cecil caught her. Her complexion had lost all its color and she looked as though she would faint. Cecil led her to the chair for her to sit.

"Come now, madam, surely you do not believe the ramblings of this madwoman? Anyone could claim these things were to come and how could we prove them or not?"

"Can you not feel the truth in them, William? She knows our future. We are her past."

"Absurd! You cannot let this woman upset you, Your Grace."

"Enough! I have made my decision and I believe it is the best one. I will honor your request, Richard. You may marry her and leave England. I do not want your blood on my hands, but I cannot allow you to claim the throne."

"Wait a minute!" Sharon yelled. "You asked her for permission to marry me? Richard, you cannot do this!"

He looked shocked himself at Sharon's predictions and now her outburst. He asked Elizabeth, "You would let us leave alive?"

"So long as you turn over the evidence you have of your claim, I will give you safe passage out of the country. You can settle somewhere on the Continent and never return to England."

"Richard, you cannot trust her! Once she has the proof, your life is worth nothing. Please, do not agree to this." She could not believe that he was willing to turn over to Elizabeth the documents that protected his own life.

"Come with me, Sharon." He took her off to the far side of the room. Once there, he looked at her and smiled.

"You asked me to trust you; now I ask the same of you. Elizabeth has given her word to me and I trust her to honor that bond. I know you think that you can return to this world of yours, but what if the passage is closed to you? I have to secure your safety and, if it has happened, any babe you carry inside you. 'Tis worth it to me."

"Those papers . . ." she began to argue.

"Are worthless compared to your safety. If you would have me to husband, I will give you the protection of my name perchance you remain behind and any ill befalls me."

"Would you return with me to my own time?"

"We must secure our release from this place and then we will try the passage. But I want you to wed me first."

He was not going to give in on this matter of marriage. She knew that arguing further would not do any good and without the marriage, his agreement for safe conduct out of England was nullified. Maybe fate would be kind to her now that she had carried out her duty? Maybe they could end up together either here in his time or there in her time?

She nodded her head and the next thing she knew he had lifted her in his embrace and was kissing her wildly. As he took her mouth over and over, she heard Elizabeth's words from across the room.

"I think we have a wedding to prepare for, milord."

Chapter 31

THEY LEFT WITH an armed escort. After a hasty wedding in the Chapel of Saint Peter Ad Vincula, they gathered their belongings together and rode off through London, across London Bridge, and southwest toward Tenby Manor in Sussex. Before leaving, Sharon had shown her eyeglasses to the queen. Elizabeth tried them on and declared them a miracle. Sharon had also shared a few other tidbits of history with her. Maybe she should not, but she felt compelled to do so.

Hours and hours of riding with a few short rest breaks brought them to the Granvilles' estate early the next day. They had decided not to tell the truth of Richard's parentage. On the pretense of leaving England for an extended visit and honeymoon in France, Richard introduced Sharon to the couple who had raised him as their own. Fighting the urge to run up to that third floor room and try the passage, Sharon accepted Richard's idea of waiting for nighttime and using it then.

Once they were greeted, Sharon was led off to a room to bathe and rest before supper. The steaming bathwater called to her and she could not resist staying overlong in the tub. The door opened and, since a screen blocked her view of the door, she waited for one of the servants to identify him- or herself. His deep voice sent shivers through her as he spoke.

"I have more hot water for you, Mistress Granville."

"You do?" she asked, shifting lower into the water.

He walked in front of her and examined all the parts of her above the water. In spite of her efforts to spread bubbles over the surface, she would swear he could see through the water as well.

"You appear to need help with your bath. Let me wash your back."

The scent of roses filled the room as he opened a small glass vial and poured an amount of liquid into the bath. The oil spread through the water and she inhaled the heady fumes. Richard moved behind her to wash her back. She leaned forward and he used a soapy cloth in ever-widening circles on her skin. Then she felt the cloth move around, teasing the sides of her breasts with each stroke.

Sharon lifted her arms, giving him access to reach further. Soon, she just leaned back and let him rub the lather over her breasts and belly. She moaned as he increased the motions around the sensitive nipples and down into the curls between her legs. A moment later, she found herself lifted from the water and laid on the nearby bed. She was panting with the desire he had built in her and watched as he stripped off his clothes and joined her there. Soon, he was moving deeply within her and they both moaned as their passion was finally satisfied.

"I think we have ruined the bedclothes," she said as she lifted her head and surveyed the damage all the water had done around the room.

"There are more beds and more rooms, if need be," he replied with a laugh. "Now, cover yourself, for the servants will soon be here with fresh water for the bath."

True to his prediction, a line of servants soon stood outside the door ready to refresh the bathwater for them. Richard stood and watched, giving her evil and lustful grins over their heads. When the bath was ready once more and the bedclothes freshly changed, Richard peeled off the few clothes he wore and sank down in the steaming tub.

They bathed and loved and slept through the rest of the afternoon. Whenever Sharon would try to dress, he would take the clothes from her and declare that, since he'd spent his wedding night in a saddle, he would spend the day after in a bed. It was an argument she never won, but, in truth, she did not mind losing.

He did allow her to dress for dinner, but because he "helped" her, they were late for the meal. His grandparents smiled knowingly as they entered the dining room. She said little as he explained that they would leave in the middle of the night since he wished to evade the escort that even now sat at the gates of the estate.

In the middle of the night, Richard woke her from a sleep she had not intended to take and she dressed in the clothes she'd been wearing when she'd come through into this time. Richard was ogling her the whole time.

"Do you not intend to dress?" he asked as he watched her tie her blouse.

"I am dressed, Richard. You know, I wonder if you will like my world."

"Do all women wear panties there?" Just great, she was married to a man with a women's underwear fetish.

"Actually yes, they do, well, most of the time. I think you will be shocked by the fashions in my time."

"Tell me what else will shock me. I would prepare myself in advance." He gifted her with the devilish smile that made her heart melt.

"Women work as equals to and sometimes as superiors to men. We travel in carriages without horses and in planes that glide through the sky."

He looked at her in frank disbelief. She knew he would marvel at the things in her world—if the passage allowed him through. In a few minutes, she would have her answer.

" 'Twill be difficult to adjust to some of these modern situations."

"Yes, it will, but I will be there with you."

"And will you wear panties for me?" he asked, kissing her once more.

"Aye, in whatever color you like. And, Richard? You can take them off of me whenever you like." Now it was her turn to laugh, as she moved away and watched the possibilities sink in.

They made their way to the third floor as quietly as possible so as not to wake anyone else in the house. He opened the door to the room where she had arrived and closed it behind them. He put the candle on top of one of the chests and looked around the room.

"Was there anything else you left here? You may want to check the cupboard or the trunks?"

"No," she said, carefully arranging the dress she carried over her arm. "I have everything I arrived with except for the papers. And my glasses."

"Are you ready, then?" he asked.

She nodded, certain that they both wore the same frown as he approached the wall that hid the entranceway to the priesthole. She had tapped on the wall, seeking the latch or other way of opening it. Now she watched as Richard slid his hand along the angle of the wall and sprung the latch. The secret panel opened silently before them.

"I saw you tapping the wall that morning we left for Windsor and wondered even then if you knew the room was here."

"I thought you did! Then you reacted strangely when I asked you about it."

"I worried that if you knew it was here, you would endanger my grandparents."

"Well, shall we go in and see what happens?"

She held out a shaking hand to him. He grasped it without hesitation and helped her up into the small chamber. Stepping inside, he let the panel close behind them. For a moment the room was thrown into pitch darkness. She lost hold of Richard's hand and panicked.

"Richard!" she called out.

"Here, my love," he answered, taking hold of her once more. "I am right beside you."

Then the room began to brighten. Light came in from a source out in the hall and Sharon could see the open doorway into the hallway. Suddenly, there was a buzzing and lights came on in the room, too.

She looked around and saw that the trunk was still there, though moved off to a place nearer the door. She caught sight of Richard staring at the lightbulb in the fixture over their heads. She smiled.

"Did I mention light that does not need candles or fire?"

"Nay, I think you neglected to mention that to me. Here now, what is that noise?"

Footsteps running down the hall in their direction became louder and louder. Then Mo burst into the cubbyhole.

"I thought we had lost you, Sharon! Where in the blazes have you been?" Mo pulled her close and hugged her tightly. "I thought you had wandered into an unsafe area in the house and been trapped somewhere."

"I am fine, Mo. Really," she said, pulling out of her grasp. "How long have you been looking for me?"

"For over three hours. It's nearly nine o'clock now."

She could tell the moment Mo finally caught sight of Richard standing in the shadows. Her mouth dropped open and she stood up staring at him.

"Mo, this is Richard Granville. Richard, this is Mo. Maureen Boylan is her full name. She is one of my dearest friends."

"Greetings, Mis— . . . Mo. I am truly pleased to meet a friend of Sharon's." He bowed gallantly to Mo, who still stared at him.

"Sharon, where did he come from in those clothes?"

"Mo, I think we have a lot to talk about," Sharon answered, laughing. Richard winked at her over her friend's head. Sharon took Richard's hand and led him into the hallway. Before they could reach the steps, a security guard met them.

"What is it, Sam?" Mo asked.

"You're not going to believe this. There are two men who say they are from Her Majesty's Government and they are asking about Ms. Reynolds."

Mo looked at her and waited for an explanation. She had none to give. She shrugged at Mo and motioned for her to lead the way.

"And they asked if a Richard Granville was here as well. Is this him?" Sam pointed at Richard.

This was strange. No one in this time knew him. Who could be looking for him?

A few minutes of walking brought them down to the main floor and Sharon found Richard gazing at the building around him. This was his family estate and when he'd seen it last, it was in its prime. This version must be difficult to accept.

Two men, in dark suits and carrying very official-looking briefcases, stood inside the main foyer waiting for them. Mo introduced herself as the project manager and suggested they move into one of the drawing rooms that had furniture in it. If either one of them thought it was strange to find a man in Elizabethan garb here, he did not show it by his expression or manners.

Sharon kept looking at Richard to see his reaction. His face was blank now. They sat on couches and the men introduced themselves. Sharon could hardly stand the tension that grew around them.

"So, what do need from me?"

"We don't need anything from you, Ms. Reynolds. We have something for you. And something for Mr. Granville."

She looked at Richard and then Mo and back to the men. "I don't understand."

"Neither does Her Majesty's Government." At her frown, the special agent continued. "This package has been held within the palace at Windsor since the time of Elizabeth. The instructions with it made no sense, but it has been passed down from monarch to monarch until today. This is addressed to you and the instructions said to bring it here on this night at this time."

Sharon thought the room was spinning. She blinked and tried to focus her vision. A package addressed to her from Elizabethan times. How? Why? What could it be? Her hands trembled as she took the package from the agent. Gently lifting the seal on it, she unwrapped the leather box and opened it.

Eyeglasses. Her eyeglasses were in the box! Elizabeth must have believed her words, for here were the very glasses she'd left behind for the queen's use. Scratched and used, but definitely hers. A small piece of parchment lay under the glasses and she lifted it to read. Holding it up to the light, she tried to make out the bold flourishes.

She held it out to Richard, knowing he was much more familiar with his sister's handwriting than she was. He peered at the note and laughed as he repeated the words out loud.

"Mistress Reynolds, my thanks for the use of these spectacles. You were correct—I have grown into a vain old woman who will not wear them and admit the frailty of age."

He held out the note and she recognized the signature, *Elizabeth R.* The date of her departure from her own time was one of the details she'd revealed to the queen before they left the Tower.

"There was also this addressed to a Master Richard Granville with the same instructions to deliver it here tonight." The special agent opened his briefcase and carefully lifted out several parchment sheets. Sharon watched with tear-filled eyes as Richard took them from the man. He turned his back on the group and walked a few paces away. She knew he was overwhelmed and she could only imagine what was in the papers he held.

"Gentlemen, is there anything else we need to do?" She stood and moved toward the door.

One of the men handed her a more modern manila envelope and closed his briefcase. They stood and followed her to the door.

"These are the papers that were filed to fulfill the instructions with his package. Our number is there; call us if we can help in any way. Her Majesty's Government stands ready to assist you and Mister Granville."

Sharon shook their hands and Mo showed the men out. When she returned, Sharon was watching Richard. Tears were streaming down his face as he read the letter enclosed in his packet.

"Richard, what is it?" she asked, fearing to open the envelope in her hands.

"She granted my request and fulfilled the provisions of my father's will. This is the original deed to Winter's Run, the estate I was to inherit." He paused and fumbled through the other papers. "And this is an official proclamation of Parliament recognizing my claim to the throne. She had this done in secret to legitimize me."

"Oh, Richard. I can't believe this. Elizabeth kept her word to you, even through over four hundred years of time."

As she took him in her arms, some papers slipped out of the envelope and onto the floor. Mo picked them up and looked at them. Looking even more stunned than a moment ago, Mo plopped on the couch and shook her head at the paper in her hand.

"This is a bank draft made out to Richard Granville," Mo said in a shocked whisper. "How much did you inherit?"

"A goodly amount," Richard replied. "My father bequeathed me three thousand pounds."

"When?" Mo asked.

"Mo, I don't think you're ready to hear this yet. Maybe after we all get some rest?"

"When?" Mo repeated her question with no indication of giving up.

Sharon looked at Richard and he nodded his consent.

"In fifteen forty-seven." Sharon waited for Mo's reaction to this preposterous date. There was none.

"I think that when you see this amount and when I hear the details of this, we'll both need more whisky than the local pub has in stock."

She handed the check to Sharon and Richard.

Sharon read the amount once and then again and again. Mo was right. There would be not be enough whisky to get through this.

Epilogue

THREE YEARS LATER

WINTER'S RUN
NOTTINGHAMSHIRE, ENGLAND

HE WATCHED HER waddle toward him and held in the laughter that fought to escape. His wife was in her eighth month of pregnancy and was somewhat touchy about her size and ungainly gait when walking. She was sensitive about her appearance and her demeanor. Actually, as he thought about it now, she was touchy about almost everything.

She dropped something on the ground as she approached him and he could finally not control his amusement as she tried several times to locate it at her feet and then debated with herself about the wisdom of trying to reach for it. His laughter rang out through the stables.

"It is rude to laugh at someone's difficulties."

He bent down, retrieved the letter, and handed it back to her. Then he took her in his arms and kissed her the way she liked it.

"But you are so lovely in your difficulties, Mistress Granville. Are you well?" She tired easily and it was no short walk out here to the stables.

"I am, Richard. I feel energetic today."

"Do not overtire yourself, Sharon. Your time approaches soon."

She rubbed her belly and he stood behind her and took over for her. She leaned against him and he felt the swell of her pregnancy. Sliding his hands over the roundness, he felt the babe move within. She laughed at him now.

"So, tell me who the letter is from and why it has you smiling." He already knew the sender; he'd seen the letter on the desk before he left for the yards this morning.

"The museum in York has offered me a position."

"And will you take this position?" He continued his motions over and around her stomach. He felt her relax beneath his touch.

"Richard, I am amazed at the difference in you in just a few short years here. I remember when you would have shouted and ordered me to take it or not to take it."

"And you would have ignored me and done whatever you pleased. As you will now."

Her laughter was music to his ears and to his heart. Their first months here had not been easy, not for her nor him. Only their love held them together as she battled to remove the taint on her name and reputation put there by Jasper Crenshaw. Then they left America and settled here, on his farm.

"I told them I could not give them an answer until after the baby's birth."

"That may not be enough time, Mistress Granville."

"Not enough time?"

"You promised to wear those new panties for me before returning to work. 'Twill be some weeks before you are ready for that."

"Richard, I love you, but you have to stop buying lingerie."

"Say that again." He paused in his massage and waited.

"Stop buying lingerie?"

"Nay, the other words."

She turned in his embrace and kissed him, the way he liked to be kissed. "I love you, Your Majesty," she said.

"And I love you, queen of my heart."

About the Author

Wife to one, mother of three (all boys), dental hygienist to hundreds and reader of thousands of romance novels, Terri Brisbin is now the author of three time travel romances. Born and raised in southern New Jersey, Terri and family live in a small town not far from Philadelphia, Pennsylvania. When not writing or working as an RDH, she spends her time reading, playing on her computer and driving her kids all over South Jersey.

If you would like to contact her, please send a SASE for a reply, bookmarks or postcards to: Terri Brisbin, P.O. Box 41, Berlin, NJ 08009-0041.

You can visit her Web site at: http://romance-central.com/TerriBrisbin, or E-mail her at Tbrisbin@aol.com. She loves to hear from readers!